ABANDON IN PLACE

Jerry Oltion

H0134

ABANDON IN PLACE

FIC
OLT

A TOM DOHERTY ASSOCIATES BOOK
NEW YORK

ABANDON IN PLACE

Copyright © 2000 by Jerry Oltion

A portion of this novel first appeared in the December 1996 edition of *The Magazine of Fantasy and Science Fiction.*

Book design by Jane Adele Regina

A Tor Book
Published by Tom Doherty Associates, LLC
175 Fifth Avenue
New York, NY 10010

www.tor.com

Tor® is a registered trademark of Tom Doherty Associates, LLC.

Library of Congress Cataloging-in-Publication Data

Oltion, Jerry
    Abandon in place / Jerry Oltion.—1st ed.
       p. cm.
"A Tom Doherty Associates book."
ISBN 0-312-87264-X
    1. Cape Canaveral (Fla.)—Fiction. 2. Rockets (Aeronautics)—Fiction. I. Title.

PS3565.L857 A64 2000
813'.54—dc21

00-034385

First Edition: November 2000

Printed in the United States of America

0 9 8 7 6 5 4 3 2 1

FOR KATHY
who asked
"What would it take to make you believe in ghosts, anyway?"

ACKNOWLEDGMENTS

Thanks to Martha Bayless for the medieval Welsh, Brian O'Leary for insight into the new science, Damon Knight and Jim Fiscus for the British rifle, Oregon Writers Colony for a week's refuge from phones (in a haunted house, no less!), and the Eugene Wordos for encouragement, brainstorming, and cookies.

Special thanks to Kristine Kathryn Rusch, who encouraged me to expand my original 7,000-word short story into a 23,000-word novella, which she then bought for *The Magazine of Fantasy and Science Fiction,* and who, after that, said, "Why don't you see what happens at novel length?"

Be careful what you ask for; you just might get it.

ABANDON IN PLACE

Part One

ABANDON IN PLACE

ix hours after Deke Slayton, the astronaut, died of cancer, his racing airplane took off from a California airport and never came down. The pilot didn't respond to the control tower, and the plane vanished from radar shortly after takeoff, but witnesses clearly identified it as Slayton's. Which was impossible, because that same airplane was in a museum in Nevada at the time.

The story made the rounds at the Cape. Engineers and administrators and astronauts all passed it along like scouts telling ghost stories around a campfire, but nobody took it seriously. It was too easy to mistake one plane for another, and everyone knew how fast rumors could get started. They had heard plenty of them over the years, from the guy who'd claimed to be run off the road by Grissom's Corvette after the *Apollo 1* fire to the Australian who'd supposedly found a piece of Yuri Gagarin's spacesuit in the debris that rained over the outback when *Skylab* came down. This was just one more strange bit of folklore tacked onto the Apollo era, which was itself fast fading into legend.

Then Neil Armstrong died, and a Saturn V launched itself from Pad 34.

Rick Spencer was there the morning it went up. He had flown his T-38 down from Arlington right after the funeral, grabbed a few hours of sleep right there at the Cape, then driven over to the shuttle complex before dawn to watch the ground crew load a communications satellite into the *Atlantis.* The ungainly marriage of airplane and rocket on Pad 39A would be his ticket to orbit in another week if they ever got the damned thing off the ground, but one of the technicians forgot to mark a step off his checklist and the whole procedure shut down while the foreman tried to decide whether to back up and verify the job or take the tech at his word when he said he'd done it. Rick was getting tired of waiting for somebody to make a decision, so he went outside the sealed payload mating bay for a breath of fresh air.

The sun had just peeked over the horizon. The wire catwalk beneath his feet and the network of steel girders all around him glowed reddish gold in the dawn light. The hammerhead crane overhead seemed like a dragon's long, slender neck and head leaning out to sniff curiously at the enormous winged orbiter that stood there sweating with dew beneath its gaze. The ground, nearly two hundred feet below, was still inky black. Sunlight hadn't reached it yet, wouldn't for a few more minutes. The ocean was dark, too, except near the horizon where the brilliant crescent of sun reflected off the water.

From his high catwalk Rick looked down the long line of launch pads to the south, the tops of their gantries projecting up into the light as well. Except for Pads 34 and 37. Those two had been decommissioned after the Apollo program, and now all that remained were the concrete bunkers and blast deflectors that couldn't be removed, low gray shapes still languishing in the shadow of early dawn. Just like the whole damned space program, Rick thought. Neil had been given a hero's burial, and the President's speech had been full of promise for renewed support of manned exploration in space, but it was all a lot of hot air and everyone knew it. The aging shuttle fleet was all America had, and all it was likely to get for the foreseeable future. Even if NASA could shake off the bureaucratic stupor it had fallen into and propose a new program, Congress would never pass an appropriations bill for the hardware.

Rick looked away, but a flicker of motion drew his attention back to Pad 34, where brilliant floodlights now lit a gleaming white rocket and its orange support tower. Rick blinked, but it didn't go away. He stepped closer to the railing and squinted. Where had *that* come from? Over half of it rose above the dawn line; Rick looked over the edge of the *Atlantis*'s gantry and made a quick guess based on his own height. That rocket had to be over three hundred feet tall.

Three hundred and sixty-three, to be exact. Rick couldn't measure it that exactly, but he didn't need to. He recognized the black-striped Saturn V instantly, and he knew its stats by heart. He had memorized them when he was a kid, sitting in front of his parents' black-and-white TV set while he waited for the liftoffs. Three hundred sixty-three feet high, weighing over three thousand tons when fueled, the five F-1 engines in its first stage producing seven and a half *million* pounds of thrust—it was the biggest rocket ever built.

And it had also been over thirty years since the last of them flew. Rick closed his eyes and rubbed them with his left hand. Evidently Neil's death had affected him more than he thought. But when he looked to the south again he still saw the brilliant white spike standing there in its spotlight glare, mist swirling down its side as the liquid oxygen in its tanks chilled the air around the massive rocket.

Rick was alone on the gantry. Everyone else was inside, arguing about the payload insertion procedure. He considered going in and asking someone to come out and tell him if he was crazy or not, but he abandoned that thought immediately. One week before his first flight, he wasn't about to confess to hallucinations.

It sure looked real. Rick watched the dawn line creep down the Saturn's flank, sliding over the ever-widening stages until it reached the long cylinder of the main body. The spectacle was absolutely silent. The only sound came from closer by: the squeak and groan of the shuttle gantry expanding as it began to warm under the light.

Then, without warning, a billowing cloud of reddish-white smoke erupted from the base of the rocket. The eye-searing brightness of RP-1 and oxygen flame lit up the cloud from within, and more exhaust blasted sideways out of the flame deflectors.

Rick felt the gantry vibrate beneath him, but there was still no sound. The exhaust plume rose nearly as high as the nose cone, roiling like a mushroom cloud over an atomic blast, then slowly the rocket began to lift. Bright white flame sprayed the entire launch pad as the thundering booster, gulping thousands of gallons of fuel per second, rose into the sky. Only when the five bell-shaped nozzles cleared the gantry—nearly ten seconds after liftoff—did the solid beam of flame grow ragged at the edges. A few final tongues of it licked the ground, then the rocket lifted completely into the air.

The shuttle gantry beneath Rick's feet shook harder. He grabbed for support just as the sound reached him: a thunderous, crackling assault that sent him staggering back against the catwalk's inner railing, his hands over his ears. The gantry shook like a skyscraper in an earthquake, knocking him to his knees on the non-skid grating. He didn't try to rise again, just stared upward in awe as the Saturn V dwindled rapidly and the roar of its engines tapered off with distance.

The glare left afterimages when he blinked. He didn't care. He watched the rocket arc over and begin its long downrange run, picking up orbital velocity now that it had cleared the thickest part of the atmosphere.

The door behind him burst open and a flood of white-jacketed technicians scrambled out. The first few stopped when they saw the enormous plume of exhaust rising into the sky, and the ones behind them piled into their backs, forcing them forward until everyone was packed near the railing. Molly, the payload foreman, gave Rick a hand up, and bent close to his ear to shout over the roar of the rocket and the babble of voices, "What the hell was that?"

Rick shook his head. "Damned if I know."

"There wasn't supposed to be a launch today," she said.

Rick looked up at the dwindling rocket, now just a bright

spark aiming for the sun, and said, "Something tells me Control was just as surprised as we were." He pointed toward the base of the exhaust plume, where the cloud had spread out enough to reveal the gantry again.

"What?" Molly asked, squinting to see through the billowing steam. Then she realized what he was pointing at. "Isn't that Pad 34?"

Molly and her payload crew reluctantly trooped back into the mating bay to see if the shaking had damaged their satellite, but since Rick was on his own time he rode the cage elevator down to the ground, climbed into his pickup, and joined the line of cars streaming toward the launch site.

The scrub oak and palmetto that lined the service road prevented anyone from seeing the pad until they had nearly reached it. Rick thought he should have been able to see the 400-foot gantry, at least, but when he arrived at the pad he realized why he hadn't. It had vanished just as mysteriously as it had arrived, leaving not a trace.

Rick drove across the vast concrete apron to the base of the old launch pedestal. It looked like an enormous concrete footstool: four squat legs holding a ten-foot-thick platform forty feet in the air, with a thirty-foot-wide hole in the platform for the rocket exhaust to pour through. Off to the side stood the foundation and the thick blast protection wall of the building that had once housed propellant pumps and service equipment. Now both structures looked old and weathered. Rust streaks ran down their gray sides, and stenciled on the pitted concrete, the paint itself fading, were the words, "ABANDON IN PLACE."

Weeds grew out of cracks in the apron, still green and vigorous even right up next to the pedestal. Rick was beginning to doubt what he'd seen, because obviously nothing had launched from this pad for at least a decade.

But the contrail still arched overhead, high-altitude winds

snaking it left and right, and when Rick opened the door and stepped out of his pickup he smelled the unmistakable mixture of RP-1 smoke and steam and scorched cement that came with a launch.

Doors slammed as more people got out of their cars. Dozens of them were there already, and more arrived every minute, but what should have been an unruly mob was strangely quiet. Nobody wanted to admit what they'd seen, especially in the face of so much conflicting evidence.

Rick recognized Tessa McClain, an experienced astronaut whom he'd dated a few times in the last couple of months, climbing out of the back of a white van along with half a dozen other people from the vehicle assembly building. When she saw him she jogged across the concrete to his side and said, "Did you see it?" Her face glowed with excitement.

"Yeah," Rick said. "I was up on the gantry at thirty-nine."

She looked up at the contrail overhead, her straight blonde hair falling back over her shoulders. "Wow. That must have been a hell of a sight. I felt it shake the ground, but I didn't get outside until it was already quite a ways up." She looked back down at him. "It was a Saturn V, wasn't it?"

"That's what it looked like," he admitted.

"God, this is incredible." She turned once around, taking in the entire launch pad. "A moon rocket! I never expected to see anything like it ever again."

"Me either," Rick said. He struggled to find the words to express what he was thinking. "But how could we possibly have seen anything? There's no tower here, no fuel tanks, nothing. And the launch pedestal is too small for a fully fueled Saturn V. This complex was for the S-1Bs."

She grinned like a child at Christmas. "I'm sure whoever—or whatever—staged this little demonstration was able to make all the support hardware they needed. And take it away again when they were done with it."

Rick shook his head. "But that's impossible."

Tessa laughed. "We all saw it." She pointed upward. "And the contrail's still there." Suddenly her eyes grew even wider.

"What?" Rick asked.

She looked across the rolling hummocks of palmetto toward the fifty-story-high vehicle assembly building—and the launch control center at its base. "I wonder if it's sending back telemetry?"

CHAPTER 2

It took a while to find out. Nobody remembered what frequencies the Apollo spacecraft broadcast on or what protocols the data streams used, and the ground controllers had to dig through archived manuals to find out. It took still more time to set up the receivers to accept the signals, but when the technicians eventually tuned in to the right frequencies they found a steady information flow. They couldn't decode most of it, since the software to do that had been written for the old RCA computer system, but they did at least establish that the rocket had not vanished along with its ground support structures.

Rick and Tessa were in the launch control center, watching the overhead monitors while programmers in the central instrumentation building frantically attempted to adapt the old programs to the new machines. What they saw was mostly a lot of numbers, but every few minutes one of the programmers would patch in another section of translated code and another display would wink into place on the screen. They had already figured out cabin temperature and pressure, fuel level in the upper-stage tanks, and a few of the other simple systems.

By this point in a normal flight the whole project would rightfully belong to Mission Control in Houston, but there was nothing normal about this launch. When the Houston flight director heard what the Kennedy team was doing, he wanted nothing to do with it anyway. He intended to keep his own neck well out of the way when heads started rolling after this crazy debacle was over.

But the spacecraft stubbornly refused to disappear. Radar tracked it through one complete orbit and part of another, when its altitude and velocity began to rise. At the same time, the fuel levels in the third-stage tanks began to drop. That could mean only one thing: The booster was firing again.

"Translunar injection," Tessa whispered. "They're going for the Moon."

"Who's 'they'?" Rick asked. So far none of the telemetry indicated a live—or even a ghostly—passenger in the command module.

"It's got to be Neil," Tessa said. "And who knows who else is going with him."

"Neil is in a box in Arlington Cemetery," Rick said. "I saw them put him there."

"And you saw the launch this morning," Tessa reminded him. "Neil being on board it is no more impossible than the rocket itself."

"Good point." Rick shrugged. Every dead astronaut from Gagarin on could be in the mystery Apollo capsule for all he knew. This bizarre manifestation was completely new territory; nobody knew the rules yet.

Enough people claimed to, of course. Psychics seemed to crawl out of the woodwork over the next few days, each with their own interpretation of the event. NASA had to close the gates and post guards around the perimeter of the space center to keep it from being overrun by curious mystics, but that merely fueled speculation that they were developing a new super-secret space vehicle at the taxpayers' expense.

The administration tried the silent approach at first, but when that charge was leveled they reluctantly admitted that for once the fruitcakes were closer to the truth than the whistleblowers. In a carefully worded press release, NASA's public relations spokesman said, "What appeared to be a Saturn V moon rocket seemed to launch from the deserted complex thirty-four. This alleged launch was not authorized by NASA, nor was it part of any program of which NASA is aware. A complete investigation of the incident is being made, and our findings will be made public as soon as we learn what actually occurred."

That was Bureauspeak for, "We don't have a clue either." Rick spent days with the investigation team, going over his story again and again—careful to say "appeared to" and "looked like" at all the appropriate spots—until he could recite it in his sleep, but no one was the wiser afterward. They examined the launch pad, which revealed no sign of a liftoff. All they could do was listen to the telemetry coming from the spacecraft and speculate.

Three days after its launch, the ghost Apollo entered lunar orbit. A few hours after that, the lunar module separated from the command module and made a powered descent toward the surface. It wasn't headed for the Sea of Tranquility. It appeared to be landing at Copernicus, one of the sites proposed for further Apollo missions before the last three had been canceled. But when it reached 500 feet, the telemetry suddenly stopped.

"What the hell happened?" demanded Dale Jackson, the impromptu flight director for the mission. He stood beside one of the consoles on the lowest of the terraced rows, looking around at the dozens of technicians who were scrambling to reacquire the signal.

Tessa and Rick were watching from farther up, sitting side by side at unused consoles and holding hands like teenagers on a date at the best movie of all time. When the telemetry stopped, Tessa flinched as if a monster had just jumped out of a closet.

"What happened?" Rick asked. "Did it blow up?"

Tessa shook her head. "Everything stopped," she said. "The command module too, and it was still in orbit."

"Five hundred feet," Rick said. Something about that figure nagged at him. What happened at five hundred feet in a normal lunar descent? "Got it!" he said, loudly enough that everyone in the room looked back up at the screens. When they saw no data there, they turned to him.

"Five hundred feet was 'low gate,' when the pilot was supposed to take over from the descent computer and actually land the LEM," he told them. "The computer couldn't take it all the way to the surface. It wasn't sophisticated enough to choose a landing site."

Jackson asked, "So, what, you think it crashed? It was still five hundred feet up."

Rick hesitated. He'd been biting his tongue for days, afraid of knocking himself off the *Atlantis* mission with a poorly chosen phrase, but he had grown tired of being timid. He cleared his throat and said, "I think when the time came for a human to take over, it went back to wherever it came from."

"Sure it did." Jackson turned to the technicians. "Get me that signal."

They tried, but it quickly became apparent that there simply wasn't a signal any longer. Not even radar could find any sign of the spacecraft. The mysterious Apollo had vanished without a trace.

NASA held back Rick's *Atlantis* mission an extra week while the ground crew checked the ship for damage from the shaking it had received, but at last they pronounced it ready to fly. On the morning of the launch, Rick and four other astronauts rode the elevator up the gantry, climbed in through the hatch in the side of the orbiter, and strapped themselves into their acceleration chairs. After a countdown that was only interrupted twice due to a defective pressure sensor in a fuel line, they finally lit the three main engines and the two solid rocket boosters and rode America's space truck into orbit.

It was Rick's first time in space. He had expected to be excited, and he was, but somehow not so excited as he had imagined. Instead of watching the Earth slide past beneath him, he spent most of his free time watching the Moon, now just past full. It had been lunar dawn at the landing site when the Apollo had lifted off, just the way it had been for the real flights over a quarter of a century earlier. That was to give the crew the best lighting angle for landing, and to make sure they had plenty of daylight to explore in. And to make emergency repairs if anything went wrong.

What a wild time that must have been, he thought as he floated between the pilot's and copilot's chairs and looked out the forward windows at the white disk a quarter million miles away. Flying by the seat of your pants, your life right at your fingertips and the entire world watching over your shoulder to see if you had the wits to keep yourself alive. Aldrin had accidentally snapped off the pin of the ascent engine arming switch with his backpack, and he'd had to poke a felt tip pen into the hole to arm the engines before he and Armstrong could leave the Moon. A felt pen! If something like that happened on the shuttle, ground control would probably order the crew to conserve power and wait for a rescue—except they still couldn't launch a second shuttle within a month of the first one. Maybe they could get the Russians to come up and push the button for them with one of *their* felt pens.

He was being unfair. The Hubble telescope repair had taken some real ingenuity, and the international space station scientists were always fixing broken equipment. But none of that had the same dazzle as flying to the Moon. Nowadays the shuttle astronauts seemed more like appliance repairmen than intrepid explorers. Rick had convinced himself that the shuttle was doing some valuable science, but after seeing a Saturn V launch only two weeks earlier, he realized that science wasn't what had thrilled him when he'd watched them as a kid, and it wasn't why he was here now. He was in space because he wanted to explore it, and this—barely two hundred miles off the ground—was the farthest into it he could get.

He wished Tessa were on his flight. She would know what

he was feeling. On their dates, they had talked a lot about their reasons for becoming astronauts, and she had admitted to the same motives as him. But she had been scheduled for *Discovery's* next launch in a month and a half.

He heard a shout from the mid-deck. *"Merde!"* A moment later, Pierre Renaud, the Canadian payload specialist whose company had paid for his ticket, floated through the hatchway onto the flight deck.

"What's the matter?" Rick asked when he saw the look of dismay on Pierre's face.

"The toilet has broken," Pierre said.

ick was on post-flight vacation in Key West when the next one went up. The phone woke him from a sound sleep just after dawn, and when he fumbled the receiver to his ear and answered it, Dale Jackson's gravelly voice said, "There's been another Saturn launch. Get your ass up here so we can compare notes with the last time."

Rick came instantly awake. Less than an hour later he was in the air headed north. By the time he crossed Lake Okeechobee he could see the ragged remains of the contrail, and when he arrived at the Cape the place looked like an anthill that had just been kicked. Cars zoomed up and down the service roads, and the public highways outside the gates were packed in all directions.

Two wide-eyed Air Force cadets escorted him from the airport to a meeting room in the headquarters building, where NASA's administrator, flight director, range safety officer, and at least a dozen other high-ranking officials were already deep in discussion over the incident. Rick noted with amusement that the flight surgeon was also present, and presumably taking notes. Jackson, the flight director, was taking about the difficulty of decommissioning a fully fueled Saturn V on the pad, should another one appear.

"We don't even have facilities there to store the fuel anymore, much less pump it," he was saying. "Especially not in the fifteen minutes or so that these things stick around. That's barely time enough to hook up the couplings."

Tessa was there as well, and she smiled wide and waved when she saw Rick. He edged around the conference table and pulled up a chair beside her. "What are you doing here?" he whispered.

"Getting the third degree," Tessa answered. "I was at the pad when this one lifted off."

"Which pad?"

"Thirty-four."

"You're kidding. You'd be toast if you were that close to the launch."

"I was in the blockhouse."

Rick supposed that would offer some protection. And besides, even that might not be necessary. The weeds hadn't been charred or blown away in the first launch. "Why were you there?" he asked. "How did you know it would happen again?"

She grinned, obviously proud of herself. "Because ghosts usually repeat themselves until they get whatever they came for, and today was the next launch window."

At the head of the table, Jackson was still talking. ". . . Nor do we have crawler capability to remove the rocket even if we *could* pump it dry. We'd have to completely rebuild the access road, and in the meantime we'd be left with a thirty-six-story embarrassment."

Rick sized up the meeting in an instant. NASA saw these ghost rockets as a threat, and wanted them stopped.

"Why don't we just put astronauts in them instead?" he asked. "There's time enough to ride up the gantry and climb inside before launch."

Jackson squinted down the table at him. "In a completely unknown and untested vehicle? No way."

"It's not unknown or untested," said Tessa. "It's a Saturn V."

"It's a goddamned mystery," Jackson said, "and there's no valid reason to risk anyone's life on one, either on the ground or in space."

"What do you propose to do, then?" the range safety officer asked. "Shoot them down?"

Nervous laughter broke out around the table, but quickly

died out. Jackson shook his head. "I propose we let them go. Assuming there are any more. They aren't harming anything except our image."

Warren Altman, latest in a string of five new administrators in the last two years, said, "Yes, precisely. Our image. We're in enough trouble as it is without Congress thinking things are out of control down here." He paused to take off his glasses, and used one of the earpieces for a pointer as he continued, "No, Dale, we can't afford to do nothing. No matter how bizarre this situation is, we've got to take control of it, show Congress that we're handling it, or we'll lose even more credibility than we already have. That means decommissioning the damned things, and if we can't do it on the ground then we'll just have to do it in orbit."

"How?" asked Jackson.

"Just as Rick suggested. Put an astronaut in one, and let him interrupt the mission once it reaches Earth orbit. We'll already have a shuttle up there next month; it can rendezvous with the Apollo and our astronaut can return on the shuttle."

"Leaving the third stage and the rest of the spacecraft in orbit," Jackson pointed out.

"Better there than on the pad," Altman replied. "Besides, maybe we can figure out a use for it. *Skylab* was just an empty Saturn third stage." He laughed. "Hell, if this continues for a few months, we could have all the habitat modules we need to build a decent space station of our own instead of that international disaster we're using now."

"And what if they disappear on us just like the last one?"

Altman's eyes narrowed. He hadn't thought of that. But he just shrugged and said, "We'll worry about that later. Chances are the damned things will fade out as soon as we interfere anyway. That's what usually happens with ghosts." He pointed his glasses at Rick. "It's your idea; do you want to volunteer?"

"Of course I do!" Rick said.

"You lucky bastard," Tessa whispered.

He thought so, too, until the training started. For the next month, Jackson kept him on sixteen-hour days in the simulators, training for a mission that hadn't even been considered in over two decades. He learned every switch and dial in the Apollo command module until he could operate the ship with his eyes closed, and he practiced every contingency that the flight engineers could come up with, including a lunar flyby and slingshot back to Earth in case the rocket wouldn't let him shut it down before translunar injection. They had plenty of data already for that kind of abort: *Apollo 13* had done a slingshot return when an oxygen tank had blown on the way to the Moon.

Rick even argued them into letting him train in a mockup lunar module, reasoning that he might be able to use it as a lifeboat in case of a similar emergency. They also let him practice using the descent and ascent engines for emergency thrust, and after he wheedled with them for a few days they even let him practice landing.

"Only because it'll help you get a feel for the controls," Jackson told him. "You couldn't actually land even if you wanted to, because if you separate the lunar module from the command module, you're dead. Rendezvous and docking is done from the command module, and you won't have a pilot."

Rick wondered about that. They didn't know who or what might inhabit the capsule atop the enormous rocket. It might be anything from Armstrong's preserved corpse to the Ghost of Christmas Future. The only thing NASA knew for sure was that they weren't going to risk more than one person on this flight.

So Rick found himself standing alone at the base of the concrete pedestal during the hour before dawn on the morning of the next launch window. He wore a shuttle spacesuit modified to allow him to lie in an Apollo couch—the best they could come up with in only a month, since the few remaining Apollo suits in the Smithsonian and other museums were over thirty years old and wouldn't hold air without major refurbishing. He also wore a parachute strapped to his back. The parachute was Jackson's idea, in case the whole Saturn V, gantry and all, faded away when Rick tried to enter the capsule 350 feet off the ground.

Pad 34 was spooky in the pre-dawn twilight. Little gusts of wind rattled the bushes that grew out of the cracks in the concrete, and Rick felt eyes watching him. Most of those belonged to the NASA personnel who waited in the blockhouse nearly a thousand feet away, but the tingling at the back of his neck made Rick wonder if other eyes were watching him as well, and maybe judging him. What would they make of him? He'd been barely ten years old when the *Eagle* landed, was never a military pilot like the first astronauts, never even a soldier. Just a kid who'd always dreamed of becoming an astronaut. And now here he stood with his spacesuit on, holding his suitcase-sized portable ventilator like a banker with his briefcase waiting at a subway stop, while the empty launch pad mocked his every breath.

Even the pads to the north were empty. *Discovery* had already lifted off three days ago, taking Tessa and five others into orbit with the Spacelab, where they were to study the effects of free fall on fruit fly mating habits—and also to await Rick's arrival. They had put themselves in the most likely orbit for the Apollo to take, but it was still a gamble and everyone knew it. If they had guessed wrong, Rick would have to go to plan B: re-entry using the Apollo capsule.

There would be no rescue if that didn't work. None of the other shuttles were even close to being ready for launch; *Atlantis* was still at Edwards, waiting for a ride home that might never come because the 747 carrier plane had developed cracks in the

wing struts, and *Columbia* and *Endeavor* were both in the vehicle assembly building with their supposedly reusable engines
scattered across acres of service bay while the technicians tried
to match enough parts to get one complete set to work.

At least Rick was there. His heart was pounding, but he
was there and ready to fly. He squared his shoulders and
checked his watch. Any time now.

Suddenly, silently, the rocket appeared. Spotlight glare
blinded Rick until he lowered his sun visor, then he turned
once around to orient himself. The gantry was right where
he'd expected it to be, and the Saturn V . . . Rick tilted his
head back and felt his heart skip a beat. It was colossal. From
right there at the base of it, the thing looked like it already
reached to the Moon.

He didn't have time to gawk. He ran awkwardly for the
elevator, his boots slapping the concrete, then climbed inside
the elevator cage and rode it all the way to the top, nervously
watching the ground drop farther and farther away. Two-
thirds of the way up, he crossed into sunlight.

The metal structure squeaked and groaned around him, just
like the shuttle gantry did. The grating underfoot scuffed
against his boots as he crossed over on the swing arm bridge to
the white room and the capsule. The hatch was open, as if waiting for him. Normally a crew of technicians would be there to
help him into his seat, but he was completely alone. Nobody
waited inside the capsule, either. Quickly, lest the rocket
launch with him on the gantry, he climbed in, unplugged his
ventilator, tossed it back out the hatch, and plugged one of the
ship's three umbilicals into his suit. He jounced up and down
on the seat a time or two. Banged on the hatch frame with his
gloved hand. Solid. Satisfied, he tossed the parachute out after
the ventilator, pulled the hatch closed, sealed it, and sank back
into the center couch.

The instrument panel was a forest of switches and knobs
before him, uncomfortably close to his face. He scanned the

readouts, looking for anomalies, while he took a deep breath and smelled the cool, metallic scent of the pressurized air. His suit umbilical was working, then. He should have a radio link now, too. He spoke into his suit's microphone. "Control, this is Apollo, do you read?"

"Loud and clear," Jackson's voice said.

"Ready for liftoff," Rick told him.

"Good. Estimated time to launch . . . uh, call it two minutes."

"Roger." Rick's pulse rate was sky-high. He tried to calm himself down, but the lack of a real countdown somehow underscored how crazy this whole thing was. He was sitting on top of a ghost!

He forced himself to concentrate on the instruments in front of him. Main power bus, green. Cabin temperature, nominal. Fuel pressure—

Amber lights blinked on, and a low rumble vibrated the walls.

"Ignition sequence starting," Jackson said.

"Roger. I feel it."

"All engines running."

Through the hatch window Rick saw the swing arm glide away, and the cabin seemed to sway slightly to the right.

"Liftoff. We have liftoff."

The rumble grew louder, and Rick felt the acceleration begin to build. The launch tower slid downward out of sight, and then all he could see was blue morning sky. He had expected the gees to slam him back into the seat, but they built gently as the booster burned its fuel and the rocket grew lighter. When the second stage ignited there was a lurch and the gees grew stronger, but still bearable.

This time Houston had gotten in on the act. Mission Control took over the flight now, and Laura Turner, the capsule communicator, said, "You're looking good, Apollo. Escape tower jettison in twenty seconds."

Rick felt the thump right on schedule, and now that the tower and its boost protection cover were gone he could see out the side windows as well. Florida was a long ways down already, and receding fast.

The third stage ignited a few minutes later, propelling the spaceship on into orbit. "Right on target," Laura said. "We track you one hundred miles uprange of *Discovery* and closing."

"Roger."

And now it was time for Rick to earn his ride. He didn't have to do much; NASA wouldn't let him fly the Apollo toward the shuttle. It was his job to disarm the engines and let Tessa bring the shuttle to him. Holding his breath, he reached out to the too-close instrument panel with his gloved index finger. Would the ship let him take over, or would it hold him prisoner all the way to the Moon? Or would it vanish in a puff of smoke the moment he touched the controls?

Only one way to tell. The switches clicked home with a satisfying thunk, and the indicator lights showed those circuits dead. The rest of the instruments, and the capsule itself, remained undisturbed. Rick took a breath, then reported, "Engines disarmed. Apollo is now safe for rendezvous."

"Roger, Apollo. Sit back and enjoy the ride, Rick."

He unstrapped himself and drifted free of the acceleration couch. The Apollo capsule might be cramped compared to the shuttle, but with only one person in it he had enough room to float from window to window and look at the blue-and-white Earth below.

And at the Moon, once again in its crescent phase. It beckoned to him stronger than ever, for here he sat in a spaceship that could take him there. Take him there and land, if only he had two more astronauts to fly with him.

The shuttle was a bright speck against the solid black of space, drawing steadily closer. Rick watched until it resolved into the familiar stubby-winged orbiter.

"Apollo, this is *Discovery*," Tessa said over the radio. "Do you read?" Her voice sounded excited, as well it might. Not every day did she get the chance to rendezvous with a ghost.

Rick smiled at the sound of her voice. He had always wanted to fly a mission with her. He had always assumed when it happened he would be the low man on the duty roster, cleaning rat droppings out of cages on a Spacelab flight or something, but here he was commander of his own ship, making space history.

He said, "*Discovery* this is Apollo. I read you loud and clear. Good to see you, Tessa."

"Are you ready for EVA?"

EVA. Extravehicular activity. They couldn't actually dock the Apollo and the shuttle; Rick would have to transfer across on his own, leaving the Apollo to coast onward alone, its engines silenced, its mission—whatever that might be—unfulfilled.

But if NASA really turned it into another *Skylab*, that might mollify whoever or whatever was behind these launches. Then maybe it wouldn't go to waste.

Rick shook his head. Who was he kidding? NASA would never use this ship for anything. He'd known it ever since he saw the look on Altman's face when Jackson asked what they would do if it faded away. Altman just wanted to show Congress—and the power behind the new Apollo—that NASA was still in control. He expected this to be the last of the mystery ships, now that Rick had deactivated it.

"Apollo, do you copy?" Tessa asked.

Rick swallowed. If he screwed with the flight plan, it would be the last time he ever flew. Worse, the spaceship could turn into gossamer and cobwebs at any moment, stranding him in cislunar space with nothing but a pressure suit, slowly suffocating as his air supply ran out. Or it could wait until he reached the Moon before fading out, just as the last two had done, the first over Copernicus and the second over the

Aristarchus Plateau. But if he didn't at least try it, could he live with himself for the rest of his life, knowing that he'd once had the opportunity to go to the Moon but had turned it down?

He had always wanted to explore the unknown; well this was certainly his opportunity for it. He had no idea whose ghost this was or what its purpose might be, but it was his ship now, by right of conquest if nothing else. So what was he going to do with it?

Tessa called again. "Hello, Apollo, are you ready for EVA?"

He took a deep breath. "Negative," he said. "Negative. In fact, I think I'm going to need a little help over here."

"What sort of help, Apollo?"

Looking out at the brilliant white crescent, he said, "I need someone to ride with me to the Moon. Preferably two someones. You know anybody who wants to go?"

essa's shriek was inarticulate, a primal whoop of surprise or relief or laughter, but before Rick could ask her which it was, Laura, in Houston, said, "Don't even *think* it, Rick. You do not have authorization for an extended mission. Is that clear?"

Rick sighed. But he could already hear the roar of bridges burning. "Clear as space itself, Laura, but I'm going. And if I can take a full crew with me, then I'm going to land when I get there. There's nothing you can do to stop me."

"Negative, Rick. You need ground control. Now that you've disarmed the engines, you have no assurance that any aspect of the mission will proceed normally. You'll have to re-arm and fire the engines yourself, but without us you won't know when to do that. Even after you're on your way, you'll need our radar for tracking, and you'll need our computers to calculate course corrections, and—"

"I get the point, Capcom." By the quickness of her response, Laura had obviously considered all this beforehand, but it didn't matter. "You're bluffing," Rick told her. "You wouldn't let us die out here if you could prevent it."

She didn't answer. Rick took that as answer enough. Tessa evidently did, too; she said, "We're coming over."

A new voice, Dale Jackson's, said, "You're staying right there. Rick, Tessa, we will not provide tracking for a lunar flight. I don't care if you drift straight out of the solar system, we will not jeopardize the entire space program just to satisfy your curiosity."

"What space program?" Tessa asked. "We're breeding fruit flies over here." That wasn't exactly fair; one of the payload specialists was an astronomer who was running a free-flying instrument platform—but she was from Japan.

"I'm not going to argue with you. Tessa, if you leave *Discovery*, you will be charged with dereliction of duty and reckless endangerment of the rest of the crew. And I'm not bluffing; if you attempt to leave Earth orbit in that Apollo, you'll be on your own."

Rick looked at the empty seats on either side of him. In a cramped alcove behind them was the navigation equipment—a telescope and sextant and a primitive guidance computer—that could theoretically provide him with enough measurements and computing ability to stay on course. But he hadn't trained to use them, and he bet neither Tessa nor whoever was coming with her knew how to calculate their trajectory with them, either.

"What do you think, Tessa?" he asked. "Can we do it without ground control?"

"I don't—"

"That will not be necessary," a new voice said, drowning her out. It had a heavy accent, but Rick couldn't place it immediately. Some foreign ham operator broadcasting on the Tracking and Data Relay Satellite frequencies?

"Who's that?" he asked.

"I am Gregor Ivanov, of the Russian Space Agency in Kaliningrad. I have been monitoring your signal, and am prepared to offer assistance."

Houston was evidently receiving his signal, too. "You can't do that!" Jackson yelled.

The Russian laughed. "I certainly can. In fact, I must. International treaties legally require that Russia offer help to any craft that has been disabled or abandoned either at sea or in space."

"You stay out of this!" Jackson yelled again. "That craft is neither disabled nor abandoned."

"Oh? Perhaps I mis-heard you. Do you plan to offer ground radar support for the lunar landing mission?" Gregor laughed again, clearly enjoying his position.

Jackson wasn't amused. "Get off this frequency, Russki," he growled. "You're creating an international incident."

"I certainly hope so," Gregor replied. "Apollo, I repeat my offer. Kaliningrad control will provide your ground support for a lunar landing and sample-return mission. Do you wish our assistance?"

Rick felt a laugh bubbling up from his own throat. Could he trust the Russians to guide an Apollo to the Moon? Would they actually help an American crew reenact the mission that had embarrassed their country over thirty years ago? Probably. The Cold War was dead and buried, with the Berlin Wall for a tombstone. Whether or not they could actually perform was the big question. Their computer equipment was nearly as antiquated as the 36K of wire-wrapped core memory under the navigation console.

But Rick really didn't have much choice. Houston would fight him every step of the way. And besides, an international mission sounded kind of nice about now. Rick would need someone on his side when he returned. If he returned. Shaking his head, he said, "Any port in a storm, Kaliningrad. I accept your offer."

"This is treason!" Jackson shouted, but Rick ignored him.

Tessa said, "We're coming across, Apollo."

"You're already suited up?" It took two hours of pre-breathing pure oxygen to purge the nitrogen from a shuttle astronaut's bloodstream before they could exit the ship; Tessa and whoever else was coming with her must have started before Rick had even launched.

"Contingency planning," Tessa replied, amusement in her voice. "You might have needed rescue, you know."

"Ah, of course," Rick said.

Jackson tried again. "Tessa, think about this. You're throwing away your whole career for nothing."

"I wouldn't call a lunar landing 'nothing.' "

"It's a goddamned ghost! It's worse than nothing. You could be killed!"

"Yes, I could, couldn't I?" Tessa said. "We could all be killed. Or worse yet, we could all give up the dream and keep flying shuttles into low orbit until they all wear out and Congress decides that manned spaceflight is a waste of time. I don't want to die in a geriatric ward, wishing I'd taken my one big chance at a real space mission."

She grunted with effort, and Rick saw the shuttle's airlock door swing open. A white space-suited figure slowly emerged, then another. Rick wondered who the second person was. Another of the shuttle's regular crew-members? Unlikely. They needed someone to fly the thing back home. That left the Spacelab scientists. Rick ran down the list in his mind and came up with the obvious choice: Yoshiko Sugano, the Japanese astronomer. Her instrument pallet was designed to fly free of the shuttle's annoying vibration and surface glow, and she had been trained to guide it by remote control. She understood docking maneuvers better than most of the regular astronauts; she would make a perfect command module pilot. Besides which, she would make the mission a truly international effort, a point that Tessa had no doubt considered long before Kaliningrad got into the act.

Sure enough, when the two space-suited figures bumped up against the Apollo and crawled around to the open hatch, Rick saw Tessa's grinning face through her bubble helmet, and behind her, swimming a bit in the one-size-fits-most shuttle suit, was Yoshiko. She didn't look nearly as pleased with herself as Tessa, but she had come along.

"Request permission to come aboard," she said somewhat breathlessly.

"Yes, yes, of course!" Rick said, helping her and Tessa through the narrow rectangle. It was a tight fit; his modified suit had made it okay, but regular shuttle suits had never been designed to fit through an Apollo hatch. Rick felt a moment's panic run through him as he suddenly wondered if they would fit through the lander's hatch. They could make it all the way to the Moon only to get stuck in the doorway.

It was too late to worry about that. Like Aldrin and Armstrong and the engine-arming switch, they would just have to figure out something on the scene.

As they struggled to fit themselves into the three seats, Jackson tried one last grandstand act, threatening to charge them and the entire Russian Federation with piracy, but Rick said, "NASA doesn't own this ship. Nobody does. Or maybe everyone does. Either way, if you're not going to help us, then get off this frequency, because we need it to communicate with ground control."

"*We're* ground control, damnit!" Jackson shouted, "and I'm telling you to return to the mission profile."

"Sorry," Rick said. "Kaliningrad is now in control of this flight. Please get off the air."

Jackson said something else, but Gregor Ivanov also spoke at the same time, and neither transmission was intelligible.

"Say again, Kaliningrad, say again," Rick said, and this time Jackson stayed quiet.

Gregor said, "You still have a chance to make your original launch window if you can prepare for boost within the next fifty minutes. Do you think that is possible?"

Rick looked at Tessa, who nodded and gave the thumbs-up. Yoshiko, her eyes wide, only shrugged. This was her first space flight, and it was obviously not turning out the way she'd expected.

"We'll have to get out of these damned suits," Tessa said. "Ours aren't modified for these chairs, and the TLI boost would probably break our necks if we tried it suited up."

"Remove your suits, then," Gregor said, "and prepare for acceleration in fifty-three minutes."

"Roger." Rick made sure the hatch was sealed, then repressurized the cabin. When the gauge neared five pounds, he twisted his helmet until the latches clicked free and pulled it off. Tessa and Yoshiko did the same.

Their three helmets alone nearly filled the space between their heads and the control panels. Removing their suits became a comedy in a closet as they elbowed each other and bumped heads and shoulders in their struggle. The control switches all had guards surrounding them, round loops of metal like old-style flip tops from pop cans sticking out on either side of the toggles to keep people from accidently tripping them, but Rick still winced each time someone brushed a panel with a hand or a foot.

"This is ridiculous," Tessa said, giggling. "Let's unsuit one at a time, and help each other out."

"Right," said Rick. "You first." He and Yoshiko unsealed the waist ring around Tessa's suit and lifted the top half over her head, then Yoshiko held her shoulders while Rick worked the lower half off her legs. That left her in the Spandex cooling and ventilation suit; not as comfortable as regular clothing, with its woven-in plastic tubes and air hoses snaking along all four limbs, but better than the spacesuit. She also left her communications carrier "Snoopy hat" on so she could still hear the radio signals from the ground. Rick stuffed the suit in the equipment bay behind the seats, then he and Tessa helped Yoshiko out of hers, and finally the two women helped him unsuit as well. It was still clumsy business, and at one point Rick found his face pressed against Yoshiko's right breast, but when he said, "Oops, sorry!" and pulled away, he bonked his head on the control panel.

Yoshiko laughed and said, "Don't worry about it. I think we will all become very familiar with one another before this is finished." Rick glanced at Tessa, with whom he'd already become pretty familiar on the ground, and saw that she was grinning.

"In your dreams, Rick," she said. "There's barely room enough in here to pick your nose."

Yoshiko blushed, and so did Rick. He said, "That's not what I was thinking."

"Sure it wasn't. Watch yourself, Yo. He's insatiable. Fortunately, the checklist will keep him too busy to paw us much."

Yoshiko laughed nervously, and Rick realized he'd been had. Nothing he could say would redeem him.

Luckily, Tessa was right about the checklist. Besides stowing the spacesuits, they had to move the Apollo away from the shuttle—which was already receding on its own as well—then orient the ship correctly for the burn that would send them out of orbit, all while making sure the rest of the electronic and mechanical equipment was functioning.

Just over half an orbit later, their panel green and the moment of truth approaching, they waited nervously for the last few minutes to tick by. The engines were armed, the guidance computer was on-line, and Kaliningrad had calculated the proper start time and duration for the burn just in case they had to go to manual control. As Rick, in the left seat, hovered with his finger near the manual fire button, Tessa said, "Hey, we haven't named the ship yet. We can't launch for the Moon without a name."

"No, that would be bad luck," Yoshiko agreed.

They both looked at Rick, who shrugged and said, "I don't know. I hadn't even thought about it. How about 'The Ghost,' or 'The Spook'?"

Tessa shook her head. "No, that sends the wrong message. We need something positive, hopeful. Like 'Second Chance,' or, or—"

"Yes, you said it: 'Hope,' " Yoshiko said. Then, looking at Rick, she said, "Or 'The Spirit of Hope' if you want to keep the ghost aspect."

Rick nodded. "Yeah. I like it."

"Me too." Tessa licked her forefinger, tapped the overhead

hatch in the docking collar—the farthest forward point she could reach—and said, "I christen thee *Spirit of Hope.*"

Gregor's voice came over the radio. "Very good, *Spirit of Hope.* Stand by for transLunar injection in thirty seconds."

The DSKY, the primitive display/keyboard, flashed, "Go/No-go?" This was their last chance to abort. Rick hardly hesitated at all before he pushed the proceed button. He had already committed himself.

The three astronauts kept their eyes on the controls, watching for signs of trouble, as Gregor counted down the time. The seconds seemed to stretch out forever, but at last Gregor said, "Now!" and right on cue, the Saturn IV-B third-stage engine automatically fired for the last time, pressing them back into their seats with a little over a gee of thrust. Rick let his hand fall away from the manual fire button and tucked it against the armrest.

The cabin rumbled softly, the acceleration much smoother than during the ride up through the atmosphere. Rick glanced out the side window at the Earth, but the gee force blurred his vision until it was just a smear of blue and white.

The burn went on and on, over five minutes of thrust, propelling them from 17,000 miles per hour to 25,000, enough to escape the Earth's pull. Near the end of the burn, Rick forced his hand out to the cutoff button, just in case the computer didn't shut it off at the right moment, but Gregor's "Now!" and the sudden silence came simultaneously. Rick's hand leaped forward with the cessation of thrust and pushed the button anyway, but it wasn't necessary. They were coasting now, headed for the Moon.

CHAPTER 5

As soon as they unbuckled from their couches, they began taking stock. They had three days of coasting to do before they reached the Moon, plenty of time to explore every nook and cranny in the tiny capsule. Every cubic inch of it seemed filled with something, and the only way to find out what was there was to unpack it, inspect it, and put it back into place. There was no room to leave things out; in fact, there was hardly room enough for them all to explore the ship at once.

Yoshiko had been right: Within the first half hour they had ceased to worry about bumping into one another. In fact, attempting to avoid it just made them all the more aware of each other, so they simply ignored the forced intimacy and went on with their work, gently brushing aside the stray elbows and feet and other body parts that got in their way. Their spandex cooling and ventilation suits at least allowed the illusion of modesty, which was really all they could ask for in such a tiny space.

Rick didn't mind brushing against Tessa, nor did she seem to mind it when he did. Both of them were grinning like newlyweds, and the air between them seemed charged with a thousand volts. They kissed once while Yoshiko was busy in the equipment bay, just a quick touch of the lips, but it sent a thrill down Rick's spine nonetheless. This was better than any Shuttle flight with her would have been.

In most ways, at least. Rick's conviction wavered a bit when Yoshiko found the food, which came in vacuum-packed plastic bags with little accordion necks to squirt water in through to rehydrate it—and to squirt the gooey result out into the astronaut's mouth. Rick and Tessa laughed at her incredulous expression when she saw how it worked. "Like toothpaste?" she asked, and Rick, who had eaten the commercially available version in his school lunches throughout the fall of '69, laughed and said, "It tastes about like it, too."

"It'll keep us alive," Tessa said. "That's what counts. I doubt I'll taste a thing anyway."

She was fiddling with something she had found in a locker. Suddenly she laughed and said, "Smile!" and when Rick and Yoshiko looked up, they saw that she had a TV camera aimed at them. "Hey, Gregor, are you getting a picture?" she asked, panning from Rick to Yoshiko and back.

"*Da*, affirmative," Gregor said. "Very clear signal."

"Great!" Tessa panned slowly around the cabin, then went to a window and shot some footage of the Earth, already much smaller behind them.

"Wonderful!" Gregor said. "Perfect. We're getting it all on tape, but if you'll wait a few minutes I think we can broadcast you live on national television."

"You're kidding," Tessa said, turning the camera back inside.

"*Nyet*. We are working on it right now. It's late night in most of Russia; so what if we interrupt a few old horror movies? This is much more interesting."

"Wow. Hear that, Houston? The Russians are showing us live on TV."

Mission Control had been silent since before the TLI burn, but now Laura Turner, the regular capcom, said, "We read you, ah . . . *Hope*. We're receiving your signal, too. Hi, Rick. Hi, Yoshiko."

"Hi." Rick and Yo waved at the camera. They could hear some sort of commotion going on in the background, either in Houston or Kaliningrad, but they couldn't tell which.

Yoshiko said, "I wonder if anyone in Japan is receiving this?"

A few seconds later, a new voice said, "Yes, we are. This is

Tomiichi Amakawa at Tanegashima Space Center, requesting permission to join communication."

"Granted," Gregor said. "And welcome to the party."

"Thank you. We, too, are arranging to broadcast your signal. And Yoshiko, I have a message for you from your colleagues at university. They are very angry at you for abandoning their observatory, and they also wish you good luck."

She grinned. "Give them my apologies, and my thanks. And tell them if any of them would have done differently, they have rocks where their hearts should be."

"Hah! They envy you. We all do."

"You should. This is an incredible experience."

Gregor said, "We are ready. Perhaps you should give an introduction, so people will know why we are suddenly getting pictures from space."

"Right," said Tessa. She pointed the camera at Rick. "Go for it, Rick. You know as much about this as any of us."

Rick swallowed, suddenly nervous. All of Russia and Japan were watching. And who knew who else? Anybody with a satellite dish and the right receiver could pick up their signal. He slicked his hair back, licked his lips nervously, and said, "Uh, right. Okay, well, hi, I'm Rick Spencer, an American astronaut, and this is Yoshiko Sugano from Japan, and Tessa McClain behind the camera, also from America." Tessa turned the camera around, let it drift free, and backed up to get into the shot. She waved, tilting slowly sideways until she bumped her head against the back of a couch. All three astronauts laughed, and Rick felt himself relax a bit. When Tessa retrieved the camera and aimed it at him again, he said, "As you've probably heard by now, NASA has been plagued with ghosts for the last three months. Ghost Apollo rockets. Well, we decided to see if somebody could ride one into orbit, and once I got there I picked up Tessa and Yoshiko from the *Discovery* and here we are." He neglected to mention that they were defying orders; let NASA say so if they wanted to. At this point, the space agency would look like the Grinch if they tried it.

Rick said, "Despite its mysterious origin, it seems to behave like a regular Apollo spacecraft. It's every bit as solid as the original article—" he thumped one of the few bare stretches of wall with his knuckles "—and as you can see, every bit as cramped. But there's an amazing amount of stuff in this little thirteen-foot-wide cone. Let's show you some of it." With that for an introduction, Rick led the camera on a tour through the command module, pointing out all the controls and the few amenities, including the waste collection bags, about which he said, "They're primitive, but guaranteed not to break down at a delicate moment, like the shuttle toilet does half the time." He waved at the control panels again, at the hundreds of switches and knobs and gauges, and said, "That's the whole Apollo concept in a nutshell: nothing fancy, but it got the job done. And God willing—or whoever is responsible for this—it'll get the job done again."

Tessa held the camera on the control panel until Gregor said, "Thank you, Rick. We've been thumbing through the manual down here, and it looks like it's just about time for you to dock with the lunar module. Are you ready for that?"

Rick wondered what manual they were consulting. Probably a copy of Aldrin's *Men from Earth,* or one of the later books published around the twenty-fifth anniversary of the first landing. Or it was conceivable that they had copies of the actual checklists from the original flights. The Soviets had had a good spy network back in the sixties.

It didn't matter. They needed to dock with the LM, that much was obvious. Rick looked to Yoshiko. "How about it?" he asked. "I've trained a little on these thrusters in the simulator, but you're our resident expert in docking maneuvers. You want to have a go at it?"

She gulped, realizing that this was her first big moment to

either shine or screw up, but she nodded and said, "Yes, certainly," and she pulled herself down into the pilot's center chair.

Rick and Tessa strapped themselves in on either side of her, and with Gregor's coaching they blew the bolts separating the command and service module from the S-IV-B booster, exposing the lunar module that had ridden just beneath them all this way. Yoshiko experimented for a few minutes with the hand controller, getting the feel of the thrusters, while Tessa filmed the whole process, showing the people back home the ungainly, angular LM perched atop the spent third-stage booster, and Yoshiko peering out the tiny windows as she concentrated on bringing the CSM around until the docking collar at the top of the capsule pointed at the hatch on top of the LM. A gentle push with the forward thrusters brought them toward it at a few feet per second, drifting slightly to the side, but she corrected for that with another attitude jet and they drove straight in for the last few feet. The docking rings met a few inches off center, but the angled guide bars sticking out from the top of the command module did their job and with a little sideways lurch and a solid clang of metal on metal, the two spaceships met.

"Latches engaged," Rick reported when the indicators lit up. He reached out and squeezed Yoshiko's hand. "That was great," he said. "Kaliningrad, we're in business!"

Yoshiko sighed and closed her eyes for the first time in minutes, and over the radio Gregor said, "Congratulations. And thank you for the live coverage. It might interest you to know that millions of people in Russia and across most of Europe were watching over your shoulders."

"And Japan, too," Tomiichi Amakawa said.

Tessa whistled softly. "Wow. People are watching a space mission? Who'd have thought. Just like old times, eh?"

Yoshiko said, "It has been a long time. A whole new generation has been born who have never seen a lunar flight. People are interested again."

Rick looked out the window at a footpad of the LM angling through his view of the Earth. People were interested again? After years of shuttle flights, the astronauts taping science shows that were only boadcast on the educational channels after they ran out of cooking and painting programs, that was hard to believe. It was evidently true, though. For now, at least, people all over the world were once more looking up into the sky.

The Earth seemed to grow brighter, more distinct, as he gazed at it. Rick blinked his eyes, then flinched when Tessa screamed in his ear.

ick whipped his head around toward Tessa to see what she was screaming about. She pointed at the control panel. "It's fading out!" she said.

Sure enough, the entire spaceship had taken on a hazy translucence. Earth could be seen right through the middle of it, without need for windows. It was like looking through heavily tinted glass, but it grew lighter even as they watched.

"Holy shit," Rick whispered. His heart was suddenly pounding. They hadn't lost any air yet, but if the ship kept fading . . .

"Spacesuits!" Yoshiko yelled, reaching around to pull one from behind the seats.

"*Hope*, what is happening?" Gregor asked, his voice tense.

"We've got—" Rick began before his voice failed. He swallowed and said, "Kaliningrad, we have a problem." He helped Yoshiko with her suit, but he knew they would be dead anyway if the ship vanished. In just their spacesuits they could survive for seven hours, maximum, before they ran out of air.

"What kind of problem?" Gregor asked.

"The ship is fading out on us," Rick said, holding the lower half of Yoshiko's suit while she stuffed her feet into it.

"Can you see it on the TV transmission?" Tessa asked, aiming the camera at the bright Earth through the spaceship's walls. She was breathing hard, but after that initial scream she had brought herself firmly under control.

"Yes, we can," Gregor answered.

"Damn. It's really happening, then."

Rick was having a lot more trouble than Tessa in keeping his fear from controlling him, but a sudden thought made him forget about his own predicament for a moment. "Cut the transmission," he said to her.

"Why?"

"You want another *Challenger*?"

"Oh." Tessa shut off the camera. She understood him perfectly. The biggest catastrophe with the *Challenger*, in terms of the space program as a whole, was not that it blew up, but that millions of people *watched* it blow up. NASA had never really recovered from that. If the whole world saw the *Spirit of Hope* kill its crew, it could destroy any renewed interest in space they had managed to create as well.

"It's too late," Tessa told him. "They already know what killed us."

But even as she said it, the walls grew distinct again. Yoshiko stopped struggling into her suit, and Rick simply stared at the metal walls that once again enclosed them.

"*Hope*, what is your status?" Gregor asked.

"It's back," Rick said. "The ship is solid again."

"What happened? Do you know what caused it?"

"Negative, negative. It just faded out, then came right back."

"Did you do anything that might have influenced it?"

Rick looked at Tessa, then at Yoshiko. Both women shook their heads. "Hard to tell," Rick said. "We screamed. We scrambled for spacesuits. Tessa shut off the camera."

"We all realized we were going to die," Tessa added, and when Rick frowned at her she said, "Well, we're dealing with a ghost here. Maybe that's important."

"Maybe so," Rick admitted.

Gregor said, "Do you have any abnormal indications now?"

Rick scanned the controls for any other clues, but there were none. No pressure loss, no power drain, nothing. "Negative, Kaliningrad," he said. "According to the dashboard, we've got a green bird up here."

Gregor laughed a strained, harsh laugh. "I begin to regret my hasty decision to oversee this mission. Never fear! I will not desert you. But this is troubling. Should I consult the engineers, or a medium?"

"Why don't you try both?" Rick said.

Gregor paused a moment, then said, "Yes, of course. You are absolutely right. We will get right to work on it."

The astronauts sat still for a moment, letting their breath and heart rates fall back toward normal. Rick looked over at his two companions: Yoshiko half into her spacesuit, Tessa holding the TV camera as if it were a bomb that might explode at any moment. Yoshiko reached out and touched the control panel, reassuring herself that it was solid again, then she turned up the cabin temperature. "I'm cold," she said.

Rick chuckled. "That's not surprising. Ghosts are supposed to make people feel cold."

Tessa narrowed her eyes.

"What?"

"I was just thinking. Ghosts make people feel cold. They repeat themselves. What else do they do? If we can figure out the rules, maybe we can keep this one from disappearing on us again until we get home."

Maybe it was just relief at still being alive after their scare, but the intense look in Tessa's eyes was kind of a turn-on. All the same, Rick tried to pay attention to what she was saying. They did need to understand the rules. "Well," he said, "they sometimes make wailing noises."

Tessa nodded. "And they leave slime all over everything."

Rick wiped at the edge of his couch. Bare metal and rough nylon webbing. No slime. "I don't think we're dealing with that kind of ghost," he said.

Yoshiko asked, "Aren't ghosts supposed to be the result of unfulfilled destiny?"

"Yeah," Rick said. "I think that's pretty clear in this case, anyway."

"You mean Neil Armstrong, right?"

"Who else?"

"I don't know. Armstrong doesn't make sense. He already made it to the Moon. If this was his unfulfilled destiny, I'd think it would be a Mars ship, or a real space station or something."

"Good point," Tessa said. "But if it isn't Armstrong's ghost, then whose is it?"

Rick snorted. "Well, NASA thinks it's theirs. Maybe the organization is really dead, and we just don't know it."

"Was there another budget cut in Congress?" Tessa asked facetiously.

Rick laughed, but Yoshiko shook her head vigorously. "No, no, I think you have it!"

"What, it's NASA's ghost?"

"In a sense, yes. What if it's the ghost of your entire space program? When Neil Armstrong died, so did the dreams of space enthusiasts all over your nation. Maybe all over the world. It reminded them that you had once gone to the Moon, but no longer could. Maybe the unfulfilled dreams of all those people created this spaceship."

Rick looked out his tiny triangular window at the Earth again. Could he be riding in some kind of global wish-fulfillment fantasy? "No," he said. "That can't be. Ghosts are individual things. Murder victims. People lost in storms."

"Shipwrecks," Tessa said. "They can be communal."

"Okay," Rick admitted, "but they need some kind of focus. An observer. They don't just pop into being all by themselves."

Tessa's hair drifted out in front of her face; she pushed it back behind her ears and said, "How do you know? If a ghost wails in the forest . . ."

"Yeah, yeah. But something made it fade out just now, and come back again a minute later. That seems like an individual sort of phenomenon to me, not some nebulous gestalt."

Yoshiko was nodding wildly. "What?" Rick asked her.

"I think you're right. And if so, then I know whose ghost this is."

"Whose?"

"It's yours."

Rick, expecting her to name anyone but himself, laughed. "Me?"

"Yes, you. You're the commander; it makes sense that you would control the, um, more spiritual aspects of the mission as well."

Both women looked at him appraisingly. A moment ago Rick had found Tessa's intensity compelling, but now those same eyes seemed almost accusatory. "That's ridiculous," he said. "I don't have any control over this ship. Except for the usual kind," he amended before anyone could argue the point. "Besides, the first two launches didn't have anybody on board. And I wasn't even there for the second one."

Tessa said, "No, but you were there for the first one, the day after Neil's funeral. And you'd just gotten back from your shuttle flight—depressed about all the things that went wrong—when the second one went up. If anybody was convinced the space program was dead, it was you."

Rick steadied himself with the grab handle at the top of the control panel. "What, you think I'm channeling the combined angst of all the Trekkies and fourteen-year-old would-be astronauts in the world?"

"Maybe. What were you thinking just now?"

"When it faded? I was thinking . . ." Rick wrinkled his forehead, trying to remember. "I was thinking how good it felt to have people interested in space again."

"There, you see?"

"No, I don't see," Rick said, exasperated. "What does that have to do with anything?"

"It's a perfect correlation. When you thought nobody cared, that space exploration was dead, you got your own personal Apollo, but when you thought maybe the rest of the world did want to go into space after all, it went away."

Yoshiko said, "And it came back when you thought our deaths would ruin that renewed interest."

Rick's head felt thick, abuzz with the crazy notion that he might be responsible for all this. The way Tessa and Yoshiko presented it made a certain sort of sense, but he couldn't bring himself to believe it. "Come on," he said. "This is a *spaceship*, not some . . . some vague shadow in the mist. It's got rivets, and switches, and . . . and . . . well, hardware." He gestured at the angular walls enclosing them.

Tessa said, "So? We already know it's a ghost. That's not the question. The question is whether or not you're behind it."

"I'm not," Rick said.

"No? I think you are. And it'd be easy enough to test. Let's experiment and find out."

Rick felt his heart skip a beat. Any emotion he had felt for Tessa a moment ago was drowned out now by unreasoning panic. Ghostly hardware was one thing—he could accept that even if he didn't understand it—but the notion that he might somehow exert some kind of subconscious control over it scared him to death. "Let's not," he said.

Tessa pulled herself closer to him. "You agreed that we should figure out the rules so we can keep it from disappearing on us again. We've got a theory now, so let's experiment and see if we're right."

Rick looked out the window again. Black space all around. No stars. Earth visibly receding. He shivered at the sight. For the first time since the launch, he really understood how far they were from help. Whether or not he was responsible for the ghost, he *was* responsible for three lives. And maybe, just maybe, a few dreams back home as well. He turned back inside and said, "We've got plenty to do already without crazy experiments. We've got to get this ship rotating or we'll overheat on the side facing the sun, and we've

got to take a navigational fix, and check out the lunar module, and so on. Right, Kaliningrad?"

"Yes," Gregor said. "Portside skin temperature is rising.
Also—" Voices just out of microphone range made him
pause, then he said, "Our engineers agree with your theory,
but suggest that you refrain from testing it at this time."

"Your *engineers* agree?" Tessa asked.

"That is correct."

"You're kidding, right?"

"*Nyet.* I—" More voices, then Gregor said, "—I cannot tell
you anything more yet. But please give us more time to study
the problem here before you do anything, ah, unusual."

Rick nodded and pulled himself down into his couch again.
Gregor was obviously hiding something, but whether he was
hiding information or ignorance, Rick couldn't tell. Either
way, he was glad to be let off the hook. He said, "I agree one
hundred percent. All right, then, let's get to work. Roll
maneuver first, so strap in."

Tessa looked as if she might protest, but after a few seconds
she stowed the camera and belted herself into her couch as
well. Yoshiko smiled and shook her head. "You beg the question," she said, but she strapped in, too.

CHAPTER 7

Rick knew she was right. As they worked to set the spacecraft spinning, he considered what Yoshiko and Tessa had said. Logically, if any single person was responsible for the Apollo manifestations then he was as good a candidate as anyone, but despite his fear of uninformed experimentation he couldn't make himself believe it. He didn't *feel* responsible for anything; certainly not the fade-out they had just seen. His own life was on the line, after all, and he didn't have a death wish.

He began to wonder about that as they went through their checklist. Would he be here if he didn't? So many things could go wrong, nearly all of them deadly. Even the most routine tasks contained elements of danger. For instance, when they blew the bolts separating the spent S-IV-B third stage from beneath their lunar module, the long tube began to tumble, spinning end over end and spraying unused propellant uncomfortably close to them. They had to use the thrusters twice to push themselves away from it before they finally watched it recede into space. The "barbecue roll" went off without a hitch, and the ship's skin temperature evened out, but when Rick unbuckled and pulled himself over to the navigation instruments in the equipment bay he discovered that all their maneuvering had driven them off course.

"It looks like we're closer to a polar trajectory than an equatorial one," he reported to Kaliningrad after he had sighted on a guide star and a lunar landmark and let the computer calculate their position. A polar course was no good; landing and rendezvous would be much easier if they stayed close to the Moon's equator. That way the command module would pass over the landing site on every orbit, and they would have a launch window every two hours without having to do a fuel-wasting plane change.

Gregor said, "*Da*, our radar confirms your measurement. Wait a moment, and we will calculate a correction burn for you."

"Roger." Rick strapped back into his couch and they used a short burst from the the service propulsion system engine to bring themselves back onto an equatorial course. That, at least, provided some relief from another nagging worry; the SPS engine was the last link in the multi-stage chain that had brought them this far, and if it had failed to ignite they wouldn't be able to brake into lunar orbit, or even make course corrections for a slingshot trajectory back home.

After the burn they had to check out the lunar module. With Yoshiko steadying her feet, Tessa opened the hatch between the two spaceships, then removed the docking probe so they could fit through the tunnel. Rick stowed the probe in the equipment bay and followed the two women into the lander, but it had even less room than the command module so he stayed in the tunnel, feeling a bit disoriented as he looked down from above on the angular instrument panel and flight controls. The ascent engine was a big cylinder between the slots where pilot and copilot stood, sort of like the way the engine in an older van stuck out between the driver and the passenger.

"Is this what you sit on during descent?" Yoshiko asked.

Tessa laughed. "No, you fly it standing up, with bungee cords holding your feet to the deck."

"You're kidding."

"Nope."

Yoshiko looked around at the spartan furnishings. To save weight, everything not absolutely essential had been omitted, including switch covers and wiring conduit. Bundles of wires were tied into place, fuel and air lines ran exposed along the walls, and the few storage areas were covered with nylon nets rather than metal panels. The whole ship looked fragile, and in fact it was. A person could shove a screwdriver through the walls if they wanted to. Yoshiko said, "I think I'm glad you two are flying this one."

They hadn't talked before this about who would stay in the command module while the other two went down to the Moon. Though keeping Yoshiko in the command module where her docking skills would be most useful was the logical choice, Rick said, "Are you sure? I was prepared to draw straws for it if you wanted."

She shook her head. "No. This is adventure enough. And who knows, if we inspire enough people I may have another chance to land later, when my own country sends a mission."

Rick wondered what a Japanese lander would look like. Probably a lot slicker than this, he figured, though to be fair he had to admit that *anybody's* lander would be slicker if it were built with modern materials. Most of the equipment—the engines and the computers and so forth—could be bought straight off the shelf nowadays. It would be so much easier to build a lunar lander now than it had been the first time, if people just wanted to.

Well, maybe they would. Who could say?

"You'll certainly have a better chance than we will," Tessa said. "Rick and I will be lucky to stay out of prison when we get—whoa!"

For a second, the Moon had shone brightly through the flight control panel. It was just a flicker, gone as soon as it had appeared, but the ship had done it again.

"It *is* you," Tessa said, pointing accusingly at Rick. "You were thinking positive again, weren't you?"

His heart had begun to pound, and a cold sweat broke out on his body as he said, "Jail isn't exactly my favorite dream."

"No, but I'll bet money you were thinking good stuff just before that."

"Well, yeah, but—"

"But nothing. Every time you think we're going to jump-start the space program with this little stunt, the ship disappears, and every time you think we're not, it comes back. Admit it."

Rick suddenly felt claustrophobic in the narrow access tunnel. He said, "No way! There are a million other factors that could be operating here. My optimism or pessimism isn't controlling the ship."

"I think it is."

They stared at one another for a few seconds, then Gregor said over the radio, "Tessa's theory may be correct. Our studies indicate that ghosts are often closely tied to emotional states."

"Your studies of *what*?" Rick asked. "You can't put ghosts in a lab."

Gregor laughed. "No, but you can sometimes take the lab to the ghosts. You forget, Russia has been studying paranormal phenomena since the cold war. We may not know everything about them, but we have learned a thing or two."

Rick and Tessa looked at each other, both clearly amazed. The Russians had actually gotten *results*? Impossible. Rick said, "I don't believe you for a second."

The Japanese controller, Tomiichi, had not spoken up for some time, but now he said, "Believe it. The Russians aren't the only ones to investigate these matters."

The Japanese, too? Rick looked at Yoshiko, but she merely shrugged and said, "I am an astronomer, not a parapsychologist."

"True enough," Rick muttered, wondering why she hadn't remembered that before when she and Tessa were brainstorming their crazy explanation for all of this. But evidently someone in Russia—and maybe Japan, too—thought they had a handle on it. "So what if you're right, Kaliningrad?" Rick asked. "What do you suggest we do?"

"Be aware that you could die out there," Gregor said. "And

if Tessa is correct, then you should remind yourself occasionally that your death will also kill any chance of a resurgence in popularity for manned spaceflight."

"I'm the one who made her turn off the camera," Rick reminded him. To Tessa he said, "I know we're in danger out here."

"You've got to *feel* it," Tessa said. "That's what matters to a ghost. You've got to remind yourself all the time that this isn't some kind of picnic."

Rick shuddered at the thought of the ship disappearing again, maybe for good, and of the three of them blowing away in opposite directions in the last puff of breathing air. "That won't be hard," he told her.

CHAPTER 8

Staying pessimistic turned out to be tougher than he thought. Over the next two days, as they coasted toward the Moon, the ship faded out twice more, once to almost transparency before whatever was responsible brought it back. Maybe it *was* him, Rick thought after the second time. It had happened while he was asleep, and when Yoshiko had shaken him awake he had to admit that he had indeed been dreaming about a colony on the Moon.

Both Yoshiko and Tessa were looking at him like hostages in a bank robbery or something. That accusing look, combined with the adrenaline rush from waking to their screams and his own fear of death, suddenly pissed him off. As he rubbed the sleep from his eyes, he said, "All right, dammit, maybe I *am* in control of this thing. And if you're right about that, maybe you're right about experimenting with it, too."

"What do you mean?" Tessa asked nervously.

"I mean if I'm God all of a sudden, then why don't I use it for something? Like make us a bigger ship, or at least a more modern one. Something with a shower, for instance. Or how about the *Millennium Falcon*? Maybe we could go to Alpha Centauri as long as we're out here."

"*Nyet!*" Gregor said loudly. "Do not experiment! It is more dangerous than you can imagine."

Rick snorted loudly. "Well, comrade, if I'm in the dark then it's because you guys are holding back on me. If you know what's going on up here, then tell me. Why shouldn't I dream up a nice, big fantasy instead of this cramped little can?"

"E equals mc squared, that's why," Gregor said. "Your ghost cannot violate the known laws of physics. We do not know where the energy comes from to create the . . . ah, the physical manifestation, but we do know that a clumsy attempt to manipulate it can can result in a violent release of that energy."

"You do, eh? And how do you know that?"

Gregor conferred for a moment with someone else in the control room with him, then came back on line. "Let us just say that not all of our underground explosions in the 1970s were nuclear."

Rick looked out the window at black space. "You've made a weapon out of ghosts?" he asked quietly.

Gregor said, "Is an industrial accident a weapon? It is not useful unless you can direct it, and that's what I'm trying to tell you now. You are the focus of this phenomenon, but not its master. If you are careful you can maintain it, but if you attempt to manipulate it, the result will be disastrous."

"So you say."

"So we have come to understand. We do not have all the answers either."

Rick's mad was wearing off, but frustration made him say, "Well why don't you come up with some? I'm getting tired of being the scapegoat up here."

Gregor laughed softly. "We are doing our best, but you will understand if that is too little and too late. We are having trouble reproducing your situation in our flight simulators."

"Hah. I'll bet you are." Rick took a deep breath and let it out slowly. "All right," he said, "I'll try to be good. But if you learn anything more about how this works, I want to know it instantly. Agreed?"

"Agreed," Gregor said.

Rick rubbed his eyes again and unstrapped from his chair. Looking pointedly at Tessa and Yoshiko, he said, "Okay, then unless anybody has an objection, I think I'll have some breakfast."

"No problem," Tessa said, holding her hands out. Yoshiko nodded. They both turned away, either to give him some privacy or to escape his anger, but whichever it was he really didn't care.

Tessa pulled herself into the equipment bay and began taking a navigational reading while he rehydrated a bag of dried scrambled eggs.

"Hey," she said a few minutes later. "We're on a polar trajectory again." She looked directly at Rick, who was sucking on a packet of orange juice.

"It's not me," he protested. "A polar orbit means we can't land. The command module wouldn't pass over our landing site again for an entire lunar day." That was twenty-eight Earth days, far too long for a crew to wait on the surface. In order to rendezvous with the command module, they would have to make an orbital plane-change in mid-launch, a much more tricky and fuel-costly maneuver. Either that or the command module would have to make a plane change, which was equally difficult.

Yoshiko acquired a rapt expression for a few seconds, then said, "Unless you land at the pole. The command module would pass over both poles on every orbit."

"We can't land at the . . . can we?"

"Absolutely not," Gregor's voice said. "Even I will not allow that kind of risk. You would have bad lighting, extremes of temperature, no margin for error in landing sites, possibly even fog obscuring your vision on final approach."

"Fog?" asked Tessa.

"It is possible. Current theory predicts water ice in some of the deeper craters near the pole, where sunlight can never reach them."

"Wow," whispered Rick. "Ice on the Moon. That would make supporting a colony a lot easier."

"Rick." Tessa was looking intently at the walls, but they remained solid.

"Look, it's a fact," Rick told her, still put out with the whole situation. "Ice would make it easier to set up a colony.

We wouldn't have to fly all our water up from Earth. That doesn't mean I think we're actually going to build one, okay?"

"All right," Tessa said. "I just want you to be careful." She looked out the window at the Earth, now just a tiny blue-and-white disk in the void. "So, Kaliningrad, what do you suggest?"

Gregor said, "Give us a minute." He took longer than that, but when he came back he said, "We want to check your guidance computer's program. Perhaps we can discover where it intends to take you."

So Rick, who had at least trained with the primitive keyboard and display, pulled himself down into the equipment bay and ran the computer while Kaliningrad talked him through the procedure, and sure enough, the program was indeed for a polar trajectory. And when they checked the computer in the lander, they learned that it was programmed for a descent to the rim of the Aitken Basin, a six-mile-deep crater right on the Moon's south pole.

"That's ridiculous," Rick said when he heard the news. "How could we be expected to land on the south pole? Like Gregor said, the light would be coming in sideways. Shadows would extend for miles, and every little depression would be a black hole."

Tessa, who had been running the computer in the lander, said, "Well, maybe this switch labeled 'Na inject' could provide a clue. If it sprays sodium into the descent engine's exhaust plume, it would probably light up like a candle flame and provide all the illumination we need."

"You're kidding." Rick pulled his way through the docking collar into the lunar module to look for himself, and sure enough there was the switch, right next to one labeled "Hi-int Floods."

Tessa said, "It looks like landing lights to me. Two separate systems for redundancy."

"Those weren't on the simulator I trained with," Rick said.

"Of course not. NASA would never plan a polar landing. Too dangerous."

They knew that NASA had been listening in on their broadcast all along, and sure enough, now Laura Turner in Houston said, "Well, maybe not, Tessa. We've been digging through the old paperwork here, and in fact one of the mission proposals *was* for a polar landing. You're right, there was a lot of argument against it, but it was considered a possibility for a later mission after we'd gained enough experience with the easy ones. Of course it got axed along with everything else when the budget cuts came down, but if we'd had the support for it, we would eventually have gone."

Rick felt a shiver run up his spine. "The last two ghosts went to Copernicus and Aristarchus. Those were on the list too, weren't they?"

"That's right."

"So basically we're re-enacting what the U.S. should have done all along."

"That's a matter of opinion, but yeah, I guess you could say that."

Gregor asked, "Houston, can those guidance computers be reprogrammed for a less difficult landing site?"

"Negative," Laura said. "The programs are hard-wired in core memory. There's only two kilobytes of erasable memory, and they need that for data storage."

"So it's a polar landing or nothing," Rick said, his breath coming short. He looked at the controls again. They were solid as a rock now.

"Looks that way," Tessa said. She grinned at him. Even with the added danger, it was obvious what she would choose.

Rick gulped. Her wide smile and intense, almost challenging stare were incredibly alluring, but at the same time he couldn't help wondering how deep a hole they could dig themselves into on this flight, anyway? Deeper, apparently, than he had first thought. But they were already in quite a ways; he couldn't back out now. "All right, then," he said. "A polar landing it is. I just hope we find something worth the risk."

Tessa laughed, and leaned forward to kiss him. "Just going is worth the risk," she said. "That's what exploring is all about."

CHAPTER 9

Both Houston and Kaliningrad were unhappy with their choice, but Houston didn't have any say in the matter anymore, and Kaliningrad was caught in a dilemma of its own making, for bailing out now would amount to abandoning an international rescue in the middle of the attempt. So they reluctantly set up their own computers to match the course wired into the onboard ones, and on the eighty-third hour of the flight Rick, Tessa, and Yoshiko strapped themselves into their couches for the long rocket burn that would slow them into orbit around the Moon. That had to happen after they had rounded the horizon, which meant they would be cut off from Earth for the burn. The computer would count down the time and fire the engine automatically, but just in case it didn't, they all set their watches to keep track as well.

The last few minutes dragged by. The Moon wasn't visible in the windows; they had turned the ship end-for-end so it was behind them now, their course missing the horizon by a mere hundred miles. Rick kept glancing at his watch, then at the computer display, then at the attitude indicators, making sure they were still lined up properly for the burn.

Yoshiko took careful notes. If Rick and Tessa crashed or couldn't return from the surface, she would have to fire the trans-Earth injection burn herself and make the homeward flight alone.

Just before the burn, the computer asked Go/No-go? again, and Rick pushed "Proceed." The three astronauts watched the countdown continue to zero, but Rick didn't feel the engine kick in. He stabbed at the manual fire button hard enough to break his fingernail on it, and then he felt the thrust.

Tessa looked over at him, her mouth open. "The computer didn't fire it on time?"

"I didn't feel it," Rick said. "Not until I—"

"It did," Yoshiko said. "I felt it before you pushed the button. The computer's okay."

"Are you sure?" It had been a split-second impression on Rick's part, and his body was so high on adrenaline that he might not have felt the thrust immediately, but he'd have sworn it hadn't fired until he hit the button.

"I'm sure," Yoshiko said.

Rick looked to Tessa, who shrugged. "Too close to call, for me."

Rick laughed a high-pitched, not-quite-panicky laugh. "What the hell," he said. "We got it lit; that's what counts. Are we still go for landing?"

Tessa nodded. "I am."

"You still comfortable with the idea of staying up here by yourself for a day?" Rick asked Yoshiko.

"Yes," she said.

"All right, then, let's do it."

They didn't mention the possible computer glitch to Gregor when they rounded the back side of the Moon and reacquired his signal. They reported only that they had achieved orbit and were ready to proceed. Gregor had them fire another burn to circularize their orbit, and that one went off automatically, so Rick began to relax about that anyway. He had plenty else to keep him occupied. The flight out had been a picnic compared to the constant checklists they had to follow and the navigational updates they had to key into the computers before they could separate the two ships. They hardly had time to look out at the Moon, its gray cratered surface sliding silently past below. But finally after two more orbits, two hours each in the lighter lunar gravity instead of the hour and a half they were used to in Earth orbit, they were ready.

They had named the lunar module *Faith*, to go along with *Hope* and to signify their trust that it would set them down and bring them back again safely. So when Gregor was satisfied that everything was ready, he radioed to the astronauts, "You are go for separation, *Faith*."

"Roger," said Rick. He and Tessa were both suited up again and standing elbow to elbow in front of the narrow control panel.

In the command module, Yoshiko said, "Going for separation," and she released the latches that held the two ships together. A shudder and a thump echoed in the tiny cabin, and they were free.

Faith's computer rotated them around to the right angle, and when the proper time came the engine lit for a thirty-second burn that lowered their orbit to within eight miles of the surface. They coasted down the long elliptical track, watching the cratered surface grow closer and closer, until their radar began picking up return signals and Gregor finally said, "You are go for powered descent."

Rick pushed "Proceed" on the keyboard, and the computer fired the engine again, slowing them to less than orbital velocity. They were committed now.

Tessa reached out and punched Rick in the shoulder. "Break a leg, buddy," she said. "It's showtime."

It was indeed. Rick gave her a quick hug, clumsy in the suits but nonetheless heartfelt, then gave his attention completely to the controls. Their course was bending rapidly now, curving down toward the surface, which this close to the pole was a stark pattern of white crater rims holding pools of absolute blackness. Rick's gloved finger hovered near the sodium inject switch, but he didn't flip it yet. He didn't know how much he had, and he wanted to save it for the actual landing.

Tessa called out their altitude, dropping rapidly at first, then slower and slower, until at six hundred feet they were only falling at twenty feet per second. Five seconds later she whispered, "Low gate," and Rick rocked the controller in his hand, switching out the computer.

He held his breath. This was when the previous two lunar modules had disappeared, at the point where the pilot had to take over. He waited for that to happen again, but the lander dropped another fifty feet, then seventy-five, and it was still there.

"Whew," he said. "We made it."

"What do you mean?" demanded Tessa. "We're still four hundred feet up!"

"Piece of cake," Rick said, looking out the window at the landscape slowly moving past. It was impossible to tell which little arc of crater rim was their target, and the tiny triangular windows were too small to give them an overview of the larger picture, so Rick just picked one that looked reasonably wide and brought the lander down toward it. It was strewn with boulders, but there were plenty of clear spaces between them, if he could just hit one.

"Quantity light," Tessa called out. He had only a minute of fuel left, less than he was supposed to have at this altitude, but it was still plenty at their rate of fall.

He slowed their descent to ten feet per second and rotated them once around. One big boulder right on the rim had a wide flat spot beside it, so he angled over toward it. Flying the lander felt just like the simulator, save for the shifting of weight, and that actually helped him get a feel for the controls.

"Two hundred feet, eleven down," Tessa said.

Too fast. Rick throttled up the engine a bit.

"One-eighty, six down. One-seventy, three down. One-sixty-five, zero down—we're going back up!"

"Sorry," Rick said, dropping the thrust again. While he was at it, he flipped on the sodium injector, and sure enough, the landscape exploded in bright yellow light. Even the bottoms of the craters were visible now, though they seemed fuzzy, out of focus.

No time to sightsee, though. Tessa kept reading off the numbers, her voice rising a little in pitch. "Forty-five seconds. One-sixty feet, four down. One-fifty, five down; one-forty, six down . . . you're picking up too much speed!"

"Got it," Rick said, nudging their thrust up a bit.

"One hundred, five down. Thirty seconds."

Rick did the math in his head. At this rate of descent he had ten seconds of fuel to spare. Far less than regulation, but still enough if he didn't waste any more. "Piece of cake," he said again, holding it steady for the spot he had chosen.

The descent went smoothly through the next fifty feet, but with only fifty feet to go, the ground began to grow indistinct. "What's that, are we kicking up dust?" Rick asked.

"I don't know," Tessa said. "It looks more like fog."

"Fog? Damn, Gregor was right." Rick held the controls steady, but they were descending into a white mist. The big boulder he'd been using for a marker disappeared in the cloud swirling up from the crater floor. Rick couldn't tell if they were still going to miss it or not; they could be drifting right over it for all he could tell.

Tessa's hand hovered near the ABORT STAGE button. That would fire the ascent stage's engine, smashing the lower half of the lander into the surface as it blasted the top half free and back into orbit.

"We're too low for that," Rick said. "We'd crash with the descent stage if we tried it. Just hang on and call out the numbers."

"Roger. Twenty, five down."

That was pretty fast, but Rick didn't budge the controller. If he shifted them sideways in the process, they could hit the boulder.

"Fifteen . . . ten . . . contact light!"

The feelers at the ends of the landing legs had touched the surface. Rick let the engine run for another half second, then shut it down. The lander rocked sideways just a bit, then lurched as they hit the surface hard. "Engine off," Rick said, his eyes glued to the ascent engine fuel level. It held steady. No leaks, then, from the shaking, and no warning lights on any other systems. Looking over at the descent engine's fuel gauge, he saw that they had six seconds left.

Tessa glared at him. "Piece of cake?" she asked. "Piece of *cake*?"

Rick, at a loss for words, could only shrug.

Yoshiko's voice came over the radio. "*Faith*, are you down?"

Tessa laughed. "Yes, we're down. Through fog as thick as soup, with six seconds of fuel left."

Fog. There was water on the Moon. Rick looked out the window, pointed. "Look, it's blowing away."

Without the rocket exhaust and the harsh sodium light to heat the ice in the crater floor, what had already vaporized was rapidly expanding into the vacuum, revealing the rubble-strewn crater rim on which the lander had touched down. Rick looked for his landmark boulder, saw it out of the corner of his window, only a few feet away from the side of the lander. They had barely missed it. In fact two of the legs had straddled it. If one of them had hit it the lander would have tipped over.

Rick put it out of his mind. They were down, and they had more important things to worry about.

Time seemed to telescope on them as they ran through another checklist to make sure the ascent stage was ready to go in an emergency, then they depressurized the lander and popped open the hatch to go outside. Rick went first, not because it was his Apollo or because he was in any way more deserving, but for the same reason that Neil Armstrong went first on *Apollo 11*: because in their bulky spacesuits it was too difficult for the person on the right to sidle past the person on the left in order to reach the door.

It was a tight squeeze, but he made it through the hatch.

The corrugated egress platform and ladder were in shadow, so Rick had to climb down by feel. He pulled the D-ring that lowered the outside camera, and Gregor radioed that they were receiving its signal back on Earth. Rick figured he was probably just a silhouette against the side-lit background, but he supposed that was about as good as the grainy picture of Neil taking his first step.

He was on the last rung when he realized he hadn't thought up anything historic to say. He paused for a moment, thinking fast, then stepped off onto the landing pad and then from there onto the frozen lunar soil. It crunched beneath his feet; he could feel it, though he couldn't hear it in the vacuum.

Tessa had made it through the hatch, too, and was watching from the platform, obviously waiting for him to speak, so he held his hand up toward her—and symbolically toward Earth, he hoped—and said, "Come on out. The water's fine!"

CHAPTER 10

The water was indeed fine. Fine as powdered sugar, and about the same consistency. Brought to the Moon's surface in thousands of comet strikes over the millennia, it had accumulated molecule by molecule as the vaporized water and methane and other gases froze out in the shadowed crater bottoms at the poles. It was too cold, and the Moon's gravity was too light, for it to pack down into solid ice, so it remained fluffy, like extremely fine snow. When Rick and Tessa walked out into it they sank clear to their thighs, even though they only weighed about fifty pounds, and they would probably have sunk further if they'd gone on. But they could feel the cold seeping into their legs already, so they had to scoop up what samples they could in special thermos bottles designed for the purpose and turn back. The sample equipment packed in the lander was designed for a polar mission, but their spacesuits were made to keep them warm in vacuum, not against ice that could conduct heat away.

So they walked around the crater rim, bounding along in the peculiar kangaroo-hop gait that worked so well in light gravity, looking for anything else that might prove interesting. That was just about everything as far as Rick was concerned. He was on the Moon! Every aspect of it, from the rocky, cratered ground underfoot to the sharp, rugged horizon, reminded him that he was walking on another world. He looked out toward the Earth, about two-thirds of it visible above the horizon, about two-thirds of that lit by the sun, and he felt a shiver run down his spine at the sight. He had thought he would never see it like that except in thirty-year-old pictures.

They were making pictures of their own now. Tessa carried

the TV camera and gave a running commentary as they explored. Gregor said that everyone in Russia and Europe was watching, and Tomiichi said the same for Japan. And surprisingly, Laura said the same about the United States. "They even pre-empted *Days of Our Lives* for you," she told them.

"Hah. Maybe there's hope for our country yet," Rick muttered.

"Watch it," Tessa said, but whether for fear of him offending their watchers or for fear of him getting too hopeful she didn't say.

Rick didn't care. He felt an incredible sense of well-being that had nothing at all to do with whether or not they made it back alive. They were on the Moon, he and Tessa, at the absolute pinnacle of achievement for an astronaut. Higher than anything either of them had ever expected to achieve, at any rate. No matter what they faced on the way home, or after they got there, nothing could alter the fact that they were here now. And Rick couldn't think of anyone he would rather share the experience with. He and Tessa would be spoken of in the same breath forever, and that was fine with him. He watched the way she bounded along in the low gravity, listened to her exclaim with delight with each new wonder she discovered, and he smiled. He wouldn't mind at all sharing a page in the history books with her.

They collected rocks and more ice from all along their path. At one stop Rick packed a handful of snow into a loose ball and flung it at Tessa, who leaped nearly five feet into the air to avoid it. When the snowball hit on the sunlit side of the crater, it burst into a puff of steam.

"Wow," Tessa said as she bounced to a stop, "did you see that? Do it again."

Rick obligingly threw another snowball past her, and she followed it with the camera until it exploded against a rock.

"Did you guys back home see it, too?" she asked. "What makes them blow up like that?"

Gregor said, "Heat, I'd guess. And vacuum. Without an atmosphere to attenuate the sunlight, a rock will heat up just as much there at the pole as it would at the equator, so when the snow touches the hot rock it flashes into steam."

"Hah, I suppose so. Looks pretty wild."

"It might also give us a good idea what gases are in the snow. Rick, could you set a sample down a bit more gently on a sunlit surface and let us see how it boils off?"

Rick did as he asked, packing a double-handful of snow and setting it on a boulder's slanted face. Steam immediately began to rise from it, then stopped after a few seconds. The snowball shifted slightly and more steam sublimed off, then another few seconds passed before the remaining snow melted into a bubbling puddle.

"Aha!" Gregor said. "Three separate fractions, at least. I would guess methane for the first, then ammonia or carbon dioxide, and finally water. That is wonderful news! All four gases will be useful to a colony."

"If we ever send one," Rick said, trying to suppress his silly grin so Tessa wouldn't grow afraid of his optimism, but that in itself made him laugh out loud.

"Damn it, Rick, you're scaring me half to death!" she said. They both turned to look at the lander, glittering like a gold-and-silver sculpture on the concrete gray crater rim, but it remained solid.

"Don't worry," Rick told her. "I may be having fun, but I'm still just as scared as you are."

"Good."

They explored for another hour, but before they had even made it a tenth of the way around the crater they had to turn back. The suits only held another two hours of oxygen, and they would need that time to return to the lander, climb back inside, and pressurize the cabin again. And after that their time on the Moon would be over, because they had to get back to *Hope* as quickly as possible and blast off for Earth again before the plane of their polar orbit shifted too far away from a return path. Their SPS engine had enough fuel for a plane-change of a few degrees, but the longer they waited the more it would take.

They had done enough already. They had discovered water on the Moon, and had gone a long ways toward proving that it could sustain a colony if humanity wanted to send one. Now all they had to do was get home alive, but that in itself was a big enough job to keep them occupied full-time.

Yet as he waited for Tessa to climb up the ladder and kick the dust from her boots, Rick thought of one more thing he could do. His heart leaped in his throat at the thought, but it would be the perfect cap to a perfect day—provided he really wanted to do it. And provided he'd read Tessa's signals right as well.

He had no time to decide. It was now or never. He gulped, muttered, "He who hesitates is lost," and moved back away from the lander.

"What?" Tessa asked. She had reached the egress platform.

"Don't go inside yet." Rick paced a few yards away, then began scuffing five-foot-high letters into the crunchy soil with his boot. They showed up beautifully in the low-angled light.

"What are you doing?" she asked him.

He didn't answer. It would become obvious in a moment, if he could just remember how to spell. That was no sure bet; his head buzzed like an alarm going off, and his breath came in ragged gasps that had nothing to do with the exertion of drawing in the dirt. This would change his life even more than the trip to the Moon. Maybe.

"Oh, Rick," Tessa said when he completed the first line, but she grew silent when she saw him begin a second. She was still silent when he finished his message:

Tessa, I love you.
Will you marry me?

He was still standing on the final dot below the question mark. He looked up at her, a dark silhouette against the darker sky, her gold-mirrored faceplate reflecting his own sunlit form and the words he'd written. He couldn't see her expression through it, couldn't tell what she was thinking. He waited for some indication, but after the silence stretched on so long that Gregor asked, "Rick? Tessa? Are you okay?" she began to climb down the ladder again.

"Stand by, Kaliningrad," Rick said.

Tessa stepped back onto the lunar surface, walked slowly and deliberately over to stand beside Rick. Even this close, he couldn't see her face, but he heard her sniff.

"Tess?"

She didn't answer him, at least not over the radio. But she shook her head a little and stepped to the side far enough to scratch a single word in the soil: Yes.

Rick echoed it aloud. "Yes!" All his apprehension died in an instant. He bounded over to her and wrapped her in a bear hug. "Tessa, I love you!"

"Oh, Rick."

"Are you two getting mushy again?" Yoshiko asked.

Rick laughed. "Mushy, hell, we're getting married."

The radio burst into a jumble of voices as everyone spoke at once, then Gregor's voice cut through the rest. "My sincere congratulations," he said, "but your launch window is fast approaching."

"Roger," Rick said. "We're going inside now."

He helped Tessa climb back into the lander, then climbed up and kicked off as much dust as he could. Before he ducked in through the hatch he looked down at the words they had written on the ground, their declaration clearly written for all to see. Those words could stay there for a billion years or so, the way things weathered on the Moon. Or if people actually came up and mined the crater for ice, they could be obliterated within a decade. That would depend quite a bit on what happened on the trip home.

Rick thought again of all the things that could yet go wrong. Engine failures, docking failures, computer failures—the list seemed endless. Despite his excitement over his and Tessa's future, if their personal welfare over the next few days made any difference then he would have no trouble staying sufficiently pessimistic to keep the ghost from fading away on them.

he number of possible disasters shrank with each stage of the mission: *Faith*'s ascent engine carried them into orbit, and Yoshiko docked smoothly with the lander, and the SPS engine fired on time to send them back homeward; but the way Rick figured it, infinity minus a few was still infinity. Plenty of things could still go wrong.

Including, of course, the ghost disappearing. Twice more on the return trip, both times right after Gregor reported that "Moon fever" was once more gripping the world, the spacecraft's walls grew indistinct around them, and both times they came back only after Rick convinced himself that their deaths could still squelch humanity's renewed enthusiasm for space. All the evidence seemed to support Yoshiko and Tessa's theory that he was somehow in control of the apparition, whether or not he was directly responsible for it.

Gregor would say no more about it, save that he should listen to them. Tessa took that as carte blanche to control his every action, including sleep, which she wouldn't let him do. She was afraid he would start dreaming of the bold new age of space exploration and they would all die of explosive decompression before he could wake up. She refused to let Gregor or Tomiichi or Laura tell them anything about the situation on Earth, and she kept inventing elaborate new scenarios in which humanity would decide not to follow their lead after all. And now that they were engaged, she seemed to think Rick's personal space was hers to invade in whatever imaginative ways she could think of as well. She would tickle him if she thought he was drifting off, or kiss him, or brush against him seductively. Rick found it alternately amusing and annoying, depending on which stage of his sleep deprivation cycle he was in at the time.

To keep himself busy, and to keep his mind on other things, he made her an engagement ring out of one of the switch guards, which were already nearly the right size and shape. He snapped one off from beside a third-stage booster control that didn't connect to anything anymore, and with a little filing on a zipper he buffed the rough edges down enough for her to wear it.

"I'll treasure it forever," she told him when he slid it onto her finger, but Rick was too befuddled from lack of sleep to know if she was fooling or serious.

Finally, less than a day out from Earth, Tessa could no longer stay awake either. As she drifted off to sleep, she admonished Yoshiko to continue the job, but as soon as her breathing slowed, Yoshiko told Rick, "Go ahead and sleep if you want. I think you'll be more valuable to us tomorrow if you get some rest now."

Rick, groggy with fatigue, tried to focus on her face. "Why?" he asked. "What's tomorrow?"

She grinned diabolically. "Reentry. Twenty-five thousand miles an hour, *smack* into the atmosphere. Sleep well."

Rick slept, but just as Yoshiko had intended, all his dreams were of burning up in a fireball as the Apollo capsule hit the atmosphere at too steep an angle, or of skipping off into interplanetary space if they hit too shallow. Or of hitting their window square on and still burning up when the ghost ship proved incapable of withstanding the heat. The gunpowder smell of the lunar dust they had tracked inside on their spacesuits didn't help any, either; it only provided another sensory cue that they were on fire.

When he woke, Earth was only a couple hours away. It still looked much smaller than it had from the shuttle, but it felt so much closer and it looked so inviting after his hours of bad dreams that Rick almost felt like he was home already.

With that thought, the capsule grew indistinct again. Tessa screamed, "Rick!" and punched him in the chest, and Yoshiko said quickly, "Remember the consequences!"

The ship solidified once more, and Rick rubbed his sore sternum where Tessa's ring had jabbed him. "Jeez, you don't have to kill me," he said. "I get scared just fine on my own when that happens."

Tessa snorted. "Hah. If you were as scared as I am the ship would never disappear in the first place."

"Well I'm sorry; I'll try to be more terrified from now on." Rick turned away from her, but there was no place to go to be alone in an Apollo capsule. After a few minutes of silence, he looked back over at her and said, "Okay, I'll try harder to control this. But don't look at me so accusingly when it happens, okay? I'm not trying to make it disappear."

Tessa sighed. "I know you're not. It's just—I don't know. I don't have any control over it, except what little control I have over you. My life is in your hands. Hell, at this point the entire space program is in your hands. And all you have to do to kill it is get cocky."

"No pressure," Rick said sarcastically.

Yoshiko laughed. "Whether you like it or not, you embody the spirit of exploration. When we get back, that spirit will probably pass on to someone else, but right now it resides in you, and you have to bring it safely home."

"With all due respect," Rick said, "that sounds like a bunch of tabloid speculation to me."

She shook her head. "No, this is really no different than any space mission. Every time someone goes into space, their nation's spirit flies with them. When *Apollo 1* killed its crew, your nation faltered for two years before going on, and when the *Challenger* blew up it took three more. When the Soviets' Moon rocket blew up in 1969, they completely scrapped their lunar program and shifted to space stations. It's like that all over the world. Every astronaut who has ever flown has had your ability, and your responsibility; yours is just more obvious than most, made physical by the same power that created this ship."

Rick studied the industrial gray control panel before him while he considered what she'd said. The truth of it seemed undeniable, at least in principle. The details could be argued—retooling after an accident wasn't exactly backing off—but it was true that exploration stopped each time an accident happened, and when it started again it almost always took a new, more conservative direction.

"Well," Rick said at last, "I'll try my best to pass the baton without fumbling. We've only got a couple hours left; after that it's somebody else's problem."

They spent the time before reentry stowing all the equipment and debris that had accumulated in the cabin throughout their week in space. While they worked, the Earth swelled from a blue-and-white ball to the flatter, fuzzy-edged landscape they were familiar with from the shuttle flights. At that point they only had a few minutes left before atmospheric contact, just time enough to jettison the cylindrical service module with its spent engine and fuel tanks, then reorient the command module so it would hit the atmosphere blunt end first.

All three of them were breathing hard as the last few seconds ticked away. They weren't wearing their spacesuits; the gee forces would be too severe for that, and besides, if anything happened to the capsule they would burn up instantly anyway, spacesuits or no. Rick reached out and held Tessa's hand, wishing he could reassure her that they would be okay, but he knew that a phrase like "Don't worry" coming from him would only make her worry all the more. So he merely said, "Ready with the marshmallows?"

"Very funny," she replied.

Yoshiko laughed, though, and said, "Never mind marshmallows, I'm getting out my bathing suit. Hawaii, here we come!"

Their splashdown target was about a thousand miles west of there, but that would be their first landfall after the recovery ship picked them up. There were two recovery ships, actually, one Russian and one American, but the Russians had agreed to let the Americans pick up the capsule if they wished. NASA wished very much, so they got the prize, though neither Rick nor Tessa looked forward to the official reception.

The unofficial one, however, would be worth every minute of NASA's wrath. The main reason for the Russian ship's presence was to televise the splashdown for the curious world, which Gregor said was even more excited now that the last, most perilous stage of the mission was about to commence. The love story didn't hurt their ratings, either.

Despite the extra danger from the publicity, Rick was glad for the attention; he was counting on public support to keep him and Tessa out of serious trouble, and maybe even provide them with a source of income from the lecture circuit until the new space program got started. Their careers in the shuttle program were certainly dead now, and only hero status would ever let them fly again.

Contact. The capsule shuddered and the seats pressed up against them. The force eased off for a second, then built again, stronger and stronger, until it was well over a gee. Air heated to incandescence shot past the windows, lighting up the inside of the capsule like a fluorescent tube, and the ship began to rock from side to side. Some of that was no doubt the guidance computer fine-tuning their trajectory with shots from the attitude control jets, but every few seconds the capsule would lurch violently as it hit a pocket of denser air. The deeper they plunged into the atmosphere, the greater their deceleration, until they were pulling nearly seven gees and struggling just to breathe.

Long minutes dragged past as the three astronauts remained pinned to their couches, barely able to move. Rick kept his hand near the manual controls mounted on the end of his armrest, but even when the buffeting became severe and the automatic system seemed to be overreacting, he didn't take over control. He trusted the ghost more than he trusted his own instincts. It wouldn't let them die now, not this close to the end of the mission.

The cabin walls flickered momentarily at that thought, and Rick cringed as he waited for a blast of flame to engulf him, but the fade-out only lasted for an eyeblink. Tessa and Yoshiko both gasped, but they said nothing. Speech was impossible with the incredible weight pressing them into their couches.

The ionized gas roaring by had cut off communications with the ground. Rick heard only static in his headphones, but the shriek of air around the blunt edge of the heat shield nearly drowned out even that. Up through the window he could see a twisting tail of white-hot flame stretching away for miles into a sky that grew steadily bluer as they fell.

Finally after six minutes the gee force began to ease off, and the flames streaming past the windows faded away. They had slowed to terminal velocity now, still plenty fast but not fast enough to burn away any more of their heat shield.

Rick looked at the altimeter at the top of the control panel. At 25,000 feet, just as the needle passed the black triangle on the gauge, the drogue parachutes opened with a soft jolt. Rick watched them flutter overhead, stabilizing the craft and slowing them just a bit more, then at ten thousand feet the main chutes streamed out and snapped open in three orange-and-white-striped canopies. The capsule lurched as if it had hit solid ground, but then it steadied out and hung there at the bottom of the shroud lines, swaying slightly from side to side as it drifted.

The sun was only a few hours above the horizon, and waves

scattered its light like millions of sparkling jewels below them. Rick let out a long sigh. "Home sweet home," he said.

"Don't relax yet," Tessa said, eyeing the altimeter. "We're still a couple miles up."

"Yes, Mom."

A new voice over the radio said, "Apollo, this is the U.S.S. *Nimitz*. We have you in visual."

"Roger, visual contact," Rick said. He loosened his harness and peered out the windows, but he couldn't spot the ship, nor the Russian one. It was a big ocean.

The altimeter dropped steadily, swinging counterclockwise through five thousand feet, then four, three, two . . .

"All right," Rick said. "We're going to make it."

"Rick!" Tessa shot him an angry look. "We're still at a thousand feet."

Rick looked out at the ocean, now seeming close enough to touch. "I don't care. I've played doublethink with the supernatural the whole way to the Moon and back; well now I'm done with that. We could survive a fall from here, so unless this thing sinks right on out of sight with us in it, I say superstition be damned: we're home safe and sound." He banged on the hatch for emphasis. It made a solid enough thud when he hit it, but a moment later it began to shimmer like a desert mirage.

"Rick, stop it!" Tessa yelled, and Yoshiko said, "Not yet, damn it, not yet!"

"I take it all back!" Rick shouted, but this time the capsule continued to fade. It supported their weight for another few seconds, but that was all. The control panel grew indistinct, the altimeter going last like the grin of the Cheshire cat, its needle dropping toward the last few tick marks, and then the couches gave way beneath them, pitching all three astronauts out into the air.

Rick flailed his arms wildly to keep from tumbling. His right hand struck one of the spacesuits and it bounced away from him, spinning around with arms and legs extended. The other two spacesuits had remained solid, too, and for a moment Rick wondered why they hadn't faded along with the ship, but then he remembered that he and Tessa and Yoshiko had worn them aboard.

He twisted around, looking frantically for the only other non-ghostly items in the capsule, and he saw them just below, falling like the rocks they were: the samples he and Tessa had collected from the lunar surface.

"No!" he shouted, reaching for them as if he could snatch at least one rock out of the air, but he suddenly got a faceful of water and he choked and coughed. The sample containers had been part of the ship, and they had disappeared, too, splashing him with their contents. He smelled ammonia, and something else he couldn't identify before the wind whipped it away.

Everything they had collected, everything they had done, had vanished in one moment of arrogant pride. They were returning to Earth with nothing more than what they had taken with them.

Except the entire world knew they had gone and knew what they'd seen; nothing could take that away.

Tessa was a few feet to the side, but she had spread her arms and legs out to slow her fall. As she swept upward, her hair streaming out behind her, Rick shouted, "Don't hit like that!"

"Of course not," she yelled back at him. "I'll dive at the last minute."

Yoshiko was windmilling her arms to keep from going in headfirst, but she was tumbling too fast. "Cannonball!" Rick yelled at her, but he didn't see if she tucked into the position or not. He barely had time to twist around so his own feet were pointed downward.

The ocean came up at them fast. Rick looked away, and this time he saw the ships, two enormous gray aircraft carriers plowing side by side through the waves toward him, their decks covered with sailors. And reporters. And scientists, and bureaucrats, and who knew what else.

Rick closed his eyes and braced for the impact he knew was coming.

Part Two

MIND OVER MATTER

The concussion when his feet hit the water sounded like a board hitting a brick wall. Rick wished he could have seen the splash, but he plunged underwater the moment he hit. His legs buckled under the strain and his breath left his lungs in one sudden whoosh, but by then the water had already slowed him enough to let him spread his arms and claw his way back to the surface.

The water was chilly, but not cold. He gasped a deep breath and shook his wet hair out of his eyes, but he was in the bottom of a wave trough. He couldn't see either rescue ship, or anything else but water. He might have been the only person in the entire ocean for all the evidence available to him.

Then Tessa bobbed to the surface just a few feet away, and a moment later Yoshiko gasped and spit out a mouthful of water just beyond her.

The next wave lifted the three of them into the air, and from atop the hill of water they saw the rescue ships less than half a mile away. This would have been the best-targeted splashdown ever, if they hadn't lost their spacecraft.

"Are you all right?" Tessa shouted over the roar of the rescue helicopter that swooped toward them.

"I'm alive," Yoshiko said, her voice full of amazement.

"Rick? You okay?"

"I guess," Rick said. He couldn't believe they'd gone all the way to the Moon and back only to lose their samples in the last few hundred feet. And it was all his fault. If he hadn't gotten cocky, they would have made it all the way down.

And *then* the capsule would have disappeared. If Rick's state of mind was in fact responsible for the ghost, then a successful landing would have guaranteed its disappearance.

Catch-22. They'd been screwed from the start; he just hadn't figured it out until now.

It was too late to do anything about it, too late to do anything but help Yoshiko climb into the orange rescue harness the hovering chopper lowered to the water. She sat on the padded collar and clung to the cable while the winch hoisted her aboard. Prop wash blew spray into Rick's and Tessa's eyes and whipped their hair into tangles while they waited for the harness again, then Rick treaded water alone while Tessa rode up to the open cargo bay. Helicopters didn't make the same noise when you were directly beneath them, he discovered. No slapping sound of rotors hitting the air; just a steady thunderous roar from the engines and the wind.

When his turn came he pulled the harness underwater with him long enough to get his feet through it, then grabbed the cable and waved to the winch operator with his free hand. He rose out of the water, spun around a few times, then felt his stomach lurch as the helicopter lifted away before he'd even risen halfway toward it. The pilot seemed to be in a hell of a hurry, he thought, then a moment later he saw why. Another helicopter swooped in right behind it and dumped a cascade of some icy-blue liquid right on the spot where they had been. The ocean boiled when it hit, and steam rose from the surface. Then the helicopter backed off and angled forward just long enough to fire a missile into the water. For a second nothing happened, then searing bright light blossomed a dozen feet below the surface and the water truly began to boil.

Rick laughed. They were sterilizing the *ocean*?

Then he spun around on the cable and his laughter died. On the flight deck of the *Nimitz* sat a familiar silver trailer house. Familiar to anyone who had watched the original Apollo missions, anyway. It was an isolation unit, as completely sealed and self-contained as a space capsule. Neil and Buzz and Mike, and the crews of the next couple of flights, had all lived for three weeks in one just like it after their return from the Moon.

But the later missions had dispensed with that, after the Moon had been determined to be biologically dead. What did NASA think it was going to accomplish by reviving that outdated practice? Was this their way of reestablishing control of the mission now that the astronauts were on the ground?

The winch kept winding while the helicopter swept around toward the carrier deck. Rick considered bailing out and swimming for the Russian ship, but he didn't want to leave Tessa behind, nor did he really want to run to the Russians again for help. Accepting their assistance on the mission was one thing, but defecting to their country was something else. He would have to bull his way through this problem himself.

The winch operator was wearing an isolation suit, and when he pulled Rick aboard he motioned him to a bench in the back with Tessa and Yoshiko, then he shoved the helicopter's sliding side door closed and sprayed the door, the deck, and the winch with pungent green foam from what looked like a fire extinguisher. Rick half expected the guy to spray him, too, but he left the three astronauts alone until the helicopter bumped down on the carrier deck. He waited until the rotors came to a halt, then he pulled open the door again and motioned his passengers out, where more navy crewmen in isolation suits ushered them to the silver trailer.

"This is ridiculous!" Rick shouted. He looked around for someone with a video camera, spotted one right beside the door of the trailer, and said, "We don't need this! The Moon is dead as a doornail. We proved that thirty years ago!"

"Sorry, sir, but we've got our orders," one of the crewmen said, shoving him firmly through the open doorway. Tessa and Yoshiko tumbled in after him, and the door slammed shut behind them.

The trailer was well insulated. Airtight, in fact. In the sudden silence, Rick said sarcastically, "Welcome home."

"You should have thought of this when you defied orders," said a voice from an overhead speaker just inside the door.

"Jackson?" Tessa asked.

"That's right."

"Where are you?"

Rick looked out the rectangular front window at the people peering in at the astronauts. He saw lots of navy faces and three journalists with video cameras, but the flight director was not among them.

Jackson said, "I'm in Florida, sweetie. Halfway around the world from you and any bugs you might have brought home."

"We didn't bring home any bugs, and you know it." Tessa sat down on the padded bench seat in the breakfast nook. No, Rick told himself, that wasn't a breakfast nook. Even though it was right across from the kitchen sink, that was their dinner table. And it probably folded down to make one of the beds, too. The couch beneath the front window no doubt made into another bed, and a third folded down over it bunk-bed style from the ceiling. At the opposite end of the trailer—maybe fifteen feet—were three narrow doors: two of them closed and probably closets, the third one open to reveal a bathroom almost as small as the shuttle toilet. The whole trailer was hardly bigger than the Apollo capsule they had just spent a week together in, but with gravity pulling everything to one surface it was going to be even more cramped.

Jackson laughed. He was in control again, and he enjoyed being there. "We don't know what all you might have brought home," he said. "You were wading through primordial comet debris up there."

Yoshiko shivered and pulled her wet hair back behind her ears. She said, "We brought back nothing that hasn't been brought to Earth thousands of times already in comet strikes."

"Maybe, maybe not," said Jackson. "We'll find out in a few weeks." He laughed again.

Rick looked up at the speaker, for lack of a better point of focus. "I didn't realize you were that petty," he said.

Jackson quit laughing. "Don't push me," he said, "or you'll find out lots of things you didn't know about me."

"I'll bet." Rick shivered. It was cold in the trailer. The window beside the table had been replaced with the air recycler, which blew a soft but steady breeze straight at him. In his wet clothing, it felt like an arctic blast.

All three of them looked like drowned kittens. He and Yoshiko were leaving puddles of seawater on the carpet, and Tessa was no doubt soaking the cushion where she sat.

Outside, the reporters and sailors and bureaucrats were struggling for position to see inside the trailer. Barely visible beyond them, the flight deck stretched off toward the horizon. Rick momentarily imagined himself at the controls of an F-15, streaking down the steel runway toward freedom.

Then a curious thought struck him. Why couldn't he? It would be no crazier than what had already happened to him. He closed his eyes and concentrated on the trailer around him, converting the window through which the gawkers peered at him into a curved bubble cockpit, the table at which Tessa sat into an ejection seat, the kitchen equipment into flight controls . . .

He opened his eyes. No luck. His surroundings hadn't changed a bit. Whatever power he'd had over the Apollo capsule didn't extend to transmutation of trailers.

There was a click from the speaker overhead, and the babble of voices from just outside cascaded in around them. Rick could only catch a word here and there among the shouted questions. "What . . . tell us . . . going . . . feel" and so forth. The usual questions; Rick didn't need to hear them to know what they were. The media never asked anything pertinent.

He turned to the window and said slowly and clearly, so the cameras could pick up his lip motion even if they couldn't pick up his voice: "Let us out of here."

If anyone heard him, they didn't let on. The babble continued uninterrupted.

"Let's at least get out of these wet clothes," said Yoshiko.
She walked the few steps to the back of the trailer, opening
cupboards and drawers along the way, eventually finding
what she was looking for in one of the tall closets beside the
bathroom door. Blue cotton one-piece jumpsuits. She took
one off a hanger and stepped into the bathroom. Bumps and
curses came from within, and Rick laughed, knowing what
was happening on the other side of the door.

"Need a hand in there?" Tessa called out.

Only slightly muffled by the thin door, Yoshiko said,
"There's no room for a hand. Or anything else, for that matter."

Rick looked around the inside of the trailer. Only the one
window, and that had a curtain. He turned to face the cameras
and said, "Sorry, guys. We've got to change out of these wet
clothes," then he drew the curtain across the window.

Tessa watched, smiling all the while, as Rick peeled out of
his spacesuit liner, dumped it in the sink so it wouldn't get the
floor any wetter than it already was, and dried himself off
with the dish towel. Then he pulled on the largest of the
jumpsuits and zipped it up. There were three pairs of soft cotton slippers on the floor of the closet, so he slipped into the
biggest pair of those, too, then rapped on the bathroom door.
"I'll trade you places," he said. "There's more room out here,
and I've pulled the curtain."

"Good." The door popped open and Yoshiko stepped out,
bare from the waist up. Even after their forced intimacy in the
Apollo capsule, Rick was surprised to see her act so casual
about nudity, but she had obviously been struggling to get
free of the wet fabric in the tiny bathroom and she wasn't
about to put the top half of her suit liner back on just to take
it off again. In different circumstances he might have joked
about the situation, or whistled appreciatively, but this was a

rotten time for it. She looked bedraggled and tired and not at all in the mood for jokes. Nor was Rick. The enormity of what they had done, and the letdown he felt at their return, was finally starting to catch up with him.

He went into the bathroom and closed the door behind him. No wonder Yoshiko had had trouble. There was barely room enough for Rick to sit on the tiny chemical toilet without bumping his knees against the door. There was only about one square foot to stand in, for the sink took up one corner beside the toilet and in the corner opposite was a shower about the size of a broom closet. Rick sat on the stool and stared at his distorted reflection in the stainless-steel shower wall. From there the clamor of voices outside sounded like the soft susurration of ocean waves against the beach just outside his vacation condo in Key West. He closed his eyes and imagined himself there, but he had no more luck with that than he had in turning the trailer into a jet.

CHAPTER 13

The trailer had a TV. Tessa discovered it in a tip-out drawer next to the refrigerator, so she turned it on and flipped through the channels. There were about fifty of them, but they were all showing the same thing: live coverage of their mission. The first view they saw came from a camera somewhere overhead, showing the crowd around their shiny trailer—a crowd that was already smaller than it had been a few minutes ago. A male announcer's voice was saying, "—still changing out of their flight gear and taking much-needed showers now that they have returned safely to Earth."

"I wish," said Rick. "You ought to see what they call—"

"Hush," Tessa said. The scene had changed to a view through the crowd, and the announcer was saying, "—minutes ago into their biological quarantine facility. Astronaut Rick Spencer was not happy with this part of the mission, though NASA officials insist that it is necessary to prevent any possible contamination from lunar disease organisms." They cut away to a picture of Rick, looking like a shipwreck victim with his hair plastered to the side of his unshaven face and a wild look in his eyes as he shouted, "We don't need this! The Moon is dead as a doornail. We proved that thirty years ago!"

"Uh-oh," Rick said. "If that's their sound bite, then we're in trouble." He went back to the window and pulled open the curtain. Nobody was even looking in now, and the crowd had begun to disperse.

"Hey, we're all changed and ready to talk," Rick said, hoping the microphone was connected to somebody's headset. It was; first one cameraman and then the others turned back to the window, and within seconds the babble had started again. "How do you . . . will you do now that . . . do you think . . . see . . . feel . . . ?"

Rick picked the last question first. "I feel wonderful," he lied. "It's great to come back home to a world that cares about spaceflight again. When we looked down at the Earth from a height nobody had been to for thirty years, and knew we were there because people *wanted* us there, well, we all felt pretty good about that."

The babble died down while he spoke, but the instant he stopped, he heard another half dozen questions. "What about the . . . Why do you think . . . was it like . . . you go again?"

"Of course we'd go again," Rick said. "Wouldn't we?" He beckoned Tessa and Yoshiko up to the window so they would be in the picture as well. Even with wet, stringy hair, they were more photogenic than he was.

Tessa put on her biggest public relations smile and said, "Sure we would. In fact, I'd love to be married up there if I could." She held up her left hand to show off the ring that Rick had made for her, and a gasp went through the crowd outside.

Rick felt an electric thrill run down his spine, too. "It didn't disappear?" he asked, incredulous.

"Nope." Tessa kissed him in front of the cameras. "We're still engaged, lover."

When the interview was over, a thousand interminable questions later, Rick pulled the curtain closed again and asked Tessa, "Did you know about the ring all along?"

"Umm-hmm," she said, smiling. "But until I was sure we were going to be safely sealed away for a while, I didn't want to bring it to anybody's attention for fear they'd take it away from me."

He took her hand in his and examined the ring. It was hard

as ever, still rough on the edge where he'd snapped it free of the control panel and smoothed it off with a zipper.

"Why didn't it disappear, too?" He looked from Tessa to Yoshiko, standing right beside her. "Have you got a theory to account for this, too?"

"I'm sure I could come up with one," Yoshiko said. "Astronomers are good at coming up with theories. But with just the one phenomenon to work from, it probably wouldn't be much good."

"That didn't stop the two of you when the capsule faded out," Rick said.

Yoshiko grinned at him. "My life was in danger then. Now it isn't." But her grin faded away too quickly, and she added, "At least I don't think it is."

Rick looked up at the speaker above the door. "How about it, Jackson? How much trouble are we in?"

There was no response. "Hello," he said, reaching up to tap the black metal grille. "*Apollo 18* to ground control. Come in, Houston."

Nobody answered.

"Well," he said, turning away. "If the lack of surveillance is any indication, I'd say the odds are good they're just going to hold us until people forget about us, then fire our asses and turn us out on the street. At least Tessa and me. They can't really touch you."

"NASA can't," Yoshiko said. "But how about your CIA? They could claim I helped hijack an American space vehicle. If they wanted to make an example of me, they could execute me as a spy."

Tessa put her arm around Yoshiko's shoulders. "They don't want that kind of example. They'll send you back to Japan before they do that."

Yoshiko nodded, but she was obviously not convinced. Rick wasn't either. This was completely new territory for him, and for the U.S. government as well. He didn't imagine anybody knew yet how it would work out.

Their hosts had at least figured out dinner. The window above the kitchen sink had been replaced with a miniature airlock, through which the ship's crew could slide trays without breaking quarantine. They wouldn't allow anything to go back out, which meant storing the used trays in sealed bags under the sink, but at least nobody had to cook.

The food was cafeteria fare, but after the stuff they'd been eating for the last week, it tasted like haute cuisine. And there was plenty of it. Rick and his crew stuffed themselves to bursting on beef stroganoff, mashed potatoes, mixed vegetables, and some kind of unidentifiable red dessert. At least they assumed it was dessert; it was sweet and sticky enough.

When they were done, Rick noticed a little pile of peas left on Tessa's plate, and for some reason the sight of it made him laugh.

"What?" she asked.

"You don't like peas," he told her.

"Right. What's funny about that?" she asked with the voice of someone who has taken far too much ribbing from her family over the years about being finicky at mealtimes.

He held out his hands defensively. "It's not the peas. Not in particular, anyway. It just struck me how odd it is that someone's personal likes and dislikes can survive an experience like we've just had."

She frowned. "It would take more than a trip to the Moon to make me like peas."

"No, it's . . ." He struggled for the words to explain it to her. "I mean, it's kind of encouraging that after all we've been through, we can still be the same people we were before. It's neat that you still don't like peas. It's reassuring. And *that's* what's funny."

She looked at him blankly for a moment, then shook her head. "*You're* what's funny."

He looked to Yoshiko for support. She was sitting on the bunk under the front window, since the seat across the table from where Rick and Tessa sat had a big wet spot from where Tessa's clothes had dripped on it.

"Am I funny?" he asked her.

She didn't meet his eyes. "I hardly know you," she said. "We were under so much stress on our way to the Moon and back that we didn't really learn much about each other's true personalities."

"That was diplomatic." Rick waited for her or Tessa to say more, but neither woman spoke. After a minute or so of silence, he leaned back and said, "Maybe I am funny. I know I'm your typical space geek. Built model rockets when I was a kid, ate 'space food sticks' in my school lunch, got signed photos of all the astronauts and swore I'd be one myself when I grew up. One-track mind all the way. Sweated bullets coming out of college because the shuttle program looked doomed from the start, but I applied for the astronaut training program anyway. And here I am."

Yoshiko smiled softly. "I guess that makes me your typical astronomy geek. My father helped me build a telescope when I was eight, and I haven't looked down since."

Both she and Rick looked over at Tessa.

"What?" she asked.

"In case you hadn't noticed, we're taking a tender moment to get to know one another," Rick said. He held his fork under his mouth like a microphone and said, "So tell us, Miss McClain, how did you acquire your irrational fear of vegetables? Were you frightened as a child by a rutabaga? Taunted in school by green beans?"

He held the fork out toward her. She rolled her eyes, then took it from his hand and set it on his tray. "My sister used to sneak her peas and carrots onto my plate when our parents weren't looking. Nobody believed me, so I had to eat hers too before I could have dessert. I heard that astronauts didn't have to eat fresh vegetables because they were too bulky for the food value they provided, so I decided that was what I wanted to be." She looked at them defiantly, daring them to laugh.

Rick didn't even try to suppress it. He snickered, then busted out with a great belly laugh. "You went into space so you wouldn't have to eat your vegetables and you think *I'm* strange?"

" 'Takes one to know one,' Dad always said."

"My dad always told me I'd come to a bad end if I didn't get my head out of the clouds." Rick rapped the back of his hand against the plastic siding of their trailer. "I wonder if this was what he was thinking of."

Yoshiko asked hesitantly, "Is he . . . ?"

"Dead. Three years ago."

"Oh. I'm sorry."

"It's all right." Rick stacked his tray and Tessa's together, leaned over and took Yoshiko's from her outstretched hand, then put all three in the waste bag under the sink, all without getting up from the table.

Through the window behind Yoshiko, the carrier's flight deck seemed to stretch nearly to the horizon, where a few puffy clouds were turning orange. Sunset came early at low latitudes. On Rick's previous visits to the tropics he had found that a bit unsettling—warm weather had always meant long days when he was a kid in Montana—but today he welcomed it.

So did Yoshiko. "I hate to—how do you say it—poop the party," she said, "but it has been a long day, and now I have a full stomach. I think I could sleep for a week."

"Me too," said Tessa.

Rick snorted. "You think *you're* tired? I should start poking you in the ribs every time you drift off and see how you feel after a couple of days of that."

"You start poking me in the ribs and we'll tie you into the top bunk, mister."

Rick looked at the fold-out bed over the window. He would have about six inches of space between his nose and the ceiling if he slept up there. And Tessa's threat implied a much more comfortable invitation.

Just to make sure he wasn't misinterpreting things, he asked, "And if I behave myself?"

She kissed him on the end of his nose. "You're so cute when you get your hopes up. Of course I want you to sleep with me, you idiot! We're engaged to be married!"

Rick's mother would have argued that that was all the more reason why they shouldn't even be in the same house together at night, but NASA had already forced their hand. And besides, what she didn't know wouldn't hurt her.

He laughed aloud at the thought that he could hide anything from anyone at the moment. They knew there was at least one microphone somewhere in the trailer; there were probably hidden cameras as well. And some poor intelligence schmo no doubt had to sort through all the tapes, maybe even type up transcripts.

Rick felt a momentary urge to stage-whisper something nonsensical just to give the guy something to puzzle over, but he let it go. He was in enough trouble already.

They searched for bedsheets and blankets, eventually finding them beneath Yoshiko's bunk. It took a little experimentation to figure out how to slide her mattress out to make a full-size bed of it, and how to lower the table to make the other bed. When they were done, there was only a tiny place next to the kitchen sink left to stand in, and they had to shuffle past one another to get to the bathroom. They took turns showering off the ocean salt and the week's worth of grime beneath it, then they switched out the lights and climbed into the sack.

Rick and Tessa slept in the nude, but it was clear from the start that the first order of business was sleeping. Tessa kissed him goodnight, said goodnight to Yoshiko, then rolled over and faced the wall. Rick put his arm around her and tried to relax, but he couldn't ignore the warmth of her bare skin against his, nor the curve of her breasts just touching his hand. Nor, he realized a few minutes later, could he ignore the air blowing across him from the recycler in the wall just above the bed. He turned his back to it and bunched up the blanket on that side, but he could still feel its chill breeze through the fabric.

As if that wasn't bad enough, he could also feel every seam separating the four sections of mattress. He and Tessa had put the wet cushion upside down at their feet, but it had soaked all the way through. Tessa's softness and warmth snuggled in next to him overshadowed all else, but as they struggled to get comfortable on the rough slabs of foam rubber, he couldn't help but giggle.

"Now what?" she asked.

"The heroes' triumphant first night back on Earth," he said. "Spent in a trailer house under military guard. It's absurd."

She turned her head toward him, which bunched her hair up against his nose. "Get used to it," she said. "I get the feeling it's going to get even more so before it gets better."

"I hope naa—achoo!"

"Yuck!" She pulled her hair away from his face.

"What do you mean, 'yuck'? I just sneezed. And besides, it was your fault anyway."

"My fault? How was it my fault?"

"You pushed your—"

Neither one of them expected the pillow that landed smack on their heads.

"Go to sleep," Yoshiko said.

Rick almost threw the pillow back at her, but checked the impulse and lobbed it gently instead. "Yes, Mom," he said, then he lay back down and concentrated on falling asleep.

Tomorrow would bring all the trouble they needed.

ure enough, before the sun even poked above the horizon they were awakened by a loud clang against the top of the trailer. Rick jerked upward, tumbling out of a dream in which the lunar module collided with the command module and ripped a foot-long gash in its side.

"What was that?" he asked when he realized where he was.

The speaker clicked on overhead and a young man's voice said, "Sorry about that, sir. We're craning you over to the *Jiménez* for the trip back to the States, and we hit the top of your habitat with the hook."

"The *Jiménez*? What's wrong with the *Nimitz*?"

"We're on maneuvers, sir. We were the closest ship to your splashdown site, so we picked you up, but we've got to get on with our mission."

Rick suspected there was more to it than that. The U.S. couldn't send a small ship if the Russians were sending a carrier. But now that they had made their impression on the world, they could put the astronauts quietly out of sight and get on with business as usual.

Then the sailor's first statement sank in. "You're craning us over? You mean like dangling from a cable?"

"Yes, sir." There was a hint of amusement in the voice. "Not to worry; this is Kevlar-reinforced towline. We do this all the time with cargo containers. You'll be fine."

Rick rubbed his eyes. "Uh-huh. It would have been nice if somebody had warned us."

"Yes, sir. Uh, you've got about five minutes before we send you over. If you need to use the bathroom or anything, now would be a good time."

"Right. Thanks for that much, at least."

They barely had time to get their clothes on before the winch reeled in the slack in the cable and with a deep bass thrumming that shook the walls, they rose into the air. Rick had never had a fear of heights, but when the trailer lifted off the flight deck and swayed back and forth over the edge, he suddenly felt himself close to panic. It was a long way down to the water. The NASA ship was a bathtub toy compared to the *Nimitz*. A tiny target for the crane to hit from so high up, even though the aircraft carrier was stable as a continent.

"We're going to die," Rick said as the gray steel wall of the carrier's outer hull slid upward beside them. He knelt on Yoshiko's bed and leaned forward to look out and down. If the crane dropped them, he wanted to see what they would hit.

"Get away from the window," Tessa told him. "You're tipping the trailer."

He was. His extra weight at the forward end was enough to tilt the floor by twenty degrees or so. He climbed back to the kitchen table bed and sat cross-legged next to Tessa. Yoshiko sat across from them, holding on to the seat back as the trailer swayed at the end of the cable, and they watched the side of the ship give way to the distant horizon while they spun slowly around.

The sky was light enough to read by and growing brighter every minute. By the time the trailer touched the deck of the *Jiménez*—and bounced twice before coming to rest—it had shaded from gray through pink to blue. It looked like a beautiful tropical day shaping up outside, for all the good it would do them.

Sailors rushed to tie down the trailer, and a moment later Rick realized why they'd been so quick about it. The aircraft carrier had been too large for waves to affect, but the smaller ship bobbed like a cork in the mid-ocean swells.

"Oh, God," Tessa said. "We're going all the way back to the mainland on this? Jackson must really have it in for us."

The trailer had landed amidship, just aft of the deckhouse.

The sailors shoved it around until its window faced the white-washed steel door, from which a half dozen people in gray suits emerged as soon as the sailors finished tying off their ropes.

One of the suits plugged a patch cord into the wall below the window, and the speaker overhead buzzed for a moment.

The suit in front said, "Hello, can you hear me inside?"

"Loud and clear," Rick said. "Who are you?"

"I'm Bernard Sonderby, CIA spook. Literally." He grinned at his own joke. "I investigate parapsychological phenomena. And these are some of my colleagues from various universities and research foundations around the country. We'd like to ask you some questions about your experience if we could." He waved casually toward the other five people; three men and two women, all of whom carried laptop computers and miniature tape recorders. Sonderby carried no props. He was apparently too important for such things.

Rick snorted. "Doesn't look like we've got a whole lot of choice in the matter."

The CIA man nodded. "I understand how you feel. I'm not happy about the quarantine, either. I'm trying to get it lifted, but in the meantime I thought we could at least get the preliminary interview out of the way."

"The *CIA* can't get the quarantine lifted?" Yoshiko asked.

Sonderby shrugged. "Contrary to popular opinion, we're not all-powerful."

"But you're working on it," Rick said. "I know your game. You want to learn how to do what we did so you can make a weapon out of it."

He had expected Sonderby to be offended—had hoped for it, in fact—but the man only nodded and said, "True enough. And to defend against one, of course. We've known for some time that the Russians have been working on psychic weapons, but until now we've had nothing substantial to study."

Before he had started seeing Apollo ghosts, Rick would have said that was because there wasn't anything substantial *to* study, but now he knew better. And he supposed the CIA man had a point. If the Russians were getting results, as Gregor had implied, then it did behoove the U.S. to learn what they knew. But making weapons was another thing.

"I will not knowingly do anything to help you build a weapon," he said.

Sonderby seemed unperturbed by his statement. "Fair enough. At this point I'm perfectly happy just talking about what happened." He turned to one of the sailors standing nearby. "Could we get some chairs here? And an awning or something to protect us from the sun and the wind?"

The sailors all rushed to comply, leaving Rick with the impression that Sonderby had more authority than he let on. Rick wished he didn't have to deal with the guy—he hated the CIA just on principle—but he had learned long ago to pick his fights. He couldn't refuse to talk to everybody, and Sonderby could just interview whoever Rick did talk to, so fighting him would piss him off for no good reason. It made more sense to talk to him directly. At least then he'd know how much the CIA knew.

He wished he could talk with Tessa about their story, brainstorm a little with her and Yoshiko about what information they should hold back, but he knew Sonderby would hear every word they said. The time to make up a story would have been when they were still in flight, but they hadn't thought that far ahead.

They would just have to wing it. But Rick could say one thing directly, and he did. He looked back inside at the two women and said, "I don't want either of you telling him anything that could be used to make a weapon, either. Okay?"

"Fine by me," Tessa said.

Yoshiko looked at Sonderby, then at Rick, and nodded.

"Okay, then. We'll talk."

CHAPTER 15

They spent the next three hours going over their experience, dredging up every innocuous detail they could think of. The trouble was, they didn't know what was dangerous and what wasn't. Maybe Sonderby did, but he and his acolytes revealed nothing. Their questions all pertained to the behavior of the ghost spaceship, and they reacted the way any group of people would to the answers. One of them kept repeating "This is so cool!" as he jotted down notes, while another muttered "That's impossible" over and over again, like a mantra.

The astronauts folded up the beds while they talked, stumbling around at first as the ship rolled from side to side. Rick tried to ignore the weightless sensation in his stomach every time they slid down a trough between waves, and finally discovered that it was better if he sat down. So all three of them settled onto the couch that had been Yoshiko's bed since it was closest to the window.

The scientists sat in folding chairs, and a blue-and-white-striped plastic tarp was tied to something overhead. Another tarp angled away to the right, protecting them from the steady east wind. Their hair still strayed in the occasional breeze, but they looked comfortable enough. Rick wished he could feel the wind on his face again.

The scientists' enthusiasm was infectious. Despite themselves, the astronauts wound up warming to the interview, growing more and more animated as they recalled the more harrowing moments of their trip, especially the reentry and their final drop into the ocean.

"That should have killed you, by the way," Sonderby said when they got to that part.

Rick actually felt his heart skip a beat. "What?"

"The fall. You were at least five hundred feet up when the capsule disappeared. From that height the impact should have been fatal."

Tessa gave Rick a look that could have frosted glass. "Oh really?" she said. "Why wasn't it?"

The CIA spook took a sip of iced tea, which the ship's crew had brought for him along with the chairs and awning. The woman in the chair to his immediate right, a physicist named Wilson, said, "Your acceleration seemed to be slowed by some unseen force. The force was nonlinear, increasing as you approached the water. From analysis of video footage I've determined that you fell at nearly one gravity to begin with, but the lower you got, the less you accelerated. In the last twenty feet, your acceleration actually became negative. So you hit with no more velocity than if you had fallen free for forty-five feet. A respectable velocity—thirty-six miles per hour—but hardly life-threatening if you land properly, as you all did."

Sonderby said, "We can only conclude that your control over reality continued after the capsule disappeared. Once you realized you were still too high to survive, you slowed your fall. It probably looked more dangerous the closer to the water you got, which would explain why the acceleration actually became negative. You panicked."

"I didn't panic," Rick said. Far from it. He remembered the wild elation he had felt at knowing he was going to live. Tempered, of course, with anger at losing their hard-won samples, but he hadn't panicked.

Sonderby didn't push. "Perhaps not. It could just as easily have been instinctive self-preservation at work. It would be interesting to see what would happen if we dropped you from an even greater height. Given time enough to realize your predicament and react fully to it, would you rise back into the air?"

"I don't want to find out," Rick said.

"I don't blame you." Sonderby grinned. "Don't worry! I know you think I'm evil incarnate, but I don't dissect kittens for fun, and I don't put people in danger for the sake of experiment."

Rick shrugged. "Good thing, because I don't think I've got any control over things anymore. I tried to turn this isolation trailer into a plane just a few minutes after we were shoved in here, but nothing happened."

The scientists all took note of that. A man named Toland, a former astronomer who had picked up an interest in the supernatural and was now a self-proclaimed psychic, said, "How can you say you have no power when the evidence is right there before you?"

"What evidence?"

"Tessa's ring."

Rick looked down at her hand, which she'd been keeping out of view of the window. The ring was still there.

"Could we take a look at it?" Toland asked.

She shrugged and held it up to the window.

Everyone crowded around, and the questions came fast and furious. "What does it feel like?" "Do you get any sensation of power from it?" "Is it cold?" "Is it hard as real metal?"

In answer to that last, she rapped it against the glass. The "click, click, click" it made said it all.

"Could we examine it first-hand?" Wilson, the physicist, asked. "I'd like to take a sample—just a tiny sliver!—for chemical analysis. We know what the actual switch guards were made of; it will be interesting to see what this one turns out to be."

Tessa laughed. "I hadn't thought of that. Jeez, what if it's gold or something?"

"If it is, then it's a damned good thing American currency isn't tied to the value of gold anymore," Sonderby said.

Tessa looked at her ring more closely. "If I let you look at it, will you promise to give it back?"

Wilson nodded and said, "Of course," but Sonderby hesitated.

"You do understand that it's the first definite, documented supernatural artifact we've ever had a chance to study. Chemical analysis is merely one of many tests we'd like to make."

"And *you* do understand that it's also my engagement ring."

"Indeed." Sonderby bit his lower lip, then slowly nodded. "It is no doubt safest with you anyway. If you will agree to let us examine it from time to time as we figure out what we need to look at next, I see no reason why you can't continue to wear it."

Tessa looked back inside the trailer. "Rick?"

He didn't like this one bit. Sonderby was talking like he owned the ring, and Tessa would only keep it at his sufferance. "I wouldn't mind finding out what it's made of either," he said, "but I don't like anybody coveting my fiancée's ring, no matter what it's made of or how we got it. It's *her* ring, and it's going to stay that way whether or not she agrees to let anyone take a second look at it. Is that clear?"

Nobody liked that idea, but they all agreed, even Sonderby.

"All right," Rick said. "So long as we understand each other. But how can we pass it outside to you without breaking quarantine? Not that I think it matters."

Sonderby pointed toward the side of the trailer where the kitchen window had been replaced by the food airlock. "We installed high-intensity ultraviolet lights in the transfer cabinet. If you would just place the ring inside it and seal the door, we can sterilize it before we open our side."

Tessa wiggled the ring off her finger, then got up and opened the cabinet. "Okay," she said. "There it is." The top and middle shelves were just wire racks, so she placed it on the bottom shelf, then closed the door.

Rick felt a queasy sensation in his stomach. He told himself it was just seasickness, but he wasn't sure he believed it.

Wilson went around to the side. She disappeared from view, but they could hear her flip the switch for the lights, and a minute later there came a thump as she opened the outer door.

They heard her voice, but she was too far from the microphone for them to make out her words. Sonderby, still at the front of the trailer, said, "She can't find it. Where did you set it?"

"On the bottom," Tessa replied. "Right in the middle."

Sonderby relayed that to Wilson, then said, "It's not there."

"What? Of course it is." Tessa grabbed the door handle, but it wouldn't open. "Close your side!" she shouted. "Close it now!"

Rick swallowed hard against a stomach that was suddenly even queasier than before. He got up off the couch and took the two steps necessary to stand by Tessa's side. They heard a thump and she yanked open the door. And there, right where she had put it, rested the ring.

"Whew!" She picked it up and slid it on her finger again. Rick put his arm around her shoulders and squeezed.

Wilson came around to the front of the trailer. "What happened?"

"It—it must have disappeared the moment I closed the door," Tessa said.

"But it was there when you opened it?"

"Yes."

Wilson pursed her lips and got a faraway look for a moment, then said, "It could have been the UV light." She turned to Sonderby. "Could we try it again without?"

Rick and the CIA agent said, "No!" simultaneously.

After a moment's thought, Tessa surprised them both by saying, "I'm okay with it. It did come back, after all."

"There is the quarantine issue," Sonderby said.

She laughed. "We all know that's bullshit. We pissed off the flight director, so he's trying to make us miserable. Come on, do you want to examine the ring or not?"

"Tessa." When she looked at him, Rick shook his head.

He'd never realized before that the phrase "gut instinct" was a literal description, but his stomach was telling him something was definitely not right.

She bent close and whispered in his ear, "I know what I'm doing. Let me try this."

He didn't like it, but as he had just reminded Sonderby, it *was* her ring. He took his arm away from her shoulder and said, "Okay."

Without waiting for confirmation from Sonderby, she pulled off the ring and set it in the cabinet again, then closed the door. "Okay, go ahead."

Wilson looked to Sonderby, who took a deep breath, then nodded, a tiny little nod. The physicist moved to the side of the trailer again, and they could hear her open the outer door. It thumped closed again almost immediately.

Wilson spoke, and Sonderby said, "It's not there." He actually seemed relieved.

Tessa opened the inner door again. This time Rick could see the ring materialize. Relief made his knees nearly buckle, but he took a deep breath and forced himself to ignore that and his stomach. "May I?" he asked, reaching for the ring. When she nodded, he picked it up and closed his fingers over it. The metal felt cool and hard, just as it had when he had snapped it off the control panel. Smoother than he remembered it, though. The zipper he'd used to file it down with hadn't really been a very good tool for the job.

Working on a hunch, he turned away from Tessa, but it remained solid.

"Close your eyes," he told her, and when she did, he opened his hand and held the ring there a moment longer. It still remained, so he moved toward the front window. When he got there, the scientists all bent close to see it. "Okay, I'm setting it on the ledge right below the window," he said, doing just that. Its gray brushed-metal finish reflected a little of the midmorning sunlight that filtered in through the awning.

"Can I open my eyes yet?" Tessa asked.

"Nope."

The moment Rick let go of the ring, it started fading out. He resisted the urge to grab it, instead leaving it alone and saying as calmly as he could, "Okay, I'm picking it up again."

The ring solidified.

Yoshiko had been silent for some time, apparently trying to stay as clear of the American political situation as she could, but she gasped when she realized what she had just seen.

"Tessa controls it!" she said.

Rick nodded. "At least partially. Okay, you can look now."

Tessa came up beside him and let him put the ring on her finger again. "What happened?"

Rick told her, and she looked puzzled for a second. "It didn't fade out until you set it down?"

"That's right."

"Then you still control it, too."

He leaned forward and gave her a little kiss. "That's entirely appropriate, considering it's our engagement ring."

All six scientists tried speaking at once. Finally Sonderby waved the others to silence and said, "Would you try letting Yoshiko hold it?"

Yoshiko shook her head. "I do not wish to be part of this experiment."

"No?"

"No."

"But it would help us learn more about how this works."

She took a deep breath, said, "I have spent the last week trying to learn how this works, with my life in peril the entire time. I am tired. I don't want anything more to do with ghosts. I want to go home, but I am being held prisoner by a foreign power, and with each passing minute we steam farther away from Japan. Please let me go. Or at least let me speak with my ambassador."

Sonderby wiped his forehead with the back of his hand.

"The situation is very complicated," he said. "You've all been charged with dereliction of duty, of course. You and Tessa have also been charged with reckless endangerment of the rest of your shuttle crew. Until those charges are cleared, we can't release you from custody even if we do eliminate the quarantine."

"I still want to speak with my ambassador."

"Yes, of course. That much I can arrange. And I promise, I will do what I can to get you all out of quarantine as soon as possible."

"Good," Rick said. Then, without warning, he sneezed.

CHAPTER 16

Everyone looked at him as if he'd just grown fangs and horns. "What?" he said. "I sneezed. Big deal. It was probably the sunlight."

"Sunlight?" Tessa asked dubiously.

"I always sneeze in sunlight."

"Yeah, right. It's really bright in here."

"It's bright out there." He pointed out the window. "And I was looking outside."

"Uh-huh."

He frowned. "Whose side are you on, anyway?"

"Earth's." She sat down on the couch. "If we actually brought something home with us . . ."

"I am not sick!" Rick stomped over to the dining table, then turned around. The boat rolled sideways just then, and he grabbed on to the seat back for support. "Jeez, give me a break. One sneeze and suddenly it's an epidemic."

Sonderby said, "I'm sure it's nothing. Why don't we take a break? We've been at this for hours."

"Now that's a great idea," Rick said, sitting on the bench with his legs out in the kitchen aisle. "And how about something to eat? They didn't feed us before they dropped us overboard." He didn't feel hungry—quite the contrary, in fact—but maybe a little food would would help settle his stomach.

Sonderby slapped himself on the forehead. "Good grief! Why didn't you say something earlier? Of course!"

"Because we could barely get a word in edgewise," Rick muttered, but Sonderby had already turned away and shouted to the nearest crewmember, "Food! Bring these people some lunch!"

While they waited for food, Tessa turned on the television, and they were surprised to find that they still had dozens of channels to choose from. The *Jiménez* evidently had a satellite dish, too, no doubt gimbaled to cancel out the corkscrewing motion as it plowed at an angle through the waves.

There was a bit more variety now, but practically every channel was still showing something related to their flight. Talk shows were full of psychics and spoon-benders, sitcoms had been hastily edited to include ghosts and magic, science shows were all about fringe research, and the news programs cut between the footage they had taken on the Moon and interviews with people on the street—most of whom were more interested in the supernatural aspect than in the idea of lunar colonization.

"Gack," Rick said. "There's more psychos than scientists out there."

"This is a surprise?" Tessa asked.

"No, but I had hoped people would pay attention to what we did as well as how we did it."

"Give them time. Going to the Moon is old news. Ghost rockets aren't."

Their lunch showed up, and they ate while they channel-surfed. The food was good enough—chicken pot pies with a salad on the side—but it didn't sit well on any of their stomachs. Rick was the first to bolt for the toilet, and he had barely flushed away the mess before Yoshiko banged on the door.

Tessa heroically held hers down, but she didn't look good. Rick weaved his way to the front of the trailer. There was nobody on the other side of the window, but he called out, "Hello, is there anybody out there?" and a sailor stepped around the side from the right. Had he been guarding the doorway? It sure looked like it: He was carrying an ugly black automatic rifle slung over his shoulder.

"Can I help you?" he asked.

"Could we get you to aim the ship straight into the waves for a while? This pitching and rolling stuff is making us all seasick."

The sailor tried to hide a grin. "Not unless we want to go to Peru instead of San Francisco."

Rick tried to imagine a globe with their ship somewhere west of Hawaii, steaming northeast. Peru would be way to the southeast. But that would put Hawaii ... "Hey, why the hell are we going to San Francisco, anyway? Hawaii's a lot closer."

The sailor shrugged. "Orders. I don't question 'em."

"Well I sure as hell do."

"With all due respect, sir, that's why I'm out here and you're in there."

"Yeah, well, questioning orders took me to the Moon and back," Rick said, but when he saw the expression on the other man's face he realized how that must have sounded. "Hey, sorry. I turn into a jerk when I get seasick."

"Oh, that's a good excuse," Tessa said from behind him. "Can I use that one next time I say something stupid?"

"As long as you're on board a ship," Rick told her. He felt another sneeze coming on, but he fought it down.

The sailor peered in through the window at them. "You know, you guys don't look very good. Let me go talk to the captain and see what we can do."

"Thanks."

He didn't leave immediately. He had to call for someone to replace him at the door first. Only when another rifle-clad sailor relieved him did he go inside the deckhouse.

Nothing more happened for at least half an hour. The three astronauts had pulled their bunks back out and were lying down and moaning by the time someone else showed up. It was a man in his fifties or so, heavyset, and graying on top.

"I'm Dr. Cortez," he said. "I've brought you something for

the seasickness." He held up a little brown bottle and a half dozen tiny round bandages in a plastic bag.

"Dramamine?" Tessa asked.

"Dimenhydrenate, which is the same thing. And scopolamine patches, in case you can't keep the syrup down. Plus I've brought something called a Seaband. It's basically an elastic bandage with a little plastic bead that pushes on a nerve about three finger-widths up from your wrist. A lot of people find that it's more effective than the drugs."

"Acupressure?" Rick said dubiously.

The doctor hefted the box of bandages gently in his hand. "Don't knock it until you've tried it. It works better than drugs on some folks. I'll send all this stuff through. Instructions are on the packages."

He went around to the side of the trailer, and they heard the door open and close. Tessa brought the medication inside and studied the label on the bottle, then got three teaspoons from the drawer beside the sink. She poured a spoonful and held it out to Rick. "Open wide."

"Yes, Mom."

She stuck the spoon in his mouth and left it there while she poured one for Yoshiko and another for herself. Rick had expected it to taste terrible, but he felt so rotten he couldn't detect much flavor at all. He licked the spoon clean and handed it back to Tessa.

"Patch," she said, handing him a light brown, round adhesive bandage about a half inch in diameter.

"Does it go anywhere specific?" he asked.

The doctor had come around to the front again. "Not really," he said. "Anywhere with a good blood supply is fine."

Tessa laughed suggestively, and Rick felt himself blush.

"Most people put 'em behind their ears," the doctor said, grinning.

Rick peeled the backing off and stuck the patch behind his left ear.

"And finally the alternative medicine," Tessa said, handing out the Seabands. They were brightly colored elastic cuffs with a marble-sized lump sewn into a little pocket on the inside. Rick got a lime green one, which was about the color he imagined his face was at the moment. He slipped it on his right wrist.

"Where does the bump go?" he asked.

"Said the boyfriend," Tessa replied, laughing.

Rick groaned. "How can you be so cheerful at a time like this?"

"I don't really feel all that ba—a—achoo!"

Rick had been trying to suppress another sneeze for the last few minutes, but when Tessa let go, he couldn't hold it any longer.

Yoshiko, still sitting on her bunk in front, whispered, "No. Please, no."

"It's the air in here," Rick said. "It's not being recirculated well enough."

"Let me check," said Dr. Cortez. He disappeared around the other side of the trailer. They heard what sounded like another access hatch being opened where the recycler was, then he came back around to the front. "Nope, it's working fine. You can adjust the air flow from inside if you want more filtration, though."

Rick looked at the vent above the table, the table that had been his bed last night, and suddenly realized what was going on. "It's the damned air flow that did us in!" he said. "We were wet and cold and we slept in a breeze all night—we're catching colds."

The doctor rubbed his chin and "hmmm"ed in thought for a moment. "Colds are viral infections. Chilling the body does make a person more susceptible, but the virus has to be there."

"So one of the guys who stocked this place before we got here had a cold. Or one of the people who made these jump-suits we're wearing, or the cook who made our dinner last night. The bug could have come from practically anywhere. All your isolation protocols are aimed at keeping bugs *in*, not out."

"True, but cold virus is airborne," said the doctor. "With the exception of your brief trek across the deck of the *Nimitz*, you haven't had a chance to be exposed to an aerosol with the virus in it."

"Achoo!" Rick sneezed again. "So we must have picked it up on deck. Either that or we're both allergic to something in here."

"That is also possible," Dr. Cortez admitted. "We can test you for sensitivity to various allergens, but for the moment I think we should just observe your progress and see what happens. It could be nothing."

Yoshiko said, "And if it's not? What if it turns out to be a new disease? Would we be quarantined forever?"

The doctor smiled what he no doubt intended to be a reassuring smile. "No. The human body totally eliminates most pathogens within a few weeks of exposure. The few that remain infectious are the ones that have evolved alongside us and learned how to evade the immune system, and it's pretty unlikely that anything you picked up on the Moon would behave like that. You'll be fine."

His smile slipped a bit. "Providing the bug's not stronger than your immune system, of course. That could be trouble. But if you survive the infection, you should be disease-free within a month."

"*If?* This is supposed to be reassuring?"

He nodded. "The odds of it being lethal are very slim. Rick's probably right; you've most likely caught colds. But we'll keep our eyes on you and be ready to head off any complications that might come along."

"Please do," said Yoshiko. She lay back on her couch.

Despite his assurances, the doctor didn't look much happier than she did. He was frowning when he left. Rick was willing to bet he was the only doctor on board. Jackson hadn't expected medical trouble—he only wanted to keep his rebellious astronauts out of the public eye—so he had probably sent only a minimal support staff.

Rick and Tessa lay down, too. Rick expected to be disturbed at any moment by reporters, but Sonderby must have forbidden them to bother the astronauts. Or maybe there weren't any on board. With Jackson running the show, that was entirely possible. He wondered if the word had gotten out yet that they were sick. That would be a public relations nightmare. Jackson's little act of vindictiveness might have already come back to haunt him if the public believed NASA had brought back a virus from outer space. He'd have been better off flying them directly home from the *Nimitz*. At least then he could claim that whatever they'd caught was an Earth bug.

And if it wasn't? Rick forced himself to consider that possibility. What if they *had* brought something home? Something new and virulent and deadly? Maybe Jackson had been right all along.

A little while later, the ship turned about thirty degrees to the south of east. It still wasn't heading quite in the same direction as the waves, but it was much better than before. There could be only one good reason why they would change course now, without even checking to see if the seasickness medication was helping: The doctor had decided to get his patients to a more capable medical facility. And there was only one place that could be in this stretch of ocean: They were going to Hawaii after all.

CHAPTER 17

Sure enough, less than an hour later Sonderby came around to give them the news.

"We've diverted for Oahu," he said. "We're setting up a better facility for you there, where we can analyze what's going on and either get you out of quarantine or provide better care for you until we know what you've got."

"Thank you," Rick said, and he meant it.

"How's the seasickness?" Sonderby asked.

Rick had to stop and think about it before he answered. "Better," he said, surprised to find that he was. But then he sneezed three times in succession, and had to pull a paper towel off the roll under the cabinet beside the sink to wipe his nose. "But I'm afraid the cold's getting worse," he added.

Sonderby said, "I can't do much to help you there, except give you time to get some rest. But I would like to continue our interview sometime today if you feel up to it."

Rick looked over to Tessa and Yoshiko. Tessa shrugged. Yoshiko said, "Aside from the seasickness, which is going away, I feel fine."

"What the hey," Rick said. "Let's go for it before we get any worse."

"Very well. I'll call the others." Sonderby turned away, then remembered something and turned back. "I have contacted the Japanese embassy. The ambassador is in Washington, D.C., at the moment, but his staff has arranged to have someone from the consulate's office in Honolulu meet you tomorrow. Is that all right?"

She nodded. "That will have to do."

Before he could go again, Tessa said, "I'd like to know how

the rest of our shuttle flight went. I assume from the lack of news about it that they must have made it down okay."

He laughed softly. "They did. The mission went off without a hitch, which of course has prompted several members of Congress to ask why NASA overstaffs its shuttle flights. They want to know why, if the crew was able to accomplish all its mission objectives with two astronauts missing, we couldn't cut those positions from the roster and save the cost of their training."

"Excuse me?" Yoshiko said. "Japan paid for my training, and we paid handsomely for launching my instrument package as well. And the reason my part of the mission was successful was because I finished it before I left."

"A fact all but lost on the type of mind—if you want to call it that—it takes to run America these days. Don't worry, nothing will come of it. I just thought you would all be amused to learn how Congress has reacted to your accomplishments."

"We saw how the rest of the country is reacting," Rick said. "I'm not sure if Congress is any more out of touch than the average voter. It looks like they're more interested in ghosts than going back to the Moon."

Sonderby nodded. "True. But I can't honestly say I blame them. We've *been* to the Moon before. How we got there this time is what's new. Don't be too hard on those of us who focus on the supernatural aspect of what you did. If we can figure out how you did it, we could go back there anytime we wanted to."

"Pardon me, but your ambition is showing," Rick said.

"Good," Sonderby said. "I have no desire to hide it from you or from anybody else. You've demonstrated something phenomenal. Literally. It could change the world. It undoubtedly *will* change the world. I want to make sure it changes it for the better."

■   ■   ■

onderby left just long enough to gather his colleagues, and the six of them resumed their questions about the mission. Rick endured it with as much patience as he could muster, but when Toland, the psychic, asked if he could bend a spoon for them, Rick blew up.

"Spoon-bending! That's all a bunch of fakery and you know it. Next you're going to want me to cast your horoscope, right?"

"That can wait," Toland said with the calm resignation of one who has been called a crackpot many times before. "But spoon-bending is certainly not fakery. I can teach you to do it."

"Not me you can't."

"Chicken," Tessa said. "I'll try it."

Toland smiled. "Very well. Here's what you have to do. Get a spoon out of your silverware drawer and hold it by the handle with the business end on top." He waited until Tessa did so, then said, "Assure yourself that the spoon is rigid. Take two or three fingers and try to bend it. Good. Now grip it tightly in one hand, with your fingers just below the spot where you want it to bend, and concentrate on softening the metal. Think about the molecules holding on to one another with their magnetic charges, and imagine them loosening up. You may feel some heat, but you're not trying to melt it. You're trying to soften it. There's a difference."

"This is such total bullshit," Rick said. "Iron is a crystalline substance. It has a definite freezing point, below which it's a solid. It's got a measurable, *predictable* tensile strength, and no amount of wishful thinking is going to change that. You can't just make it—"

"Shut up," Tessa told him. "I'm trying to violate the laws of physics here."

"That's the point I'm trying to make."

"What do I do next?" she asked Toland.

He said, "When you feel it starting to soften, you'll have maybe a second to bend it before it becomes rigid again. It might go on its own, but if it doesn't you can push it over. Just use one finger so you'll know you couldn't have done it without psychic help."

"Psychiatric help, you mean," Rick muttered, but Tessa ignored him. So did everyone else. Sonderby and Toland and the four other scientists watched intently through the window as Tessa held the the spoon in her right hand and willed it to bend. She pushed on the inside of the bowl with her left index finger, but it didn't go anywhere.

"Keep concentrating. You'll know when it's ready."

"Should I close my eyes?"

"No. It helps to focus on what you're doing."

Tessa held the spoon about eight inches in front of her nose. Her forehead wrinkled as she squinted in concentration, and the hand holding the spoon began to shake. Suddenly she sneezed, and the bowl fell off and bounced on the carpet.

"Yow!" Tessa shouted, dropping the handle as well and sticking her fingers in her mouth. "Uhnn! It got hot!"

"Did it burn you?" Toland asked.

She pulled her fingers out of her mouth. "Not bad."

Rick saw a red line across the fleshy part between the first and second joints of her top two fingers, and another red line running down the pad of her thumb. They could have come from holding the spoon so tightly, but they weren't fading.

"Are you okay?" he asked. "Do you need some ice?"

"No. I think it scared me more than it burned me." She bent down to retrieve the pieces. "Wow. It does look all melted."

She was right. The ends looked rounded and bubbly, rather than ragged the way they would be if someone with superhuman strength had ripped the spoon in half. Rick took the handle from her and inspected it closely. It certainly did look melted. But how could somebody melt stainless steel with her mind?

Maybe it wasn't stainless steel.

"Gallium," he said. "It's made of gallium. Melting point just about body temperature. You hold it in your hand and it softens up just like that."

"Try it," Toland said smugly.

Rick did, taking the handle in his right hand and pressing the melted end of it into his left palm. At first it didn't melt, but then suddenly it did. He enjoyed watching Toland's expression change from smugness to surprise to alarm as he kept feeding the spoon handle into the growing silver puddle in his palm.

"Gallium," he said again. "It has to be."

"Po—pour that out, please," Toland said. "Quickly."

"Why?" Rick asked. "Don't like to see your little magic act exposed? Maybe I should—yeeeooowww!" His palm suddenly felt like he'd stuck it in an open flame. He yanked his hand out from under the liquid metal, splashing some of it up against the kitchen counter, but the bulk of it dropped to the floor, where it lit the carpet on fire the moment it touched the fabric.

"Shit! Shit, shit, shit!" Rick yelled as he reached for a drinking glass to fill with water, but his fingers wouldn't close around the glass. He looked at his palm, saw the angry red burn, and suddenly felt the pain redouble.

Tessa tried to stomp out the fire, but she leaped back when her slipper also started to smolder. She had knocked down the flames, but black smoke still rose from the floor, stinking of burned sheep.

Rick turned on the cold-water tap and stuck his left hand under it until the pain receded a little, then cupped both hands together and splashed water on Tessa's foot and on the floor until the smoke stopped rising. The air recycler switched to high, sucking it out.

Rick looked down and saw a Rorschach blot of silver metal, its fingers frozen into the blackened pile of the wool carpet.

"Damn it," he said, cradling his injured hand and looking

out the window at Toland. "That sure as hell wasn't gallium. What was it? What happened here?"

"I have no idea," Toland said, then he reconsidered and added, "No, actually I have a pretty good idea, but it's untestable unless you want to try burning your other hand."

It was hurting like hell now. Rick squeezed it with his right hand, wincing with the pain. "What are you, nuts?"

Toland sighed and rubbed his forehead. "Quite possibly. Welcome to the world of psychic research."

CHAPTER 18

The ship steamed into Pearl Harbor the following afternoon. The isolation trailer was once again craned overboard, this time onto a camouflage-painted flatbed truck, and as soon as it was tied down a crew of soldiers unfurled a green canvas top that covered the trailer as if it had been made for it.

Rick had been growing steadily more nervous as he'd seen the vast expanse of gray ships, green vehicles, and camouflage uniforms in the harbor, but when the canvas flopped down over the back of the truck and cut off most of their light, he felt a moment of true panic.

"Hey, wait a minute," he yelled. "Where are you taking us?" His voice didn't sound like his own anymore; the cold had reached his sinuses and stuffed him up. At least he wasn't sneezing as much as he had been yesterday. Tessa was at the coughing stage, which had kept Rick awake half of the night— a night spent on the floor to avoid the draft from the air recycler.

The soldier tying down the tarp didn't act as if he heard him. The intercom had probably been turned off when they'd unplugged the trailer from the ship's power. Rick thumped the window with his right hand, but the soldier tied the last corner of the tarp down, and the darkness was complete.

"This doesn't look good," he said.

"What do you think they're going to do with us?" Yoshiko asked.

"I don't know. But wherever they're taking us, they apparently don't want anybody to know about it, and I don't like that." He thumped the window again. "I could bust this easy enough. We could wait until the truck slows down at an intersection or something and then jump out. It will probably be our only chance to escape if we're going to, because wherever they're taking us, I'll bet it's crawling with military just like this place."

"We don't know that," Tessa said. "Sonderby's played straight with us so far."

"Yeah, and he may be about to lose control of us to some military commander who wants a new weapon even more than he does."

"I don't know," she said. "But I do know if we break quarantine, we're going to be in even deeper trouble than we are now. And we may *cause* more trouble than we want, too. We are sick, after all."

"You and I are." Yoshiko hadn't showed any symptoms yet.

The truck's engine rumbled to life. A few seconds later, it started to move, accelerating smoothly. Apparently the driver was at least trying to spare them a rough ride.

Soft scraping sounds came out of the darkness as Tessa felt her way along the wall next to the door until she found the light switch and flipped it on, but nothing happened. "Doesn't this thing even have battery power?" she asked.

"It's got to," Yoshiko pointed out. "The air system is still running."

Rick tried the light above the sink. It took him a few seconds to find the wall switch, but there was no power to that light, either. "Maybe I should heat a spoon until it glows," he said sarcastically.

Yoshiko drew in a sharp breath.

"Don't worry, I was kidding." He now wore a bandage on his left hand big enough to use for a baseball mitt, and he was popping pills every hour to dull the pain. He had no urge to injure himself further. Tessa still had red marks on her fingers, too, but those weren't burns.

Yoshiko said, "I wasn't worried. I was just thinking, what

if you were to try the same thing you did yesterday with a light bulb?"

"What good is a melted light bulb?"

"No, just concentrate on making the filament glow."

"I'd just melt it inside the bulb," he said. "Assuming anything happened at all."

"How do you know?"

He sighed, then had to sniff and cough for a few seconds. "I don't know, but I'm not interested in trying it. Who cares if we're in the dark literally as well as figuratively? Unless you want to bust out of here and risk spreading what we've got to the whole damned planet, we're stuck."

"I'll try it, then," Yoshiko said. "Give me a light bulb."

"All right," Rick said dubiously. He fumbled for the fixture above the sink, unscrewed the bulb behind the plastic shade, then reached out in the darkness toward the sound of Yoshiko's voice. He encountered her hand reaching for his, then felt her fingers slide along his to grasp the bulb.

"Okay, here goes. I'm holding the bulb in my hand and imagining the filament inside, imagining it getting hot this time instead of getting soft. Getting so hot it glows . . . getting hot . . ."

Rick and Tessa waited, both holding their breath, while Yoshiko concentrated on the light bulb. The truck turned a corner, then began picking up more speed.

"Come on, *glow*," Yoshiko said, and Rick heard a desperation in her voice that made it clear this was about far more than simply producing some light. She had been a passenger this whole time, a bystander caught up in vast and bizarre events beyond her control, and now it was her turn. She was going to command some of this psychic energy if it was the last thing she did.

For just a moment he wondered if this whole thing was some kind of hallucination, if the three of them were patients in an insane asylum somewhere, fueling each other's delusions while doctors and nurses peered at them through one-way glass and took notes for condescending articles in psychology magazines.

Then the light bulb began to glow.

"Yessss," Yoshiko said, making the word one long exhalation.

She held the bulb in both hands, like a supplicant holding an offering to a higher power. It glowed with only a few watts, just enough to illuminate her round, smiling face, dark eyes sparkling with delight.

"Glow!" she whispered, and like a candle that receives pure oxygen, the light grew stronger. It filled the trailer with soft, warm illumination.

"I can do it!" she said. "I can make it light up just by thinking about it!" The light waxed even brighter as she spoke, becoming too brilliant to look at.

"That's, uh, that's great," Tessa said, "but that's a sixty-watt bulb you've got there. I don't know how much heat the filament can—"

The bulb burst with a loud *bang*, plunging the trailer into darkness again. Rick felt glass shards strike his face.

He stepped forward. Glass crunched underfoot. "Yoshiko! Are you all right?"

"I . . . think so." She didn't sound like it.

"Did you get glass in your eyes?"

"No. I had them closed because it was so bright next to my face."

"What about your hands?"

"I've—ow!—got some slivers in the sides of my fingers."

"Tessa?" he asked.

"I'm okay."

The truck lurched and Rick reached out to catch himself, grabbing the edge of the countertop without even thinking about where it was in the dark. He wondered if it had been there all along or if his mind had created something to hold on to right where he'd been reaching for it. It would be hard to say, unless it faded away beneath his hand.

He reached out for the table and sat on one of the benches next to it. "I am so tired of this crazy stuff," he said. "I just want the world to be normal again. I want to be able to count on something working the way it's supposed to."

"I'm sure it is," Yoshiko said. "We just don't understand the rules yet."

"Rules! I'm even more sick of wacko rules than I am of the wacko stuff that keeps happening to us. 'Don't feel good about life or we'll all die.' What kind of warped rule is that?"

"Just as warped as the Heisenberg uncertainty principle, or the Pauli exclusion principle," Yoshiko replied. "You can't know the position and momentum of a particle at the same time, and you can't have two electrons in the same quantum state—quantum physics is just as counterintuitive as this is."

"Maybe to you," Rick said, then a moment later he realized how that sounded. "Sorry. That was the jerk speaking again."

"You're forgiven again. This upsets me, too. But there's no denying anymore that it exists. We have to learn the rules and make them fit what we already know about how the universe works, or we might as well go back to living in caves and cowering from thunderstorms."

She had a good point. Rick had always scoffed at spoon-benders, but now he had a big burn on his hand as a painful reminder that he had become one himself. He couldn't deny that any more than he could deny their trip to the Moon and back. Even if the evidence of it was gone, *he* knew it had happened, and he couldn't live the rest of his life in denial.

"That poor bastard Toland," he said softly in the darkness. "I wonder how long he's been able to bend spoons without anybody believing it's for real?"

"Somebody must believe him," Tessa said. "He's here, isn't he?"

"True enough," said Rick. He listened to the truck rumble along the highway for a few seconds, then said, "I wonder how much they already know?"

CHAPTER 19

"Negative thoughts bring negative results," said Toland later that evening.

They had been driven to a military base called Schofield Barracks in central Oahu. There had been some confusion at first when they thought that was the name of the building they had been transferred into, but Sonderby insisted that was the name of the entire base, and even showed them a map to prove it. He pointed out the medical center on Wai'anae Avenue, saying, "You're in this building on the end. Used to be the urgent-care clinic until they built a new one over here, but the old TB ward still had all the negative-pressure hardware installed, so it was a piece of cake to set up a quarantine unit for you. We even had time to stick up some partitions to give you private bedrooms."

Rick absorbed as much of the map as he could: The main gate was to the east and a smaller gate was northeast, but that one was actually a straighter shot since the roads all ran at an angle. There were rows of barracks to the southeast, and undeveloped space to the north. Or maybe whatever was there just wasn't shown on the map.

Sonderby's description of where they were matched Rick's memory of their arrival. Their trailer had been pulled into a small parking lot next to a two-story building, where a long plastic tunnel waited to be sealed around the door. The astronauts had been allowed to walk through the tunnel into a suite of rooms; two small bedrooms, each with a window looking out into a small grass courtyard between their building and the next one, a bathroom for each bedroom, a dining area that still retained the sinks and countertops of the lab it had once been, and a living room with a floor-to-ceiling window that faced not outside, but into a conference room.

That's where Sonderby and his crew, plus three more military people, sat in what looked like luxury classroom chairs while they debriefed the astronauts. Rick and Tessa and Yoshiko sat in overstuffed recliners on their side of the glass and sipped chilled fruit juice. They were still in quarantine, but the new quarters were so much larger than anything they had been in for the last two weeks that it almost felt as if they had been turned loose outdoors.

Doctors had taken blood samples through a glove box in the lab, and were working on isolating the pathogen in their systems while they settled in.

Toland had just been explaining the few things he knew about psychic powers. "Negative thoughts bring negative results," Rick repeated. "You know this for a fact."

"We do in certain cases. In others, such as your Apollo mission, the rule appears to be reversed. However, in most of the turnabout cases we've been able to study before this, there has been another interpretation of 'negative' that overrides the obvious one and makes the general rule apply."

"Such as?"

"People harming others with psychic powers, for instance. Usually if you try it, nothing happens. But occasionally people are able to if they believe that they're helping more people than they're harming, or righting a wrong, or helping the victim in some way."

"Helping the victim? How could that be?" asked Tessa.

Toland smiled. "You've heard the phrase, 'tough love'?"

"Ah. Of course. Spare the rod and spoil the child."

"Exactly. Discipline is high on the list of repeatable psychic phenomena. So are ghosts guarding dangerous crossings and psychic healing."

"You've got repeatable, documented evidence of this?" Rick asked incredulously.

"Of course not. One of the basic laws seems to be that none of this is reliable. The one time you absolutely need it, that's when it will fail. That's why we want to learn how you kept your Apollo capsule tangible for so long. Not only is it a record for size, but for duration as well."

Tessa snickered, and Rick blushed.

"So why did my light bulb blow up?" Yoshiko asked.

"What light bulb?"

She explained what had happened on the trip from Pearl Harbor.

"That one's easy," Toland said. "Rick is a strong negative polaron—that's our term for someone who doesn't believe in psychic phenomena—and Tessa was worried that you might somehow hurt yourself like Rick did. With that much negative energy working against you, I'm surprised you got it to glow at all."

"But she did," Rick said, waving his bandaged hand as he spoke. "That's the thing. How come she got it to work in the first place, and then it suddenly turned bad? How come I was able to melt an entire spoon handle into a puddle before it burned my hand? How come Tessa's spoon left her with stigmata?"

Toland shrugged. "The energy has to go somewhere. In each of your cases, once you started channeling it you were stuck with it. You couldn't cut it off fast enough when things started to go bad."

"So we tangled with the dark side of the Force? Come on."

"No, no. There's no light side or dark side. There's light and dark uses for it, but it's just energy."

"Uh-huh. But where does it *come* from?"

One of the military men spoke up. "That's what we'd like to know." He had enough stuff on his shoulders and pinned over his breast pockets that Rick knew he had to be fairly impor-

tant, but he couldn't read rank insignia to know how important. He guessed the guy must be a general, though. A little
brass plaque above all his medals had MARCUS etched on it.

"Got any theories?" Rick asked.

The general's short burst of laughter sounded like a dog
barking. "Oh, we've got dozens of 'em. The best one so far
seems to be the 'quantum foam' theory. You know about
quantum foam?"

"Are you talking about the zero-point energy in free space?
Particles popping into existence in matter-antimatter pairs,
and then instantaneously annihilating each other so the net
energy of the vacuum is zero?"

"That's the stuff. And that much we know is true. There's
more energy buzzing around in a cubic inch of space than in
a cubic inch of plutonium. It's just a bitch to get at. *But.*" He
paused dramatically. Rick thought of William Shatner playing
Captain Kirk, but he kept the smirk off his face. "But. A couple of guys in Utah figured out how to tap it nearly twenty
years ago. They just didn't know what they'd discovered.
They thought it was cold fusion. And when other laboratories tried to reproduce their results—*skeptical* laboratories,
because they didn't discover it first—they of course got nothing. The Utah guys couldn't sell used cars after that."

He shifted a little in his chair, which squeaked under his
weight. "We picked it up and started fiddling with it, and
eventually figured out that it wasn't fusion at all. It was just
free energy, and it only worked when the people running the
experiment expected it to work. We kept fiddling with it, trying different configurations on new recruits, until we learned
that you could stick two plain wires in a beaker of distilled
water and get juice out of 'em if the guys running the experiment genuinely thought it would work."

Rick would have called him a liar yesterday. Now he just
said, "That's going to be handy when we run out of oil."

"Tell me about it. Trouble is, to get more juice, you need

more people believing in it, and it's not a linear function. It increases as the square root of the credulous audience."

"Run that by me again?" asked Tessa.

The general nodded. "One person by himself can generate about a volt. Two people generate one point four, You need four people to generate two volts, nine to generate three, and so forth. The square root of the number of participants."

"Oh. So you'd need . . . thirteen, maybe fourteen thousand people just to generate house current."

"Right. Not practical. And of course every dubious adherent to the old physics damps the reaction as soon as they learn somebody's trying it. Or distorts the energy into the wrong form." He held out his hands, palms up. "Boom. As you've seen; when things start to go bad, the inverse square law seems to fly right out the window."

Rick remembered Gregor Ivanov talking about Russian underground explosions that had hadn't been nuclear.

"So you *could* make bombs with this business," he said.

General Marcus nodded. "Theoretically. We haven't had much luck making anything blow up on purpose."

"Neither have the Russians, according to Gregor," Rick said.

Marcus would have said more, but he was interrupted by Dr. Cortez, who entered the briefing room wearing a white lab coat and waving a sheaf of papers in his right hand as he said, "I've got some interesting results on the, um, the virus that Rick and Tessa have."

"Have you identified it?" asked Sonderby.

"Yes and no." Cortez held a transparency up to the light so everyone could see it. It showed a hexagonal array of little bubbles, maybe a hundred of them altogether. It was in black and white; Rick guessed it was an electron microscope image.

Cortez said, "This is definitely the pathogen. We've found it in both Rick and Tessa's blood samples, and not in Yoshiko's."

The doctor's words somehow made Rick feel even worse. He could smell the virus in his breath, feel it clogging his lungs.

"Is it a known virus?" asked Sonderby.

Cortez laughed. "Well, there's the rub. It's not really a virus. It's what somebody who knows a little about microbiology might *think* a virus looks like, but it's missing a few key components."

"You're saying it's an alien lifeform after all?" the general asked.

Cortez shook his head. "No more than Mickey Mouse is an alien lifeform. This thing is a caricature of a lifeform. It's artificial."

"What?" asked Rick, suddenly convinced he could feel little nanomachines crawling around in his bloodstream.

"Artificial like your spacecraft was artificial," said Cortez, turning toward the window. "It's a ghost virus, and not a particularly good one at that."

"You're kidding."

Cortez looked to Sonderby, then back at Rick. "Nope. It makes perfect sense when you think about it. Billions of people saw you hustled into that isolation chamber, and then they didn't hear from you again. Some of 'em were bound to think the worst. Enough of them, evidently, to provide the psychic energy to create just what they expected. They don't know enough micro to get the bug right, but that doesn't matter because everybody knows what 'sick' feels like. So you feel sick even without a real bug in your system."

"That's gratitude for you," Tessa muttered. "So what do we do about it?"

"Find the focus," Toland said. "Group minds don't create things by themselves. They need a spokesman to focus their energy. Like Rick was the focus during your mission, and Tessa seems to be the focus for her engagement ring."

"So who wants us to get sick?" asked Rick.

Toland shrugged. "It's not that simple. I doubt if anyone

actually wants you to be ill, but someone evidently believes it would be in your best interest."

"Who?"

Almost apologetically, he looked at Yoshiko. "Well, since one of you didn't catch the virus, I think that's pretty clear."

Yoshiko leaped up from her chair and approached the window. "I do not want them to be sick! I am terrified of catching it myself!"

"But you were also afraid of what Dale Jackson would do to all of you when you returned to the States. So it would be in everyone's best interest if something diverted you to Hawaii instead."

"That's ridiculous."

"Is it?" Toland took the transparency from Dr. Cortez and stuck it up against the glass. "Have a look at this. Doctor, could you explain its deficiencies in detail, please?"

Dr. Cortez was shorter than him. He had to stretch to point, until Toland realized the problem and lowered the micrograph. "Okay," Cortez said, "for starters, there's no way for it to attach itself to a host cell, and no DNA to inject once it got there even if it could. Instead it's got these little ball things all the way through. They're made of cellulose, like plant cells, instead of the usual protein coat, and they've got no DNA in them either. The whole thing actually looks more like a plankton skeleton than a virus."

As he spoke, Rick became aware of an amazing sensation coursing through his body. His stuffed-up nose opened again, the tightness in his chest loosened, and the muscle aches faded away as if he'd just slid into a whirlpool bath.

"Holy shit," he whispered. "Faith healing, too."

"What?" asked Sonderby.

"All of a sudden I feel fine."

"Me too," Tessa said. She sniffed, made a face, and swallowed. "Gack. Evidently the snot was real."

Rick thanked fate that his cold had already progressed

beyond the wet stage. He laughed. "This gives a whole new meaning to the phrase 'psychosomatic illness,' doesn't it?"

Yoshiko looked at him, confusion written all over her face. "But I didn't do anything."

"Except lose faith in the virus," Toland said.

"Faith!" she yelled, backing away from the window. "Faith! If faith could create something out of nothing, then a thousand Buddhas would walk the Earth. A million Allahs would sire a billion Jesuses. Miracles would happen all the time. But they don't."

"A man is a lot more complex than a virus," said Toland. "And religions always split into factions. There's a thousand different faiths all trying to create a mutually contradictory reality. Thank God for that, or your worst nightmares could come true the next time the Pope decides women should all be barefoot and pregnant again."

"I don't care about that," Yoshiko wailed. "I don't care about any of it. I'm an astronomer, damn it! I study what *is*. I don't need a God, not to thank nor to fear. I don't need faith in anything but the universe itself. I'm tired of this craziness and I want to go home."

Rick recognized his own words from earlier that same day. He knew just how she felt. "I want to go home, too," he said. "And now that we know what made us sick, there's no reason to keep us here."

General Marcus cleared his throat and stepped up to the glass. "Well, we'd like to keep you under observation for a few more days at least, in case any real lunar pathogens have been masked by the fake ones. And we would really love to look at that ring. We haven't been able to actually get our hands on a physical manifestation in all the years we've been studying this ghost stuff."

"They all blow up on you?" Rick asked.

Marcus snorted. "You talk like they're a dime a dozen. I've seen exactly one ghost in all my life, and it was thin as cobwebs. We're getting fairly good at making electricity and softening metal and so forth, but that old e=mc^2 business really makes it hard to create something out of nothing. Yours is the first documented case I've heard of since Deke Slayton died, and we didn't get a chance to do more than bounce radar beams off his plane before it disappeared."

Rick looked around at the plush living room. It had a stereo, a big-screen TV, a wall of books, a phone, a computer—all the comforts of home. But knowing it was also a prison made the walls feel like they were closing in on him. He could imagine how it felt for Yoshiko, imprisoned in a foreign country.

"We'll make you a deal," he said. "Tessa and I will stay for two more days, but Yoshiko gets to go home immediately."

"We can't break your quarantine—" the general said, but Tessa cut him off.

"The quarantine is total bullshit. We already broke it two days ago on board the *Jiménez*. Let her go."

General Marcus looked at Sonderby, visibly controlling an angry outburst, but Sonderby merely shrugged and said, "She's right, you know. It *is* bullshit. Jackson imposed it and we all went along with it because it kept them where we could get at them, but we know there's nothing on the Moon that hasn't been delivered to Earth hundreds of times a year in tektites and meteorites. So I allowed the biological seal to be compromised for about five seconds to see if we could examine Tessa's ring close-up."

The general rolled his eyes upward. "CIA," he growled. "I swear, you guys will destroy the world yet." He looked back through the window at Yoshiko. "All right. Your consul is about to beat the doors down anyway. We'll let you go—in a self-contained isolation suit. If you or the consul decide to open it up, that's your problem, but *I'm* not authorizing a breach of quarantine until two full weeks have passed."

"Two *weeks*!" Rick protested.

"If you want to buy your friend's freedom, that's the price," the general said. "Take it or leave it.

"You don't have to do anything," Yoshiko said. "They'll have to release me anyway."

Tessa laughed. "She's right. You're bluffing."

Marcus colored slightly. "Try me. Two weeks is the minimum we could keep you here, provided you cooperate and we start learning what we want to know. If I decide to declare you a national security risk, I could keep you here forever."

The threat hung in the air like a fresh fart, one which everyone but Marcus and his prisoners tried to ignore.

Rick tried to think it through. Could he get them out of there any sooner? He couldn't imagine how. Marcus held all the cards. The fact that he was willing to bargain at all meant that he wasn't invincible, but Rick had no idea where the chink in his armor might be. It would probably be better to pin him down to an agreement, witnessed by others, before he withdrew even that.

"All right," he said. "Two weeks. But I have one more request."

"What's that?" Marcus asked, his tone of voice making it clear that he was not in a mood to bargain.

"I want to call my mom."

CHAPTER 20

W ell hello, stranger," she said. Rick pictured her sitting at her kitchen table, the bright Montana sun reflecting off the snowbanks outside and filling the room with light. Her silvery hair would be curled in front, and if she'd been baking when she answered the phone she would be wearing a flowered apron. Floured, too, most likely.

He leaned back in his armchair and threw one leg over the side the way he'd always done when he was a teenager hogging the phone at home. "How you doing, Mom?"

"Fine, fine. Except you never call." Her voice sounded the same as he always remembered it. Rich, full of inflection, still just a little raspy from the years of smoking before she gave it up.

"I've been kind of busy."

Tessa, sitting on the other arm of the chair, could only hear his half of the conversation, but she laughed when she heard him say that. He smiled and put his free arm around her.

"So I've heard," said his mother. "You didn't tell me you were going to the Moon."

He chuckled. He hadn't told her he was riding a ghost into orbit, either. The last time he'd called he had merely told her that he would be going into space again sooner than he thought. Now he said, "It happened kind of fast. And once we decided to go all the way, I figured you'd hear about it."

She laughed with him. "Lord, that's true enough. You're all over the news. And the reporters are all over my yard, too. They've just about ruined my crocuses. I turned the hose on 'em yesterday."

"You didn't!" Rick could just imagine the video of that.

"I did. Just the sprinkler, but it kept them off the grass." She sighed. "Of course now they've churned it into mud."

Rick's mental picture wavered. "Mud? I thought there'd be snow. It's winter, isn't it?"

He heard something click against the tabletop. A coffee mug, probably. "It's supposed to be, but we haven't had any snow for weeks. Must be that global warming everybody's talking about." She paused, and he heard her take a sip, then she said, "I also see you're getting married."

Rick gave Tessa a little squeeze around the waist. "That's right."

"The TV is full of it. You'd think you were Charles and Diana."

It took him a second to place the reference. His mom lived in a timeless world anymore. Then he remembered and said, "Well, she makes me feel like a prince."

"Good. You treat her right and you can be happy your whole lives."

"I plan to, Mom."

"Good. You misspelled 'marry,' by the way."

"What?"

"When you scuffled your proposal in the moondust. You wrote 'Will you m-a-i-r-y me.' "

"No I didn't!"

"Looked like it to me. 'Course you were the one who got C's in penmanship, so maybe it was supposed to be an 'r.' "

Rick hadn't even been aware that Tessa had taken pictures of it. In fact, come to think of it, he was almost certain she hadn't. Gregor hadn't known why they had paused before re-entering the lunar module. He looked up at Tessa. "Did you film what I wrote on the ground up there?"

She shook her head. "I was too stunned to think of that."

"Somebody faked it, then. Mom says she saw it on TV."

"Not the TV," his mother said. "It was in a newspaper."

"A newspaper?" Rick laughed. "Oh, you mean like the *Enquirer*?"

"I don't remember which one it was, dear. Your pictures were on all of them there at the checkout stand at Safeway. I couldn't afford to buy them all."

"Jesus, Mom. I keep telling you that stuff is all baloney."

Her voice took on an edge he remembered from childhood. "What do you mean? You *are* getting married, aren't you?"

"Yes, of course we are. But the paper lied about the photo. We didn't take any pictures of what I wrote."

"What do you mean? I saw them with my own two eyes."

Rick knew when he was beat. He sighed, then said, "It doesn't matter. Hey, she's right here. You want to talk to her?"

Tessa raised her eyebrows.

Rick's mother perked right up. "Why sure, dear. Put her on."

"Just a sec." He covered the mouthpiece with his bandaged hand and whispered to Tessa, "It's all right. She's a sweetheart. Just don't argue with anything she says."

"Right." She picked up the phone as if it were a live snake and held it gingerly up to her ear. "Hello, Mrs. Spencer? Okay, Violet it is. Fine, thank you. How are you?"

Rick listened to her half of the conversation, growing more and more curious as she said things like, "Yes, he does. Oh, I don't mind that. Actually, I kind of like it. Oh, does he? I'll remember that." They chatted like old friends for maybe ten minutes, then Tessa said, "It's been a pleasure talking with you. Would you like to speak to your son again? Okay, I'll tell him. Yes, ma'am, we will. Goodbye."

She hung up the phone and said, "She said to tell you to call more often."

"Uh-huh. Sounds like you two got along okay."

"She seems like a nice woman."

"Mmm-hmm." He pulled her down into his lap. "What do you know, here's another one."

"Rick!"

He nuzzled the side of her neck. "Mmmmm. There's something erotic about listening to my fiancée talk to my mother for the first time. I get all these . . . I don't know, all these *woman* vibes. It's like a primal force of nature."

"Don't talk like that, or Toland and Sonderby and their kind will want to study that, too."

"Ha. Good point." He stretched upward to kiss her. She met him halfway, and the kiss was just starting to show some promise when the door opened on the other side of the glass wall and someone cleared his throat self-consciously.

Rick looked over to see Sonderby standing there, a smile on his face. "Yoshiko is on her way," he said.

"And now it's time to pay the piper, eh?" He leaned his head against Tessa's shoulder. "All right. The sooner we get to work, the sooner we can get on with our lives."

CHAPTER 21

The first thing they did was a chemical analysis of Tessa's ring. The lab techs who did the testing quickly discovered that it only worked if they performed every step within Tessa's sight. Rick had to file off a few flakes of metal for them, then put the sample in a clear test tube and transfer it through the Plexiglas airlock in the lab while Tessa watched every step. The techs had set up their gas chromatograph and mass spectrometer just on the other side of the window, and they took off the access panels so she could see the samples right up to the moment they were vaporized.

Finally Wilson, the physicist who was overseeing the whole operation, looked at the readouts and whistled softly. "Look out, economy," she said.

"Gold?" asked Tessa, who still held the ring in the palm of her hand.

"Gold, silver, and platinum, in about equal proportion."

"That's not what the originals were made of, were they?" Rick asked.

"Not by a long shot."

Tessa said, "It is, on the other hand, what most engagement rings are made of, isn't it?"

"Gold and silver, maybe," said Wilson, "but platinum? I don't think so."

"It's a precious metal. More so than gold or silver, if I remember right."

"That's true enough. But if Rick was going for precious—"

"I wasn't going for anything in particular. I was practically delirious from lack of sleep."

"Your subconscious mind, then. If it was creating precious metals on purpose, why not palladium or strontium or iridium?"

"It's just as well he didn't include strontium," Tessa said. "That's radioactive, isn't it?"

Wilson nodded. "Strontium 90 is, but how did he know that? How did he know anything in the state he was in? It's like he was tapped into some hidden source of knowledge as well as power."

Rick laughed nervously. He wasn't sure he liked having two women discussing his abilities. "Maybe I'm smarter than you think," he said.

Wilson looked at him critically. "All right, name the elements in order. Alphabetically."

"Uh, maybe I'm not."

Tessa rescued him from further embarrassment. "Whatever the ring is made of," she said, "I'll always treasure it." She picked it up from her palm with her right thumb and index finger, rotated it so she could see the top, then flipped it around and slid it on her left ring finger.

"What was that all about?" Rick asked her.

"What?"

"Turning it around. Does it fit better one way than the other?"

She blushed. "No. But I remembered which way it went when you put it on my finger, and I want to keep wearing it that way."

"Oh. That's . . . well, that's really sweet." He felt a slow tide of warmth spread over him. It was going to be fun sharing life with a person who thought the way she did.

The experiments were kind of fun, too, except for one. They were back in the living room, and on the other side of the glass Toland and the others were speculating why the ring hadn't disappeared along with the rest of the capsule, when

Toland suggested that it might be a physical manifestation of Rick and Tessa's attraction to each other.

General Marcus snorted. "Typical New Age theory. It's all touchy-feely and absolutely untestable."

"We can test this one easily enough," Toland said.

"How?"

"Make them fall out of love."

Rick laughed nervously. Tessa was sitting right beside him in a loveseat that they had pulled around to face the window; he reached out for her left hand with his right and laced his fingers through hers. He could feel the ring pressing against his index and middle fingers. "That might be more difficult than you think."

"I'm not talking a permanent change of affection here. A few seconds ought to be enough."

"Even so, I don't think we can just switch it on and off like a light."

Toland laughed. "You haven't been married before, have you?" He stood and approached the glass. "Try this. Just for the sake of experiment, I want one of you to say something, and the other to deny it."

"Like what?"

"Anything. Say 'The sky is blue.' "

Feeling foolish, Rick nonetheless said, "The sky is blue."

"No it's not," Tessa said without prompting.

He looked over at her, saw her grinning, and said, "Yes it is."

She pointed at the ceiling. "There isn't even a sky here."

He felt like he was in the middle of a Monty Python sketch, but he supposed there couldn't be any harm in trying it, so he said, "Outside there is."

"How do you know? We could be under a dome."

"On the other side of the dome, then."

"It's probably cloudy."

"You don't know that."

"Ha! You don't know it's blue, either."

"You're right," he said before he could help it. "Damn it! I'm sorry, we're supposed to be arguing."

She picked up the thread without a hitch. "That's right, you screw-up! What's the matter with you? You never get anything right."

"Do too!"

"Do not. You couldn't even make a spaceship that didn't disappear on us half a dozen times. You scared poor Yoshiko to death."

That hit a little close to home, which was no doubt just what she'd intended. "Scared her to death?" he asked. "What is she now, a ghost?"

She disengaged her hand from his and scooted away from him on the couch. "I was speaking metaphorically, but I wouldn't expect you to understand that, mister so-literal-he-has-to-think-the-space-program's-dying-in-order-to-keep-the-ghost-alive."

"I understand metaphor," he said, floundering for a snappy comeback. "I understand lots of things. Maybe better than you."

"Oh yeah? Well if you're so smart, why didn't you think to safeguard our lunar samples any better than you did? Any fool should have known to put them inside one of the spacesuits."

She couldn't have hurt him more if she had hit him in the nose. Rick sat back, stunned by the sudden realization that she was right. The spacesuits were real, handcrafted hardware, built the good old-fashioned way. They had fallen into the ocean right alongside Rick and Tessa and Yoshiko. Rick *could* have brought the samples home safely if he'd only been thinking clearly.

Then Tessa said "Uh-oh" in a voice that cut through everything, and he looked at the hand she was holding up.

No ring.

She reached toward him. He flinched back, but she said, "Kiss me, you idiot!" and planted her lips on top of his. She was all over him, holding his head in her hands, giving him tongue, pressing her body against his, but when she backed away for a second and they looked at her hand the ring was still missing.

"I'm sorry!" she said, her eyes filling with tears. "Jesus, Rick, I'm sorry! I didn't think of it either, not until just now. It's not your fault, okay? Rick, talk to me!"

He had to remember to breathe first. "I . . . don't know what to say. I was stupid. We were all stupid."

"I don't give a shit how stupid we were! I love you. Damn it, Rick, listen to me. I love you."

He looked at her. She was crying in earnest now, tears running down her cheeks. Something melted inside his chest, and he reached out to take her in his arms. "I love you, too," he said.

"Are—are you sure?"

"Of course I'm sure. How could you ever doubt that?"

"I didn't."

He looked at her hand, and a great weight lifted off him. The ring was back.

"Did too," he said.

She jerked away from him. "What?"

"Just kidding."

"Just *kidding*? Damn it, Rick, this is my ring we—" In that instant she realized it had returned. "My ring," she said softly.

Rick turned to Toland and the others, who were watching with the morbid fascination of children with a jar full of ants. "Satisfied?" he asked.

"Quite," said Toland.

The general sighed. "One of these days I'm going to transfer out of this woo-woo shit, I swear it. But not today. Okay, people, let's try to quantify what we've just seen. Rick, did you at any moment feel your *love*—" he rolled his eyes at the very idea of such a term having a military application "—for Tessa diminish?"

"No!" Rick said. He wiped the tears from her eyes.

"Tell the truth, now. This is important."

"I said 'no,' and I mean 'no,' damn it!"

"Subject says 'No . . . damn it,'" Marcus said, scribbling on his notepad.

"How 'bout you, Tess?"

"That's 'Tessa,'" Rick snapped.

"My, aren't we touchy all of a sudden? Okay, *Tessa*. Did you stop loving Rick?"

"No," she said.

Marcus tossed his pencil pinwheeling over his shoulder. "Then somebody kindly tell me what the hell just happened here."

Toland, still standing by the glass, said, "Tessa, were you afraid you'd hurt Rick by what you said?"

She nodded.

"Afraid you'd hurt him bad enough that he might not love you anymore because of it?"

She nodded again.

"QED" said Toland with smug satisfaction.

Rick looked him right in the eye and said, "I hope you get run over by a bus on your way home tonight."

"Negative thoughts bring negative results," Toland reminded him.

"What if I think the world would be a better place without you?" Rick stood up, lifting Tessa to her feet as well, and led her into the bedroom. Behind them he could hear an angry conversation starting up, but he slammed the door on it and lay on the bed with Tessa, holding her close in the darkness.

"Are you all right?" he asked her.

"I guess," she said. She sniffed. "I'm sorry. I thought it was just a silly experiment, but all of a sudden it flew out of control."

"It was a dumb experiment. For one thing, it *had* no control. That's just one of about a million things that bug me about these guys. They've got no controls, no double-blind testing, no uniform methodology. They're just poking around in the dark, each one trying to describe their particular patch of elephant, but they don't have a clue what the big picture is."

"Neither do we," Tessa pointed out.

Rick took a deep breath and let it out slowly. "That's the only reason I'm willing to stay here."

CHAPTER 22

After three days without contact with the astronauts, the press was getting nervous. Yoshiko was en route to Japan, where she had consented to remain in quarantine but refused to give interviews, which left Rick and Tessa under the media bug lens. The trouble was, the bug lens couldn't find its focus, so the stories were getting fuzzier and fuzzier as reporters speculated on what might be happening behind closed doors.

Sonderby and Marcus apparently had a riotous argument about it not long after Rick and Tessa had left for the bedroom, because only an hour or so later they were rousted from sleep by the telephone, and when Rick answered it—padding into the living room in the nude—it was Sonderby on the line, asking if he and Tessa would speak with the media. There was nobody on the other side of the glass, which vaguely disappointed Rick. He'd wanted someone to witness his act of disdain.

He put it into words instead. "Do you really want us to tell them what's going on here?" he asked.

"I wouldn't be asking if I didn't," Sonderby replied.

"Come on, what's the real agenda? You guys never want press coverage. Something's come up and you want us to fix it. What?"

"Have you always been this suspicious of the government?" Sonderby asked. "It's surprising that didn't make it into your file."

"Don't give me that shit. I'm sure there's lots worse than that in my file. And you're dodging the question. What do you want us to tell the press?"

Sonderby sighed. "Nothing you don't want to say. This is your chance to tell your side of the story. Give it a human face. Correct some of the misinformation that's going around."

"Aha! Now we're getting somewhere. What 'misinformation' are you talking about?"

Sonderby *hmmed* for a moment, choosing his words before he spoke. "Perhaps I used the wrong word. 'Misdirected attention' would be a better term. The media are focusing almost exclusively on supernatural phenomena, and forgetting the real science that you accomplished. Your voyage seems in danger of being forgotten in the general clamor over ghosts and so forth."

Rick twirled the phone cord around his index finger. "That does sound like a problem," he admitted. "So you want us to play booster for the space program."

"Yes. So to speak. And for hard science in general. There's a danger that people will use this as yet another excuse to reject Western technology."

Rick didn't like that idea any more than Sonderby, but there was an edge to the other man's voice that Rick didn't understand. "You talk like that's a threat to national security or something."

"It is," Sonderby admitted.

"You're kidding. How? So a few more people start eating granola and reading by candlelight. So what?"

Something squeaked on Sonderby's side. He must have leaned back in an office chair. Rick sat on the arm of the recliner next to the phone while Sonderby said, "Have you ever heard of consensual reality?"

"No, but I can figure out what it must mean."

"Good. Well, have you ever wondered why so many nations seem so resistant to change for generations, and then all of a sudden everything's different overnight?"

"That's a no-brainer. It's called revolution."

Sonderby chuckled softly. "True, true. But what leads to revolution? Not just one man with an agenda. Revolution starts with the masses. Their view of reality changes, and one day what they were happy with for generations suddenly becomes intolerable. It happens practically overnight. Some critical number of converts is reached, and the consensual reality of the whole nation shifts. *Then* more often than not one man with an agenda takes advantage of it and twists it to his own ends, but that's a different problem. The people at the top of the old heap are already on the way down."

Rick scratched an itch in the middle of his back. "What does that have to do with us?"

"You're a bright guy. You figure it out. Put what I just told you together with what you've learned in the last couple of days. What do you think could happen?"

Rick let it stew for a few seconds. "You're telling me you're afraid if enough people start believing in ghosts there'll be a revolution?"

Sonderby sighed. "You can really be obtuse sometimes, you know that? Look, it isn't just ghosts. We've been tracking patterns of thought in America for decades now, and we're seeing a real shift away from technology. People still want their microwaves and their VCRs, but they don't want all the infrastructure that goes with them. It's too complicated. So they're constantly looking for an easier way. We've spent two hundred years building up a society that believes in rationality, science, and law and order, but it's teetering on a knife edge because it takes so much work to keep it all going. Too much work for some people. They'd rather believe in gods and magic and free lunches."

"And we just offered them a free lunch," said Rick.

"Bingo."

Rick felt a cold chill sweep through the room. He knew it was just the effect of his hair follicles standing up in an old evolutionary response to his own fear. If he'd had the thick body hair of his ancestors he would look twice as massive as he had a moment ago; instead he merely felt the air against his skin more easily. He knew that. But how easy it would be to attribute it to a ghost. And if four hundred million people thought ghosts were more real than, say, rockets . . .

He shivered. "We'll talk to them," he said.

CHAPTER 23

The interview did not go well. Rick had never learned the trick of leading the media where he wanted them to go. Tessa was a little better at it, and Sonderby had planted a ringer in the crowd, but even when they focused on his questions about spaceflight and scientific inquiry into the paranormal, they knew their message was being drowned in the general hysteria. Rick felt like shaking a few of the more obnoxious reporters by their necks and saying, "Look, people, the entire basis for Western civilization is at stake here!" but he knew that would do more harm than good.

He felt uncomfortable in his one-piece jumpsuit, too. It wasn't like the coveralls some of the astronauts wore; it was more like a pair of pajamas. It had felt fine in the little trailer, and when he'd found the bedroom closet in their new apartment stocked with more of them he hadn't asked for anything else, but now he felt a little like Hugh Hefner, lounging around the Playboy mansion in his bathrobe all day. He supposed it added a homey look to the proceedings, but it left him feeling somehow exposed, unprotected in front of the media wolves.

He endured the questions about what it felt like to control a ghost ("Scary," he told them honestly enough. "I was terrified the whole time."), and whether or not he would do it again ("I'd rather do it in a real rocket."), and breathed a sigh of relief when the topic shifted to his and Tessa's engagement.

It was a short-lived sigh. "Have you set a date yet?" someone asked.

Rick looked at Tessa, and she looked back at him with the same surprised expression. They hadn't even talked about it.

"I guess we've been too busy to think that far ahead," Rick said.

"What about children? Are you planning a family?"

"Yes," said Tessa, just as Rick said, "No."

The reporters laughed. Rick quickly said, "I mean no, we haven't talked about it yet."

"Hey, how about toilet paper?" asked someone else.

"What?"

"Over the roll, or under?"

"Are you serious?" Rick asked.

"Sure! More marriages are killed by minor incompatibilities than all of the affairs and financial crises combined."

"And 68.3 percent of statistics are made up on the spot," said Rick.

That got a laugh, but it didn't get them off the hook. "Which way?" someone else shouted, and someone else said, "On the count of three! One . . . two . . . three!"

Rick and Tessa were sitting side by side on the loveseat again. He squeezed her hand and said "Over" just as she, predictably, said "Under."

"Uh-oh. How about the toilet lid? Up or down?"

"Come on," Rick said, "that doesn't really matter, does it?"

"Spoken like a true man," said a female reporter.

"What do you think *does* matter?" the ringer asked.

"Love," Tessa said. "Trust. Respect."

Rick nodded. "I'll go with that."

The questions shifted to other topics, like what they planned to do once they got out of quarantine. When Rick answered, "Get married and look for new jobs," that led to a surprised silence, broken by someone in back who said, "You're quitting NASA?"

"We're fired, last I heard," said Rick.

"But—don't they want to keep you there to create more spaceships for them?"

Rick would have loved to use that opportunity to skewer Jackson and Altman, the flight director and administrator who wanted only to decommission the ghost Apollo rockets, but he couldn't give up the opportunity to make a more important point. He took a deep breath and said, "Just because we got a free ride once doesn't mean we should expect it all the time."

He smiled, knowing he'd scored a direct hit, until another reporter asked, "Why the hell not?"

The news programs that night and the newspapers the next day were just as bad as Rick and Tessa had feared. They were national heroes, spiritual guides who would lead the country into a new age. The millennium had come and gone long since—even the one a year later that the stuffy scientists had insisted was the real one—but suddenly millennial fever was back, and Rick was the new messiah. Several programs even said so straight out.

"How come the messiah is never a woman?" Tessa asked playfully as they watched the Chase-Miller news hour on TV.

"There was Joan of Arc," Rick reminded her.

"Yeah, and she was burned at the stake, wasn't she?"

"Jesus got hung out to dry," he pointed out.

"And Moses and Mohammed lived to ripe old ages, surrounded by harems full of beautiful women."

"Did they?"

"I think so. Didn't they?"

He leaned up against her. "I don't know. But it does sound good. I could go for a harem."

"Oh you could, could you? I thought I was supposed to be your one and only."

He searched for a good comeback, finally deciding on, "You think you can handle all that miraculous libido?"

She punched him playfully in the ribs. "Bring it on, holy man."

"Don't mind if I do." He'd been sitting with his right arm around her shoulders; now he slid his hand down through her collar, glancing over to the big window as he did, but the conference room beyond was empty, lit only by one soft overhead light.

"When do you want to get married?" he asked.

She leaned up against him, resting her hand on his thigh. The easy familiarity with which they touched one another somehow made the thrill of it even stronger. Maybe it was knowing they could do it whenever they wanted to, now and for the rest of their lives.

"I think I'd like to get married as soon as we get out of quarantine," she said. "Maybe right here in Hawaii. What do you think? Would your mother like to fly all this way for a wedding?"

He kissed her softly on the cheek. "Are you kidding? An excuse to come to Hawaii? You'd be her favorite person right from the start."

"Then let's definitely do it here."

"All right." He kissed the soft hollow between her neck and collarbone. "I think there's something else I'd like to do here. Right now, in fact. In this very couch." He cupped her left breast in his hand, and kissed her on the lips.

She slid her hand farther up his thigh. "You know, I was joking back in the capsule when I told Yoshiko you were insatiable, but now I'm beginning to think I was right."

"Is this a problem?" He unzipped her jumpsuit just enough to kiss the top of the hollow between her breasts.

"Of course not."

They began fumbling with zippers and tugging at sleeves and pant legs, giggling like teenagers at Rick's clumsiness with one hand still bandaged. He made up for it with his teeth, tugging her clothing off and growling like a wild animal while she shrieked, "That tickles!"

Rick was distantly aware of the TV droning on about the world's new spiritual leaders, but Tessa soon commanded all of his attention. And a few minutes after that, she truly made him feel like a god.

CHAPTER 24

The next day, he learned how to shoot fire from his fingertips. They were in the lab/dining area, with Toland, Wilson, Cortez, Sonderby, Marcus, and a few others watching from the full-blown laboratory on the other side of the window. Toland had him imagine a line of air molecules between his finger and his target—a wooden stirring stick clamped to a ringstand on the table—and then imagine heating them to incandescence. It worked like a charm, and Rick giggled like a kid with a new toy while the stick burned . . . until the ringstand suddenly burst into flame as well.

"Jesus!" he shouted, while Tessa, standing by with a fire extinguisher just in case, sprayed foam on it. It fizzled and spit for a second, then the flames subsided. Smoke roiled up toward the ceiling, to be sucked into the air intake and scrubbed clean.

The stick was gone, turned to ash instantaneously. The clamp that had held it was missing the front half of its rubber-coated jaws, too. The back half—including the rubber—was still intact. "How could it do that?" Rick demanded. "That's stainless steel!"

Toland, looking up from the video camera that was capturing the day's experiments, said, "Stainless steel is mostly iron. And iron oxidizes. Get it hot enough and it oxidizes rather quickly, as you've just seen."

"But . . . holy shit, how hot?" Rick gingerly touched the heavy base of the ringstand, then the vertical rod holding the clamp. Both were cool to the touch, but that was probably from the fire extinguisher foam that still covered them.

Behind Toland, Wilson said, "Well over its melting point. You essentially vaporized it."

Rick wiggled his fingers nervously. They weren't even singed. He looked up at the people watching through the glass. They all looked a little shell-shocked, especially Marcus, who was scowling, obviously upset as well as impressed that more "woo-woo shit" was proving possible.

"Tessa, could you try it as well?" asked Toland.

She looked at the mess on the table, then handed Rick the fire extinguisher. "I suppose so. Shall I just use the stand itself for a target?"

"That would be fine."

"Okay, here goes."

She stood back and pointed at it. Rick waited to the side, extinguisher ready, and even though he knew what she was trying to do, he nearly fired in reflexive surprise when a bright red beam crackled out from her hand and a scintillating cloud of fire engulfed the top of the ringstand.

Flame-retardant foam spattered and hissed, and the rubber jaws of the clamp dropped off to land wetly on the tabletop, but nothing burned this time. Tessa let the flame play over the clamp for a few more seconds, then lowered her hand and the line of fire disappeared.

"It didn't burn," she said.

Rick's laugh had a high edge to it. "You just sprayed flame from your fingers, and you're complaining that the metal didn't burn?"

"Well, you did it. Why shouldn't I be able to, too?"

Toland said, "I suspect the group mind that's providing the energy to power your abilities is somewhat sexist. Most people are, after all. And Rick was the one controlling the Apollo capsule, so they naturally see him as the leader."

"Shit," she said, extending her finger and flaming the ringstand again. It didn't burn this time, either, nor even melt.

"The group mind," Rick said when she gave up. "You think that's what's responsible for all this? People all over the world believing we can do it?"

"That's my guess. You're ten times more powerful today than you were yesterday, and the only thing that's changed is the public exposure."

"So when our fifteen minutes of fame are up . . . ?"

"Back to cooking with microwaves." Toland grinned. "But for now, you're hot. Literally. Could I get you to try manifesting something?"

Rick set the fire extinguisher on the dining table. "I guess so. What would you like?"

Toland rubbed his chin, thinking it over, then said, "How about something you've already made once?"

"I don't think a Saturn V would fit in here," Rick said wryly.

"Not the real thing," Toland said. "But how about a model?"

"No," Marcus said quickly from the back of the lab. Everyone looked over at him, and he said, "What if he miscalculates? Or what if he makes it small enough, but perfectly accurate? There's hydrazine and liquid oxygen and liquid hydrogen on board a Saturn. You want that in here?"

"Ah. Good point," said Toland. "Okay, how about something else familiar, but not so dangerous. Like . . ."

"An apple," Dr. Cortez suggested.

"An apple?" Rick asked.

"Yes. It's actually quite a complex object to attempt. If you succeed and it persists long enough to study, we could learn a great deal from it."

Rick supposed they could. He wondered if his apple cells would be any more realistic than Yoshiko's virus. "Fair enough," he said. "An apple. How do I go about it?"

Toland said, "I would suggest clearing your mind and envisioning it as you would like it to appear. Think about what an apple is. Skin and flesh and core, with seeds and a stem and the remains of the blossom on the bottom. Maybe the wax coating if it's a store-bought apple."

Rick let the psychic's words help him form an image. Apple

on the teacher's desk. Don't want a desk in here too!—so change that to the dining table. Bright red apple, maybe not quite as red as the fire extinguisher, woody brown stem curving up to the left, little bumps on the bottom, always the sweetest part . . .

The air above the table shimmered, and over the course of about five seconds became the very thing he had pictured.

"Holy shit," Tessa whispered. She picked it up and turned it around in her hand, then burst out laughing. "Red delicious, large, number 4016, Washington," she read aloud. She turned it around so Rick, and then the people on the other side of the glass, could see the tiny oval supermarket label on its side.

Rick had to lean against the counter to support his weight. He felt sick to his stomach, but not from exertion. He said, "That's what, half a pound or so? If that's real matter, then how much energy did I just channel from nowhere?"

"$E=mc^2$," Toland said. "But if it's any consolation, I suspect you pulled it already formed out of an alternate dimension or something. Much less energy involved that way."

Alternate dimensions. Wonderful. There went one more aspect of reality out the window. Rick supposed he should be amazed by it all, but what he felt was stunned. This couldn't be happening. The universe didn't work this way. He didn't want it to work this way.

Toland obviously did. Rick had just violated half a dozen laws of physics, and the parapsychologist was grinning from ear to ear. And already explaining it with talk of alternate dimensions as if he'd dealt with the concept all his life.

"How do you know all this stuff?" Rick asked. "Have psychics been doing this sort of thing all along?"

Toland laughed. "We wish! Most of what the world-renowned psychics do is fake. There may be a few legitimate ones, but they don't share their tricks. No, I'm just making this up as I go along."

General Marcus snorted. "That's encouraging." Something

in his voice made Rick suspect he wasn't being entirely face-
tious. The idea of a bunch of wackos knowing more than the
military about how the universe really worked probably
scared him as much as it did Rick.

Marcus glanced from Toland back to the apple in Tessa's
hand. His frown deepened as some new thought occurred to
him, and it looked as if he was about to share it, but Dr.
Cortez asked if they would try sending the apple through the
sample airlock and the moment passed.

The apple tested out as real as anything, except when the
researchers left it out in the open air. It didn't turn brown the
way a normal apple would. Instead, as soon as both Rick and
Tessa stopped paying attention to it, it vanished.

They tried it again, this time with Tessa, who was pleased
to learn that she could make an apple, too. Then they tried it
together, both of them concentrating on the same thing, and
discovered that it appeared faster and lasted longer.

"That corroborates some earlier studies done at Princeton
with random-number generators," Toland said. "Emotionally
bonded couples were up to seven times better at influencing
the outcome than single subjects."

"Does that mean we'd be able to generate seven volts
instead of 1.4 in a cold-fusion experiment?" Tessa asked. "Or
would it be the square root of seven?"

"I don't know," Toland said. "Good question. General
Marcus, you must have experimented with bonded pairs,
didn't you? What kind of results did you get?"

"The classified kind," Marcus said, still frowning.

Toland returned his expression. "Classified? I thought we
were trying to learn something here. If you already know—"

"I know I could lose my job if I told you," Marcus said.
"Let's just say that yes, we had some anomalous data, but the
official 'Don't ask, don't tell' policy toward sexual orientation
killed further research down that line of inquiry."

Toland thought that over for a second. "Are you saying

that gay couples have the same enhanced power as hetero couples? You measured this?"

"I'm not saying anything."

"But you're not denying it, are you?"

Marcus looked toward the ceiling and hummed softly, "Dum de dum de dum."

"I'll be a son of a bitch." Toland laughed. "That news ought to upset a few religious applecarts."

"If you can duplicate it. *Off* this base." Marcus looked through the glass again at Rick and Tessa, his expression still serious. "Right now I'd like to try it with these two. Something tells me they'll get considerably more than seven volts."

There didn't seem to be any reason to go to all the trouble to use palladium electrodes and heavy water, so Toland just stuck a couple of wires in a beaker of tap water and hooked it to a voltmeter while Rick and Tessa concentrated on making electricity flow through the meter. The experiment lasted about ten seconds, during which the output climbed beyond ten thousand volts before the meter exploded in a shower of sparks.

Tessa giggled. "Woo, baby, are we hot or what?"

Rick looked at the smoking ruin of the voltmeter. Marcus looked at Rick and Tessa, the same expression on his face that he'd had when Rick had made the first apple.

Toland was oblivious. "It's definitely the group mind," he said happily. "And it's not the number of believers in the experiment; it's got to be the number of believers in the *experimenters* that counts. This is great!"

This is getting way too strange, Rick thought, but he kept his opinion to himself.

CHAPTER 25

The next morning, Tessa woke him up with a scream.

"What?" Rick said, disoriented from sleep and trying to see in the dim twilight that just barely hinted of dawn through the bedroom window. "What's the matter?"

"My ring is gone!"

"Gone?" He sat up and reached for the light on the nightstand, clicked it on, and turned toward her.

She held out her hand. "It's not there."

"Could it have fallen off?" He lifted her pillow, but saw only the wrinkled white sheet.

"I don't think so, but maybe." She patted the mattress beneath her, then looked over her side of the bed. "I don't see it."

He checked his side, then leaned out and peered under the bed in case it had slipped down next to the wall, but he didn't even see any dust bunnies.

Then a speaker clicked on overhead and a female voice said, "Are you okay?"

"No, we're not okay," Rick yelled, angry at being awakened to bad news and at the revelation—hardly surprising, but now confirmed—that their bedroom conversation was being listened to.

"What's wrong?" the voice asked. Rick looked upward and decided the speaker must be behind the ceiling light shade.

"Tessa's ring is gone. Did someone take it in the night?"

"I—don't think so. I'm just the person on watch, but there's been no breach of security that I'm aware of."

"Well, get me Sonderby. Whatever happened, I'll bet he's behind it."

The woman hesitated. "Uh, sir, it's five A.M. He's still in bed."

"Where the hell do you think we are? Wake him up."

"Yes, sir."

He turned to Tessa. "Did you feel anything?"

She was holding her left hand in her right and rubbing her fingers, but she shook her head. "Nothing. When I woke up I noticed that something didn't feel right, and that's when I realized it was gone, but I didn't feel anything before that."

"It must have just faded out, then."

She looked at him speculatively, saying nothing aloud but speaking volumes just the same.

"What?"

"Do you still love me?"

"*What?* Of course I do."

"Then why . . . why did it disappear?"

"I don't know, but we're going to find out. Sonderby!"

There was another click from overhead, then the sound of a sleepy voice over a telephone. The security woman must have called him, then patched his phone into the intercom system.

"Hello?" he asked.

"What did you do?" Rick demanded.

"I *was* sleeping," the CIA agent said. "Or do you mean before that?"

"Tessa's ring is gone. What happened to it?"

"Ah." He said nothing more.

"That's a mighty damn pregnant silence. What did you do?"

"Nothing, personally. But General Marcus decided your abilities posed a security risk, so he . . . well, he leaked a rumor to the press that your engagement had, um, been called off."

And the news had just hit the streets. Actually, it had probably been hitting for hours; it was midmorning on the mainland. People all across America were losing faith in their heroes as they read their morning paper or listened to the radio on their way to work.

Tessa and Rick both shouted, in stereo, "You bastards!"

Rick wondered if he could shoot flame through the phone line and fry Sonderby on the spot, but he checked that thought before it could become more than a momentary urge. No matter how good it would feel, he didn't want murder on his conscience.

"Come now," Sonderby said. "You'd think you were the first celebrities to be maligned in a tabloid. So the public has lost confidence in you; what difference does that make in your private lives? I would think you'd be thankful for a return to normality."

"We'd be thankful if people would stop meddling with us," Tessa yelled. "I want my ring back."

"I'm sure the government will buy you a replacement. We'll make you another just like the first one if you'd like. We have enough photos and the metallurgical report to go by; I'm sure it would be indistinguishable from the original. I'll—"

"*I'd* know," Tessa said. "I don't want something made in a lab somewhere. I want the one Rick made for me on the way home from the Moon."

Sonderby had no response to that, but the words "security risk" still echoed in Rick's ears. He remembered what General Marcus had said a few days earlier: "If I decide to declare you a national security risk, I could keep you here forever."

He leaned over to Tessa and whispered softly in her ear, "Put your clothes on. We're getting out of here."

"What?" She turned her head to whisper in his ear. "How? We're in the middle of a military base!"

"I don't care," he whispered back. "We're busting loose of this place before Marcus decides to report our deaths."

"What was that?" Sonderby asked.

"I said you're a heartless son of a bitch and I hope a horde of rabid rats comes and eats your testicles," Rick said aloud. He switched out the light again in case there was a camera in the room, then got up as quietly as he could and picked up his jumpsuit off the chair beside the bed. It rustled as he put it on, but Sonderby was talking again so he didn't hear it.

"I told you, I had nothing to do with it. I learned about it after the fact. But Marcus has a good point; nobody should have the kind of power you have. In the wrong hands, it could be—"

"Shut up," Rick said. "You had us hold a press conference to see if it would boost our ability, and when you got the information you needed you switched us off like a light. I don't like being manipulated like that."

"I—"

"Just shut up. Don't dig yourself in any deeper."

"Look, I'm sorry it had to happen this way, but—"

"Shut up!" Rick yelled. He snatched up a pillow and stuffed it in between the light shade and the ceiling, wedging it in all around, and sure enough, Sonderby's voice fell to a muffled buzz.

Tessa had pulled on her jumpsuit and slippers. Rick put on his own slippers, cursing the bandage on his left hand, and motioned her toward the door, where he whispered in her ear, "If we're lucky that'll cover the microphone, too, but just in case we aren't . . ." He raised his voice and said, "I want to see just how much damage those bastards have done. Come on."

He led the way into the living room and turned on the TV. Some anonymous early-morning talk show host was saying, ". . . apparently couldn't stand the public scrutiny. All I've got to say is they should be glad they're not in show business!" A laugh track rose and fell, as if what he'd said was actually funny.

Morbidly curious, Rick switched channels and found a "conversational drama" where four improbably cheerful couples (one gay) talked about the annoying sexual habits that had made them split up, and an early-morning soap in which an actor and actress who could barely remember their lines threw dishes at each other while they argued about whose distant ancestor was haunting the upstairs bathroom.

Tessa, standing at his side, her light blue jumpsuit looking snow-white in the TV's electron glow, said, "We're doomed."

"Negative thoughts bring negative results," Rick said. "Stand back. I've always wanted to do this." He stretched his right hand out toward the TV, and in a soft voice that was nonetheless full of steel, he said, "For the good of the country."

He imagined a line of fire reaching out from his fingers straight into the heart of the picture tube. Elemental, wrathful fire, the avenging fire of every child who had been set down in front of a boring program and told to stay quiet, every mind that had been filled with an inane advertisement jingle, every boring, beer-drinking fool who had soothed his inferiority by watching something more mindless than he rather than educating himself instead.

For a moment he was afraid he had no power left, but finally a flickering bolt of lightning reached out in slow motion and gently caressed the television, splitting into branches that reached around it on all sides. The program twisted as if in a heavy magnetic field, but it didn't go out. Rick clenched his fist and snarled "Die!" but what happened wasn't at all what he expected. Instead of the lighting reaching inside the set to fry the electronics, it constricted around it, compressing the television like a wad of paper. The plastic case screeched and cracked, and electronic parts inside flared and popped like a string of firecrackers. And finally, wheezing like a punctured balloon, the picture tube lost its vacuum and went dark.

"Remind me never to get you mad," Tessa said.

Rick laughed, momentarily giddy with delight. "Never

fear, I must use my powers only for good!" he said in a mock-superhero voice, then, realizing where he'd heard most super-heroes, he said, "God, what a contradiction in terms that just was, huh?" He nodded back to the bedroom and whispered, "Come on, time to go."

Part Three

ALL SYSTEMS GO

The quarantine quarters had been designed to keep in microbes, not people. That was one advantage to being cooperative up until now. Rick and Tessa needed no super powers to heave a chair through the window and drape their bedding over the sharp edges while they crawled out onto the lawn. They looked to either side, sizing up the stucco exterior of the building they had been in and the long covered walkway that stretched off into the distance between two rows of buildings on either side of their own. Dim lights at every building's entrance cast enough light for them to see that theirs was on the very end, smaller than the others and tucked in between them like a cork at the end of a bottle.

It wasn't a tight fit. There was at least twenty feet of grass and bushes between their building and the next one. Rick nodded toward the corner and they padded softly toward it.

The grass was wet with early morning dew. It soaked their slippers before they made a dozen steps, but Rick didn't care. He reveled in the sensation of grass underfoot and fresh air in his lungs again. A light predawn mist gave it a chilly bite and softened the edges of anything more than a few yards away. That would no doubt burn off with the first light of day, but sunrise was still a ways off. They'd picked the perfect time to make their escape. Nearly everyone would still be in bed.

Around the corner was a concrete sidewalk, then the parking lot they had arrived in. The silver quarantine trailer was gone; now six or seven cars clustered under a single yellow streetlight. There was a huge tree in a grass strip between the lot and the street, a banyan or something similar with multiple trunks all wrapped around each other before they split apart into separate branches, some of which stretched out over the parking lot. Smaller trees lined the street, beyond which were more buildings that looked like offices or residences. A sign just opposite the street entrance said BOY SCOUTS OF AMERICA.

"Jeez," Rick whispered, pointing at the sign. "I had no idea the Army had Boy Scout divisions."

Tessa squinted to see what he was talking about, then whispered, "It's probably for their kids, dummy."

Rick shrugged. Maybe.

The parked cars looked inviting. They didn't look like they belonged to military people. They looked like rental cars: new and sleek and anonymous. They probably belonged to Toland and Sonderby and Wilson and the rest. Perfect, if he could get one to run. He wondered if he could yank the right key out of an alternate universe.

It was worth a try. He jogged up to one, hunkering down between it and the next car to avoid being seen, and looked at the lock. Gazed at the lock. Bonded with it, understood it, *grokked* it—and imagined a key sticking out of it.

Tessa caught up with him a moment later, peered inside, and said, "Hey, hotshot. There's a key in the ignition."

"Huh? I was trying for the door lock."

"Looks like you missed. Either that or we just got really lucky."

Not as lucky as they might have been, it turned out. The doors were locked. Rick and Tessa both tried to move the automatic lock button with their minds, and Rick even tried shorting it out with a blast of electricity, but he succeeded only in scorching the upholstery. Their power was fading fast as Marcus's false news story spread.

"Damn it," he said. "This is getting us nowhere. Let me kick in the window." He moved toward the back, but Tessa stopped him. "No, do the driver's window. We'll probably have to go past a guard post."

"What does that have to do with anything?"

"It's cold. Nobody would be driving with their windows down this time of morning. But they might roll down the driver's window to wave at the guard."

"Oh. Good point." During their careers as astronauts, he and Tessa had been to dozens of military bases. Security was far less rigorous than most people had been led to believe—which was probably why the bases could get away with letting it be so lax. Most people who wanted to sneak in or out made up elaborate schemes to distract guards or cut fences, and wound up drawing more attention to themselves than if they just drove by and waved. And from the Boy Scout sign and the VISITORS sign on the entrance to the lot, this looked like an open post, where people could come and go at will anyway. Getting out would be a piece of cake . . . if they could just get into the car.

Rick moved back to the driver's window, braced himself against the next car, and struck out with his right foot. He felt the impact all the way up into his thigh, and bit down on a reflexive "Ow!"

The window barely cracked. Worse, the alarm in the car he had been leaning against began to wail.

"Shit, shit, shit!" he yelled, kicking at the window again, but it obviously wasn't going to break. He looked for a rock or a board or something to smash it with, but there wasn't any loose debris in the manicured lawn.

His heart had been pounding all along, but now it started to race. Sonderby must know by now that he and Tessa were gone, and the alarm had just pinpointed their position. He and Tessa had a few seconds at best before someone came to investigate.

They were standing in the pool of yellow light from the street lamp. It was time to give up on the car. But where could they go? This place was going to be crawling with people soon, but the buildings across the street were too far away to hide behind. The medical buildings clustered behind the one they had been quarantined in would provide some cover, but that's exactly where everyone would look for them. Maybe they could dodge from tree to tree down the street, but he doubted they'd get far doing that, either.

The alarm set his teeth on edge, rattled his bones. No time to think; just *do* something.

He decided. "Quick, into the tree." He pointed at the huge banyan next to the parking lot.

"You're kidding."

"That's the only cover in this whole damned place. Go!"

She took off running. He wasted a second trying to fry the alarm, but in his panic he couldn't even generate a spark. Cursing, he chased after her, his wet slippers flapping against the pavement. She jumped up onto the knobby mass of roots, then grabbed one of the trunks as he came up behind her and boosted her up with both hands on her butt.

He leaped up after her, scrabbling out onto a branch until he was shrouded with leaves. The branch wasn't quite as wide as he was; he lay straight along it, his arms stretched out over his head to make him as thin as possible.

Tessa had taken a branch next to him. Both of them angled out toward the parking lot.

"What now?" she asked.

"I'm wide open for ideas," he said, just as the door of the medical building they had escaped from burst open and a uniformed guard rushed toward the shrieking car, his rifle in hand. He was just a silhouette under the streetlight, but that somehow made him seem all the more ominous.

"Ducking would be good," Tessa whispered. They both hunkered down behind their branches, just as the door on the building to their left flew open and hit the stop with a clang.

"You there!" a voice shouted from the darkness. "Halt!"

Rick froze, but it was pure instinct. The soldier who had been running toward the car did, too, then he looked over and shouted, "It's me, you dumb shit. I'm checkin' out this damn alarm." His voice sounded young, and a little scared behind his bravado. He kept moving past the car as he talked, putting it between him and the other guard.

"Who's 'me'? I don't know you from Jack, Jack. You just put down that gun real slow-like and come show me your ID."

Rick leaned his head slowly over the edge of the branch until he could see out of the corner of his eye who was speaking. It was a kid maybe nineteen years old, skinny and nervous, with eyes as big and white as full moons. He held his rifle leveled at the equally young kid who was standing practically beneath his branch.

This was getting way out of hand. The two guards had been inside brightly lit buildings, so their eyes weren't adapted to the relative darkness of a single streetlight yet, and the one beneath him was looking into that light, but even so, if Rick or Tessa moved they would be spotted in an instant. And if they didn't move they'd be spotted in an instant and a half when more people showed up. Rick didn't take the time to come up with a plan; he just did the only thing he could think of: He dropped off the branch and landed on the kid with the gun.

They both tumbled to the ground. Rick's elbow cracked painfully against a tree root, but he gritted his teeth and snatched up the gun, then rolled to his knees, jammed the barrel into the kid's side, and growled, "Don't move."

The guard across the street was running straight for them, unable to get a clear shot between the parked cars. "Both of you hold it!" he shouted. "Don't nobody move or you'll both get hurt."

"I ain't movin', man," said the one Rick held at gunpoint.

The other one ran up to the back of the car they had been trying to break into, but he stopped just out of leaping distance for Tessa, who was crouched on her branch like a leopard ready to pounce.

The car alarm kept screeching. For the first time in his life, Rick thanked fate that a lifetime of false alarms had conditioned most people to ignore them. If Sonderby *hadn't* yet figured out his captives were gone, they might still have time to get free.

"Drop it," said the kid.

"You drop it," Rick said back.

"Nu-uh. We here is trained to die for our country. We ain't lettin' you go just 'cause you got a gun on one of us."

"Speak for yourself," said the kid on the ground. "I don't want to die to catch some fuckin' car thief."

"You're a damn poor MP then, Jack."

"My name ain't Jack."

"I don't give a rat's ass. Now both of you, just—"

The alarm chose that moment to switch off. In the silence, Rick said, "Tell you what we'll do. Me and not-Jack here will just slide into this car, gentle as can be. Then I drive to the end of the block, let him go, and take my chances on the street."

"Bullshit. I'm going to shoot your ass if you don't drop that gun. I give you to three. One . . . two . . ."

Tessa stood up on her branch, took one long step to get into range, and leaped. The kid with the gun whirled around, brought the barrel up, and pulled the trigger.

"No!" Rick cried, reaching toward them.

The click echoed off the medical buildings as Tessa fell onto him feet first, knocking him to the pavement behind the parked cars. Rick growled "Stay put" at the one he'd taken the gun from and got up to help Tessa with the other one, but he needn't have bothered. She had knocked him out cold.

Rick kept the gun pointed at his captive as he helped Tessa to her feet. She grabbed the other gun and moved past him to point it at the first kid while Rick reversed his own gun and smashed its stock into the window of the car they had been trying to steal.

The glass shattered into thousands of fragments, but the plastic layer in the middle held them all together until he hit it again and punched through. Heedless of the edges, he reached inside and found the lock button, opened the door, and jumped into the driver's seat. Tessa waved her gun at the kid on the grass and said, "Drag your buddy out of the way so we don't run over him. In fact, take him inside. He may need help."

Silently, the kid got up and picked up the limp body in a fireman's carry, hauling him across the parking lot toward the medical building Rick and Tessa had escaped from. While he did that, she hobbled around to the passenger side of the car and jumped in, panting, "Jesus, this Bonnie and Clyde stuff is hard on the feet. Let's get the hell out of here."

Rick reached for the ignition switch, but felt only a depression with wings on either side and a narrow slot in the middle.

"Uh-oh."

"What?"

"The key's gone."

CHAPTER 27

Tessa klonked her head on the dashboard. "Son of a bitch. You can't count on any of this ghost crap! The moment you need it most, *poof*!"

Rick tried to concentrate on the lock, imagining another key in it, but nothing happened. He was way too rattled to focus.

"Where's that guard?" he asked, craning his neck around to see behind the car. "Where'd he go?"

"I don't know," Tessa said, opening her door.

"No, help me here," he said, trying again to make a new key, but she got out and stood up.

"Come on," she said. "It's time to do what we should have done in the first place."

"What's that?"

"Run!" She turned away and tried to do just that, but her left ankle gave out beneath her and she fell to the pavement.

"Tessa!" Rick scrambled across the car and out her door, helping her up just as the guard they hadn't knocked out slammed into him from behind. Rick's gun skittered under the car, and the three of them fell in a kicking, biting, cursing heap between the car they were trying to steal and the one next to it.

Rick came up on top through sheer weight and determination, but it didn't matter. He heard a door bang against its stop, and a voice that didn't sound at all like a young kid shouted, "Split up. Move!"

Rick stuffed his bandaged hand in the kid's mouth before he could yell. It took both him and Tessa to hold him down.

"We've got to split up, too," Tessa whispered.

"They'll catch us anyway," Rick whispered back.

"They'll catch *me*. I twisted my ankle. But if I can make enough trouble for 'em, maybe you can get away."

"I can't leave you!"

"You're going to have to. Unless you can turn one of these cars into a helicopter in the next couple of seconds, we aren't both getting out of here."

"Shit," he swore. "Helicopter? I can't even make a damned key that'll last."

The kid they'd caught suddenly quit struggling. Maybe he'd realized who had captured him, and was afraid of being turned into a toad. Rick didn't let him up, nor did he lift his hand when the kid started making soft "Uh, uh, uh," sounds beneath the bandage.

Footsteps echoed off the buildings, and someone shouted, "Here! Someone's hurt." That would distract at least a few of the people looking for them, and the cars would hide them for a little while, but not forever. Rick shook his head angrily and said, "Damn it, there's got to be a way out of here."

The kid rolled his eyes upward, then back, up and back, tilting his head as much as he could each time and making the same grunting sound. It was obvious he had something to say. Rick was at such a total loss for a better idea that he looked down and said, "One shout and you'll be swallowing teeth," then he lifted the bandage.

The kid licked his lips, then whispered, "Listen to her, man. You're cornered. You ain't both gettin' loose, but one of you can still make it."

"How?"

"Let me take her in. I'll tell 'em you ran off 'cross the street. When they all go chasin' off after you, you haul ass the other way."

It wasn't much of a plan, but it was better than nothing. "Why the sudden change of heart?" Rick asked.

"I didn't know it was you," the kid answered. "Shee-it, if I had, I'd of gave you the keys to *my* car."

"That's not such a bad idea," Rick said.

The kid paused, clearly realizing he'd overstated his devotion to the new media heroes, but then he shrugged and said, "Right pants pocket. Fits a brown Datsun pickup over in the lot on the other side of F quad. That way about two blocks, and 'cross the street. Washington plates." He stuck out an elbow that Tessa hadn't been able to pin down, pointing diagonally across the parking lot they were in, past the building on the left.

Rick looked at him, wishing he could believe it would work. Wishing he could believe that the kid would actually help them.

"Go, damn it!" Tessa whispered. "Go. One of us free is better than neither of us. You can get help and come back for me."

"Wait a second." Rick had never thought so fast in his life. Shouting voices, footsteps, and banging doors seemed to fade into slow motion as he said, talking almost as fast as he was thinking, "Why can't I come back for you right away? If he leads everyone off on a wild goose chase, you can just hide right here until I drive by."

"Oh, yeah, and I get my fuckin' ass court-martialed," hissed the kid.

"I'm not letting you turn Tessa in so I can get away."

The kid growled with inarticulate frustration, but then he shook his head and said, "All right, we try it your way, but you better remember me in your fuckin' wills."

Rick let out a deep breath he hadn't even known he was holding, then leaned back and let the kid up.

He didn't shout. Instead he reached into his pocket, dug out his keys, and gave them to Rick. Tessa handed him her gun, but first she jacked the bullet out of the chamber. She looked at the base of the cartridge and visibly shuddered.

Rick reached for it, examining it under the streetlight's yellow glow. Its fully jacketed bullet was still perched atop the necked-down case, yet the primer on the bottom had a circular dent in it where the firing pin had struck. He shook it and heard powder swish inside. Had their psychic power somehow stopped it from firing, or had it just been a dud?

He gave it back to Tessa. "I'd keep this as a good luck charm if I was you."

"No shit," whispered the kid. Then he patted Rick on the shoulder. "Good luck, man. Wait 'til I lead everybody out o' here, then go for it."

"Thanks, Jack."

"It ain't Jack," the kid said, but this time he was grinning.

Rick was about to ask him what his name *was*, but he was already gone, running behind the parked cars and shouting, "There they go! I see 'em!"

They heard more shouts and people running. Rick peeked under the car and saw a dozen or so booted feet rushing off across the street toward the Boy Scout building. He retrieved the rifle he'd taken from the first kid and gave it to Tessa.

"Hold tight," he said. "I'll be back as quick as I can."

Tessa kissed him, her cold nose against his cheek the total opposite of her warm lips. "Be careful!"

"*You* be careful. Stay out of sight until I get back."

"I plan on it."

He kissed her again, then peeked out over the hood of the car. Through the thinning mist, he could just see the backs of the soldiers chasing off after their improbable benefactor.

He looked the other way. Nobody on the steps of the buildings facing the parking lot. They must have taken the person Tessa had knocked out to the infirmary.

There was no better time. He sprinted to the corner of the building, expecting a bullet in the back the whole way, but he made the hundred feet or so of open space and grabbed the rough edge of painted cement, pulling himself to a stop behind it and panting for breath. A quick peek to confirm that nobody was looking, then he sprinted for the first palm tree in a row of them along the street, then the next one, and the next one. He looked to his right at the buildings as he passed them. Identical medical wards, by the look of them. Stenciled on the wall next to their doors were the words, OFF LIMITS AFTER 16:00 HOURS. He chuckled softly. This whole place was off limits to him now.

By the time he made it halfway down the block he was hidden in the mist, so he slowed to a jog to let his burning lungs recover until he reached the end of the block, then he crossed the street and looked for the F quad parking lot. It was easy to spot. There were four long buildings facing one another from the four sides of a city block, and hundreds of cars parked to the southwest side of them. The cars were decorated with bulldog stickers, chrome skull hood ornaments, and crossed-missile mud flaps. F quad was obviously soldiers' quarters, and these were their personal vehicles.

It took him a couple of minutes to find the pickup, which turned out to be brown from rust as much as from paint. There was only one sticker on its bumper, a faded yellow-and-black one with the enigmatic slogan: EDDIE WOULD GO. Rick had no idea what it meant. The back end held two spare tires and a milk crate full of engine parts—not a good sign. The hinges squeaked when he opened the door, and the passenger side of the bench seat was filled with drink cups and newspapers and CD cases, but to his surprise the engine started right up. It ran much smoother than he expected, too. The kid wasn't much for neatness, but evidently he was a decent mechanic. Rick unlocked the other door, made sure it would open for Tessa, then backed up and drove out of the parking lot.

The street next to F quad was one-way going the wrong way. Rick followed the sign, figuring he'd draw less attention to himself if he at least followed the traffic rules.

The headlights threw everything into sharp relief. He turned left at the next cross street, then left again and drove slowly down the street toward the medical center, cursing softly when he saw more people milling around in the parking lot, no doubt looking at the car with the smashed window. From this angle he could clearly see Tessa hiding under one of the other cars. It looked like she'd picked the farthest one from the one they'd broken into, but with them all huddled together like they were, that hardly mattered.

And slowly, like watching a train wreck on a distant bridge and being totally powerless to prevent it, he saw someone bend down to look under the cars.

He honked the horn and flashed the lights. That drew the attention of everyone but the person who had bent down, but when that one saw Tessa he must have shouted the alarm because everyone turned back to help drag her out from under the car.

Rick briefly considered running them all down, but they held Tessa in their midst. He thought about jumping out and wrestling her free, but there were six or seven of them; more than he could overpower even if they weren't armed, which they were. In fact, one of them was already raising his rifle toward Rick and motioning him to stop.

He was only a dozen yards away; he had to stomp on the gas or the brake, and with a gun aimed straight at him he reluctantly chose the brake. Then he realized that the headlights were no doubt blinding everyone but him, so he rolled down the window and leaned out, shouting with a lousy imitation of a Southern accent to disguise his voice, "Hey, somebody's hidin' 'hind that tree back there!"

Tessa picked up on it in an instant, looking past the pickup and screaming, "Run, Rick! Run!"

"Damn it, kill those lights!" shouted the soldier who had been aiming his gun at Rick. Rick flashed the brights at him instead, yelled, "Whoops, sorry," then turned them off and rolled by, slouching down and turning his head away from the streetlight until he was well past so they couldn't see his blue pajamas or get a good look at his face.

"Keep running!" Tessa shouted, keeping up the deception, then he realized she had probably meant exactly what she'd said. He looked in the side mirror and saw two soldiers racing down the street in the direction he'd come from, but the rest still held on to their prisoner. One looked after the pickup, raised his rifle, then lowered it again, apparently not willing to risk a shot at what might actually be just another soldier on his way to work.

Rick wanted desperately to go back and rescue Tessa, to leap from the truck with a handful of thunderbolts and drive her captors to their knees in a heroic display of blazing glory, but he knew he had about as much chance of making that work as his attempt at stealing a car.

No, this time he would listen to her. He rubbed tears from his eyes as he drove away, watching her dwindle in the mirror, watching the soldiers lead her back toward the main doors of the building they had just escaped from, but he continued driving to the corner and turned to the right, looking for a road that would lead him out into civilian territory, already scheming how he would return to break her free again.

He realized they were farther apart now than they had been for two weeks, and with that realization he felt something stretching thinner and thinner, something almost physical, and he thought, *These are heartstrings. My God, those are real, too.*

CHAPTER 28

H e didn't even see a guard post. The streets funneled together past a baseball field, then dumped him onto a two-lane road with signs pointing to Honolulu or Waialua. Rick turned right toward Honolulu, and a few minutes later found himself on H-2, the southbound Interstate highway. At any other time, he would have laughed. *Interstate?* In Hawaii? But that's what it said.

He dug through the debris in the seat beside him while he kept one eye on the road. It was all fast-food trash and music. He didn't find anything of interest until he opened the glove box, where he discovered the vehicle registration slip. The truck's owner was Mark Benton, and though the paper was smudged and wrinkled from months of abuse, Rick could still read an address on Liliha Street.

Mark had been a lot smaller than Rick, but some kids his age still wore their clothing baggy. The chain dangling from the ignition held four or five more keys; Rick was willing to bet one of them fit Mark's front door. It was worth a shot. He couldn't stay there long, but if he could get some real clothes and enough spare change to make a few phone calls, he could probably make a clean break.

Where he would go from there was anybody's guess, but he would just take it one step at a time. Step number one was to find Liliha Street, which meant finding a phone booth so he could look at a map.

The sun peeked over the horizon as he approached the outskirts of Honolulu. It looked like it could be a glorious day. It *would* be a glorious day if he could spring Tessa from the government's clutches. He had no idea how he would do that, but he would think of something.

He kept his eyes out for a shopping center where he could find a phone, but instead he came to a freeway interchange and had to decide which way to go. Definitely not Pearl Harbor! He turned east on H-1 toward downtown Honolulu.

The speed limit was just 50 mph, but none of the cars around him were speeding. He supposed there was little point in it; you could probably cross the island in an hour at that pace. He kept his own driving under control until he spotted a promising exit, then turned off and looked for a phone booth, eventually finding one outside a convenience store with bold blue-and-white letters proclaiming ABC STORE over the doors.

The phone was in a small blue rectangular enclosure on a post rather than a Superman-style booth. He parked the pickup close to the phone so he wouldn't be too conspicuous in his light blue pajamas. There was a newspaper dispenser beside the booth, and sure enough the headline read: SPACE ENGAGEMENT'S OFF! in three-inch type. He started reading the article, feeling his anger at Marcus and Sonderby rising with every lying word. They claimed he had gotten cold feet and dumped Tessa! And then they quoted her as saying she had never intended to go through with it anyway, that she had just agreed to marry him on the Moon because she'd been afraid she wouldn't get home alive if she didn't.

There was more, but it was cut off by the fold. Rick didn't need to see any more anyway. He felt like driving straight back to Schofield Barracks and blasting those two lying bastards into ashes right then and there, but given the way his last few attempts at paranormal phenomena had gone, he doubted if he could do more than singe their hair.

He couldn't fix this by playing Rambo. He took a deep breath and stepped over to the phone, where he picked up the directory and thumbed through it for a map.

It had been torn out, of course. Rick hoped whoever had done it had had an emergency bigger than his own, but it didn't seem likely. No doubt the other guy thought his navigation problems were big enough to warrant stealing a map, but Rick doubted if he'd had a newspaper headline advertising his problems in the stand beside the booth.

He looked at it again. The *Honolulu Advertiser*. He turned to the yellow pages, looked up "newspapers," and found their ad, which gave the street address on Kapiolani Boulevard. Of course he still didn't have a map, but he imagined it would be somewhere downtown. And there were other phone booths. Surely every directory in Honolulu couldn't have the map ripped out of it. Eventually he would find the newspaper office, and when he did, he would give them the real story.

He never found it. Once he was back on the freeway, he turned on the radio to see if he could find any news about his escape, and instead he heard a deejay say, "How about you, ma'am? Where are you from?"

"Wallace, Idaho," a querulous old woman's voice said.

"And what do you think about Rick and Tessa breaking up?"

"I think it's a damn shame. They got us all worked up for nothing. There ought to be a law."

"And how about you? What's your take on this?"

A younger male voice said, "Hey, what can I say? Rick's an idiot, 'cause Tessa's a major babe. But, like, now maybe I've got a chance, you know? So it's not necessarily such a bad deal, right?"

The deejay laughed. "Now there's what I call an optimist. How about you, sir?"

An older man said, "When I was a boy, we took engagement seriously. None of this 'here today, gone tomorrow' crap. They ought to be ashamed."

"*Me?*" Rick shouted at the radio. "*Marcus* ought to be ashamed. Hell, you old coot, *you* ought to be ashamed. Believing everything you hear."

The deejay said, "Once again, this is Larry Iritani at the International Marketplace, asking early risers from all over the world what they think of the situation. What's your opinion, ma'am?"

There was a long silence, then, "No talk English good, so sorry."

"International Marketplace, is it?" Rick muttered. He suddenly wished he'd stolen the whole damned phone book. If he could find out where this radio jock was broadcasting from, he could nip this situation in the bud even faster than by going to the newspaper.

He felt the rumble of Botts dots under his tires just as a car horn honked from the lane beside him. Rick yanked the pickup back into its own lane and waved apologetically at the passenger in a blue Accord, then he suddenly cranked down his window and shouted, "Hey! Hey there!" He made window-cranking motions, and nearly swerved into the other lane again.

The passenger, a teenage girl with blond hair and too much makeup, looked afraid to roll down her window at first, but then she did a wonderfully theatrical double-take and the glass slid smoothly into the door. Her hair immediately started whipping in the wind, but she pulled it behind her head with her left hand and yelled across the three or four feet of space between cars, "Aren't you Rick Spencer?"

"That's right!" he said. "Where's the—?"

"What happened?"

What happened? How could he condense it all to a few words shouted between cars? He couldn't. He just shouted, "Where's the International Marketplace?"

"The what?"

He had to weave to avoid the other car as the driver accidentally swerved into his lane. He'd flown jet planes in formation before, but it was harder to keep two cars side by side on the freeway. "The International Marketplace," he shouted again.

"Oh. It's in Waikiki," the girl shouted back.

"How do I get there?"

Just then he noticed the sign on an overpass: Liliha. He'd missed it!

The girl laughed. "How do you get to Waikiki? Straight ahead!"

"How far?"

She shrugged. "Couple of miles. Take the . . . exit if you want . . . Marketplace." A jacked-up pickup with knobby tires on the other side of her car drowned out her words.

"Which exit?" he yelled.

"The second one!"

"Got it. Thanks!"

"You're welcome!"

Rick rolled up his window and eased off the gas a little to let the other car past him. He looked back at the Liliha overpass. Should he go back? But Waikiki and the radio reporter were only a couple miles ahead. And he was instantly recognizable in the blue bodysuit. If he stopped to change clothes, it might be harder to prove he was who he said he was.

He drove on, growing more and more furious with each person he heard interviewed on the radio.

Just a mile or so later, a huge green sign across half the highway said WAIKIKI NEXT 3 EXITS. The blue Accord pulled in front of him as they passed the first one, and he followed it off the second. The girl leaned out and shouted something back to him as they went down the off-ramp. He couldn't hear her, but he knew a "follow me" situation when he saw one.

The Accord led him down a palm-shaded street that jogged to the right, then left again to join a main thoroughfare. Not long after, they crossed Kapiolani Boulevard, and Rick looked for any sign of the newspaper office as they crossed it, but he didn't see any. *Later*, he told himself.

They drove into a thicket of hotels, the ones on the left dozens of stories tall with balconies looking out to sea, the ones on the right shorter but with elegant entrances presumably leading to beachfront rooms. People filled the sidewalks, some of them already wearing bikinis and swim trunks this early in the morning.

The Accord stopped at a stoplight, even though it was green. When Rick pulled up behind it, the driver honked the horn and the passenger pointed over the roof to the left. Rick saw a bunch of shops, then a brick courtyard with a bunch of vendor's booths in front of a huge banyan tree, in which a tree house had been built. A curving wooden sign hanging from the tree house said "International Marketplace."

And sure enough, there was a guy with a remote transmitter on his back, headphones over his ears, and a microphone in his hand, surrounded by a thick crowd of people who wanted to talk about Rick and Tessa's "breakup."

Rick looked for a place to park the pickup. There were no spaces on the street, and there was no side street at the light. He supposed he would have to drive around until he found a parking garage or something, but when he watched a gray-suited yuppie speak into the microphone and heard his voice on the radio saying, "I think it's a classic case of cold feet," he killed the engine right there on the street and leaped out of the truck.

"Hey!" he shouted, striding through the crowd. "Hey you!"

aces turned toward him. He watched recognition pass among them like ripples in a pond.

"It's him!" a woman said, pointing, and another woman beside her said, "It can't be. He's in quarantine."

"It is me," Rick growled.

People backed away from him, whether out of fear of Moon bugs or the sound of his voice he didn't know. Nor did he care. He marched straight up to the radio jock—a slender Asian kid who couldn't have been over eighteen—and took the microphone from his hands.

"This is Rick Spencer," he said into the microphone. "I just escaped from Schofield Barracks, where Tessa and I have been held captive for the last week. Everything you've heard about us has been lies."

The crowd erupted into a babble of voices. Rick held up his hands for silence, nearly strangling the reporter before he realized the microphone had a short cord. People kept talking, so he shouted, "Quiet!" and concentrated on making a line of fire above his hand.

For a moment nothing happened, then there was a bright flash and a loud *bang* echoed off the sides of the vendors' booths. It wasn't what he'd been trying for, but it got people's attention.

Unfortunately, it was the wrong kind of attention. The noise had sounded like a gunshot, and now people screamed and pushed backward away from him, and someone in the crowd yelled "He's been shot!"

"No I haven't!" Rick shouted. "Everything's fine, just quiet down and listen." He spoke into the microphone again, hoping that it would at least pick up his voice even if the crowd couldn't hear him, but when they realized he wasn't going to shoot anyone they quieted down and listened to him.

"The military has been testing us to try to figure out how we do what we do," he said. "We went along with it at first because we want to know what's happening just as badly as they do, but after the press conference three days ago our abilities started to grow even stronger, and it became apparent that the power comes from *you*. The more of you who believe in us, the more power we have."

He couldn't tell whether they were getting any of this or not, but at least they were listening, so he plunged on ahead. "That apparently scared the government, so they leaked a rumor that we were splitting up. It worked. Tessa's engagement ring disappeared last night, and our strength grew much weaker. That little flash you saw was about all I can do now."

He paused, searching for the right words, then went on before the reporter could take the microphone back. "We never broke our engagement. We're getting married whether the government wants us to or not. But they're still holding her up at Schofield! I need your help to get her back."

About half the people cheered at that, but he could see the skepticism in the others' faces.

He shrugged, knowing how silly it all sounded. "I know, I know, I would swear it was all hooey, except I just rode all the way to the Moon and back in a ghost, and I've been conjuring up all sorts of other stuff all week."

"Show us," a young woman in a bikini said.

"Yeah, do it," said a middle-aged black man in a suit beside her.

Rick chewed his lower lip. His attempt to get their attention hadn't gone the way he'd expected. "This stuff never seems to work right when I want it to," he muttered, "but I ought to be able to at least make something. Stand back."

He handed the microphone to the reporter. The crowd

inched closer rather than away, and Rick realized they were being forced together as more and more people abandoned their cars and rushed in from the street.

Two of the people rushing toward him were a camera crew from one of the TV stations. They bulled their way past everyone until they stood next to Rick, then the cameraman backed into the crowd opposite him, making room to get him in the picture and incidentally clearing enough space for him to feel comfortable trying to create something.

"Okay," he said, looking around for inspiration. The booths were full of puka shell necklaces, gold chains, coconuts carved into monkeys, and the like. Tourist kitsch. Rick saw a row of coffee mugs and decided to try for one of those.

There was no table to do it on, so he simply held out his right hand, palm up, and concentrated on making a colorful mug with red, yellow, and blue flowers and the word HAWAII in bold white letters across it. It would have straight sides and a semicircular handle, and be just the right size for sipping coffee from. He imagined the weight of it in his hand, the feel of cool glazed ceramic against his skin.

The air seemed to waver, then the mug actually stood there, teetering in his outstretched hand. Hot coffee splashed over the sides, but he snatched the handle with his bandaged left hand before reflex made him drop it.

"Oh, man," someone said, "that is just too crazy."

The woman who'd asked for the demonstration reached for the mug. He let her take it, but he said, "Careful. This ghost stuff has a habit of disappearing at the most inconvenient times."

Everyone laughed, the woman a bit nervously, but she bent forward so she wouldn't get spilled on if it slipped through her fingers and took a cautious sniff. "Smells like coffee," she reported. "Is it safe to drink?"

"I wouldn't," Rick said. "We ate and drank the food on board the Apollo capsule, but that was before things started going so wacko. That could be battery acid in there for all I know."

She handed the mug back to him again.

It chose that moment to fade away, but true to form, the coffee remained. It quivered there like cylinder of jiggling brown Jell-O, mocking Rick's effort to banish it along with the cup, and then with a soft *sploosh* it washed over his right hand and spattered to the bricks.

Rick shook his hand and patted it with his bandage to get the hot coffee off it. "Damn it!" he yelled. He stepped back to avoid getting wet feet, too, but with one last wisp of steam the coffee vanished, leaving no trace that it had ever been there.

The TV news anchor, a gray-haired Hawaiian man, had been standing right beside Rick the whole time. Now he raised his own microphone in front of him and said, "Gordon Carlson for News 9 here with Rick Spencer, who has just demonstrated his amazing psychic ability to make things appear and disappear at will. Rick, you said earlier that the military is trying to undermine your ability to do this sort of thing by spreading false rumors about you, but it still works, however unpredictably. Why do you suppose that is?" He shoved the microphone in Rick's face.

Rick laughed nervously. "That's a damned good question. If I had to make up a woo-woo answer for it, I'd guess it's because enough people still believe I've got the ability, but now they think I'm a screw-up for breaking my engagement with Tessa. So I can still make things appear, but everything I make now screws up, too. But that's just a theory. I don't claim to understand how any of this works."

The radio reporter said, "Now that the true story is out there, do you think your ability to make a fully functional rocketship will come back?"

Rick shook his head. "I don't care about that. I just want to get Tessa free from the military. If we can make more rockets after that, we'll do it, but that's a problem for another day. She needs help now!"

"What do you want us to do?" he asked.

At the same time, the TV reporter asked, "How do you expect to get her away from the U.S. Army?"

"I don't know," Rick said. "I barely got away myself, and that's because we caught them by surprise." No need to mention the guard's sudden assistance, he thought. "Now they know I'm coming back for her, so they'll be ready for us. The only thing I can think of to do is get as many people as we can to go back up there and storm the base. They can't keep us out—the fence around it is just chain link, and they can't shoot at a whole crowd of civilians. If we occupy the base and refuse to leave until they give her up, they'll have to—"

"What about your quarantine?" someone with a loud voice shouted.

"The quarantine was total bullshit. There are no pathogens on the Moon. They just used that as a convenient excuse to hold us."

As he spoke, Rick felt a surge of adrenaline pour through his system. He was so buzzed already it was hard to believe he could grow any more so, but then he realized it might not be adrenaline. He felt the same way now as he had after the news broadcasts they had made from the Apollo capsule.

Could it be the power of people's belief he was feeling? There were at least a couple hundred people here, but if Marcus could be believed, that would only give him the magical equivalent of about twenty volts. It would take thousands of people to make him feel this strong.

He looked into the TV camera, then glanced over at the radio reporter. How many people were watching and listening? And how many other stations were picking up their report and bouncing it around the world?

The marketplace buzzed with voices as people talked among themselves. The TV reporter had to shout to be heard over the noise. "Do you seriously think you can get her back by storming the base with a bunch of tourists?"

"What else can we do?" Rick said. "The law won't work fast enough. They can stall for months. We've got to go get her *now*."

The voices grew louder as people began hotly debating whether or not to join him. He could almost feel the waves of anger and fear washing over the crowd. The army was holding their heroine prisoner! But it would take a lot of people to overpower an entire military base, way more than they could muster right there in Waikiki. Maybe people from other parts of the city would join in once they heard what was happening, but if they didn't, Rick's little parade would simply end in jail.

"We've got to *try*," he said, looking straight into the camera.

The TV reporter said, "Uh-oh." He was looking over Rick's shoulder. Rick turned around to see two policemen approaching him. The crowd was giving them a wide berth.

"Is that your truck?" one of the cops asked.

Jeez, what should he say? A hundred people had seen him drive up in it. Then he glanced across the street and realized that the cops had probably seen him, too, because there was a police station only half a block away.

There was only one answer he could give. "Yeah, it is."

"I'll have to ask you to move it," the cop said.

Rick stared at them in disbelief. In Florida, they would have handcuffed him and dragged him off to jail. Either Hawaiian cops were a different breed of cat, or these guys were on his side.

"I'm about to do just that," he said. He turned back to the camera and the radio microphone, and looked into the thickest part of the crowd around him. "Who's going with me?" he shouted.

The marketplace fell nearly silent. Rick heard scuffling feet, an embarrassed cough, and a woman whisper louder than she'd expected, "Brian, don't you dare ruin our vacation on some quixotic rescue attempt."

Then the TV cameraman said, "Jesus, look at that." He aimed the camera past Rick, past the cops, walking steadily closer to the pickup and zooming in on the back bumper.

A gasp went up in the crowd.

What the hell was that all about? Rick felt a moment of panic, knowing he had lost them, but then someone behind him said, "Bah! Eddie would go!"

Someone else shouted it. "Eddie would go!"

"Yeah, Eddie would go!"

Most of the people around him looked as puzzled as he, but not the shopkeepers. They obviously knew what the bumper sticker meant. And so did the Hawaiians in the crowd. And the surfers. Every male in swim trunks and half the women as well picked up the chant, and soon the marketplace echoed with their cry: "Eddie would go!"

Rick had no clue what it was all about, but he knew opportunity when he saw it. "Yeah, let's go!" he shouted, striding toward the pickup. "Follow me!"

He grabbed the radio reporter on his way and whispered in his ear. "Ride with me. I don't have a clue how to get there from here."

The reporter laughed hysterically. "Are you kidding? I wouldn't miss this for the world!" He ran around to the passenger side of the pickup, swept the fast-food junk to the floor, and climbed in. A half dozen more people piled into the back among the spare tires and engine parts.

"Hang on," Rick told them. He slid into the driver's seat and started the engine. Shoved the transmission into gear. He had to honk the horn a couple times to clear a path, but people jumped out of the way. The blue Accord he'd followed there was parked on the right, the driver evidently waiting for him to take the lead this time. He looked in his rearview mirror and saw people streaming for the cars that had stopped behind him, piling in eight and ten to a car. Others were racing for side streets, where they had no doubt left their own vehicles.

The TV crew ran back down the street to their van, then swerved onto the sidewalk and drove it toward Rick, the cameraman leaning out the passenger window and filming the whole thing.

It was time to go. Rick let out the clutch and the pickup rolled through the light—green, he noticed happily—drawing the street full of other cars behind him like the train of a king's mantle.

CHAPTER 30

So who the heck is Eddie?"

They were approaching the end of the strip of hotels. It looked like parkland beyond, with more banyan and palm trees shading a grassy lawn. The reporter pointed left at the boundary between city and park, and Rick turned that way, leading his impromptu invasion force back toward the freeway. The cars behind him were honking horns, and the passengers in the back of his pickup were shouting and waving at them with just their thumbs and little fingers extended. Another Hawaiian custom, Rick supposed. He wondered if he and Tessa would have a chance to learn some of these customs like normal tourists after this was all over.

Then he looked in the mirror again and realized he was kidding himself. This wouldn't *be* over. What he and Tessa were going through was not the sort of thing a person could shrug off and then continue their lives as if nothing had happened. They were different now, and even if they lost their ability to do these bizarre things, the world was different because of them. All of humanity had finally seen a ghost, and like the person who encounters a long-dead uncle in the upstairs study, no one could ever go there again without thinking of it.

"Who is Eddie?" he asked again, raising his voice to be heard over the din behind him. He was coming up on a red light, but he couldn't imagine stopping the entire procession, so he gritted his teeth, honked the horn, and drove on through.

"Eddie was a surfer," the reporter replied when they were past. He slipped the left side of his headphones off his ear so he could hear Rick better. "Used to go out in the craziest weather. He was eventually lost at sea trying to rescue someone else, but he's become a local legend. Sort of the embodiment of foolish optimism. Now whenever somebody's having a hard time making a decision, people remind them that 'Eddie would go.' "

Rick rolled his eyes. "Great. The god of foolish optimism stands firmly behind me."

The reporter rolled down his window and stuck his remote transmitter antenna out the window, saying, "I don't know about you, but if I was storming a military base, I'd want Eddie on my side." Then he laughed. "What am I saying? I *am* storming a military base!"

He clicked on his microphone and said, "Sarah, can you hear me?" He cocked his head, listening to the voice in his headset, then replied, "Yeah, good." To Rick he said, "She wants another live broadcast when she breaks out of commercials."

"Do we really want to tell the Army exactly what we're doing?" Rick asked.

The reporter laughed. "You think they don't know? Look up there." He pointed to a dark green helicopter flying slowly along the ridgeline of a volcanic cone to the northwest, then to the TV van right behind their pickup. When Rick turned to look, the passengers in the back waved and shouted, "Woohoo! Go, dude!"

The reporter said, "At this point, what you want is coverage. Get the word out as far and as fast as you can. Work up that divine juju of yours to maximum power."

"It's not divine," Rick said quickly.

"Whatever. Coming up in five ... four ... three ..." He was silent for the last two seconds, then he said, "Hello again, Sarah. This is Larry Iritani reporting live from the cab of Rick Spencer's pickup as Rick leads an army of angry tourists toward Schofield Barracks to rescue Tessa McClain."

He listened to his headphones for a moment, then said, "That's right, Sarah. Rick is driving, I'm riding shotgun, we've got six people in the back of the pickup, and there are at least fifty cars behind us, all packed with people. We're headed up Kapahulu for the freeway right now, so anybody who wants to join us, come on down!"

He listened to Sarah again. Rick suddenly realized he could find out what she was saying if he turned up the radio, which had been nattering softly in the background the whole time, but the moment he did that he heard an echo that built quickly to a howl of feedback. Larry switched off his microphone and said, "Can't do that."

"Sorry." Rick turned off the radio.

"'Sall right." He clicked on the microphone again. "So Rick, what do you plan to do once we get there?" He stuck the microphone between Rick's face and the steering wheel.

Rick had no idea how to answer, but he had to say something. "I guess I'll give them a chance to be reasonable," he said. "But if they won't give her up, then we'll have to go in after her."

"Go in after her," Larry repeated. "That sounds dangerous. You don't have any weapons, and your supernatural powers seem unreliable at best."

Rick held his bandaged hand over the microphone. "Don't say that! Public perception is what makes it work or not."

"Ah, right." Rick uncovered the microphone and Larry said, "Rick doesn't want to tip his hand, but he's definitely got some surprises in store for the Army. He's working on it right now, so I'll turn it back over to you, Sarah, and let him make his plans."

Rick felt a brief pang of conscience at the thought of using the media to boost his power. He was feeding the fantasy that Sonderby had convinced him was dangerous only a few days earlier. But dammit, Sonderby had forced his hand here. Science and law and order weren't fast enough to rescue Tessa. Rick wasn't sure he could *get* a court order for her release, and even if he could, he didn't think Marcus or Sonderby would actually honor it. He had to move faster than the law. If it took New Age mysticism and public sentiment to spring her from captivity, then that's what he would use.

But despite Larry's quick recovery, how he would use it was still anybody's guess. Rick felt time racing past while he waited for inspiration, but short of leading his posse of civilians to the Army base and demanding her release, he still didn't know what he could do. That was the frustrating thing about this psychic business: not knowing what he was capable of.

Could he make himself invisible and sneak past the guards? He'd never tried that, but Toland's method for doing practically anything was simply to imagine himself succeeding at it. It would be worth a try. After all, he'd had plenty of experience with stuff fading away; how difficult could it be to make the same thing happen to himself?

"Left here," Larry said as they passed under the freeway. Once again, Rick didn't wait for the light. He accelerated up the ramp and hit the freeway at 70 mph. The road was concrete here, and bumpy in the heavily loaded pickup. He looked into the mirror and saw his passengers hunkered down behind the cab, hanging on to the sides of the box. Behind them, a river of cars streamed onto the highway; more than there had been when they started. Good. Word was spreading, then.

He tugged the mirror over until he could see his own reflection and concentrated for a moment on making it disappear. He imagined it growing less and less substantial, squinting his eyes to start the effect, letting his vision blur and grow dim while he remembered what the Apollo capsule had looked like when it had faded out. He fought down a moment of panic when he remembered what had ultimately happened to the capsule, but he reminded himself that it hadn't actually become less substantial the first few times. It had continued to hold air, after all, so he didn't have to actually disintegrate either.

He could feel something happening. The hair stood up on the back of his neck as he realized he was actually changing. He opened his eyes, and sure enough, the image in the mirror was hazy, as if the first blush of fog from a hot shower was just starting to settle on the glass. Then he realized the entire reflection was doing it. The people in the back, the cars behind them, all were fading out.

"Uh-oh," Rick whispered, looking straight ahead to see if it was just the mirror or if it was really happening. Everything still looked fuzzy. He could see well enough to drive, but not if it got much worse. Trying hard not to panic, he said, "Sorry, let me see if I can undo this."

"Undo what?" Larry asked. He had been looking out his side window; he turned toward Rick and jerked back in shock. "Whoa! What'd you do to your eyes?"

"My eyes?"

"You look like Lil Orphan Annie."

Rick looked back in the mirror to see what he was talking about and flinched hard enough to jerk the pickup halfway into the next lane. The people in back yelled and grabbed on to one another for support, but Rick's attention was riveted to the mirror. His eyes were as white as boiled eggs all the way from edge to edge. Not until he leaned in for a closer look could he see even a hint of his green irises, and gray dots where his pupils should be.

"Oh, fuck," he said. He felt himself starting to sweat. "I should've known better."

"What were you trying to do?"

"I thought maybe if I could make myself invisible, I could sneak in and get Tessa while everybody else provided a distraction."

Larry looked at him again, then shied away at the sight. "So you made the rest of the world go away instead, but just from your point of view. Man, those look like the mother of all cataracts. You'd better hope that's not permanent."

Was it? Rick swallowed hard. "Nothing else has been," he said hopefully. "Let me see if I can blink them back to normal." He closed his eyes hard, rolled them around in their sockets a little, and opened them again. Was the fog any thinner? It didn't look like it.

"Undo, damn it," he growled, closing his eyes again. Maybe if he imagined them normal again? But what if that just added more bad magic? No, better to stop while he could still see at least a little bit.

Larry grabbed the wheel and helped steer. Good. Rick peered into the mirror again, afraid to will his eyes normal with more supernatural power, but equally afraid not to. He forced himself to just watch what happened, leaning in close so he could see more clearly.

Nothing happened for at least ten seconds, which felt like forever in the speeding truck, but then his mind inevitably started to drift from his immediate condition to thoughts of what it would be like living the rest of his life like this, and he saw a hint of color return to his irises. He waited, breathing hard, while his pupils grew more well defined. Behind his head, like a photographic print developing under a darkroom safelight, the reflected cab of the pickup slowly took on its normal definition again.

"I hate this shit," he said softly, then he took a deep breath and shouted, "I *hate* this shit! All I wanted was to go to the Moon. I didn't ask for this ridiculous supernatural crap."

Larry tried to stifle a giggle, but failed. Rick glowered at him, but that just made the reporter burst out laughing. " 'All I wanted was to go the Moon,' " Larry quoted. "Listen to yourself! Most people just want to get the rent paid."

Rick supposed that might have sounded kind of pretentious. He realized he had been clenching his fists, unclenched them, and took over the driving again, "All right, so maybe I asked for more than usual, but I didn't sell my soul to get there. And I most certainly didn't agree to become some kind of spectral schlemiel after I got home."

Larry reached out and clapped him on the shoulder. "Don't take it so hard. You touched a ghost. People who do that come away changed."

Rick sighed. "Yeah, maybe so. But I don't have to like it. This stuff goes against the grain of everything I believe in. Besides, it never works right."

"Maybe that'll change now that you're getting your reputation cleared up. Take 78 here."

Rick followed his directions, wondering how far they would get before the Army threw up a roadblock. Damn it, the whole situation had been a total fuck-up from the moment he and Tessa had tried to escape. They were complete amateurs at it. They needed professional help, and lots of it, not a bunch of tourists in sandals and bathing suits.

He took a deep breath. Negative thoughts bring negative results, he reminded himself. "Are there alternate routes up there in case they block the interstate?" he asked.

"Oh, sure," Larry said. "Don't worry; we'll get there." He listened to his headset for a moment, then said, "How about another segment? Boost your ratings a little bit more."

Rick had nothing more to say, really, but he knew the exposure couldn't hurt. He hoped the TV crew were tapping into the radio station's audio. If they were doing that, then he could be speaking to millions of people all over the world.

"Let's do it."

CHAPTER 31

Larry raised his microphone and said into it, "Okay, we're ready on this end. Sure, say when. Okay." He waited a few seconds, then his whole demeanor changed like someone had just thrown a switch. "Hi, this is Larry Iritani again, live with Rick Spencer, who has just shown me an amazing new ability. I can't yet say how he's going to use it—" he said this with a wink at Rick "—but I will say it's the most unnerving of his psychic talents I've seen yet. And as he's explained to us, every new listener who believes in him boosts his strength even more. By the time we get to Schofield, I wouldn't want to be in the Army's shoes! Rick, tell me—" He paused, listening, then said, "Who? Rambo? How many? Yes, by all means, go!"

He switched off his microphone and turned on the pickup's radio again. "You've got to hear this," he said, just as a female deejay—presumably Sarah—said, "We're now going to William Parker, a civilian visitor at Schofield Barracks, who reports an army of—well, you tell it, Will."

"I'll try," an excited male voice said. "This is almost too incredible for words." From the static in the signal, it sounded like he was talking into a telephone rather than a remote broadcast transmitter. "I'm parked just across the street from the medical building where Tessa is being held, and I'm seeing an entire platoon of Rambos appearing like popcorn out of thin air and advancing on the building. They've got the place completely surrounded, and they're smashing windows to get inside. The guards inside are firing at them, but their bullets don't even slow them down."

"What exactly do you mean by 'Rambos'?" asked Sarah.

"I mean six-foot-tall, overmuscled soldiers. Commandos. I'm seeing them from behind so I can't tell if they look like

Sylvester Stallone, but they're bare from the waist up except for bandoliers of bullets and grenades, just like the classic movie poster. They've got machine guns in both hands, but they're not firing at anyone. They're just forcing their way into the building. I can't see what's going on inside, but I don't hear any screams. Just gunfire and shouting."

Rick looked over at Larry, whose eyes were as wide, if not as blank, as his own had been a few minutes ago. "Holy shit," Larry whispered.

"Thank you, Mr. Parker. Larry, what does Rick have to say about this?"

Larry wiped sweat from his forehead.

"Larry?"

He turned on his microphone and a howl of feedback swept through the cab, then he switched off the radio and said, "Sorry. We're both stunned here. I don't think Rick had any idea that was happening. Or did you, Rick?" He held out the microphone.

Rick made an instinctive decision. He didn't like lying to the source of his power, but if it helped win Tessa's freedom without bloodshed, he would do it. He winked at Larry so at least he would know, and said, "Yes, actually, I did. I just didn't want to let on until they were in place. Now that they've secured the area, it'll be safer for the rest of us to approach. And now that the Army has seen what they're up against, maybe they'll be a little more willing to let Tessa go."

"Without firing a shot," Larry said. "Speaking as the passenger in the lead vehicle, that sounds good to me. Let's hope it works out that way." He listened to his headphones for a moment, then replied, "If not, I'm sure Rick has plenty more surprises in store for us all. We're coming up on the H-2, so it won't be long now."

The road had smoothed out some, but after they negotiated another interchange it became bumpy concrete again. Rick was still doing seventy. He looked back at the passengers and at the cars behind him. Everybody still seemed to be hanging on and packed tight. There didn't look to be more than half a length between cars as far back as he could see. It seemed like most of Honolulu was behind him. Even the people who weren't intentionally part of the exodus had been swept up in the tide.

Something didn't feel right, though. The closer they got to Schofield Barracks, the worse he felt. This wasn't going to work. The phantom commandos were going to disappear at the crucial moment, or the Army would open fire on the crowd, or . . .

He didn't know what. But something wasn't right.

"We should have hit a roadblock by now," he said.

"Don't look a gift horse in the mouth," Larry told him.

Rick shook his head. "This feels like a trap. They're not putting up any resistance at all. They *want* us to go in."

"They're going to get more than they bargained for if they do," Larry said confidently. "I can't believe you created a bunch of ghost commandos like that. It's incredible."

"It'd be more so if I knew what the hell they were doing." Rick saw a flash of something out of the corner of his eyes, turned to look, but there was nothing there. Then he realized it had moved with his head. It was an image *in* his eyes, just a faint ghost overlaid on reality. Was he getting some kind of response to his desire to see what was going on ahead?

He closed his eyes for a second and tried to make sense of the afterimage on his retinae, but all he saw was the negative image of the highway and the trees alongside it. Except there was motion. He tried to make out what it was, but it just looked like more highway and trees.

"Shit," he said.

"What?"

"I'm seeing visions now, but it's the same damn thing I see with my eyes open."

"Well, maybe that'll be useful in the dark," Larry said.

"Yeah, right." Rick kept driving, but he couldn't shake the feeling that something was going awry. Schofield was coming up fast, though. It was too late to back out now.

Maybe it was just nerves. Larry looked tense, too, as he switched on his microphone again and said, "Okay, we're just about there. Put me on live again."

"You're going to give the play-by-play?" Rick asked him.

"You bet I am. In three . . . two . . . Hi, this is Larry Iritani, riding shotgun with Rick Spencer only a mile from the main gate of Schofield Barracks, where an army of phantom commandos is already softening up the resistance while we lead at least a couple thousand people from Honolulu on a rescue effort to—whoops, get ready to turn left."

Rick felt almost sick to his stomach. It was a trap. The double vision was getting worse. Was Toland or some Army psychic messing with his mind somehow? He could see another steering wheel now, as clear as his own, except for the head in the way. It was as if he saw it from the back seat. Trees whipped past the windows, but then they suddenly gave way to fields of some prickly, cactus-like plant. The bare ground between plants was red as blood.

"Turn here!" Larry said.

Someone was definitely playing with his mind. Rick let up on the gas, but the sickness felt like a gunshot to the chest. He couldn't breathe. He couldn't see where to turn anyway. The image in his mind was stronger than the view through his own eyes. It was a nightmare vision of hand grenades on knife-bladed plants, all growing in blood-soaked dirt. He saw a line of telephone poles on the roadside, and laughed hysterically. Telephone poles in Hell?

"Turn! Turn!" Larry yelled. "Shit, we missed the main gate."

"I . . . can't do it," Rick said, fighting for control.

Larry was breathing hard. Completely forgetting the microphone, he said, "All right, all right. There's another gate up ahead. But get ready, it's coming right up."

"I'm . . . trying." Rick lifted his foot to press on the brake, but the feeling of impending disaster nearly overwhelmed him. "There's . . . something wrong!" He squinted, trying to see through the increasingly realistic vision of the highway to Hell, but it just became even sharper. He saw a female hand on the back of a car seat, and for a moment it felt like his own. He was bracing himself with it while he looked out the windshield, desperately trying to see where they were taking him.

"Slow down," Larry said.

On the hand's third finger a silvery ring, scratched and rough on the edges, caught the low morning sun.

"Tessa," Rick said.

"Slow down! You're going to miss this one, too."

"Tessa's not there."

"What?"

"She's in a car. They're taking her somewhere else."

"How do you know that?"

How did he? He had no idea. Telepathy? What if it was just a hallucination? He was stressed, he'd only gotten a few hours of sleep last night, he hadn't eaten anything since yesterday evening; of course he was hallucinating.

He knew he should turn onto the military base. He would never get anyone to help him again if he didn't. This was a one-shot chance to rescue Tessa, and he was about to blow it on some ridiculous vision. On a hunch and an upset stomach.

But that was her hand, and her ring, beckoning him onward.

"Dammit!" he yelled. How much more of this psychic crap could a person take? He had a split second to choose between phantom Rambos and unclear portents, and Tessa's life could be on the line if he messed up. He moved his foot an inch toward the brake, and instantly felt worse. Toward the gas pedal, and the oppression lifted.

"I just *know*," he said. "She's ahead of us." He stomped down on the accelerator.

The last gate shot past on the left. The road dipped, then rose up a steep hill. The pickup's shocks bottomed out at the base, and the passengers in back yelled in surprise. The stream of cars behind them slowed, then came on.

The road forked. Rick stayed on the straight path. The pickup rocketed up the hill, breaking out of the trees into the exact same landscape he had seen earlier. A row of telephone poles stood along the roadside, and in the fields on either side, plants with leaves like knife blades, hand grenades nestled in their centers, grew in brilliant red soil.

"Pineapple!" he shouted, recognition releasing his tension like a bomb burst.

"What?"

Rick didn't answer. There was a car up ahead.

He kept his foot on the floor. The speedometer passed eighty, then ninety. Larry held the microphone up and said, "We're—we're going on. Rick thinks they're ahead of us. There *is* a car about half a mile away."

"Not for long," Rick muttered as the pickup's speed crept toward one hundred.

The driver of the car saw them coming and floored it as well. "Oh, no you don't," Rick growled. Now that he was committed, now that he knew he was right, he felt the strength pouring back into him. He rolled down his window and stuck his left arm out, fighting to keep it from whipping backward in the wind. He imagined a line of fire reaching straight ahead, engulfing the other car's tires, melting them right off their rims.

A thunderbolt the width of his arm lanced out like a Star Trek phaser blast from his bandaged left hand. Larry cried out, "Jesus Christ!"

"You ain't seen nothin' yet," Rick said, firing another shot straight into the fleeing car's trunk. The lid blew off and pinwheeled away, slicing down a row of pineapple before it veered back toward the road, smacked a telephone pole, and broke it in two halfway up. The trunk lid fell to the ground, but the pole toppled over toward the highway.

"No, you son of a bitch!" Rick yelled. He reached forward and imagined himself grabbing it, shoving it the other way. The pickup swerved as if it had been hit, but the pole arced over and slammed into the red dirt, leaving the road clear.

"Glad to see that Newton's laws still work *some* of the time," Rick said.

"What?" asked a totally bewildered Larry.

"For every action, there is an equal and opposite reaction."

"If you say so."

His first blast had blown out at least one of the other car's tires. The car swerved as the driver tried to keep it on the road, but he was going way too fast for that. The back end spun around, fishtailed left and right, and then the car skidded through the ditch and plowed into a row of pineapple plants.

It looked like a vegetable bomb had gone off. Green and yellow pulp blew out on all sides. Rick kept his foot on the gas until the distance between cars closed to only a few hundred feet, then let off, pumped the brake a couple of times, yelled, "Hang on!" and swerved off the road after them.

The pickup bounced like a rocket with bubbles in the fuel lines. Rick could hear tools and engine parts clanking around in the back, and the surprised shouts of the people there hanging on for dear life. He aimed for the path left by the first car, but he misjudged and hit a row of pineapple himself, and the view out the windshield became a green explosion.

The pickup lurched to a halt. He and Larry threw open their doors and jumped out, but the people in the back had already leaped over the cab and were rushing toward the car. It was a gray two-door sedan with no markings on it. Through the back window, Rick could see three or four people struggling to restrain someone.

They weren't having much luck, probably because fire kept dancing over their hands every time they touched her. Rick heard them scream and curse, and heard Tessa shout, "Let me *go!*" just as the top blew away like a hatch with explosive bolts.

The car sank deeper into the volcanic soil. Action and reaction, Rick thought inanely as he sprinted through the trail of smashed pineapple to the back of it. That hadn't been his work. Tessa must have felt claustrophobic.

The roof landed wetly a dozen yards out in the field. The air smelled like an explosion in a salad bar. Rick stepped up into the lidless trunk, then reached over the back window toward Tessa. Her ring glittered in the sun as she reached toward him.

It had come back. She was safe, and her ring had come back.

His heart was pounding a mile a minute. He had to swallow before he could find his voice. "Are you all right?"

"I think so." She stood up.

The two soldiers in the back seat with her were in no shape to resist. Both of them were nursing burned hands. But the driver and the front-seat passenger both held short, ugly pistols pointed right at Rick.

Neither of them was Marcus. Rick felt almost disappointed.

"Back off," said the driver.

Rick gave him a withering look while he tried to stop panting long enough to say more than a couple words at a time. "You're not . . . stupid enough to pull the trigger," he said. He heard cars pulling up on the roadside, doors slamming, then people saying "Ow, ow, ow!" as they picked their way through the pineapple to the scene of the accident. The TV van plowed another path straight toward them, the cameraman still leaning out the side window. Somebody was going to owe the plantation for an acre or so of ruined crop.

One of the people who had been in the back of the pickup reached out and opened the getaway car driver's door. The driver whirled and pointed his gun at him, and his buddy turned his head to see what he would do, but neither one fired. Then while the second soldier was distracted, one of the other rescuers snatched the pistol right out of his hand.

It went off with a loud bang. Rick saw the muzzle flash and felt the bullet pass through his hair just above his left ear, but he was already reaching out mentally for the driver's gun.

The driver was fast. He got off three shots, but they all went into the door as Rick focused on his hand and shoved. Then Rick squeezed, and the driver's hand crackled like a bug under a boot heel.

He screamed "Aaahh!" and dropped the gun.

Still struggling to control his voice, Rick said, "Are we though playing games?"

Nobody answered.

He might not have been able to hear them if anyone had. A helicopter swooped up over the ridge, just a few feet off the ground, headed straight for them.

Rick and Tessa both reached out toward it at the same time, and a single bolt of flame lanced out to meet it. Rick imagined the firebolt exploding just in front of it, a shot across the bow, but Tessa wasn't feeling so generous. The blast took off the tail rotor and the helicopter slewed sideways, then spun the other way as the pilot fought to control it with only the main rotor. He made a split-second decision and brought the nose up, then cut the power entirely and ditched into the pineapple field.

They could feel the thump in the soles of their feet when it hit, but the helicopter stayed upright on its skids. The pilot popped open his door and stepped out, but he just stood there beside his wounded machine, staring toward the car and the pickup and the people swarming toward them.

Rick turned back and reached for Tessa again, helping her climb over the back window. Just when he thought he might be able to get his breathing under control, she smiled, and suddenly he couldn't trust himself to speak again.

She looked at him, her eyes glistening in the sun. "Rick," she said.

"Tessa."

He put his arms around her. Even through her coverall, touching her sent shivers through his hands. The air seemed to crackle with energy as everyone around them held their breath.

And then they kissed, and the crowd burst into applause.

CHAPTER 32

They held the wedding three days later. That was barely time enough to organize anything, but most of the people who had helped in the rescue were there on vacation, and Rick wanted to hold it while they could still attend. Fortunately it turned out there was a thriving business in arranging Hawaiian weddings. No fewer than ten separate companies offered to do it for free, and when Rick and Tessa asked if they could all work together, they jumped at the chance to stage a blowout event like none other.

The only thing Rick and Tessa had to do was pick the place. People were full of suggestions. The Fern Grotto on Kauai. The top of Mauna Loa on the Big Island, or Haleakala on Maui. In the crater of Diamond Head, or beside Waimea Falls right there on Oahu. But when they imagined thousands of people trying to crowd into any of those places, they all seemed like logistical nightmares.

It was Rick's mother who solved their dilemma. When they called to tell her to hop the first plane to Honolulu, and told her about their trouble in picking a spot, she said, "You're in a tropical paradise, for Pete's sake. Hold it under a palm tree on the beach."

And with that advice, the place became obvious. Most of their potential guests were already staying in hotels along Waikiki, or lived within driving distance. All the buses stopped there. The place was touristy as hell, but part of the reason for that was because Waikiki was one of the prettiest beaches on the island. Tourism hadn't ruined that. If anything, the careful landscaping around the glitzy hotels added to the magical image.

Picking which stretch of beach to use proved hardest of all, until Rick, Tessa, and Larry walked the entire length of it from the Hilton Lagoon to the aquarium. The beach curved gently around the shallow bay, providing anyone who stood anywhere along it at least some view of any other spot. They had just about decided on the stretch in front of the Royal Hawaiian until they came to a concrete pier jutting out into the ocean at the very end of the hotels, at the boundary between city and parkland. The curve of beach continued on beyond it—the widest stretch of it, in fact—and there was a huge open park behind that.

"There," Tessa said, pointing to the end of the pier. Shallow waves washed against it, and kids on boogie boards swept along its gray flanks. A seawall extending parallel to the beach on the right side made an enormous swimming pool for people who didn't want waves.

"That?" Rick said. "It's concrete. There's not a palm tree within a hundred yards."

"And it's also the most prominent spot on the whole beach. You can see it from everywhere. Plus boats can anchor just beyond it, so even more people can get up close. It's perfect."

"It's concrete," Rick said again, but she didn't act as if she'd even heard him. She started talking about flowers and awnings and cake and catering, and Rick realized they'd found their wedding place.

They stayed at the Park Shore, the last hotel on the beach, and right across the street from the pier. Rick watched the preparations from their top-floor suite, marveling as entire truckloads of flowers were brought in, transforming the drab cement into a riot of fragrance and color. The morning of the wedding, caterers in the park began assembling a cake in the shape of a Saturn V at least fifty feet long. A bright silver tank truck pulled up next to it, and Rick nearly fell off the balcony when the driver unfurled a banner that read, CHAMPAGNE WAGON.

"I've heard that weddings always get out of hand," he said, "but this is ridiculous."

Larry looked over the railing to see what he was talking about, then laughed. "I could use some of that right now."

Larry had been with him all morning, nervously patting the breast pocket of his white tuxedo every thirty seconds or so, for Rick had drafted him for duty as his best man, and as such he had to carry Tessa's ring. They had experimented with it the day before, letting him carry it through their rehearsal dinner, and it hadn't vanished then, so Tessa had made him take it this morning. She wanted a traditional wedding, and that meant the best man carried the ring.

"That's your engagement ring," Rick had told her at dinner. "You should let me buy you a decent wedding ring."

She had nailed him to the spot with a withering glare, and said, "This is the only ring I want. Now, or ever."

Her father, a round, cherubic man with a bald head and a wide smile, had laughed and said to Rick, "You'll have to get used to that temper of hers. Her mom's the same way."

"I am not," Mrs. McClain had said, and Tessa had laughed. "No, I'm far bitchier, right?"

"I didn't say that, dear."

Rick couldn't tell if they were having fun or getting ready to claw each other's eyes out. Life around them would be interesting, to say the least.

On the balcony, Larry checked his watch for about the millionth time. "Are you doing something to the flow of time?" he asked.

"Not that I know of," Rick said. "Relax."

Larry grinned. "Why aren't you nervous?"

"Who says I'm not?" Rick held out his hands—the left one finally free of the bandage. Both shook just a little.

"You're calm as a clam compared to me."

Rick shrugged. "Believe it or not, this is something I really want to do." He looked back out at the bustle of preparation going on outside. People were already lining up on the beach all the way up to the police station and beyond. The ocean was packed with boats. "Maybe not quite on this scale, but I do want to get married."

"Good thing, because there's no backing out now. Everybody who's anybody is here."

That wasn't quite true. Dale Jackson had declined their invitation to attend, and while Sonderby and General Marcus hadn't been invited, they had made it clear they weren't joining the party, either. They had in fact threatened to have the astronauts arrested on outstanding warrants ranging from dereliction of duty to reckless endangerment, but Rick and Tessa suddenly found themselves represented by lawyers they hadn't even heard of, who talked the district attorney into issuing warrants for the government men's arrest on exactly the same charges.

The judge had taken one look at the whole mess and told everyone to get the hell out of his courtroom, so that was that, at least for the moment. Rick knew that wouldn't be the end of it, but maybe they could at least get married before the legal hassles started up again.

Yoshiko had barely arrived in Japan, only to turn around and come back to be Tessa's maid of honor. Now, her quarantine suit abandoned, the two women were in the room next door, giggling like teenagers as they dressed for the ceremony. It seemed to be an involved process. Rick was glad the groom just had to wear a tuxedo.

He and Larry watched the setup team put the finishing touches on the pier: a podium for the priest to use as an altar, chairs for Rick's mom and Tessa's parents, and another couple rows of chairs at an angle for the most important guests. Rick wondered how many of his astronaut friends had managed to make it. He and Larry and at least a dozen of them had gone out for an impromptu bachelor's party last night, but he knew more were coming today.

People started filling the seats. Rick wished he had a pair of binoculars to see who all was there . . . and a moment later an eight-inch reflecting telescope on a tripod appeared on the balcony between him and Larry.

"Jesus!" Larry shouted, jumping back. "Where did that come from?"

"Sorry," Rick said, grinning at the absurdity of it. "I wanted to get a closer look, and the next thing I knew . . . poof." He aimed the telescope between the balcony rails at the end of the pier, looked into the eyepiece, and got the closest view of his mother's back that he'd had since he was a baby slung over her shoulder.

He nudged the tube to the side and saw a blur of motion, which stopped on a white flower lei. A glimpse of another woman's face came into view, a Hispanic woman, but it was gone before Rick could recognize her. She looked vaguely familiar, like someone he should know, but he couldn't place her and he couldn't track her, either. She must have been another one of Tessa's relatives walking toward the chairs.

"This thing's useless for anything less than astronomical distance," he said.

Larry took a peek, then lifted the business end of the 'scope to point out to sea. He panned along the boats for a moment, then said, "Oh, I don't know about that. Have a look."

Rick did, and saw a sailboat with twenty or thirty people on board, all of them nude. A blue-and-white banner stretched along the railing at knee height read, WEDDING BELLS AND NOTHING ELSE! THE ALOHA SUNSHINE SOCIETY.

When he looked up again, Larry laughed at his silly expression. "Like you say, weddings tend to get out of hand."

"I guess." He looked again, then turned the telescope away. If Tessa caught him literally scoping out babes on their wedding day, she'd . . . he didn't know what she'd do, but it wasn't worth risking it.

Finally the phone rang. Larry picked it up, said, "All right, we're on our way," and hung up. He patted his breast pocket again and said, "Showtime."

Both of them looked in the mirror before they left. Hair okay? No spinach in the teeth? Boutonniere on tight? Rick felt his heart beating harder than it had during the Apollo launch. All systems go. Showtime.

CHAPTER 33

They emerged from the hotel into a mob of well-wishers. The first couple dozen dropped flower leis over their heads as they passed, and people waved and cheered all along the narrow path left open for them to walk in. They waved with that same thumb-and-little-finger wave, which Rick clumsily tried to return, much to everyone's amusement. Larry was better at it.

They crossed the street—packed with people as far as they could see—and started down the pier. Now Rick started recognizing faces. Laura Turner, from Mission Control. He stopped long enough to drape one of his leis around her neck and say, "Thank you," and was about to move on when she nodded to a tall, heavyset man at her side and said, "This is Gregor!"

"Gregor! My God!" Rick reached out and gave him a bear hug, which Gregor returned with enough enthusiasm to relocate vertebrae.

"Congratulations!" Gregor said.

"Thank you. I mean thank you for everything! *Spacebo!*"

Gregor blushed. "*Eta nichevo.*"

Rick wanted to say more, but Larry nudged him forward. He was right. Thousands of people were waiting. But Rick felt lighter than air as he walked the rest of the way to the end of the pier. Gregor was here!

So was Mark, the kid who had loaned him his pickup. Rick hardly recognized him in daylight in civilian clothes, but when he did he stopped and said, "Sorry about all the pineapple. I must have dented up the grille pretty good, too. I'll pay to have it fixed."

"Are you kidding?" Mark said. "That pickup's worth a fortune now! I've got offers for over a million bucks already. Thank you!"

Totally bemused, Rick said, "You're welcome, I guess."

"Same to you, dude. Anytime you need to borrow some wheels, give me a call." Mark slapped him on the back, and Larry urged him onward.

The last hundred feet were a blur. More astronauts pounded him on the back and whooped as he passed. Aunts, uncles, and cousins smooched him on the cheek or shook his hand. Rick recognized half a dozen movie stars, cheering and hollering like everyone else.

Only the last couple dozen people closest to the altar got chairs. Immediate family, in Tessa's case. There was an empty chair next to her mother for her father to sit in after he walked her to the altar. Rick, as an only child with just one parent left, wondered who else was sitting with his mother, then he nearly tripped over his own feet when he recognized President Martinez looking at him from the chair beside her. That was the woman he had seen in the telescope! There were four or five people he didn't know sitting behind her and behind Tessa's mother. Secret Service agents, or heads of state? He suddenly wished he paid more attention to politics.

One slender, dark-haired girl in her mid-twenties had to be Tessa's sister, Elise, just in from New York today. She was the one who had sneaked her vegetables onto Tessa's plate when they were young. The family resemblance was amazing, except for the color of her hair. Rick smiled and waved, then waved at the President and at his mother, who looked pleased as could be even though Rick knew she had voted for Martinez's opponent. He and Larry took their places next to the priest, who was covered in a white robe, hood drawn over his head, which he held down in prayer.

The podium held only two microphones, but both were no doubt connected to every broadcast network in the world. Television crews on scaffolds—also covered with flowers—

filmed the whole scene from either side. Helicopters hovered in the distance, prevented by air traffic control from approaching closer than a mile.

Waves lapped at the end of the pier. The water was full of people clinging to boogie boards. The walkway back to the beach was a sea of faces, turning away now to catch their first glimpse of Tessa. The aroma of fresh flowers filled the air, even with the sea breeze sweeping it inland through the palms.

The familiar "Ba dum da dum!" of "Here Comes the Bride" rang out from the hotel side of the street. Rick looked for the source of it, saw enough speakers to stage a rock concert stacked atop their hotel, and hoped Tessa had gotten out of her room before they had fired them up.

She had. The moment the music started, a cheer went up from the crowd near the hotel, and spread toward them in a slow wave as Tessa and her father walked arm-in-arm toward the pier. Rick thought the applause for him had been something, but this was unbelievable. It was a roar of voices and applause that spread up and down the beach, echoed off the buildings, and nearly drowned out even the amplified music. It was a primal force of nature. Rick suddenly realized that at the moment Tessa was probably the most popular person on the planet.

They didn't need flower-bearers. People threw enough leis ahead of her to carpet the ground at her feet. Two of her youngest cousins carried her train, and Yoshiko stayed busy scooping errant flowers from its billowing folds before they could weigh it down to the ground.

Larry checked the ring again. Rick concentrated on simply breathing as Tessa approached.

Her white satin dress glowed in the sunlight. Lace along the sleeves and shoulders softened it, and her veil and the folds of sheer fabric falling from her waist gave her an ethereal look, as if she were walking through clouds. Beneath the lace, opaque white satin sheathed her body close enough to show off the curve of her hips and her long, slender legs. More lace and satin accentuated her bustline, and five strands of pearls winked from under her veil, sparkling from her neck to the tops of her breasts.

Her face was clearly visible behind the veil. Rick had never seen such an expression of expectant eagerness before. She looked up and saw him, and her lips turned upward in a smile that outshone her dress.

Her father led her to Rick's side, then sat down next to her mother. The music stopped, the last notes echoing up the canyon of hotels to the left. Rick took Tessa's hand, and they turned toward the priest. There was a long silence, then the priest raised his head, drew back his hood, and said, "Dearly beloved."

A gasp travelled like a wave down the length of the pier. It was the Pope.

His name was Thomas. People called him the "Doubting Pope," and he professed to be comfortable with that title. He had, after all, started out agnostic, and he was the first to admit that God had never spoken to him in a clear and unambiguous way. He was fond of saying that most religious experiences could be attributed to inspiration or indigestion, but that the difference was impossible to discern.

He was American, and in his late forties. Just beginning to turn gray, he was a new Pope for a new millennium, and his youth, candor, and humility had drawn more people into the fold than all the Johns and Pauls and Piuses before him combined.

Rick felt a brief moment of panic at the thought that getting married by the Pope would make him a Catholic, but the ceremony was exactly the same as the one he and Tessa had practiced the night before with the wedding services' rent-a-priest. They managed to say their vows without stumbling over the words, and before they knew it they were exchanging rings.

Larry handed Tessa's ring to Rick with such a sigh of relief that President Martinez had to stifle a laugh. Rick slid it onto her finger, then let her slip a matching band, taken from a real Apollo control panel on display at Kennedy Space Center, on his finger.

Then the Pope pronounced them husband and wife, Rick lifted her veil, and they kissed.

Rick thought the fireworks were all in his imagination, but when he opened his eyes he saw bright firebursts blossoming all over the sky. That plus the cheers and the applause seemed to shake the ground, but he supposed his wobbly knees were adding to the effect, too.

There was no way to do a receiving line, so Rick and Tessa were supposed to simply march back down the pier, greeting everyone they could on the way. They started with Pope Thomas, who congratulated them and then said, "We need to talk."

"We do?" Rick asked, then he blushed and said, "I mean, sure. Um . . . when?"

"Tomorrow will be soon enough. There are some things you need to know about your new abilities."

He turned them around before they could ask what he meant, and gently shooed them onward. Their parents and Tessa's sister all had to get hugs, and then President Martinez hugged them as well. She was holding a roll of paper in her hand, tied with a bow. "A wedding present," she said, handing it to Tessa, who slid the bow off the end and opened it. Rick glanced over and caught the words, ". . . absolved of any crime related to . . ."

"A pardon?"

She nodded. "Just in case. I don't want anything to spoil your honeymoon."

"Thank you!" Rick and Tessa said in stereo.

"My pleasure. You did a heroic thing. I'd love to talk with you more about it when you get back to the mainland."

"Of course," Rick said. "We'll, uh, call and set up a time right away."

"At your convenience."

She stepped back and they walked on, hardly feeling the ground beneath their feet. There were a good six inches of flowers there anyway, and more coming down like rain. When they reached the end of the pier it became a flood, until they were wading through carnations and gardenia blossoms to the reception area in the park.

Rick felt intoxicated before he even had a sip of champagne. The Pope and the President both wanted to talk to them! And thousands of people pressed close in the park, eager to get even a glimpse of them. It would have been scary if everybody hadn't been smiling and congratulating them.

Fifty feet of Saturn-V-shaped cake didn't even begin to feed everyone. The caterers gave Rick and Tessa the escape tower anyway to freeze and eat on their first anniversary, then set out hundreds of sheet cakes, but the rumor started to spread that the newlyweds had multiplied the original cake like Jesus had the loaves and the fishes.

They managed to squelch that rumor, at least in their immediate vicinity, but even so everyone wanted to see them perform some kind of magic trick. Finally they relented and conjured up a flock of doves, which circled the park twice before vanishing.

"Do something everybody can see!" someone called out.

"Like what?" Rick asked.

"Spell something out with clouds!"

"No," someone else shouted. "Make a fire-breathing dragon with your names tattooed on its wings!"

"You're kidding," Rick said, laughing at the silly image that brought to mind, but a moment later he jumped as a dark shadow swept over the crowd, heading up the beach. He looked upward and sure enough, there it was, big as a 747, with bat wings, a long, sinuous tail, an equally serpentine neck, and a rough, scaly head that belched flame at least fifty feet when it roared.

If the words JUST MARRIED hadn't been there in gold letters on its wings, it would probably have started a panic. As it was, people gaped up at it in awe as it flew just above the treetops toward Pearl Harbor, circled around the airport, and flew back to circle Diamond Head before vanishing in a huge puff of smoke.

Nobody asked for another demonstration.

CHAPTER 34

The dragon was probably a mistake," said the Pope.

They were in his room at the Sheraton, at the forward point of its ship-like prow. The view out the windows was a postcard scene of Waikiki, with sunlight glittering off the waves, sailboats on the bright blue ocean, and Diamond Head in the distance.

Pope Thomas was dressed in a red-and-blue aloha shirt and Bermuda shorts, clearly enjoying the chance to let down his hair a bit in a tropical paradise. Rick had bought a gray suit—using his mother's credit card, since his wallet was still at Schofield Barracks—and Tessa had borrowed a modest blue dress from her sister that made her look like a political candidate.

"We, um, didn't make it on purpose," she said. "Somebody suggested it, and it just sort of happened."

His Eminence nodded. "That's a problem. You'll have to learn to control that. You'll also have to watch your own whims."

Rick told him about the telescope he'd created yesterday.

"Just so. Had it gone away by the time you got back to your room?"

"Yes."

"Things like that usually do. But until they disappear, they're just as real—and as dangerous—as the real thing."

Tessa leaned forward in her chair. "You talk like this happens to you all the time."

Thomas shook his head. "I'm afraid not. It's been decades since a Pope could do more than transubstantiation. That's the business with the wine and the cracker turning into the blood and body of Christ."

"You mean that's for real?"

"Used to be. We live in a more rational world nowadays. People take things like that metaphorically instead of literally. Pius XII could supposedly do it, but nobody after him. I think it was the ascendence of science after the atom bomb that damped his power. And now of course secular humanism is taking an even bigger bite out of religion."

"You don't sound particularly upset by this," Rick said.

The Pope shrugged. "I'm not. Religion is merely a vehicle for guiding people's belief in the supernatural. The less of that belief there is, the less guidance they need."

"Excuse me?"

Thomas looked out the window at the ocean, gathering his thoughts, then turned back to face Rick. "You don't honestly believe that your ability is anything new, do you? Psychic power has been around as long as there have been minds to focus it. Pharaohs, shamans, prophets—I'd be willing to bet most of their abilities came from the same source yours do. The notion of the divine right of kings probably derives from it. Anybody who could get a big enough following had the potential, if not the ability, to wield it, and other people seem to be able to tap into a limited amount of power just on the strength of their own belief. You and Tessa are just the latest in a long line of practitioners."

He smiled softly. "I'm not particularly worried about you—you're good people, and you have the best interests of humanity at heart—but in the wrong hands your ability could be very dangerous. The Church realized that long ago, so we've taken it upon ourselves to teach people a basic sense of morality, to direct the power of consciousness toward good. We try to make people believe in a just and powerful God who won't tolerate selfishness or petty desires. That way if another focus comes along, they'll only be able to use their abilities for good."

He laughed. "We should have known that the next focus would be technological instead of metaphysical. This is the twenty-first century. But we naïvely assumed that rationalism would preclude the belief in psychic abilities. We were worried about astrologers when we should have been watching out for astronauts. We even had advance warning, but we ignored it just as NASA did."

"What?" Rick asked, suddenly even more alert than before. "NASA has had ghost rockets before this?"

"No," said the Pope. "But they had a psychically induced disaster that nearly cost three men their lives. Remember *Apollo 13*?"

"That was caused by a wiring failure in an oxygen tank," Tessa said.

"Undoubtedly," Thomas agreed. "But if it hadn't been that, it would have been something else. Think for a moment. *Apollo 13*. It lifted off at precisely 13:13. It's almost as if NASA was trying to prove they weren't superstitious. But it didn't matter what NASA believed; America thinks the number 13 is bad luck. So *Apollo 13*'s oxygen tank blew up two days into the flight, which—surprise, surprise—just happened to be the 13th of the month. If that's not evidence that the group mind affects reality, then nothing is. Not to disparage their training or anything, but it's a good thing people also believed that the astronauts were all heroes, or the crew might not have made it home alive."

Rick, who had just ridden to the Moon and back on a rocket apparently powered by the angst of Trekkies and Heinlein readers, didn't know what to say. It sounded preposterous, but . . .

Tessa shifted uncomfortably on her chair. "So what does this have to do with the dragon we made?"

The Pope sighed. "There are seven billion people on Earth. At least half of them saw what you did yesterday on TV. Now three and a half billion people believe in dragons." He shivered and said, "I am glad we have supersonic fighter jets with heat-seeking missiles nowadays. If either of you has a nightmare, we may need them."

Rick flinched as he heard a sudden roar from outside, but it was just another plane taking off from the airport. "Are you serious?" he asked.

"I don't know if it's quite as bad as all that," the Pope answered. "After all, most of those people know you made it up. But the human soul does have a dark side to it, and there are more than enough dark images to populate our imaginations. Demons and devils are pretty much passé these days, but there are plenty of movie monsters and UFOs to take their place. Any of which—like yesterday's dragon—could become real at a moment's notice if you let them."

Rick was getting over his awe. Maybe it was the matter-of-fact way that the Pope spoke about such bizarre things. "Why are you telling us this? It would seem to me that planting those images in our minds is the worst thing you can do."

"I want you to be aware of the danger. I want you to be able to recognize the source of it if something like that happens. You are the focus for the world's thoughts at the moment, but it's *their* thoughts as well as yours that determine what you can do."

"For better or for worse," Tessa said. The words sounded much more foreboding today than when she had spoken them yesterday.

"Exactly. It's a responsibility I wouldn't wish on anyone, but now that you've got it, you had to be warned."

Rick snorted. "Don't think of pink elephants, is that it? How are we supposed to prevent casual thoughts from becoming real?"

Thomas had been resting his elbows on the arms of his chair. Now he steepled his fingers in front of his face and said, "Prayer is fairly effective. Prayer and meditation. In centuries past, people prayed to prevent divine intervention as often as they did to solicit it. And meditation is a useful way to clear the mind of unwanted thoughts."

"More woo-woo shit to go along with the rest of it," Rick muttered.

"Rick!" Tessa kicked him in the shin.

"Sorry," he said to Thomas, then he repeated it to her, "Sorry. I still have a hard time with all this."

The Pope laughed. "I sympathize. Imagine my surprise when I accepted my appointment to the Vatican and learned what was really going on."

Rick tried. He imagined it could be quite a shock. "Is that why you named yourself Thomas?"

"Part of the reason." He smiled enigmatically, and Rick realized that was as much of an answer as he was going to get.

Thomas stood up. "I'm glad we had this little talk. Call me if you have any problems. In the meantime, enjoy your new-found abilities. You may be the first people since Jesus to actually deserve them."

"That can be taken two ways," Rick said with a wry grin.

Thomas laughed. "Most things can. Be careful."

CHAPTER 35

The President was much more pragmatic. When Rick and Tessa had settled into their chairs in the Oval Office, only three days after their audience with the Pope, she leaned forward across her desk and said, "Would you be willing to take another flight into space?"

"In another ghost?" Rick asked. "No way."

"Tessa?"

"Not without a very good reason."

"How about the future of the human race?"

For a moment, Rick was afraid someone had discovered an asteroid on a collision course with Earth, and a moment later he was afraid he had just *created* one, but the President blew that fantasy out of his mind.

"We all know NASA's a dead horse," she said. "We're not going to beat any more performance out of it. If we want to get into space again, we're going to have to find a different way." She twiddled a wood-barreled pen between her right thumb and forefinger. "What you did two weeks ago strikes me as a radically different approach. And much more cost-effective than the old way."

"Much more dangerous as well," Tessa said.

"Is it?" She tapped the pen against her desktop. "You made it there and back without even knowing what you were doing. I've talked with the people who, ah, debriefed you after you returned, and they assure me this 'quantum observer effect,' as they're calling it, can be quantified and controlled."

"Sonderby would say that," Rick snorted. "I'll bet Marcus wasn't so optimistic."

She stopped twiddling the pen. "He has offered his resignation. I turned it down, but you're right, he's not enthusiastic about our chances. However, he did admit that he has been able to measure the effect and reproduce it in the laboratory. Mr. Toland thinks he can refine the process so it becomes more reliable. All we need, he says, is someone with enough public backing to channel the necessary energy into useful forms."

Rick held out his left hand, the bright red scar on his palm facing her. "He also thought bending spoons was safe, but look what happened to me."

She didn't flinch. "We can proceed cautiously."

Tessa cleared her throat. "Uh, there's one big problem with this idea that nobody seems to be thinking of. Our power apparently comes from the public, whose attention span is about a week long. Thanks to Sonderby and his cohorts we've lasted a bit longer, but by this time next month I doubt if we'll be able to make a paper airplane."

The President shook her head, her expression a mixture of amusement and sorrow. "The public believes what they're told to believe. The media can herd them like sheep."

Rick didn't like the sound of that. He said, "Isn't that a bit cynical?"

"It's a fact. Politics is a media game. You don't get to be President without learning how to control what people think about you."

After what Marcus and Sonderby had done to him and Tessa, Rick supposed she was right. He wondered how much of a science it had become, and imagined rows of lab-coated spin doctors running computer simulations and releasing specially concocted rumors to select tabloids and talk shows. Hell, they probably *ran* the tabloids and talk shows. Government intervention could at least account for their inane contents.

Martinez resumed tapping her pen. "I'm surprised at your reluctance. You're astronauts. I'm offering you the chance to rebuild the space program."

"No offense, ma'am, but Tessa's right. I'd love to kickstart an honest exploration program again, but if we build it out of smoke and mirrors, it'll eventually go *poof*, no matter how well we understand what we're doing."

"Before or after we've been to Mars?"

He couldn't help laughing. "Mars? We just barely made it to the Moon and back. We have no idea how far away this—what did you call it; this 'quantum observer effect'—persists, even if we could get the public to stay interested long enough to make the trip. The power source is still on Earth, after all."

"So let's test it. We can send an unmanned probe first if you want. It wouldn't cost us a cent."

Rick looked over at Tessa. She was tilting her head and winding a lock of hair around her finger, frowning slightly as she listened to him debate with the President. When she realized they were both looking at her, she straightened up and said, "Why not? As long as nobody's life is in danger, I don't see a problem with it."

Rick wished he could remove his jacket. He was growing hot inside his suit. He might have gotten away with it with the Pope, but not here, so he ignored the sweat under his arms and said, "Remember what Gregor said about explosions. $E=mc^2$. We've been lucky so far, but if one of our little creations turns into energy all of a sudden, we're screwed. A rocket big enough to get to Mars could take out half of Florida if it blew up on the pad."

"Who said anything about launching from Florida?" Tessa asked. "We can create it in space. If it blows up there, who cares?"

He still didn't like the idea. He couldn't explain why, though. He should be excited about using his newfound ability for the one thing in life he had always wanted to do. Going to the Moon hadn't fulfilled his dream; it had only whetted his appetite for more. So why did he balk at the idea of going to Mars? Was it because they would essentially be cheating? Did he fear the cultural backlash that Sonderby had warned him about if people began to expect a free lunch?

"Have you discussed this with Sonderby?" he asked the President. "Why aren't you worried about the economic consequences of this? Why aren't you trying to suppress it instead?"

She laughed. "Like any good government official should? We're not all afraid of the future, Mr. Spencer. Sonderby shared his concerns with me before you escaped from quarantine. He may even have been right. We're probably going to have a social and economic upheaval like this country has never seen before, but it doesn't have to be a terrible thing. We can either embrace it or stick our heads in the sand, but it'll happen whether we try to stop it or not. The genie is out of the bottle. The only real question now is what we do with our three wishes."

Maybe that was it. Martinez had been careful to say "our" three wishes, but it was clear that she wanted her share of the goodies. So would everyone else who could bend Rick's or Tessa's ear. They were going to have to learn how to dodge pitches or they would be spending the rest of their lives performing miracles for people.

He shivered despite the heat. That would be one way to keep the power flowing. If they gave everyone what they wanted, they could probably keep it indefinitely.

That way lies martyrdom, he thought. Nobody, no matter how much power they drew from the void, could satisfy everyone. Martinez was *starting* her agenda with Mars. What would she ask for next? A working nuclear-fusion power plant? Electric cars that actually worked? Replacement trees for the clearcut rain forests? Or would it be something more sinister? A natural disaster in the Middle East for instance, or a revolution in China.

And what if they balked? Would they find themselves merely maligned in the press, or visited by CIA agents in the night? The only thing he knew for sure was the deeper they got into government intrigue, the deeper their bodies would be buried when they were no longer useful.

"I'd like to think about it," he said. "We're new at this. We don't know if we're even capable of that sort of thing. I don't want to leap blindly into something we'll all regret later."

Martinez wasn't happy with that, but she couldn't very well advocate throwing caution to the winds, either. She did the next best thing, though, saying, "As Tessa pointed out, one of the unknown variables is how long you'll have this ability. Don't wait too long to make up your mind, or we could lose a golden opportunity."

"Understood," said Rick. "We'll definitely think it over." He stood up and held out his hand for her to shake, as though he had been dismissed. It worked; she set down her pen, shook his hand, shook Tessa's as well, and watched them let themselves out of her office.

Tessa waited until they were in the limousine to the airport before she exploded.

"Do you realized you just blew off the President of the United States?"

"Oh yeah, I'm fully aware of that." He tugged off his tie and loosened his collar, then searched for the air conditioning vent and turned it so the cold air blew straight at his face.

"What the hell were you thinking?"

He mopped the sweat off his forehead with his sleeve. "I was trying to figure out how to get out of there without a radio collar around my neck," he said. "She wants us, lover. She wants us bad. She'll give us a little time to come back to her on our own, because she'd love for us to join her voluntarily, but she's got an agenda as long as her arm in tiny little print. Mars is just a carrot to lure us into her web. Her real target is right here on Earth."

"Ooh, I love it when you mix metaphors," Tessa said

seductively, but her body language betrayed her true emotion. And her next words. "Damn it, Rick, she just offered us Mars on a platter!"

"Big deal. She's using our platter." He took her hands in his and looked into her eyes. "Everybody who's ever had any experience with this stuff has told us to be careful. Do you really think we should blow *them* off just to make the President happy?"

She didn't reply immediately. When she did, she said, "What do *you* want to use it for?"

"What?"

"You've got the power of a minor deity. What do you want to use it for, if not a flight to Mars?"

He had already asked himself that question many times, late at night after Tessa was asleep, but he hadn't come up with a satisfactory answer then, and he didn't have one for her now. A nice house? A jazzy car? His own interplanetary spaceship? It all seemed so petty. Even the spaceship.

"To tell you the truth, I don't want to use it for anything. I wish it would just go away. I've already *got* everything I want."

"Damn it, Rick, I'm serious."

"So am I." He gripped her hands tighter. He watched her try to maintain her frown, but it slowly lost ground to the smile that crept over her features.

"Damn it," she said again. "How am I supposed to stay mad at you when you keep saying things like that?"

He didn't answer her. Not with words, anyway. He knew enough to quit while he was ahead. Which, he supposed as she kissed him, was the whole point he'd been trying to make.

CHAPTER 36

They were standing in the ticket line when Tessa said, "Jesus, I just realized we haven't even talked about where we're going to live."

Rick scooted his bag a few feet forward as the line moved. Only in Washington did the counter for ticket purchases have a longer line than for already-ticketed passengers. Politicians on expense accounts, no doubt, making last-minute flights home on "official business." That spoke volumes right there about the trouble with giving the government a blank check.

He tried not to let it get him down. He looked over at Tessa, who wore a hat and sunglasses to keep from being recognized, just as he did, and said, "So what do you think? Your place or mine?"

She lived in Orlando; he in Houston. They were headed for Orlando today, but that wasn't necessarily their final destination.

"Texas is too hot," she said. "Besides, if we're not working for NASA, there's no reason to be there anymore, is there?"

"We haven't actually gotten our pink slips yet," he reminded her.

"Yeah, right. Are you planning on showing up for work on Monday?"

He nudged his bag forward again with his foot. "Altman's new policy entitles us to two weeks post-flight vacation. I don't think imprisonment by the government counts. So we've got over a week left before we have to report."

"Good point. So where do you want to spend it?"

He thought it over for a moment, trying to imagine them in his house or in Tessa's apartment, but neither place felt right. "How about Key West?" he asked. "I go there a lot to relax.

And it's far enough removed to keep all but the most determined people away. We might not even have to go incognito
there." He didn't like wearing sunglasses indoors.

"I've never been to Key West," she said.

"Then we should definitely check it out. If you like it, we
can buy a condo there or something."

"Just like that?"

"Hell, the owner'll probably give it to us if we do a magic
trick or two."

They reached the head of the line, and a minute later a
counter opened up. The ticket agent hardly blinked when
they presented their ID, but when she handed them their
boarding passes they saw that she had put them in first class.

"Hey, thanks!" Rick said.

"You're welcome," the agent said. "And congratulations."

Tessa smiled at her, made a little flourish with her right
hand, and handed her a pink carnation.

The agent's eyes grew wide. "Wow! Thank you! I'll treasure it forever."

Rick laughed softly. "I'm afraid it probably won't last more
than a few minutes. But you never know."

As they walked toward their gate, he said, "Why did you
do that?"

"Because I wanted to." She looked over at him and sighed.
"Look, we've got the ability. Why not use it?"

"I keep thinking about the Russian explosions. 'Industrial
accidents,' Gregor called them. How big a bang would we get
if that carnation decided to let go of its mass all at once instead
of fading away gently?"

"It doesn't work that way," she said.

"How do you know?"

"Look, how much stuff have we manifested since this
whole business began? Starting with a fully fueled Saturn V.
Has any of it blown up? No. It all fades away."

"So far."

They reached their gate and sat down in the last row of chairs with their backs to the waiting room.

"What's the real issue here?" she asked. "Something's obviously bugging you, but I don't think it's explosions."

She was right. He *was* worried about the danger, but that wasn't the source of his reluctance. Neither was Sonderby's gloom-and-doom scenario about the end of Western civilization. That was too abstract a concept to really scare him down at the instinctive level where his motivations came from. No, what bothered him was something much more primal.

"I guess what it is," he said, "is that this whole business somehow offends me. The universe shouldn't work this way. All my life I've been taught that the basic workings of nature were understandable, and I always thought I understood them pretty well. Now this comes along and blows all that right out of the water."

"No it doesn't," Tessa said. "I'm sure we're not violating any of the *real* laws of nature. Just the ones that people have made up to describe the way they thought things worked. So we have to expand the picture a little bit to account for something new; big deal."

He watched a 747 taxi in toward the gate to their left. It looked improbably huge and ponderous to fly. Would it have offended the Wright brothers? "It's a big deal to me," he said. "Maybe because I'm the one responsible for it. A lot of scientists are going to lose their jobs before this is over."

"Scientists? I'd think they'd be at a premium now while we try to figure this out."

"The ones who can adapt to the new paradigm will be. The ones who can't are going to be serving hamburgers. And that's probably most of them."

She thought it over. "Maybe. I've heard people say that science advances by funerals. But even so, it's not your fault. What is, *is*. Whether or not people can adapt to it isn't your responsibility."

He snorted. "I'm sure the asteroid that wiped out the dinosaurs was just minding its own business, too. But if I was the asteroid, I'd still feel guilty."

"If you were the asteroid?" She laughed. "Jesus, Rick, are you a classic case of assumed guilt or what?"

The walkway nosed out toward the plane like a turtle sticking its head out of its shell. Rick said, "All right, that was a silly analogy, but I do feel responsible for this. If I'd followed orders and left the Apollo in orbit like I was supposed to, we'd have had a minor curiosity to deal with. Now we've got a global crisis." She started to speak, but he went on. "And the worst part of it—the worst thing for me, personally—is that I've got to watch every thought I have. The Pope says he's not worried because we're nice people, but he doesn't know me. I get mad sometimes, just like anyone else. Somebody cuts me off in traffic and I want to shove him out of my way. Well now I can do it. I *will* do it if I'm not careful. If I dream about something, it's liable to show up on my doorstep in the morning. Or worse, in the middle of the night. I don't like having to worry about that."

"Well, me either," Tessa said, toying with her hair again. "But come on, Rick. I think it's a fair trade."

"I don't."

They left it at that. There really wasn't much more to say. On the plane to Orlando Tessa amused the other people in the first-class section by creating flowers and rings and watches for them. One man asked if she could create a copy of Ryan Hughes's latest book, *If Wishes Were Rockets*. She had never heard of the author nor that particular book, but she concentrated hard and pretty soon a thin paperback appeared in her hand. Sure enough, it had the right name and title on it, but when the astonished man who had requested it opened it up, he laughed and showed her the blank pages inside.

"That's odd," she said. "You'd think if I could create a

dragon that actually breathed fire, I could create a book with the right words in it."

The man laughed and said, "Well, if it helps your ego any, *I'm* Ryan Hughes, and I don't know what goes in here yet either. I just got the idea for it a couple days ago and I haven't started writing it yet." He looked at the cover and said, "I'd love to show this to my editor. This is the best cover I've gotten yet."

"It probably won't last that long," Tessa told him. "Sorry, but that's the way it seems to work."

"Here," said the woman in front of him. "I've got a camera. Hold it up." He did, and she took a snapshot of him pointing proudly at his name in big, bold type.

They exchanged addresses and phone numbers, and Tessa gave them hers, too. "I want to see if that photo comes out," she said. "And if the book is actually printed with that cover on it, I think we've just demonstrated time travel."

"Cool," said Hughes.

Rick grunted and looked out the window. A tiny flying saucer dropped down from overhead, hovering just on the other side of the glass. It couldn't have been more than eight inches across, with a classic bubble top and three landing legs sticking out the bottom. A proportionally tiny green-and-white-spotted alien waved at him, and blinked three of its six eyes.

Rick pulled down the shade and tried to sleep.

CHAPTER 37

Two days later, the dogs died. Rick woke to the sound of the telephone, which startled him enough by the simple fact that he had told nobody where he and Tessa were staying. When he picked it up, a woman asked him, "Do you hate dogs?"

"What?" he asked groggily. "Who is this?"

"Andrea Winston of the *Eugene Register Guard*. I was just wondering if you'd ever been bitten by a dog, or had a neighbor with a barking dog, or anything like that."

"You woke me up to ask me that? How did you even know where I was?"

"I'm a reporter, Mr. Spencer. So do you or Tessa have anything against dogs?"

"No! Why?"

"About half an hour ago, every dog in Eugene suddenly fell over dead. I was wondering if you had anything to do with that."

"Dogs? Dead? What?" Rick tried to get his mind up to speed. "Where did this happen?" he asked.

"Eugene, Oregon," she replied.

"I've never even been to Oregon. No, wait, I think I changed planes once in Portland. But I didn't have anything to do with killing any dogs."

"How about Tessa?"

"No!"

Tessa raised her head from her pillow. "What's wrong?"

He didn't bother to cover the phone. "A bunch of dogs died in some little town in Oregon, and this reporter thinks we did it."

"No, sir," said Andrea. "I'm just asking questions. We've

got a lot of upset people here, and we're trying to figure out what happened."

"Dead dogs?" Tessa asked. "Why does she think we did it?"

"I don't know. Why do you—"

"Because they *all* died. Every dog in town, as near as we can tell. Even ones who never go outside. And it apparently happened at the same exact moment everywhere."

Rick relayed that information to Tessa. "What time was that?" he asked, intrigued despite the accusation that he was behind it.

"Five-thirty-seven A.M."

He looked at the clock on the nightstand: 9:03. If Oregon was on Pacific time, that put it less than half an hour ago.

"We were both sound asleep at the time," he said. "And no, before you ask, there weren't any dogs barking around here to annoy us subconsciously, either. We're in a condo that doesn't allow pets."

The reporter's tone softened somewhat. "I see. I'm sorry if I sounded like I was accusing you, but it's so bizarre I couldn't think of anybody else who could be responsible."

"It's all right," said Rick. "It does sound suspicious." He ran a hand through his hair, shoving the sleep-tangled forelocks off to the side. "If I had to make a guess—and this is just a guess, mind you—I'd say that you've got someone living there in Eugreen who accidentally became a focus of power."

"Eugene," said the reporter.

"That makes sense," Tessa said. "Think of all the people in America who stick their dogs outside first thing in the morning. They almost invariably bark and wake up the neighbors. So there's this wave of irritation traveling across the country, picking up momentum with every person who's awakened. By the time it gets to Oregon, half the people in the country are pissed. Somewhere along the way it reaches critical mass, and one person who really wants some peace and quiet focuses that power—probably without even knowing he's doing it—and *skrrk*." She drew her finger across her throat.

The reporter could apparently hear her over the phone. She said, "Somebody else besides you can do that?"

"Who knows?" Rick said. "If Dennis Toland's theories are right, then the power is out there for anybody to use if they can tap into it. Anger is a pretty powerful force. I'm surprised nothing like this has happened before."

"Nobody knew it was possible before," Tessa said.

Rick could hear Andrea typing. "Umm-hmm," she said. "That makes sense. It also scares the hell out of me, but I suppose it makes sense. So do you predict a rash of violence as people learn that they can take out their frustrations on one another with psychic power?"

"Jesus, I hope not," Rick said. He wondered what they could do to head it off. An idea came to him and he immediately hated it, but he also realized he had to try it. "Look, I don't know what Tessa and I can do from here, but it's only been half an hour or so since the dogs all died, right?"

"That's right."

"We could try to bring them back to life."

She gasped, and Rick realized that she hadn't had nearly as much time to get used to the idea of supernatural events as he had.

"I have no idea if it'll work," he said. "When we create stuff, it disappears again in just a few minutes, but if these dogs haven't been dead too long, maybe it'll be like zapping them with a defibrillator. If we can just get them moving again, maybe they'll be okay."

"Oh yes!" Andrea said. "That would be wonderful."

Rick realized one of the dead dogs must have been hers.

"Give us a minute to concentrate on it," he said.

"Okay."

He set the phone down on the nightstand. "You want to try this?" he asked Tessa.

"Of course I do." She took his hand, and they both closed their eyes.

"Okay," Rick said, "Let's try to imagine a bunch of dogs lying on their sides, then getting up and wagging their tails again. Ready?"

"Ready."

"Go."

They tried. Rick imagined as many different kinds of dogs as he could. St. Bernards, German shepherds, Labradors of all colors, boxers and terriers, and even poodles and Chihuahuas, which he would have been just as happy to leave dead.

Maybe that little bit of hypocrisy was enough to spoil the attempt. Or maybe it was impossible to revive dead animals, or to do it from three thousand miles away. Whatever the reason, nothing happened, not even when they got out a road atlas and found Eugene so they could attempt to concentrate their power on the town itself.

"I'm sorry," Rick said when they finally gave up. "I guess our ability doesn't extend to life and death."

Andrea sniffed. "I . . . that's all right. You tried. Thank you for that."

"You're welcome. And we're truly sorry," Rick said. "If we learn anything more that might help, we'll definitely let you know."

She thanked them again and hung up. Rick set the phone back in its cradle and lay back against his pillow. "I have a bad feeling about this," he said.

Part Four

ONE GIANT LEAP

Eugene was just the beginning. Once the news got out, there were mass die-offs in cities throughout the country. But Eugene was the only town where every dog had died. The number involved in each instance shrank steadily as the day drew on, which led Rick to speculate that owners who truly cared about their animals were able to protect them somehow once they learned there was a threat. Either that or people were focusing their rage on specific targets now.

Quite a few people claimed just that, saying they had exhausted every other effort to get their neighbors to shut up their dogs, and so had resorted to psychic measures once they realized it was possible.

Predictably, a rash of murders followed those announcements. All but one of those murders involved conventional methods—which lent a little weight to Rick's theory and reassured him a little at the same time. He had been hoping that an individual person's will to live would protect them against someone else's will to kill them, but there had been no good way to test that.

He still didn't know if that's how it worked, but the one psychic murder didn't disprove his theory. It was hard to even call it murder. Rick imagined that it—and more cases like it—were going to mess up the courts for years to come. An elderly woman whose neighbor claimed to have wished her six Pomeranians to death responded by wishing *him* dead, and a hundred-foot fir tree had later fallen on his house, crushing him as he gave an interview on national TV. The kicker: The fir tree had been only twelve feet tall a moment earlier.

There were also plenty of dead cats, usually in proximity to avid flower gardeners. There were far fewer cats than dogs, however, and one university biology professor proposed studying the feline brain to see if they did indeed have some latent psychic ability that protected them from harm, as folklore often said they did.

The psychic vigilantism wasn't limited to animals, either. Within hours of the revelation that people other than famous astronauts could control reality, there was a rash of engine failures in muscle cars and jacked-up pickups, blocking roads all across the nation. The stereos in low riders with subwoofers began exploding in spectacular electrical short circuits. All the gas-powered leaf blowers in America turned into boa constrictors, which luckily faded away before they could break more than a few ribs of their startled handlers. And in northern Idaho, an enclave of white supremacists suddenly found their faces glowing bright green.

The one shared factor in all the occurrences seemed to be the pent-up frustration of people who had had to live with such blatant violations of common decency for too long. Pundits in England suggested that America was about to become a civilized country at last, and plenty of Americans agreed with them, but the people who lost pets, cars, stereos, and the like weren't so jolly.

Rick and Tessa broke their seclusion to go on TV to urge people to control their tempers, but it did little good. They received thousands of death threats, most of them from dog owners who accused them of masterminding the demise of their darling companions. For one alarming moment Rick collapsed with chest pains that felt like classic heart-attack symptoms, but Tessa rushed to his side and he instantly felt better.

"Don't you dare let those bastards touch you!" she said fiercely. "Ignore them!"

"I will if you will," he said, trying not to let his fear show. He told himself he'd just gotten a bad case of indigestion, and refused to let himself dwell on any other possibility.

Even so, he kept her within sight as much as possible from

then on. Not just for his own good, either. He didn't know if he could help if anything happened to her, but her presence had certainly revived him, and he didn't want to risk either of them getting hurt if he could prevent it.

In other countries, the arguments weren't so petty. Dogs and cats and cars weren't nearly as important in nations still struggling for basic human rights. In the Middle East, women quickly discovered that they could strike out at their fundamentalist tormentors from behind the veil; and Eastern Europeans learned that even if they couldn't kill one another directly with the sheer force of their mutual hatred, they could burn each other's houses down and make refugees out of everyone, then kill each other with conventional weapons.

Internet sites sprang up as quickly as their programmers could upload the files, urging people to band together behind this cause or that. Print media weren't far behind. The ads weren't even all selfish. The *New York Times* gained an immense amount of good will, if only modest success, with its front-page photo of a homeless man sleeping on a steam grate over the caption, "Could you spare a kind thought today?"

Television ministries also got into the act, with evangelists exhorting their flocks to "Dig *deep* into your psychic pockets and *divest* yourselves of your worldly encumbrances!" That stopped when one in particular, the Reverend Bob "Bobby" Bobbison, said, "Jesus tells us that it is easier for a camel to go through the eye of a needle than for a rich man to enter into the Kingdom of God. So let *me* shoulder the burden of your earthly wealth so that you may pass unhindered into Heaven! Don't imagine riches for yourselves; send it all to me! Everything you've ever wanted, send it to me!"

It wasn't embarrassment that stopped the others, though that should have been reason enough. No, they only toned down their pleas for money after Bobby wound up crushed under $10,358,464 in cash, seven tons of miscellaneous jewels, a kilo of cocaine, three speedboats, and a double-wide trailer. All of which vanished not long after his bikini-clad "disciples" finished counting it.

Rick and Pope Thomas got a good laugh out of that, but the rest of their phone conversation wasn't as mirthful. Rick had called to ask for advice, but he wound up giving more than he received.

The Pope had problems of his own. Two thousand years of attempting to guide the lives of mankind had put the Catholic Church in the midst of practically every crisis on the globe. They were revered by their followers and hated by their detractors, and Thomas had inherited the whole mess.

"The good news," he said jokingly as he described the interplay of forces that had come to bear on him, "is that I can manifest real doves of peace now when I give a public audience. But the bad news is, they turn into bats about twenty feet away from my hand."

"That's, um, that's a problem," Rick admitted.

"You're telling me. Pigeon shit is hard enough to clean off your miter, but have you ever been hit with fresh bat guano?" Thomas chuckled softly, but then he said, "I wish that was the worst of my problems. People have always loved killing each other over what they think everybody ought to believe, but now that they can see how the number of believers affects the way the world actually works, they're going crazy trying to wipe out anybody who doesn't agree with them. And the worst part of it is, in my capacity as leader of the Church, I haven't got a moral leg to stand on. Killing infidels to boost our own power used to be official doctrine."

"Used to be," Rick said. "But it's not anymore. I've never been happy with the idea that an organization can't leave its old baggage behind if it changes its ways."

"Original sin is another one of our founding principles." Thomas sighed. "Man, I sometimes think I should just close the doors and turn out the lights."

Rick could hardly believe his ears. This was the Pope talking! "Hey, are you all right?" he asked.

"Oh, sure," Thomas said. "Medically, at least. I've got enough faithful followers to keep me from succumbing to the hatred of the rest. But it's depressing to see the world heading back into chaos again so quickly after all we've done to make it a better place."

Rick looked at the television, which he had left on with the sound down low. A cop show he didn't recognize showed yet another car chase. "People have a short attention span," he said.

The Pope took a sip of whatever he was drinking, then said, "What we need is something to focus their attention again. Something positive for them to get behind instead of dwelling on how much they hate their neighbors. Your wedding drew people together like never before, but we need something that'll last longer."

"Like another Apollo flight?" Rick asked.

"Been there, done that."

Rick laughed. How true. But another thought came to him, one he wasn't sure he wanted to voice. He bit his lip, trying to decide, but finally said, "How about a trip to Mars?"

The Pope was quiet for a long few seconds before he said, "That might be a start."

CHAPTER 39

The President grinned from ear to ear when her secretary ushered Rick and Tessa into her office again.

"I assume your presence here means you've re-thought your position," she asked.

"Got it in one," Rick replied, pulling up a chair for Tessa and then one for himself. He hardly felt self-conscious at all in the Oval Office this time.

"I've already assembled a phase 1 team for you," Martinez said, opening a drawer and taking out a folder. "If you don't like any of the people I've picked, we can give the bushes another shake, but these guys should be able to shoulder the management burden and most of the grunt work and let you two get on with the real work of designing and building the hardware."

She handed the folder to them, and Rick saw a list of titles and names, most of whom he recognized as mavericks within NASA. One, Delia Rose, a former talk-show host, would be their public relations guru. A couple names were new to him. Like the CEO. "Who's Allen Meisner?" he asked.

"Chairman of the International Network of Scientists Against Nuclear Extermination."

"International Network of . . . INSANE?" Tessa asked, laughing.

"That's right. I thought it would be appropriate to have a mad scientist running the project." She held up her hand. "Now before you get your panties in a knot, let me say he's a damned fine administrator. He knows how to delegate, and he also knows how to do the jobs he's delegating. Something very few people in management do. His only weakness is that he loves wacky science and he'll want to spend most of his time in the lab with you rather than pushing paper in his office. If that gets to be a problem, let me know and I'll wind him back up and set him on track again, but you should at least give him a chance first. He's good."

"He sounds perfect," Tessa replied, still giggling.

"He is." Martinez reached out and flipped over the page of names, showing them a tentative timetable. Rick saw that the first item was "Unmanned landing," dated less than three weeks in the future.

"Uh . . . that won't work," he said. "Mars is a *long* ways away."

"I'm aware of that," she said. "Last time we talked, Tessa suggested creating the probe in space. Why not start out with it most of the way there?"

Rick leaned back in his chair. Was it possible? He and Tessa hadn't been able to revive a townful of dogs from just across the country. But this would be different. Rick really *wanted* to explore the other planets.

"Why don't we just create the thing already on the ground?" he asked.

Martinez laughed. "Because we want a space program, not a spy mission. We want to learn how to do this even without magic tricks if we have to. Use it for what you can—and for the sake of public interest, make it as glitzy as possible—but try to build us a solid foundation that won't vanish the moment I get caught diddling an intern."

Rick felt himself blushing. Martinez saw it and laughed. "That was a figure of speech, Mr. Spencer. Now go. *Boldly* go where no one has gone before. Let's see if we can't take the human race to the stars while we've got the chance."

She was serious, wasn't she? Rick felt a thrill run up his spine at her words. For the first time since he'd felt the thrust of the Saturn V press him into his seat, he felt like he might actually be going somewhere. It might be another publicity stunt geared as much toward placating the masses as leading them into space, but he could hear the conviction in the President's voice and he heard it in his own as he said, "We'll do it." He'd been reluctant only a few days ago, but now he realized the President had been right all along. You don't look a gift horse in the mouth, and you don't let opportunity stand on your doorstep in the rain. Not when there are so many other people willing to take them in and use them for their own agendas.

Okay, the first problem is durability," said Allen. "We don't want to make something that'll disappear on us halfway to Mars. I see two ways of doing that. One: Build real hardware for the back end of the mission, and use the power of positive thinking just for the launch."

He rubbed his nose, a gesture no doubt left over from his days in high school when he wore black plastic glasses with electricians' tape around the bridge.

He, Rick, Tessa, and the eleven other scientists in their phase 1 group were gathered in the meeting room of their new office building: in reality the living room of a modular home parked beside a warehouse-style lab on the flat volcanic plain east of Taos, New Mexico. That was one of the few stretches of open desert left that wasn't already a military reservation or a national park, and it had the added advantage of being smack-dab in the middle of an ancient place of psychic power. Nobody knew if that would make any difference or not, but they figured it couldn't hurt.

Plus there was Los Alamos just to the south if they needed any conventional science done. It had been a long time since the Manhattan Project, but the place had been designed for a rush job and it could no doubt be cranked up for another one if necessary.

In the meantime, a baker's dozen scientists, astronauts, and publicists—plus one for luck, Hobbit style—were giving it their best shot on their own. They were seated around the dining table, drinking coffee and munching corn chips while they brainstormed. With its carpeted floor and textured walls and comfortable furniture, the place had a homey feel that beat the heck out of most meeting rooms.

"Option two," said Allen, standing by the head of the table "and by far the cheapest if we can figure out how to do it, is to make the stuff you create last for good. Like Tessa's ring. How did you do that?"

"I have no idea," said Rick. "It didn't actually last for good, anyway. When people lost faith in us, it vanished like everything else."

"Yeah, but it's been solid as a rock ever since, even after the dead-dog business. At least I assume it has. Any flickers, Tessa?"

"No," she said, turning the ring around on her finger.

"So it's fundamentally different from the other stuff you've made. We ought to see if we can figure out how and why." There was a white dry-erase board on the wall beside him; he wrote RING on it in green ink, then said, "Not everything else disappears, either. The effects last. A photo of something you create doesn't disappear when the thing itself does. You didn't come to a screeching halt every time the Apollo capsule faded out on your way to the Moon, so we know momentum doesn't disappear." He wrote MOMENTUM on the board.

"Also, when you burn something or blow it up, it doesn't get better afterward, either. The effects of psychic intervention are durable." He wrote EFFECTS on the board. "So we could use psychic stuff to create real stuff, and the real stuff would stick around."

"Von Neuman machines?" Rick asked.

"Maybe. We don't necessarily want gadgets whose only job

is to make more gadgets, but if you can make a gadget that makes a gadget that makes something useful, that would be cool."

Rick had to take a moment to parse that out. He finally got it, but he wondered if it would be possible to create something that required such an abstract concept to describe. All the things they had created so far, no matter how complicated, had been easy to conceive of and easy to visualize.

He would try it, of course, but he didn't have high hopes. Like making a photocopy of a photocopy, he imagined the fidelity of what they were trying to achieve would suffer the farther it got from the original act of creation.

They brainstormed a while longer on general concepts, then switched over to their first actual mission: to create a probe already most of the way to Mars, land it, and beam images back to Earth. They sketched out a few basic concepts for an orbiter and a landing craft, the NASA people excitedly describing some of the ideas that had never made it past the design stage for lack of a development budget, but when they started talking about ion drives and Orion braking and BIS code burst data transmission, Rick held up his hands and said, "Wait a minute. I haven't got a clue what any of this stuff looks like. I don't even know what some of it *is*. How am I supposed to create something I don't understand?"

The conversation in the room came to a sudden halt. "Pictures?" someone asked.

Tessa laughed.

"What?"

"When I was a kid, *Mad* magazine had an article where they took kids' drawings of what they wanted for Christmas and built them exactly the way the kids drew them. Wacky perspective, parts extending right through other parts, stuff like that. I remember a red wagon with a triangular box, and jagged wheels with spokes that stuck out past the rims, and a handle that looked like a couple of sticks because the kid had used brown crayon and that's what it looked like in the drawing. If we try to make something we're not familiar with, you're probably going to get the same sort of thing."

"We'll make the drawings accurate," one of the engineers said.

"Down to the last bolt and wire?"

"Come on, you made a complete Saturn V," he said. "You can't tell me you knew where every bolt and wire on one of those went. Nobody does."

"Rick made the Saturn V," Tessa said.

Everyone looked over at Rick. "I know a lot about the Saturn stack because I was a total space geek when I was a kid," he said, "but I don't know it that well. I had to be drawing on someone else's knowledge when I made it."

"Precisely. And you can draw on ours when you make the Mars probe."

"Maybe," he said. "We'll see. Put that on the list of things to test before we go for the real thing."

Tessa said, "What if we can't make something just from design specs? What then?"

"Do another *Mars Observer*?" Rick asked. "*Pathfinder*?"

"Been there, done that," said Delia, their media handler. "We're supposed to be building excitement toward a manned mission. Maybe we can drive another Sojourner around to survey a good landing site, but that won't get much attention. We need glitz. Something the media can put on the front page."

They kept talking, and eventually ended up with a dry-erase board full of ideas, but Rick felt a blanket of gloom settle over him at the prospect of intentionally staging a media circus in order to gain support. He knew all the reasons, even agreed with them, but he still wasn't sure if the end justified the means. Or in this case, if the means justified the end. After all, who were they to use saving the world as an excuse to build a new space program?

CHAPTER 40

Despite his doubts, he and Tessa went on television the next day to promote their new endeavor. They described the President's mandate to lead humanity back into space, and outlined the various methods they had discussed to achieve it. Throughout their interview, they stressed the importance of public support, urging people to set aside their differences and pull together for a common cause.

"This could be the next stage in human evolution," Rick said at one point. "We've got an amazing opportunity to choose where we go next, metaphorically as well as physically; let's not blow it over barking dogs and ancient feuds."

Tessa went on to describe some of the obstacles they still faced, chief of which was the ephemeral nature of everything they created with psychic power. "We still don't know all the rules," she said, "but it's looking more and more likely that psychic creations only last as long as the creator is actively aware of them and the people who lend their support to them still care." She waved her left hand, and suddenly held a bright red balloon. "The moment either condition ceases to be met . . ." She waved her right hand, held up a pin, and popped the balloon.

Then she held up her left hand again, the ring on her next-to-last finger glittering under the stage lights. "I'm wearing proof right here that you still care about Rick and me, and I'm very flattered that you do. But I'd like to ask you to extend that concern to include the welfare of the entire human race. Let's look toward the future instead of the past or the present, and let's take this opportunity to lift humanity out of the cradle once and for all."

After the cameras were shut down, they gathered with their

publicity department—Delia—and went over their presentation.

"You used too many big words," she said. "People think 'ephemeral' is the stuff bugs use to communicate with. Saying 'evolution' was probably a bad idea, too. We lost half the South over that one. And Tessa, I'm sorry to say it, but you looked more smug than flattered when you held up that ring. People don't like smug."

"Sorry," she said, her face falling. "I was trying to look sincere."

Delia laughed. "Oh, honey, you've got a lot to learn about TV. Sincere *always* looks smug in front of a camera. Smug looks shifty, and shifty looks nervous. I think it's the bright lights or something. But listen, I don't mean to sound like you guys choked out there. It went great. We just want to refine your performance for next time."

Rick groaned. Next time. He'd known when he became an astronaut that the job would occasionally involve public appearances, but he'd never learned to like them. Now that his job depended on public support, he was going to be doing it more than ever.

Fortunately, it also involved real science. Real woo-woo science, which Delia urged him to call *new* science from now on, but it was still science. They tested their ability to manifest objects at greater and greater distances by making ordinary radio transmitters appear in Earth orbit, on the Moon, and beyond. The transmitters failed almost immediately because they weren't built to withstand the cold and vacuum of space, but that was part of the plan. Tessa's public entreaty notwithstanding, they had enough public support nowadays that when they both concentrated on something it lasted a couple of hours, and they didn't want a couple dozen radios beeping away incessantly, adding to the background noise of an already-jammed electromagnetic spectrum while they worked.

All they needed were a few beeps that they could time for distance and measure for signal strength; after that the transmitters could die and quietly fade back into the quantum foam.

They quickly discovered that they could manifest things all the way out to Mars, so that part of the project wouldn't be a problem. They also discovered that the radios were appearing the moment Rick and Tessa concentrated on bringing them into existence. Their signals returned at the speed of light, but if the distance measurement was even remotely accurate—and the attenuation of signal strength confirmed that it was—then the speed of thought appeared to be infinite.

That one observation alone should have shaken mainstream science to its core, but by that point there was very little core left to shake. University physics departments were struggling to maintain credibility without crossing the line into credulity, but it was a losing battle. Anyone willing to sacrifice their silverware drawer to a little experimentation could prove that there was much more going on in the world than physicists were willing to admit even now. Faster-than-light communication was just one more item in a rapidly growing list of things that scientists had missed or been too conservative to accept.

Naturally the Taos group continued onward, manifesting radios farther and farther out into the solar system and beyond. Distance simply didn't seem to matter; their Pluto signal came in five days after they concentrated on sending a radio out to it, just as faithfully as all the others. Just for the fun of it they imagined one going all the way to Alpha Centauri, and made a note to listen for the beeps in 4.2 years.

Their attempts to create a real space probe were less successful. They were able to make a *Sojourner*, which everyone had fun directing around through the sagebrush outside their lab, and they were able to make half a dozen other existing deep-space probes as well, but no matter how well the design team drew their pictures of the new hardware, neither Rick nor Tessa could bring it into existence.

The designers even tried it themselves, under the theory that since they knew what they wanted, they might have more success coaxing it out of the quantum foam, but even though they could bend spoons with the best of them, without the intense public support that Rick and Tessa commanded, making things appear was beyond their ability.

It looked like they might have to resort to bugging the universe from home after all. But that wasn't what they were after. Like President Martinez had said, they wanted a space program, not a spy mission. This wasn't about exploring the planets so much as exploring human potential.

"Maybe we need to start closer to home," Rick said during another of their brainstorming sessions. "We discovered ice on the Moon; why don't we go back there and build a colony? We can do that with Apollo technology while we figure out how to go to Mars."

Allen shoved his imaginary glasses up his nose. "I don't know. A permanent Moon base is pretty sexy, but not as sexy as going to Mars. Besides, we don't know for sure if that ice is real, either."

"What?" Rick asked, shocked. "You think we faked it?"

"No, of course not," Allen replied. "But what about wishful thinking? Who's to say you didn't *make* it?"

Jesus. It was possible. How would they know? They had only been there a few hours; the whole crater full of snow could have been just as chimerical as the spacecraft that took them there.

"We need to send another probe back to find out," he said.

"And how do we know that the ice won't reappear just when the probe's there?" Allen asked. "We've proven beyond a shadow of a doubt that expectations lead to all sorts of odd occurrences."

"If it appears every time someone looks for it," Tessa said, "then does it matter if it's not there the rest of the time?"

Allen laughed. "This whole situation does lead to radically different notions of permanence. Offhand, I'd say it doesn't matter as long as we can count on it. But the moment we need it most—and thus fear its disappearance most—that's when it's likely to vanish for good."

xperience certainly seemed to bear him out. But one artifact—Tessa's ring—stubbornly refused to follow the rules. It
was as real as rocks now. It didn't even fade out the day that
Tessa, angry at yet another failed attempt to build even a habitat dome for their Mars mission, blamed it all on Rick, called
him a "pessimistic throwback to the Newtonian era," and
stormed off to sulk in their bedroom with the door closed.

Their first glimmer of understanding came from an unusual
source just a day after their next televised progress report.

World news was not good—a new leader had risen to
prominence seemingly overnight in Eastern Europe, promising the war-torn Balkan states independence and revenge
upon the powers that had oppressed them for so long—but
Rick and Tessa tried to put a good spin on what was going
on in America, at least. People seemed to be adjusting to the
new science much more readily than anyone had expected.
Sociologists had predicted that people would have to go
through a grieving process for their former belief system
before they could accept the new, and that was certainly true
in many cases, but the vast majority of Americans had
always believed in paranormal phenomena. Ghosts were
nothing new to them, and they had seen Uri Geller bend
spoons on TV. Maybe one in fifty had also seen James Randi
demonstrate how how it was all fakery, and maybe one in
ten of those had believed him, but the vast majority had
accepted the self-proclaimed psychics at face value. Like
Rick's mother and the photos of his wedding proposal, they
trusted what they had seen with their own two eyes, no matter what the source.

So the most heavily industrialized nation on Earth was

having surprisingly little trouble accepting the paranormal into their everyday lives. Agreeing what to do with it was tougher, and state legislatures were full of hastily drawn bills attempting to regulate it, but that was a doomed effort and everybody knew it. People were going to do what they damn well pleased inside their own heads, and if the effects of that were suddenly more apparent in the outside world, well, the world would just have to learn to deal with it. If that meant being more polite to one another for fear of supernatural retribution, so be it. Only assholes needed to worry, right?

It wasn't that simple, of course, but that was the mind-set that prevailed when it came time for Rick and Tessa's progress report. So the world's most popular couple described what they were doing in Taos, and urged everyone to keep them in their thoughts while the Mars team tried to assemble some order amid the chaos. At Delia's suggestion, they stressed how difficult it was to keep things from fading away, and how they were struggling to figure out how to make their creations permanent. ("A little drama goes a long ways toward winning hearts," Delia had told them.) They concluded with a plea for support, and a promise to televise every major step they took "toward humanity's collective goal to break free of the bonds of Earth and become true citizens of the galaxy."

As if they had any other choice. If they didn't televise their progress, they would be forgotten in days.

They had barely switched off the cameras when the phone rang. Normally Delia answered the phones, but she was busy with the camera crew so Rick picked it up. A hesitant male voice said, "Hi, this is Walter Jimson from Grover's Mill, New Jersey. I've got something in my barn you might ought to have a look at."

"What kind of something?" Rick asked, already wondering how he could get this kook off the phone gracefully.

"Well, sir, have you ever heard of Orson Welles?"

"The movie director? Yeah, sure I have, but what does that have to do with—"

"He was a radio announcer back when my grandfather was about my age. Did a broadcast on Halloween of 1938 about an invasion from Mars."

"Oh, sure," Rick said. "He did H. G. Wells's *War of the Worlds*. I heard a tape of that once."

"Then you know it caused quite a panic around these parts."

"I'd heard that, yes."

"My grandfather owned this farm back then. He was listening to the radio that night when he heard something out in the pasture. So he grabbed up his shotgun and went out to have a look, figuring it might be somebody tryin' to steal a cow for the meat, you know, since the Depression was still going on back then, but when he got outside he saw this huge water tower walking around on three legs, shooting his dairy cattle with a heat ray."

Rick couldn't help laughing. "You're telling me he saw a Martian?"

Walter stayed perfectly calm as he said, "There's no way to tell if it came from Mars. Given what's been going on the last few weeks, I'd bet it didn't come from any farther than my grandpa's imagination. But wherever it came from, I've still got its armor in the barn."

The hair on the back of Rick's neck stood straight out. "What? You've still got it?"

"Yep." Now the satisfaction was evident in Walter's voice.

"Holy shit. You're darned right I want to have a look at that. How do I find you?"

Walter gave him directions, which involved landmarks like "the old Steigler place" and "the white Texaco station with the CO-OP sign still painted on the side." He gave Rick a phone number to call in case he got lost, and Rick promised to be there just as soon as he could gather up a crew and jump in the plane.

Six hours later, he, Tessa, and Allen stood under the glare of a floodlight in the middle of a hay-filled post-and-beam barn, staring at a pile of rusty metal on a tarp on the ground. At first glance the pieces looked like tractor fenders, or maybe wedges of an old-style satellite dish, but on closer examination it was easy to see that the three big curved sections fit together to form a mushroom-shaped tank about fifteen feet across. Tiny slits near the top looked like eyeholes in medieval armor. A ragged hole the size of Rick's fist dimpled the side of one section, and three hollow, articulated legs lay folded beside it, one of them twisted and crushed as if a heavy weight had landed on it.

"Shotgun blast?" Rick asked, pointing to the hole.

Walter, a thin, weathered man in bib overalls and a John Deere cap, nodded. "Yep. Grandpa was using double-ought buck. He told me he hit the leg first and the thing fell forward, and when it hit the ground one of the tentacles wrapped around his leg so he shot it point-blank in the side."

"Tentacles?" Tessa asked.

"Big bullwhips that came out from underneath."

"What did you do with the body?"

"Body, hell, what did you do with the heat ray?" said Allen.

"The body went into a hole in the ground out back," Walter said. "It started to stink real quick. The heat ray is long gone. It never worked after the Martian fell on it anyway."

Rick stared at the dark brown metal. "I can't believe this. I mean"—he added hastily—"I believe it well enough, but *man*, who'd have thought? The public hysteria that night when people thought they were really being invaded must have been way worse than the history books let on."

"It was pretty bad," Walter said. "Grandpa said he only told one person about the Martian, because after everybody learned the radio show was a hoax he didn't want to stir up any more trouble."

"Who did he tell?" asked Tessa.

"FDR."

"Roosevelt?" said Rick. "The President knew about this?"

"Yep. That's what happened to the heat ray. When we got into World War II, Grandpa reminded him he had it, and Roosevelt had him send it to the Army. They apparently couldn't make it work."

"The Army?" Rick laughed. "That's why those buggers already had a secret psychic weapons program! They knew this sort of thing could happen!"

Tessa asked quietly, "Your grandfather. Is he still alive?"

Walter shook his head. "No, he died back in '63 or '64."

"But this is still here."

Allen reached out and rapped a knuckle on one of the curved metal sections. It gave out a deep, resonant "dong." "We'd love to take a piece of this back with us to study in the lab," he said. "If we can figure out why it didn't fade away, we'll be a whole lot closer to learning how to make a reliable spaceship."

"To go look for real Martians?" asked Walter.

Allen stood up. "No, we already know there aren't any— uh-oh."

"What?" Tessa asked.

"There aren't any *now*. What if people learn about this? Will they suddenly start believing in Wellsian Martians again? And if they do, will there suddenly *be* Wellsian Martians again?"

Four people looked at one another under the floodlight glare. "Shit," said Rick.

CHAPTER 42

Walter obviously knew how to keep a secret. That left Rick, Tessa, Allen, and the rest of their group as potential leaks. They trusted each other, but fourteen people couldn't keep a secret for long, especially when the whole world was looking over their shoulders. So they only took one piece of the carapace back to Taos with them. That much didn't look like anything unusual, and even if word got out that it was part of something supernatural, nobody would guess what it was.

They quickly learned why it was so ineffective as armor. Wells's Martians fought with heat rays, so their armor was designed to reflect light rather than deflect projectiles. The surface had oxidized over the years, but a little polishing brought back the silvery shine, and a few minutes with a cutting laser revealed the ability to remain reflective even when the top layer vaporized under a prolonged assault.

"It's really battle armor," Allen said when they discovered that. "I thought it would just be sheet metal, the sort of thing a farmer would make it out of if he did it the hard way, but it's the real thing."

So how come a farmer could make laser-proof battle armor before the invention of the laser, but a couple of astronauts couldn't make a new kind of spaceship? Rick had no idea, but if they could learn how he'd done it, it would sure make their job easier.

They had no clue why the stuff hadn't disappeared like a bad dream the day after it had killed Mr. Jimson's cattle, either. They analyzed the metal and found it mostly iron, with traces of carbon, manganese, chromium, and tungsten, but that didn't tell them why it persisted. They tried making duplicates of it, and the duplicates tested chemically identical, but they also faded away if Rick or Tessa ignored them for more than a couple of hours.

Finally, in desperation, Rick called the Pope again. Maybe he would have an idea.

Rick was on hold for nearly twenty minutes before Thomas came to the phone, and when he did he sounded like he had been asleep. "Sorry to wake you," Rick said. "It could have waited."

"Wake me?" Thomas said, laughing shrilly. "Oh, what I wouldn't give for even an hour's sleep. I haven't slept in days."

"What's the matter?" Rick asked.

"Haven't you heard? We're fighting a war over here."

Rick had heard about the "Slavic uprising," as the papers had been calling it, but he hadn't realized it had reached all the way to Italy. "You mean right there, in the Vatican?" he asked.

"Not yet, but it's getting close," Thomas said. "They took Venice today to the north, and Brindisi to the south. They'll be coming at us from both directions as soon as they can build up their supply lines again."

Rick could hardly believe his ears. How could somebody invade Italy? "Jesus Christ! Pardon my French, but isn't the Army doing anything to stop them?"

Thomas said, "Oh, yes. They're fighting valiantly. They're also outnumbered and outgunned. And they're finding it rather difficult to kill ghosts."

"What?"

"Bagdonis is calling up phantom warriors to do his fighting for him. Like you did with the commandos in Hawaii. Only his aren't as civilized as yours. And everyone who opposes him adds to his strength with their anxiety."

"Bagdonis? Who's he?"

The Pope sighed. "No offense, but Americans really ought to pay more attention to the rest of the world. I know; I used to be one." He cleared his throat. "Sajudis Bagdonis is a Lithuanian, who sort of resented it when his country disappeared in the last round of border-shuffling. He's decided to bring it back, and expand its borders to make up for old debts. Like all the way to Portugal. He's already taken Poland and everything south of it, and now he's working his way east."

"Aren't the Lithuanians Catholic?" Rick asked, proud of knowing at least that much.

Thomas laughed. "Quite right. They'll no doubt spare the Vatican when they invade. Unfortunately I doubt if they'll extend the same courtesy to me. I'm not exactly the most popular pope in history."

"Sure you are," Rick said, but he knew he was speaking only for himself. Tradionalists hated Thomas, who had endorsed birth control, women in the priesthood, marriage for priests, and any number of other reforms designed to bring the Church into the twenty-first century.

"So what are you doing?" he asked.

"Oh, the usual attempt to rally the forces of good against the forces of darkness," Thomas answered flippantly. "But unfortunately, what we have here is the ideology of freedom against the ideology of dictatorship, and the quantum observer effect strongly favors the rigid structure of dictatorship. Everything freedom stands for is exactly wrong in this kind of war."

Rick remembered Toland's admonition about negative thoughts, but he didn't really think Thomas needed to hear it. He knew that already.

"What about NATO?" Rick asked. "Aren't they able to do something?"

"They have most gallantly offered to drop nuclear bombs on Bagdonis's army whenever Italy gives the word, but unfortunately Bagdonis has a nasty habit of quartering them in cities we would really rather not obliterate."

"How about *me*? Can I do any good?"

The Pope thought it over for a good long time before he said, "This isn't your war."

"It sounds like it could become my war soon enough if he tries to take over all of Europe. Besides, it sounds like this Bagdonis guy is using my bag of tricks. No pun intended. I can't stand back and watch him do that."

Thomas's voice grew more intense, as if he were talking to an audience. "You do not know war, my friend. You have not watched your friends killed in battle, nor seen your wife and daughters raped and murdered, nor witnessed your home burning to the ground while enemy soldiers roast your baby on bayonets in the flames. Americans try to make war a civilized entertainment to be televised back home, but it never stays that way for long. If you come here, you will see these things, and worse. It may not be your family and your home, but if you come here, you will see it happen. And you will probably die yourself, possibly without striking a blow. That, too, is war."

Rick's stomach lurched at the images Thomas's words evoked. His heart was speeding up and he was starting to sweat at the thought of what he was getting into, but he said, "I believe you. And I'd much rather stay here and build rockets, but I don't know if I could do that knowing that people were dying over there because I didn't help." He swallowed. "Like it or not, Tessa and I are probably the most powerful people on the planet right now, at least in terms of psychic ability. If we sit on our thumbs over here and let you guys go down in flames, we're not going to be able to live with ourselves."

Thomas actually yelled into the phone. "Do not allow Tessa to come over here!"

"I can try to talk her into staying," Rick said, "but she's not mine to order around."

"Then if you love her, stay home with her."

"I can't do that. Not now."

"You don't know war," Thomas said again. "Stay home,

Rick. I mean it. If you must go somewhere, go to Mars. You'll do humanity more good in the long run by providing hope than by fighting evil."

Someone spoke to him for a moment, then Thomas said, "I have to go. They need me to decide which holy relics to ship to America for safekeeping." He spoke to the other person on his end for a moment, then said, "But I forget my manners. You called me, not the other way around. What did you call about?"

"I don't even remember," Rick said. "Jesus, I can't let you—"

"You can. I insist on it. Give us hope, not just another warrior. Yes, coming! I have to go. I'll speak with you again when I get the chance. I said I'm coming!" He hung up before Rick could say anything more.

Rick sat there in his chair at the conference table, looking out over the sagebrush plain. The Sangre de Cristo Mountains rose high in the east, dwarfing the town at their base. Blood of Christ. A pretty name, here; about to become reality over there. How could he sit by and let some pissant dictator march all the way across Europe again? The last time America had tried that they'd wound up in the war anyway, and they'd had to drop nuclear bombs on Japan to stop it.

He got up and went looking for Tessa.

CHAPTER 43

She wanted to go. Allen told them both they were being stupid. He had been in Vietnam; he had seen war. He described some of what he'd seen in such gut-wrenching detail that the Pope's description seemed tame by comparison, but he still didn't convince them to stay put.

"I feel responsible!" Rick said.

"Tough," Allen replied. "Fighting for peace is like screwing for celibacy. Even if you *are* responsible, which you're not, going off into battle isn't going to help anything."

"How do you know?"

"Because I've *been* there, damn it!" Allen slapped the piece of Martian battle armor, which he'd clamped to a workbench to study. It rang like a gong. "You want to know how come this damn thing stuck around? Because it's a war relic, that's why. It's full of fear and anger and uncertainty. The people of New York and New Jersey were terrified that night! They thought the worst war in history was happening all around them. The strongest emotions in the world made this—" he slapped it again "and it'll take a lot more than another weapon to make it go away." He took a couple of deep breaths, then said, "If you want to help, find a way to make this fucker *dis*appear. Then maybe you'll have something you can use on Bagdonis."

Rick could not think of a single word to say in response to that. He looked at Tessa, who didn't seem inclined to say anything else, either.

Allen cleared his throat. "Sorry I yelled at you. But going over there would be the stupidest thing you could possibly do right now. The Pope is right: This is an ideological battle. So make love, not war, okay?"

"Here? Now?" Tessa asked, smiling weakly.

Allen blushed. Still a geek at heart. "Get out of here," he said.

They got. They had to dodge the six or seven paparazzi who had set up shop in the sagebrush outside their lab, but that was easy enough to do. Rick had already trained them to keep their distance after they had first arrived, threatening to fog their film if they became obnoxious. He had only had to follow through once. So he and Tessa drove past their camp on the way out, let them take a few close-ups, then told them they didn't want to be followed. As they drove away they could see the paparazzi debating it, and one even got into their car, but when Tessa made a few sparks dance on the hood the others dragged him out again before he could put it into gear. Fogged film was one thing, but doing engine repair in the prairie on a hot day was something else.

Rick and Tessa headed for the Rio Grande Gorge, a thousand-foot-deep notch in the volcanic plain that the river had carved after the lava flow had blocked its path. It was hardly visible until you reached it. Drivers on the road to Tres Piedras sometimes drove right onto the bridge before they realized it was there. Skid marks showed the spot where most people noticed.

There was a trail to the north of the bridge that led to a hot spring at the river's edge. Rick and Tessa checked for more paparazzi, concentrating on the back-of-the-neck feeling of being watched that they got when any were about, but they felt none so they walked down the trail, only to find another couple already in the spring.

These were locals. The man, a shaggy, dreadlocked and bearded type, just said "Hi." The woman, a long-haired brunette with freckles all the way down as far as Rick could see, said, "Come on in."

At least they weren't photographers. Feeling just a little self-conscious, Rick and Tessa said "Hello," stripped off their clothes, and slid into the water beside them. It wasn't hot-tub hot, but in the intense midday sun it felt fine. Moss covered the rocks, smoothing their edges and giving them a shaggy appearance.

They introduced themselves, just to be polite. The other couple, Mike and Star, knew them already. Star asked how the Mars project was going.

Tessa answered her, and then their talk turned to psychic healing, which Star was more interested in. She claimed to have been doing it for years, but her credibility had gone up immensely after Rick and Tessa had blown open the doors for mainstream acceptance.

Rick let himself drift as he listened to them talk. The west wall of the gorge was in shadow, and birds kept appearing and disappearing as they flew into and out of the sunlight. Cliff swallows, he supposed, though he imagined they could be hawks. It was hard to judge scale in a canyon this immense.

The rush of the river and the heat of the spring lulled him into a trance. It was hard to imagine that a third of the way around the world, people were killing each other over an ancient border dispute. That someone he knew was evacuating their home at this very moment, packing their valuables and fleeing the advancing army. Or that that someone was the Pope. The world was too strange.

Star's voice broke into his reverie. "So, do you guys mind if we make love? That's kind of why we came down here."

He pretended to be asleep while he waited for Tessa's reply, though he imagined his involuntary reaction would give him away pretty soon.

He thought about Allen's admonition just an hour or so ago to make love, not war. Tessa was no doubt thinking of that, too, because she said, "So did we," and scooted back to lean against Rick. Her bare skin felt even warmer than the water.

He put his arm around her. Kissed her. And on the other side of the world, the Pope fled the Vatican. The world was definitely too strange.

Rick called the President when they got home, just to make sure they weren't making a stupid mistake. The day's events seemed to be getting weirder by the moment, and just ringing up the President on the phone didn't help any, but they needed a reality check and somehow the notion of looking for it in Taos seemed counterproductive.

He got put on hold a few minutes this time, too, but in a surprisingly short time the President picked up and said, "I sure hope you're calling to report success. We need a major feel-good story."

"Well, uhh . . ." Rick said, looking across the dining/conference table at Tessa, "actually, the reason we called was to ask your opinion of the Balkan situation. Don't you think we should go over there and try to stop this Bagdonis guy?"

"Absolutely not," she said without hesitation. "Let the military take care of Bagdonis. Your job is to give us something to look *toward*. Now tell me you're going to do it."

Rick swallowed. "We're still working on it. But we're making progress. We've found something besides Tessa's ring that didn't fade away. Once we figure out how that works, we can start making actual, durable hardware. And once we do that, we're on our way."

"Good. What's your timetable?"

"It's, uh, still too early to say."

"Wrong answer. I want something in space in three days."

"Three days! That's imp—that's even sooner than our original projection."

"World events change fast, Rick. We can either keep up or get left behind. Your fifteen minutes of fame are ticking away."

"The only thing we could possibly cobble together in three days would be some meaningless spectacle," he protested.

"That's what they said about *Apollo 8*," Martinez replied. "They didn't have the LEM ready to flight-test, but they needed another launch to keep the public interest up. So they sent it around the Moon on Christmas Day. People called it a silly spectacle, but you know what?"

"What?"

"The crew of *Apollo 8* took the first photograph of the entire Earth. For the first time in history, people could see our planet all at once and think about how fragile it looked floating there in space. That one photograph spawned the entire environmental movement. So don't tell me a spectacle has to be meaningless."

"Hmm." He shifted uncomfortably in his chair. Tessa tilted her head, her eyes questioning. "We'll see what we can do."

"Good. Give Tessa a hug."

"We already tried that."

The President laughed a bit uncertainly. "Okay," she said. "You're obviously way ahead of me. Let me know when you're ready to launch. I'll need to make a speech."

"Right."

They said goodbye, and Rick hung up the phone.

"Well?" Tessa asked.

"We've got three days to get to Mars," he told her.

CHAPTER 44

They gave it their best shot. They worked around the clock trying to create something, anything, that could land on the red planet and do something that hadn't already been done there, but new hardware continued to be beyond their ability.

Old hardware, on the other hand, was getting easier and easier. Rick discovered that he could make a lunar module on command, fully fueled and ready to fly, just by waving his arms and imagining one sitting among the sagebrush outside their lab. In a fit of pique he made a full dozen of them, one right after another—more than NASA had in its entire program—and watched them like a hawk, defying them to disappear on him. He climbed inside one, checked its controls, even powered it up. In a what-the-hell mood he fired the descent engine, running the thrust all the way up to maximum, but it only generated a third of a gravity so of course it didn't go anywhere. It roared and rattled the thin metal walls and torched a few sagebrush, but that was it.

He climbed back out and looked at the smoldering remains of the gnarled bushes. Now why the hell had the rocket exhaust burned them, when an entire Saturn V lifting off from Pad 34 hadn't even singed the weeds growing there? Because he hadn't imagined them burning? Because back then he hadn't been aware he was controlling anything at all? Who could say? None of it made any sense.

"I *hate* this shit!" he yelled into the blue New Mexico sky. A couple of paparazzi out in the sagebrush snapped his picture, but he didn't care. Drama was good for the ratings, according to Delia.

Allen, who had been watching from the lab's open garage

bay, walked out to stand next to him. "It's certainly a challenge, isn't it?"

"Yeah," Rick said, feeling foolish now for losing his temper.

"But you just gave me an idea."

"What?"

"What if we plumb the fuel tanks together so we can burn all of it in the bottom stage? There'd be more than enough for a powered descent onto Mars, wouldn't there?"

Rick tried to imagine what that would be like. "I don't know," he said, looking at the ungainly spacecraft as he spoke. "It would take a long, long burn to lower the lander's velocity so it wouldn't go up in flames when it hit the atmosphere, and a continuous burn all the way *through* the atmosphere so it doesn't fall out of control, and then a full-throttle landing because the engine can barely outdo Mars's gravity even with empty tanks. That's a lot of fuel."

"Not if we start with less than orbital velocity to begin with," said Allen. "And we could put a parachute on the top to lower it through the atmosphere. Hell, the only time we really need the engine is for the landing."

"And then what do we do? This is a manned vehicle. After it lands, it just sits there."

"It's got a rover, doesn't it?" Allen walked up to it, searched a moment for the D-ring next to the ladder, and gave it a tug. The trapdoor dropped outward like felled tree, and the spindly rover bounced out, nearly tipping on its side when it hit a sagebrush. "The springs were designed for lunar gravity," Allen said. "They'll be fine on Mars."

"We still don't have a driver," Rick pointed out.

Allen reached into his hip pocket and pulled out a black-plastic case about the size of his wallet, opened it up, and showed Rick his day planner. "Ten megabytes of memory, fully programmable, with a USB port for controlling external devices," he said. "If we can't plug this into the steering system, I'm not a mad scientist."

Rick looked at the tiny gadget in his hand, imagining it controlling the thirty-year-old technology at his side. It didn't seem any crazier than the rest of this.

It took a few attempts, but in less than a day Allen had the rover driving around their lab, bumping into walls, backing up and going off in new directions, broadcasting a TV picture from the camera mounted on a pole in front. In the lander, the engineers plumbed the fuel tanks together and attached a parachute to the top hatch, which wouldn't be used for anything else anyway since there wouldn't be a command module to dock with.

Allen patched another palmtop computer into the flight control systems, stealing most of his code from an old landing simulator program popular in the eighties. It wasn't pretty, but it could read the radar altimeter's input and direct the engine's thrust for a soft landing, and that's all it needed to do.

He and the other engineers walked Rick and Tessa through the completed spacecraft, showing them exactly what they had done and how they had done it, then the two astronauts stood back and concentrated on making another one just like it.

The air shimmered—not unusual in the desert heat—then a second lunar module appeared next to the first. Allen climbed the ladder, peered inside, then leaned back out and said, "Looks good!" With his car alarm remote he sent the signal that activated a servo that released the rover, and it bounced out onto the ground, the camera on its post in front swiveled left and right, and it drove out into the sagebrush.

"Call the Prez," Allen said, sticking his thumbs in the waistband of his pants and puffing out his chest. "We've got a mission."

They launched it two days later. The plain around their lab had become an impromptu campground in the day since the President's announcement, with curious onlookers arriving by the busload, but that really didn't matter since the actual spacecraft was going to appear in Mars orbit anyway. Delia arranged for Porta-Potties and a tank truck of fresh water, after briefly considering and rejecting the idea of having Rick and Tessa make them from scratch. The more public support they got, the longer their creations seemed to last, but nothing would make them lose that support faster than having a toilet disappear on someone in mid-use.

They did at least make television sets so people could watch the landing, and they manifested a lander on the roof of the lab just for practice. The crowd cheered, and Rick decided that was as good a moment as any to do the real job.

They stood outside the lab, speaking into a microphone connected to a public address system with speakers on all four corners of the building. Cameras captured the proceedings from three angles, and one focused on a huge liquid crystal monitor showing the real-time image from the Hubble telescope of Mars in all its glory. Beside that, another monitor waited for the signal from Mars. Both image feeds came from JPL, who already had the downlink facilities in place, but that was the limit of their involvement. With luck, that would be all that was necessary.

"Okay," Rick said into the microphone, wincing as a howl of feedback built up before he could cover the screen with his hand. Allen quickly adjusted the volume and he tried again. "It may seem a little backwards, but as the President outlined in her speech yesterday, we're going to test the *middle* part of a mission to send people to Mars using this new technology we've discovered. Getting there and getting back with actual passengers is going to require a lot more careful planning, but we can at least test the landing phase remotely, which is what we're going to do today. In just a minute Tessa and I are going to make the actual lander in orbit around Mars, so if you all want to concentrate with us, link hands or whatever, we'll give it a try."

Another cheer rolled through the crowd, then died into an expectant hush. Someone started singing a single, deep-pitched "Ommmmmmm," and more people picked it up until the desert seemed to vibrate with energy. And this was just the local crowd. People all around the world—maybe even in Eastern Europe—were also watching, and lending the power of their consciousness to the project.

Rick and Tessa linked hands. A swirl of light, like fog in a breeze, twisted around them, and sparkles like tiny strobe lights burst out around them. Rick looked to Tessa, who winked at him. "Martinez wanted a spectacle," she whispered in his ear.

"Right. Let's give her one. You ready?"

"Ready."

They looked at Mars in the monitor. The Valles Marineris made a ragged, dark slash through the red surface to the right, and the four major volcanos pocked the left. Dark and light splotches marked the rest of the landscape, softened at the edges from millennia of blowing dust. They would try to bring the lander into existence a hundred miles up and directly over Olympus Mons. It would move eastward as the planet turned, coming down somewhere on the volcano's gentle flank. There was no reason to choose that spot over any other, except that it gave them a visual target to shoot for, someplace they could focus on while they worked their magic.

Feeling self-conscious about performing something so unusual—so *woo-woo*—in front of so many people, Rick closed his eyes for a moment and tried to banish his embarrassment. It never felt like he was doing anything special when he made things appear. He felt like a charlatan, waving his arms while someone else did the real work behind the scenes. He probably could do just that and let Tessa make the Mars lander on her own, but as they had discovered early on, their results were more powerful and more reliable when they both concentrated on the same thing.

So he tried to ignore the crowd at his back while he looked again at the monitor and imagined a lunar module appearing in space above the Martian surface, the planet's red glow reflecting off the gold foil covering its lower panels.

He had grown used to the sensation that came with a successful manifestation. It was sort of a prickling at the top of his spine, almost like being spooked, which he supposed was appropriate. He felt it now.

He relaxed. Tessa exhaled and looked away from the monitor. They would know in seven minutes whether or not they had succeeded.

The time ticked slowly away, the cameras recording the two astronauts as they watched the Hubble image and the still-blank lander monitor for indications of success. The national TV feed was showing a simulation of what they expected to happen so people wouldn't grow bored and switch channels, but Rick and Tessa and the crowd around the lab were content to watch the real-time monitors and wait.

At last the signal arrived. It flickered, and lines scrolled through it from signal degradation over interplanetary distances, but they could clearly see the landing legs sticking out into the triangular window's view, and the huge volcanic caldera below it.

"Altimeter reads 99.98 miles," Allen said, peering into the computer they had set up to monitor the flight instruments. "You guys are good!"

It certainly looked like it. Allen's pocket computer fired the engines automatically, then throttled down to let the planet's gravity draw the lander in. It rode the rocket down until the atmosphere grew thick enough for the parachute to do some good, then the computer shut down the engine and deployed the 'chute. Rick wished he had created a camera outside the lander so they could see more than the tiny patch of craters through the pilot's window, but it was still quite a view. For the first time in weeks, he felt the thrill of honest discovery. They might have gotten there with smoke and mirrors, but this was the real thing. That was really Mars on the monitor.

A few minutes later, the picture flickered and was replaced by a full view of the lander from directly overhead. The crowd gasped at the awe-inspiring view of Olympus Mons sliding past below, with the glittering spacecraft hanging from its tether in the middle of the picture.

"Did you switch to a simulation?" Rick asked Allen.

"No. That's coming from Mars."

"Well I'll be damned," Rick said. "I wanted a better view, but I didn't realize I was going to get one. I must have created a camera on the underside of the parachute."

Tessa laughed. "Be careful what you wish for in this business. You just might get it."

They watched the lander descend until it seemed that it had to crash. The surface details were so crisp it looked like they couldn't be more than a few feet away. But the engine didn't fire for a landing. "Allen?" Rick asked, his heart beating a little faster. "Altitude?"

"Nineteen thousand feet," Allen replied.

"Nineteen thousand? It can't be!"

"That's what it says. Eighteen-fifty now."

Rick tried to believe the instruments. He was too far away to pilot the ship remotely; he would be reacting to seven-minute-old data. The thing had probably landed already, or nearly so. But man, it was hard to watch it drop like this and trust a control system cobbled together at the last minute they way they had done.

He took Tessa's hand and held on tighter and tighter as the lander approached the surface. Finally, long after it looked like the LEM had to crash, they saw rocket exhaust billow out below it.

The view tilted when the explosive bolts blew the top hatch loose, and with it the parachute, but the weight of the hatch kept the 'chute from collapsing. From their bird's-eye view they watched the lander drop closer to the red surface, its shadow drifting lazily over the eroded landscape below.

Then something odd happened. The lander suddenly rose into the air again. The rocket throttled down to practically nothing, but the vehicle continued to rise until it struck the hatch still dangling from the parachute. One of its legs snagged a shroud line just as the lander started falling again, tipping it sideways. Attitude jets fired to correct for it, but they couldn't hold up the whole weight of the craft. It tipped farther and farther, its main engine throttling up at the same time, until it slipped free at an angle of maybe sixty degrees.

The view bounced as waves worked their way up and down the shroud line, but the watchers on Earth could see the lander racing across the ground, turning as the computer tried to bring it upright again, but it was too late. The lander merged with its pursuing shadow, a wave of red dirt blew outward ahead of it, and then the whole thing exploded in an even redder ball of flame.

The parachute camera continued to show the scene as metal panels rained back to the ground and the smoke cloud billowed out and drifted away on the breeze. It zoomed in slowly as it descended, like the end of a disaster movie where the credits are supposed to roll over the final image of death and destruction, but this just went on and on without interruption, focusing ever closer on Rick and Tessa's failure. Finally, about five minutes later, the picture flickered and went out.

"Loss of signal," Allen reported matter-of-factly.

Rick knew what had happened. In his moment of panic when he thought it was going to crash, he had lifted the lander back into the air, just as he had done with himself and Tessa and Yoshiko when they had fallen into the ocean. He had caused the crash.

He looked out at the crowd. They had watched, as stunned

as he, through the entire spectacle. Now he braced for a prolonged "Boo!" as they vented their frustration, so he was taken completely by surprise when they began applauding instead. Some of them cheered wildly, and one man with a particularly clear voice shouted, "Do it again!"

CHAPTER 45

Well, I guess Martinez got what she wanted," Rick said that night. He and Tessa had finally gone to bed, content with a job well-done—on the fifth try.

The person in the audience had been right. It didn't cost them anything to try again, even when the next lander set down in a crater and promptly tipped over, creating another fireball. So they had tried it again. ("Third time's a charm," Tessa had said to their TV audience, which Delia later reported had increased in number the minute word of their difficulties got out on other channels.) This time they managed to get one onto the ground safely.

Then the rover had dropped out of its bay, the computer had powered it up, and promptly driven it off a six-foot cliff.

The next landing went smoothly, but one of the rover's wire wheels caught on the ramp and the other three simply spun there, digging into the sandy soil until it was buried up to the fenders.

"Give it a push!" someone shouted, and Rick considered trying just that, but by now this was becoming personal. He was going to get one to work from the beginning if it took him all day. So, all embarrassment at performing in public gone in the heat of frustration, he and Tessa concentrated on making yet another one, and this time it performed flawlessly. The lander set down on a level site, the rover deployed correctly, and the computer drove it nearly ten miles before it ran out of battery power, its onboard camera beaming back hours of pictures of the rocky terrain the whole time.

That the whole thing was a total publicity stunt didn't matter a bit. The public had seen a proof of concept for future exploration, and had given it their seal of approval. And they had been entertained with drama and explosions on the way. Delia pronounced the whole thing a complete success, and said she couldn't have come up with a better production if she'd been allowed to stage the whole thing.

President Martinez took it from there in another speech the next morning, pointing to their project as an example of the positive potential for New Science. Their difficulties proved it was still new, but she urged the nation to look toward the future, when they could expect further refinements of the power of thought to provide limitless energy, an end to the degradation of the environment, and a better life for everyone. The first step toward achieving all of that, she told them, was to believe it could happen.

Unfortunately, Bagdonis and his followers preferred the more conventional method for improving their standard of living: taking it from someone else. Italy fell to his two-pronged attack just as Pope Thomas had said it would, and Austria, Switzerland, and Germany dropped like bowling pins behind it. France was gearing up for a massive defense of its borders, but Bagdonis had learned how to disable jet and rocket engines in flight, so they were already reduced to infantry before they had fired a shot.

"How does he do that?" Rick asked when heard about it on the morning news, but the moment he asked, he realized the answer. Like the people who had learned to kill their neighbors' dogs and disable their loud cars, or like himself with the paparazzi, Bagdonis and his followers no doubt simply imagined some vital component malfunctioning in the intricate engines driving the machines rallied against them.

What was next? Bullets that wouldn't fire? Why not? Tessa had already done that trick.

But apparently nobody on the NATO side could do it, or else Bagdonis's will was stronger than theirs, because otherwise his army wouldn't be able to capture city after city as fast as they could drive to them.

He looked at Tessa over their morning bowls of Cheerios and said, "I don't know if I can sit back and send more lunar modules to Mars while this guy is running around loose in Europe. We've given Martinez what she wants. Now I think it's time to go put a stop to this business, don't you?"

She looked out the window before answering. Rick followed her gaze. It was going to be another sunny day. The tent city that had sprung up around them in the last week was diminishing as people packed up after yesterday's excitement. A few would hang on, hoping to absorb some of Rick and Tessa's mystical powers, but the rest would go home, back to their jobs and their families. If they even paid any attention to what was happening in Europe, they would no doubt think it was not their concern. Other countries could use the new energy source for warfare if they wanted to, but America was going to the stars. After all, the President was telling them just that.

The problem with her plan was that there seemed to be a nearly infinite amount of power available. People could go to the stars *and* kill their neighbors if they wanted to. It hadn't happened in America yet, but it wouldn't be long before another focus of power came along, promising a better world if he could just get rid of all those pesky blacks, or Asians, or Baptists, or whatever minority the focus wasn't. The longer Bagdonis was allowed to run free overseas, the more likely it became that someone like him would start the same process here.

Or that he would start it himself after he was done with Europe.

Rick said, "What do you think?"

Tessa looked back inside. "Martinez will be pissed if we go."

"So what? At least we'll be able to live with ourselves."

"Yeah. But . . . she's the President."

"You know what I think the deal is with her? I think she's still in denial. She's willing to use this for fun and games, and she's got all sorts of great justification for it, but when it comes to counting on it for something vital, she backs off. She doesn't believe in it yet. Not down deep where it really counts."

Tessa laughed. "Does anybody? Do you?"

"I'm starting to. I wouldn't be suggesting we go fight a war in Europe if I didn't."

"Yeah," she said again. "I suppose you're right. So how do we go about actually beating this guy?"

That was the question, wasn't it? Just like going to Mars, it was one thing to say they wanted to use their psychic ability, and another thing entirely to actually do it. They would need professional help. Fortunately Rick knew just the person to call.

CHAPTER 46

General Marcus was no longer at Schofield Barracks. It took a few phone calls to track him down, but when they did, they were not surprised to find him in France, helping prepare for the big assault.

"Well, well, well," he said when he realized who was calling, "if it isn't Superman and Wonder Woman. Congratulations on your wedding."

"Thanks," said Rick. Tessa, on a second phone right next to him, said, "Sorry we messed up your clean room."

He snorted. "That's not all you messed up. This whole damned situation is your fault, you know."

"Maybe," Rick said. "I get the feeling something like it would have happened whether we were at the focus or not, but I'll admit we're the ones in the spotlight. We want to help stop it. What can we do?"

"You can't put the genie back in the bottle," Marcus said. "We're stuck with it for good now. Or do you just mean Bagdonis?"

"That was sort of what we were talking about," said Rick.

"Yeah, well, he's trouble enough for one day, that's for sure." He *hmmmed* for a bit, then said, "I really don't want the President breathing down my neck any more than she already is. Tell you what. You sent a LEM all the way to Mars; how about you see if you can drop a bomb on Bagdonis's head from right where you are."

"We don't know where Bagdonis is," Rick said. He didn't even know for sure where Lithuania was, but he wasn't about to tell Marcus that.

"Unfortunately, neither do we," the general said. "But you

were able to track down Tessa easy enough when I tried to move her. Think you'd be able to do that for him?"

"I don't know. Neither one of us knows him. We've really got no connection to him. I doubt if we'd have any luck at that."

"Why don't you try?" Marcus suggested sweetly, but his voice was full of mockery.

"All right, all right," Rick said, remembering why it had been so easy to hate this guy. But he closed his eyes and tried to imagine where Bagdonis might be. He got a vague image of a gray concrete building about five-stories tall and half a block on a side, with a four-lane street in front of it, but it was such a generic Eastern European city image that he knew he had just made it up in his own head.

Tessa had tried it, too, but a moment later she opened her eyes and shook her head. "Nothing," she said.

"Me neither."

Marcus said, "Why am I not surprised? That would have been way too easy. Well, then, come on over and join the party. I think we've probably got a day or two before he advances again, so maybe you can sense something from here before he does."

"We're on our way," Rick said. "Where do you want us?"

Marcus mulled it over, then said, "She'd skin me alive if I put you on the front lines. Paris ought to be safe enough. Fly to Paris. I'll have somebody meet you there."

They didn't tell Allen what they were doing. They told him they were driving to Albuquerque for an overnighter, and when they got there they bought plane tickets for Paris. They called Marcus again and gave one of his aides their flight number, then settled in for the long flight across the U.S., changed planes in New York, and flew on across the Atlantic. They didn't talk much on the plane. There wasn't much to

say. They had no idea what they would face when they got
there, and if they talked about it they would just scare each
other more than they already had.

Then the captain came on the intercom and did it to them
anyway. It was after dark by then, and the plane had just
started to descend when he said, "Ladies and gentlemen, I
regret to inform you we've had a slight change of plans. The
Paris airport has apparently been closed due to a . . . security
threat of some sort, so we've been diverted to London. We'll
be landing at Heathrow Airport in about thirty-five minutes.
There will be agents waiting at our arrival gate to assist you
with hotel or alternate travel arrangements, and there will
undoubtedly be more information available by then as well. I
apologize for the inconvenience."

Rick and Tessa looked at one another, and Tessa said the
one word they were both thinking: "Bagdonis."

They should have known they couldn't keep their presence a
secret. The first person who saw them in the airport recognized them and said, "Thank God you've come!" She
rushed up and gave them both hugs, and more people followed her until the waiting area was jammed with people calling out to one another, "They're here, they're here!"

They endured it with as much grace as they could despite
their embarrassment, but as the crowd swelled and cut off any
hope of a quick exit, Rick found himself wishing for a security
guard or someone to lead them out of there. The only officer
in sight was busy spreading the word, though, and as Rick saw
the expressions of relief on the faces around them he realized
just how threatened the Britons must feel. They had been
invaded from the Continent over and over again since Roman
times—hell, since before that. They knew just what sort of
atrocities were breathing down their necks yet again.

He tried pushing through the crowd, but people kept wanting to hug him or shake his hand, so he had only made it a few feet when he heard an even bigger commotion at the fringes of the crowd.

"Look out, he's got a knife!" someone shouted, and someone else said, "Knife? Go on, that's a sword!"

That got the security guard's attention. He waded into the crowd, saying, "Well, well, well, what have we here?" in an authoritative, situation-under-control voice.

"He's a loony!" someone called out. "Look, 'es wearing chain mail!"

Rick tried to see who they were talking about, but even when he stood on tiptoe he couldn't spot anyone carrying a sword. He could see the focus of the disturbance, though, as people backed away to give him room. Whoever it was must have been short.

He considered taking the opportunity to slip away, but if there really was someone with a sword there, he supposed he and Tessa had better stick around in case they could help to keep him from hurting anyone. So he pushed his way after the guard, with Tessa right behind him, until he came to the edge of the circle around the swordsman.

He was only five feet or six or so, but he had a commanding presence just the same. Not because of the sword, which remained sheathed at his side, nor because of the glittering silver chain mail that covered his leather shirt and hung below his waist. It was his eyes that drew Rick's attention; eyes that had seen everything, yet still glittered with curiosity and determination. His entire face, wrinkled with time and covered with a close-cropped gray beard, gave off such an expression of calm confidence that Rick found himself instantly liking the man, despite his odd clothing and his presence with a weapon in an airport.

Then he realized who it had to be.

"Arthur?"

The crowd noise drowned out his voice more than few feet away, but the man looked up at him and smiled. He said something in a deep, resonant voice, but it was so heavily accented that Rick couldn't make out the words.

"Sorry," he said, shaking his head. "I didn't catch that."

The man tried again, but what little that Rick caught sounded like, "Dyd da itt, a unbenn."

"Do you speak English?" Rick asked him.

"I think he *is* speaking English," Tessa said. "Old English."

"Oh boy." Like any tourist convinced that he could be understood if he only spoke slowly and loudly, Rick tried one last time. "What . . . is . . . your . . . name?"

The man shook his head slightly, his brows knitting together. The voices around them diminished as people listened for his response, but when he spoke again, it was more gibberish: "A pwy ytwyt di?"

Rick tried again. "Your name? I'm Rick. Rick Spencer." He thumped his own chest, then pointed at the other man's chain mail.

"Arthur vrenhin," the man said. Rick felt the hair rise on the back of his neck, and the crowd began to buzz with voices again, but they hushed completely when the man said again, more loudly, "Arthurus rex."

He spoke a few more sentences, addressing everyone. He seemed just as puzzled as they at his appearance in their midst, but he spoke like a man determined to make the most of it. The language barrier didn't prevent him from making it clear that he was a no-nonsense sort of guy, a fact that became even more evident when he drew his sword and held it high over his head. Its polished blade and wide, jeweled cross guard glittered under the bright lights. A couple of camera flashes startled him for a moment, but he held his ground and turned once around, presenting the sword for all to see.

A few people backed away, but he didn't really look like he

was trying to threaten anyone; and when he noticed their reaction he slid it back into its sheath again. A little brightness seemed to vanish along with the blade.

"Excalibur," Rick whispered.

"Excalibur!" the man answered happily, patting its hilt.

"I think it's really 'im!" said a woman next to Tessa.

"Me too," she replied.

The security guard stepped forward, clearly unsure what to do next. "Come along," he said, holding out his hand. "I think we'd better take this up with the port authority."

CHAPTER 47

Neither man protested when Rick and Tessa offered to accompany them. Half the crowd followed at least as far as the "Authorized Persons Only" door, then apparently ran off to join the others in telling the tale. By the time a medieval scholar arrived to interpret for them, the news had already hit the street that King Arthur had returned from Avalon to protect England in its time of need.

The university professor, a surprisingly young man named Derek Hobbs, was quick to correct their misconception about one thing, at least. "He's speaking medieval Welsh, not Old English," he pointed out. "And he has a fair command of Latin as well."

Rick could speak neither, so he didn't particularly care, but Derek seemed fascinated more with the language than with Arthur himself.

Arthur seemed fascinated with everything. He examined the metal detectors as he walked past them, the electric lights overhead, the neon lights in the shop windows, even the knob on the security room door with the curiosity of a small boy. The only thing that didn't surprise him was the one thing that would have surprised anyone else: When they reached the office and found too few chairs for everyone to sit on, Rick and Tessa manifested extras for themselves.

Arthur laughed and said something in Welsh, and Derek said, "He says Merlin could do that, too, but he sometimes wound up on his, er, bottom when he got distracted."

Rick, still struggling to believe the evidence of his own eyes and ears, said, "Tell him it works the same way for us."

It took a surprisingly short time to convince the authorities that arresting King Arthur for a weapons violation would be a disastrous public relations move, especially now when England was facing a real threat from the Continent. In no time at all he was released into Rick and Tessa's custody, who in turn begged Derek for help in figuring out what to do next.

Arthur suggested reviewing the troops and meeting the knights who would be leading them in the upcoming battle. Derek tried to convince him that perhaps he should learn a bit about twenty-first-century England first, but he would have none of that. "I am here to fight, not to observe," he said.

So Derek made a few phone calls, and within the hour they were whisked off to a military base where an RAF lieutenant showed him row after row of Harrier jets, tanks, artillery guns, and so forth, all under the watchful eye of a BBC camera crew who were careful to focus on Arthur so they wouldn't give away military secrets to Bagdonis.

The cameras kept cutting to Rick and Tessa as well, and the interviewer kept saying how wonderful it was to have such phenomenal support in Britain's hour of need. He kept stressing again and again how the tide was finally turning, saying things like, "We'll soon have Bagdonis on the run," and "The forces of darkness have obviously seen their last day," until Rick wanted to strangle him. But he knew what it was all about. This was a war of the mind as well as on the ground. If they could swing public opinion around to a more hopeful stance, they might rob the invaders of some of their power without having to actually fight them hand to hand. And maybe with a little luck they could put some fear into the enemy for a change. If Bagdonis knew he was facing supernatural power equal to his own, perhaps he would lose confidence, and with it his seeming invincibility.

After half an hour of continuous coverage, their guide sent the camera crew away and took his guests inside to a briefing room, where he said to Arthur, "Thanks for putting up with that. It should boost morale a bit, if anyone believes you're for real. I admit to a little trouble in that regard myself, and you're standing right here."

"Dioer," Arthur said when Derek translated that for him, and Derek burst out laughing.

"What?" Tessa asked.

"I believe the Americanism would be, 'No shit.' "

"Ah."

The lieutenant smiled, but it was short-lived. Sitting down heavily, he said, "Now that we're not in front of a camera, I can give you the straight story. The truth is, the planes and the tanks aren't worth a damn in this war. As soon as Bagdonis knows they've been deployed, he shuts 'em down. We've been reduced to guns and our own two feet." He nodded toward Excalibur and said, "Swords are pretty much obsolete these days, but I wouldn't advise you to trade that in on an SA-80 anytime soon. At the rate this is going, that could easily become the most useful weapon in the country."

"Dioer," Arthur said again after Derek translated.

They began talking strategy, which mostly involved trying to keep Bagdonis from getting a foothold on the island. Arthur received the news that there was now a tunnel beneath the English Channel with more alarm than he had shown over the jet planes, but he nodded happily when he learned that it had been blocked. They discussed England's naval capability, and when Arthur asked if their supplies of flame arrows were adequate, the RAF officer assured him they were.

Rick, listening to all this, finally understood the meaning of the term "boggled." He had known it intellectually before, and he had felt it a time or two on the way to the Moon and back, but now, sitting in a war room with King Arthur on the eve of battle, he knew for certain that his mind was filled to capacity. The foundations of his worldview had survived blow after blow, emerging battered but essentially intact every time, but he knew one more impossible occurrence would topple the whole works right on over the edge.

So it was a great relief when the door opened and General Marcus stuck his head in. If ever there was a person with a solid view of reality, he was the man. "There you are," he said. "I've been looking all over for you. Come on, let's get to— who's that?"

Rick smiled. "King Arthur. Arthur, this is General Marcus."

"Dyd da itt," Arthur said.

Marcus squinted at him, then shook his head and said to the RAF lieutenant, "You Brits always seem to have an ace up your sleeve. Let's hope he's tougher than he is tall."

Derek prudently didn't translate that. Marcus didn't stick around for conversation, either; with hardly another glance at Arthur, he ushered Rick and Tessa out of the room and outside to a waiting car, which took them to another part of the base.

"What happened in France?" Tessa asked as they rode along in the darkness.

"What didn't happen?" Marcus replied. "Let's see, we tried nukes. Dropped two of 'em from an SR-71 so high the bastard didn't even know it was up there."

"And?"

"And the fuckers didn't go off." He sounded offended at the very idea.

"How could that happen?" Rick asked.

"How can he kill an airplane or a rocket engine in mid-flight? You tell me. All he needs to know is that it's there, and he can mess it up so it doesn't work."

"But he can't see a bomb coming, can he?"

"He's got radar."

"Oh. Well then, how about cruise missiles? They fly below radar, don't they?"

"When they fly. Remember what happened to the dogs back home? He apparently hates cruise missiles. He can't seem to affect them out here where we're still in control, but as soon as we send one into his territory, it fails."

"Oh. So then what?"

Marcus sighed. "So we tried chemical explosives. Just plain old dumb bombs. We had better luck with that, but he figured out where they were coming from before we could do much good with 'em. We lost our SR-71, and we haven't tried sending up another one. You can't do a saturation bombing without planes. And besides, there are still millions of civilians on the ground."

"Haven't they been able to fight back?"

"Sure they have. But half of Bagdonis's army won't go down when they're shot, and the ones that do are back on their feet in minutes. They only last a half hour or so, but while they're up they don't go down a second time until you blow their goddam legs off. It's the spookiest damned thing you've ever seen." He looked over at his passengers, as if trying to decide if that was true or not, then said, "But we've finally got a lead that might prove useful."

"Oh, what's that?" Rick asked, eager for some ray of hope in the gloomy news.

"We're zeroing in on Bagdonis."

"Oho! That's something. Where is he?"

"He keeps moving around, but we're narrowing it down."

"How?" Tessa asked.

"Let's just say I've gained a little respect for the CIA," said Marcus.

Rick suddenly got a bad premonition. Sure enough, when their car pulled up to an office building and they went inside, there was Sonderby seated at a computer on which a map of France held dozens of blinking red and yellow dots. There were six other people in the room with him, each with a computer of their own, and more people rushed in and out of other rooms like it all the way down a long hallway.

Sonderby stood up and extended his right hand toward Rick. In a fake German accent he said, "So, Mr. Bond, we meet again."

Tessa giggled, and Rick couldn't help smiling, but Marcus said, "Cut the spy versus spy crap and fill him in on Project Peekaboo."

"You have all the patience of a boiling teakettle," Sonderby told him. "But since Peekaboo is my baby, I don't mind cutting right to the chase. As its name implies, this project involves playing hide-and-seek with the enemy. We've learned that he isn't staying safely behind in Lithuania like we'd originally thought. He apparently can't guide his army from that far away. Like you, he can *affect* things at practically any distance, but as Rick learned when we tried to move Tessa, he has to be a lot closer to sense what's going on. He's got a hell of a range, but it's not infinite. More like fifty miles."

He waved toward the computer screen. "So just before a major offensive he positions himself where he thinks he can do the most good, and relies on radio to keep tabs on the rest. When his soldiers get in trouble he sends phantom reinforcements, and when they detect incoming planes or missiles he knocks 'em down. He's smart enough not to transmit anything, but we're able to listen to the incoming reports, and those tell us where he *isn't*."

He pointed to a yellow-shaded oval about halfway between Reims and Dijon. "There aren't any calls for help coming from this region. That can only mean his troops aren't getting into trouble there. They're sending regular reports, because even they don't know where he is, but he's catching all the shit we throw at him before they have to ask him to."

"A fifty-mile radius circle is still a pretty big area," Rick pointed out.

Sonderby nodded. "Sure, if you had to search the whole thing. But it's a *circle*. That puts him right in the middle. Of course it's a fuzzy circle, and flattened in front where the worst of the fighting is, so the target is still a mile or two across, but that should have been close enough."

"Should have been? That's where you dropped the nuclear bombs?"

Marcus said, "This morning he was in Strasbourg, but yeah, you get the idea."

"You tried to nuke Strasbourg?" Tessa said indignantly.

"We waited until he was fifteen miles west," Marcus said. "The blast radius wouldn't have reached the city. But like I told you, he managed to detect the bombs and disable them before they went off."

"So what do you plan to do next time?" Rick asked.

Marcus smiled. "Have you send him a little present by Cerebral Express."

CHAPTER 48

It was a good plan, except for one thing: Rick and Tessa couldn't create a nuclear bomb. They tried dozens of times, even over open ocean where the only things hurt would be a few fish, but they just couldn't do it, not even when Marcus took them out to the arms depot and showed them an actual bomb, nor when a technician opened it up and described the internal workings. They could manifest the casing easily enough, but the plutonium core stubbornly refused to appear with the rest of it.

"What's the deal?" Marcus demanded. "Is this some kind of weenie peacenik thing? You can't contribute to nuclear proliferation? What?"

"I don't know!" Rick said, just as exasperated as Marcus. He certainly understood that a single nuclear blast was preferable to losing all of Europe. Intellectually the choice was obvious, but apparently it wasn't so clear an issue emotionally. He and Tessa had both spent the first years of their lives afraid of a runaway nuclear war with the Soviet Union; apparently that fear still lived in their subconscious minds, refusing to allow them to take the first shot.

"How about an 'accident' bomb?" Marcus asked.

"Accident bomb?" said Tessa.

"That Russki space controller said if you weren't careful when you tried to make something out of nothing, you could get a big explosion. Is there anything to that, or was he just blowing smoke?"

"I don't know. We've tried hard not to do that."

Rick said, "Wait a minute. I thought you guys had a few explosions of your own when you were doing your cold-fusion experiments. Or were *you* blowing smoke?"

Marcus colored slightly. "We had one explosion. We were never able to duplicate it."

"Aha."

They tried it anyway. They tried manifesting things underground, figuring that maybe two objects occupying the same space at the same time would cause an explosion, but after a dozen failures they tried it close enough to investigate and saw that the ground just bulged upward to make room. Rick tried manifesting something while Tessa tickled his ribs to distract him, but they got nothing at all. They tried imagining something inherently impossible, like a flaming ice cube, but they got nothing that time, either.

In frustration they tried making a regular chemical bomb, but they had no better luck at that. Even conventional explosives were apparently beyond their emotional capability.

"Now that makes no goddam sense at all," Marcus growled as they drove back toward the office where Sonderby had set up shop. "You can make a fully fueled lunar module, which has just as much explosive potential as a decent-sized bomb. You can even blow 'em up—on Mars. Why the hell can't you do the same on Bagdonis's head?"

"Maybe we can," Tessa said.

"What?"

"Drop lunar modules on him."

Marcus started to laugh, but stopped in mid "ha." "You're serious."

"Not entirely," she said, "but let's think it through. We know we can make lunar modules. Rick made a dozen of them one time when he got mad. How many would it take to make sure we actually hit Bagdonis?"

Marcus narrowed his eyes, thinking it through. "Let's see, the blast radius is what, a couple of hundred feet at best? I doubt if it's even that, since there's practically no containment to speak of. And we'd have to saturate at least three or four square miles to ensure we got him. We're talking thousands of 'em. Can you do that many at once?"

Rick shook his head. "One at a time. Maybe two if we each concentrate on a separate one."

"Then we might as well forget it. Unless you hit him with your very first one, he'll know we're onto him and skedaddle. And if he realizes how we tracked him, he won't make the same mistake twice."

"Then we need to pin down his position better the first time," said Tessa.

Something connected in Rick's mind, then immediately fled. When Marcus had said "your very first one," he'd gotten a glimmer of an idea, but it was already fading away. He tried to bring it back, but it stubbornly remained just out of reach. "First one," he murmured. "First one."

"Rick?"

"Hmm?" He looked up to see Tessa watching him curiously. "Oh. Nothing. Stray thought. You were saying?"

"If we're going to drop a lunar module on him, then we need to know exactly where he is."

"That's true. Can we narrow down that circle any?"

Marcus shook his head. "Not unless you've got any bright ideas. We tried pressing an all-out attack to see if we could define the edges of his range a little better, but plain old battle chaos drowned out any meaningful information."

"Hmm," Rick said again. "I wonder if I could sense him if I were to get close enough. Have you got any stealth planes left?"

Marcus snorted. "Oh, sure, but they're like the cruise missiles. They run fine over here, but as soon as we cross into occupied territory, they flame out and drop like rocks."

"I bet they wouldn't with me on board."

Both Marcus and Tessa looked at him like he'd lost his

mind, but he said, "Look, he's using psychic power against us, and we can't seem to fight back on his terms. So let's fight back on our own terms. We know I can sense things; maybe not as well as he does, but I can do it. And even if I can't make a bomb, I can probably make another engine if the plane quits in flight. But I'll bet you it doesn't quit in the first place with me on board."

"With *us* on board, you mean," Tessa said.

He shook his head. "Me. Now before you—"

"Damnit, Rick—"

"—get all bent out of shape, I'm not just being chivalrous. For one thing, there's only one extra seat in the plane, am I right?" He looked at Marcus.

Marcus nodded. Something in his eyes told Rick he was wrong about that, but Marcus was going along with him. Good enough.

"And for another, you don't load both your secret weapons on the same plane anyway. If something does go wrong, they'll need you to help try plan B."

"If we both go, there's a hell of a lot less chance that nothing will—what's plan B?"

"I don't know. We probably won't come up with one until we find out what happens this time."

"Plan B sucks rocks," she said. "And plan A is just as bad. Besides putting you in danger, it's totally ridiculous to think we can fight a war with lunar modules."

"It was your idea," Rick pointed out.

"Well, it was a stupid one."

"It's better than anything else we've come up with. Unless you've got a better one. One that doesn't involve losing any more countries to Bagdonis."

She didn't answer. Rick gave her time to think it over, hoping she would come up with something that meant he wouldn't have to fly over enemy territory, but finally, just as they pulled up in front of Sonderby's office, she shook her head and said, "No, I don't."

He took a deep breath. "All right then, let's do it. With the excitement over Arthur and you and me all showing up here at once, our power is probably as strong right now as it's going to get. And we'll have a lot better luck avoiding detection if we go while it's still dark, right?" He looked over at Marcus.

Marcus nodded. "Right again."

"I assume Sonderby can track the plane?"

"He can. From above they're not as invisible as from below."

"Then Tessa, you watch from here. When I figure out where Bagdonis is hiding, I'll drop an LM on him, but that may not be enough to punch through whatever building he's in, so when you see the flash, you start dropping them on the same spot. Between the two of us, we ought to be able to burn him out if nothing else. Okay?"

She clearly wasn't happy, but she nodded.

He took her in his arms, hugged her tight, and kissed her. "Don't worry, I'll be all right."

"You'd better be," she said, then she kissed him again hard enough to bruise lips.

"I'll definitely be back for more of that," he said.

Marcus gave them their moment, but no more. "Come on," he said to Rick. "Let's get you checked out on your plane."

"Right."

Tessa got out, closed the door, and Marcus told the driver to take them back to the RAF side of the base. Then he settled back into the seat and laughed. "You've got more spunk than I thought, boy. *Extra* seat. That's good."

Rick waved at Tessa as they pulled away. He knew she couldn't see inside the car, but she waved anyway. "What do you mean by that?" he asked, trying to ignore the sensation of something stretching thinner and thinner.

Marcus laughed even louder. "You don't know? The F-117 only has *one*."

t took him two hours to get ready, most of it spent going over the controls. He flew T-38s all the time, he'd trained extensively for shuttle landings, and he'd even had the front seat in an F-16 for about an hour, so it wasn't like he was going into it blind; but all the gauges and dials were in different places—most of them replaced with heads-up displays— and there were a few controls he had never worked with before. Like weapons triggers. He was going in hot, in the hopes that he could get a bomb to blow after all if he could sneak it in before Bagdonis became aware of his presence. His reluctance to create one that worked might not extend to damping the explosion of one that was already built the hard way. It wasn't a nuclear warhead—Rick doubted if he could let one explode even if he could push the button to launch it, but a precision strike with a conventional bomb might be within his emotional ability. Like the whole mission, it didn't have a great chance of success, but it was worth a try.

The pilot who checked him out made sure he knew how to run one final system: the ejection seat. "If you even *think* you're going down, hit it," he urged. "These things have the glide ratio of a brick without the engines, and if you lose electrical power you've got no control at all."

"Just like the shuttle," Rick said.

The pilot grinned and gave him the thumbs-up. "All right, then. You're as ready as I can make you in one night. Go get 'im."

"Will do."

It was three A.M. at that point. The fighting in France had not stopped, but Sonderby reported that Bagdonis's circle of influence had gone away in the last hour, and his troops were apparently mopping up while he slept. Rick input the coordinates of his last known position into the satellite navigation system, fired up the engines—surprisingly quiet, even though he knew they had been designed that way—and taxied out to the runway. Then, without fanfare, he shoved the throttles forward and roared into the sky.

There could be no radio contact with the ground. The moment Rick transmitted anything, he would blow his cover. Sonderby and Tessa could send messages to *him*, but whatever he said had to be innocuous enough to pass as normal radio traffic, because they had to assume that Bagdonis's people were listening in. Coded frequencies were probably still secure, but they didn't know that. And even if they were, a sudden increase in traffic on frequencies that were normally used for airplanes would warn them that something was going on, and that alone would put them on heightened alert.

So Rick had a quiet half hour to learn how his plane handled as he streaked across the Channel and into French airspace. He'd heard the F-117 called the "Wobblin Goblin" before, but it seemed solid as a rock to him. In fact, with its flat triangular underside, it flew a lot like the shuttle. He didn't plan to test its aerobatic capabilities anyway; this was going to be a straight-in, straight-out mission.

The infrared night-vision monitor showed him only dark water across the channel, but when he reached the coast he could see the land beyond in such clear detail he had to look out the window to assure himself it was still night. It was like running a high-resolution simulator, except he could feel the reality of it in every vibration. He could sense things that weren't in a simulation, either. Instinct or intuition or something warned him about obstacles even before they came into view on the screen, and he found himself flying more by feel than by conscious thought.

He flew to the east, behind enemy lines, figuring anyone who heard the plane would assume it was one of Bagdonis's.

He would be over the target area before anybody was the wiser, and if he circled wide he could probably make more than one pass without arousing suspicion. He didn't think he would need more than that. He had sensed Tessa more than a mile away, and while he had no guarantee that he could sense Bagdonis at that distance, he was willing to bet he could. He was more used to having psychic ability now, more willing to accept his hunches as real. He was using them at that very moment, hugging the ground with the ease of a practiced pilot. He would find Bagdonis. He would find him, and before the night was over, there would be one fewer bogeyman to haunt the world's dreams.

The plane felt his malevolent presence before Rick did. Only a few miles after he had crossed into France, the engines suddenly stuttered, then the right one flamed out completely.

"Oh, no, you don't," Rick said, restarting it and focusing his thoughts on keeping the plane running. It kept lurching and threatening to die again until he pictured a bubble of safety surrounding it, imagining his thoughts deflecting whatever bad vibes were directed at him like the wings deflected the wind. That seemed to help, though it was a constant struggle to keep it in place. Whatever Bagdonis was throwing at him was like some kind of radio-jamming device, only this one jammed mechanical things. Rick tried to imagine how that could work, but all he got was a mental image of a UFO flying over a freeway, leaving a string of dead cars in its wake. He snorted derisively, then berated himself for having such a closed mind. When was he ever going to learn? People claimed that UFOs stalled cars and damped the current in power lines all the time. And Rick had actually seen one, even if it was only a figment of his imagination. Now he regretted not pursuing it further when he'd had the chance. Bagdonis had obviously discovered the trick, whether or not he'd gotten it from a UFO.

It was apparently selective. Rick saw city lights off to the side, and the lights of individual farms and country estates scattered below. A few cars drove along the highways, even at this time of night. It hardly looked like a country that had just been invaded. But as he flew past the city he saw more evidence of it: Six or eight blocks of the downtown area were in flames, and a few other buildings scattered farther out also burned. Rick guessed they were police stations, and maybe radio and TV stations as well. If he were leading an invasion, those and military bases were what he would hit. He would use his shock troops to smash the country's ability to fight back and to communicate, then move on while a second wave came along behind to mop up any pockets of resistance that were left. It had worked for Hitler, and it looked to be working even better for his spiritual successor.

If he concentrated, he could feel the emotions of the people below him. Fear and anger, probably from both sides in the struggle. Sorrow over the dead. Cold, dark hatred. And regret. Rick concentrated, trying to decide if he was imagining it. He could be fooling himself; none of these feelings could exist beyond his own overly credulous brain, but if he was reading true emotion from below, somebody was having serious regrets about what they were doing.

Well, well, well. There were a few human beings in Bagdonis's army after all. Maybe the monolithic new Eastern bloc wasn't so monolithic as the West had thought.

It was strong enough even so. The plane kept trying to die. The navigation screen flickered, as if even satellite signals were having a hard time. It didn't matter. Rick knew he was drawing close. The hair started standing up on the back of his neck, but he couldn't tell yet if it was from Bagdonis's presence or just from excitement. It could easily have been excitement. In another couple of minutes, this whole war could be over.

He lined up his path through the center of Sonderby's circle, then lifted the nose, pulled back on the throttles, and glided ballistically across the target zone. Radar couldn't spot him, and now they could barely hear him on the ground. Even if he didn't pick up anything on the first pass, he could turn around and try again a mile or two to the side until he did.

The tingling at the back of his neck grew stronger. He watched trees and roads and fields sweep past in the night-vision monitor, examining each building as it slid into view, but none of them drew his attention. They were all just houses and barns. The hostility he had been feeling since he entered enemy airspace was stronger here, and the monitor became shot through with snow, but Rick couldn't sense a distinct source. He looked directly out the windows, but the land here was pitch black. For a second it seemed like the darkness was a physical thing trying to seep in through the glass, but he looked back inside and the sensation went away.

He was already past the prime target area, headed toward the battlefront. He closed his eyes and tried to extend his senses, thinking that maybe watching the infrared image had drowned out whatever signal he might be receiving subconsciously, but a few seconds later the heads-up alarm snapped him alert with a recorded voice saying, "Terrain. Terrain." He was coming down the other side of his ballistic arc. He throttled up and banked to the left, choosing that direction completely at random. He swung around 180 degrees, lined up two miles to the south of where he had crossed the first time, and repeated his climb and throttle-down.

The radio had been silent the entire time, but now it crackled with static, then Tessa said, "Go north 4.7 miles."

The sound of her voice seemed to dispel the darkness a little. They must have learned something after he left. He itched to bank the plane and head straight north, but to do that he would have to use the engines, which would give away his current position. Better to finish his arc and do another one to the north.

He closed his eyes again, trying to sense anything up there, but his joy at hearing Tessa's voice overpowered his other emotions.

He didn't wait for the terrain alarm this time. While he was still at the top of his arc he banked left, letting himself drift northeast so he would come down closer to the point where he could begin his third run. From there he banked hard, goosed the engines just long enough to set him up again, and coasted along a line 4.7 miles north of the one he had just been on.

He could feel his pulse rate rising and his skin starting to flush with the increased blood flow. Something awaited him up there. Something dark and full of hate. He checked the laser-guided bomb: armed. Ready to drop, but where?

Up ahead. He could feel it now. The irrational hatred he had been feeling all along grew crisper, divided into distinct components. There was a core of cool, calm, pure ambition, glazed with rationalization and fired with anger. Try as he might, Rick couldn't feel anything he could label "evil." Just impatience, frustration—and fear. Whatever else Bagdonis was, he was also afraid.

As well he should be. Rick banked to the right a little, letting his subconscious mind guide his actions, until he saw a long, rambling château draw into view on the monitor. A wide lawn dotted with trees extended forever in front of it, and manicured gardens surrounded it on the other three sides. Four cars stood in the circle driveway in front.

He instantly knew that was it. He had no rational reason to be so certain, but he had no doubt. Bagdonis was there.

CHAPTER 50

The château was less than a mile ahead. He moved the weapons guidance crosshairs onto it, made sure they locked on, then pressed the FIRE button. He felt a lurch as the bomb bay doors opened, the bomb dropped into the night, and the doors closed again—all in barely a second. There would be a brief flash on the enemy radar screens if any were pointed his way, but it would be gone already.

His weapons screen gave him a laser sight to mark what part of the house he wanted to hit. The château had two wings leading off at angles from a central three-story tower. He tried to sense which wing Bagdonis was in, but couldn't get a feeling for it. There was no time to search for him; Rick aimed directly for the center, figuring an explosion there would blow flame well into either side.

The picture broke up for a few seconds, then came back, but it was long enough that the laser had lost its lock on the target. Rick aimed it again and concentrated on holding Bagdonis's jamming field at bay, barely remembering in time to throttle up the engines and gain some altitude.

It didn't matter. The bomb punched through a third-story window, then a moment later appeared on the other side of the château, knocking a big hole in the wall as it exited, but not exploding.

"Damn you!" Rick cursed, not sure if he was damning the bomb or Bagdonis. He banked the plane around hard, already imagining a lunar module appearing over the château, and when the building came into view again he saw that he had been successful at that much, at least.

Tessa's materialized just above his. Both of them fell like

rocks onto the central tower's flat roof and burst into a satisfying fireball.

"All right!" Rick shouted, slapping the canopy overhead with his palm. He laughed at the absurdity of it as well as the success. Lunar modules! But they worked. He imagined another one over the north wing, and a few seconds later there it was, its fragile skin bursting open like a water balloon on the peaked tile roof and showering flame down both sides.

People came streaming outside the building, some fully dressed, others pulling on clothing. Rick dropped another lunar module on the south wing just a moment after Tessa's second one hit a little ways down.

Then a line of fire lanced upward toward his plane. In the infrared image, it was a solid bar of bright purple light.

"Shit!" he yelled, jerking the stick hard to the left. The firebolt shot past his right wing. He rolled the plane completely over, banked hard to keep the building in view, and imagined another lunar module crashing down into the courtyard in front. He hadn't had a chance to tell if that had been an anti-aircraft missile or a blast of elemental fire, but either way, those spotters on the ground outside had to go.

He dropped another lunar module on the north wing of the château, but it was becoming clear that the building was too strong for them to punch through. They were burning merrily on the flat rooftop in the center, and flame was rushing off the ceramic tile on either side, but they weren't actually doing much damage.

He switched on his transmitter. "Manifest them inside the building!" he shouted. "Inside!"

"Radio silence!" Tessa replied.

"Screw radio silence; he knows I'm here, but we're not doing any damage!"

Another beam of fire shot upward. He wasn't able to dodge this one completely; it hit his left wingtip and blew a three-foot chunk off. The plane dropped into a hard bank, but he advanced the throttle a little and brought it back to level. He could probably fix that wing if he had a second, but at the moment he needed the time to concentrate on another lunar module, because this time he had seen where the fire had come from.

"South wing!" he yelled. "South wing, just one or two rooms from the center on the second floor."

"Roger." He imagined Tessa peering at a satellite image, and felt a moment of comfort as he thought of her watching over him. He wasn't doing this alone.

The flames weren't even close to Bagdonis's room. Rick imagined a lunar module inside with him, imagined it crashing down through the floor from the room above, its fuel tanks rupturing and the hypergolic propellant bursting into flame the moment the two components mixed. It worked just like he'd imagined, too, but Bagdonis didn't stick around for the explosion. The moment he realized something was happening in the room with him, he leaped out the window, threw another burst of flame at Rick in midair, then fell into a burning bush directly below.

Rick couldn't see what happened after that. There was enough illumination just from burning rocket fuel to light the building and its grounds like day, but his own motion carried him around to the side of the château before he could see if Bagdonis made it free.

He tried to dodge the incoming streak of flame, but it roared through the back of the same wing that had been hit before and the plane started into a spiral. Rick gave it hard right aileron, but he remembered a second too late that on a delta-wing like this the ailerons did double duty as elevators. With the left control surfaces gone and the right ones pointing upward for a right bank, the whole plane dropped straight for the ground.

At least it was banking to the right. He let it tip about a third of the way over, then straightened it out and gave it hard left rudder, shoving the throttles all the way forward at the same time. The plane had no afterburners, but it still kicked him back in his seat and leaped ahead, wobbling for real now as he constantly adjusted the controls to keep it aloft, using the right wing for lift and the tail for attitude.

Fortunately Bagdonis was on the other side of the building. Rick took the moment he needed to work on the left wing, craning his neck around to look out the side window at it so he could imagine it whole again. It was too dark to see more than a faint outline, but apparently that was good enough: A few seconds later the plane tipped sharply to the right as the left wing started providing lift again.

He leveled off with less than a hundred feet of airspace left and did a climbing bank back toward the flaming building. He would put some distance between him and Bagdonis this time, and give himself a little more cushion in case he took another hit.

He roared past, manifesting lunar modules one after another as quickly as he could along the entire front of the château, and when he circled around to that side he saw that Tessa had already been busy there as well. The whole front of the the building was aflame. If Bagdonis hadn't gotten away, he was toast.

It looked like maybe that was the case. No more firebolts shot up at him. He allowed himself to hope, but the moment he was past and couldn't see the building anymore, he felt a sudden burst of panic and shoved the plane into a hard right dive. Sure enough, another violet lance of flame roared past, and this time he couldn't see where it came from.

"Did you track that?" he asked,

"Negative," Tessa said. "The fire is washing out the satellite picture that close to the building."

"Damn it!" Rick said. Lunar modules weren't causing enough damage. If Bagdonis ran off into the bushes, he could play hide-and-seek with them all night. Marcus had been right. They had needed to hit him with their first shot, and they hadn't done it. Now it was too late.

They needed a nuke. Why the hell couldn't he make a nuke that worked? He'd already killed half a dozen people with rocket fuel; why couldn't he do it wholesale with a bigger explosive? Because the subconscious part of his mind that controlled that sort of thing was a peacenik. Probably the only reason he could make lunar modules was because he was an astronaut, and down at the level that counted he didn't think of them as weapons.

Well, then, he needed a bigger lunar module.

And with that thought he remembered the flash of inspiration he'd gotten and then immediately lost back at the RAF base. Marcus had said, "Unless you hit him with your very first one," and for that brief moment Rick had thought back to his very first manifestation.

He banked the plane around. This was going to be fun.

"Watch your eyes," he said to Tessa. "I just got a bright idea."

"What?"

"You'll see."

His very first manifestation, before he even realized it was him doing it. Rick smiled there in the cockpit, remembering the stats. Three hundred sixty-three feet high. Three thousand tons, most of it fuel. The energy equivalent of a nuclear bomb. He imagined what it would look like poised over the château. Not right side up, supported by its gantry. Oh, no. This one would be pointed straight down, its escape tower aimed right at Bagdonis's head.

He flipped the F-117 on its back just to make sure he got it right. The rocket would no doubt blow up either way, but style was important. He leaned back in his seat, looked out the window at the burning building, and imagined a brilliant white rocket pointed right at it. A huge spike, engines lit, 7.5 million pounds of thrust shoving it deep into the ground.

Yeah. Give the third stage a little *containment*, as Marcus would say.

It appeared before him, just as it had the first time, only now it was a lot closer. That could be a problem, he thought, banking the plane a bit so he wouldn't fly right through the fireball when it exploded.

The engines stayed lit. He hadn't expected that. The fuel intakes were on the bottom, after all, and the rocket was upside down. But it was also under thrust. A tongue of flame shot up hundreds of feet into the sky, and this time, with gravity helping it along, the whole stack accelerated like a rifle bullet—straight down.

It crumpled when it hit. The thirty-three-foot-wide first stage didn't even slow down. As Rick swept past upside down he watched all five engines fire all the way to the ground, slamming a solid sheet of flame out in all directions. The château vanished as if it had been made of tissue paper. The trees and cars in front of it made momentary silhouettes before they, too, vanished in the conflagration.

Something else winked out of existence as well. An impatient, angry, and terrified vortex of darkness screamed momentarily in frustrated rage, and was silent.

Rick heard Tessa shout, "Woo-hoo!" but over her voice the heads-up alarm said, "Terrain. Terrain."

The plane was too low to roll and climb out of it. Rick shoved the stick forward, bringing the nose up, but the horizon didn't drop away the way it should have.

He couldn't eject upside down. He would beat the plane to the ground if he tried it.

His last conscious thought as he watched the forest surrounding the estate rush up at him was, *This thing doesn't fly inverted worth a damn.*

is first thought after that was surprise that he could think anything. He should have been dead. You don't drop a jet fighter upside down into a forest at flight speed and walk away from it.

Then he tried to sit up and he realized he hadn't walked anywhere. He couldn't feel his body at all. Not just his legs, but his arms, chest, lungs, eyelids—nothing. Not even a heartbeat.

He listened. No hearing. He detected no smells, either. He would have a hard time proving he wasn't dead, except for Descartes. *I think, therefore I am.*

Okay, so he was. But what was he? Comatose?

He didn't hurt. Under the circumstances, that was probably bad news.

Someone needed to turn down the lights. He couldn't see any details, but it was bright here. A grainy kind of brightness, like reflected laser light full of interference patterns, or . . .

. . . a memory settled into his mind from his childhood. The health club where he learned to swim had a steam room, and he had used to sit in there to warm up after he'd done his laps in the outdoor pool. He wore glasses back then, but not in the pool, so he was blind as a bat in the steam room, too. Not that it mattered, because he couldn't see more than a few feet through the steam anyway. But just at the edge of his vision, he could see individual droplets of water condensing in the air. They swirled around when he waved his hand through them, billowed away when he exhaled, popping into and out of existence as they passed through his field of view.

The light was like that. Particles rather than smooth whiteness. Too small to focus on individually, but there, just on the edge of perception.

Pixels? Was he seeing with some kind of computerized implant? Just how long had he been unconscious, anyway?

Tessa? he asked. He couldn't speak aloud, but he thought it as strongly as he could. Maybe he was hooked to some kind of neural implant, or maybe she could sense his mind directly.

He got no answer, not from her anyway, but he could feel a more general response to his call. Somebody was out there. A lot of somebodies. Millions of them. Billions. Not all of them human. In fact, only a tiny portion of them were human. He could feel their combined consciousness surrounding him, pressing in on him, suffusing through him like gravity or some kind of life energy. Like a force of nature.

Whoever they were, they weren't talking, but as he became more aware of them he realized they didn't need to. He was starting to understand where he was without words.

He wasn't dead. His *body* was dead—vaporized, probably, in the crash—but the information that was him hadn't died with it. Now that he contemplated it from the other side, it seemed silly to have assumed that it would. Everything he had ever interacted with, from the food he had eaten to the other minds he had communicated with, had come away altered by the experience; that influence still remained. Even the atoms that had made up his body retained their connection to him, if not to each other. His body wasn't self-aware, never had been, but it had forged a set of connections that were, and those connections persisted.

Physicists had known about the connectedness of the universe for decades. Paired particles somehow knew what each other experienced and instantaneously changed state to match, even if they were light-years apart. Einstein had called that aspect of quantum physics "spooky action at a distance," and had tried to disprove it, but it had finally been proven real instead.

Rick *was* Einstein's "spooky action at a distance." He knew that now. So was every other mind that had ever lived, on Earth and elsewhere. Consciousness never died; it only expanded as it made more and more connections with the rest of the universe. That's what Rick felt surrounding him: the universe itself, growing more self-aware with each mind that joined it.

Perhaps the biggest surprise of all was the realization that he had already been part of it all his life. Every time he had interacted with any part of the cosmos, the whole thing had responded. He had known that emotionally, had even expressed it in the brief flirtation with solipsism that every child goes through, but experience had convinced him it wasn't true. He had never thought that its converse might be true, that instead of being the only consciousness in the universe, he held a part of every other consciousness in him. That's how he had known how to build a Saturn V even though he didn't know all the minute details of its construction; all the people who did know were sharing information with him.

For a moment he felt afraid of losing his identity in the universal mind, but so far he had lost nothing; only gained the knowledge of those who had joined before him. Gained awareness of the knowledge, actually; he had always been connected to it. He couldn't recall anyone else's memories, couldn't hear individual voices, but if he concentrated on the right questions, he could understand how things worked.

Permanence, for instance. Allen had been exactly right about the Martian battle armor. It remained because of the depth of emotion in the people who had lent their belief to it. Tessa's ring was the same way. There was a threshold, not merely of numbers, but of passion, beyond which the quantum foam wouldn't reclaim its own.

The quantum foam. The graininess of his vision wasn't vision at all. He was witnessing the zero point where mass and energy traded places, where particles popped into and out of existence in empty space, joining the cosmos for a brief moment before vanishing again. Joining *him*.

He wondered if he was still able to tap into their energy. What should he create?

Tessa! he thought, then immediately squelched that idea. There was only one way for the real person to get here, and he would never wish her dead for his own gratification. He didn't want a duplicate, either, even if it were possible. But a duplicate Earth would do for now. Someplace to stand, with trees and grass and a stream nearby, with birds in the trees and a sky overhead with white puffy clouds drifting lazily past.

The particles swirled as if stirred by a spoon. They coalesced, became solid matter, slowly gaining definition until he stood in exactly the scene he had imagined. He felt the grass between his toes and realized he had inadvertently re-created his own body to go along with the rest of it. He hadn't bothered to re-create his flight suit, he noted.

Heaven, it seemed, was literally what a person made it. Lonely, though. He could probably learn to communicate with the individual minds in the universal consciousness, but he would always wish for one mind in particular. He'd only spent a few months with her, but she had already become the most important person in his entire life, and now he'd gone and lost her.

The sudden flood of sorrow took him to his knees, then forward to lie prone, clutching the grass and breathing the rich, earthy scent of the ground. When he'd been a disembodied point of view he had taken it all stoically, intellectually, but now he had hormones again, and tears.

He almost banished himself back to the quantum foam again, but it was better to feel sorrow than nothing at all. And here he could also feel triumph at stopping Bagdonis, even if it had cost him his life. Even if it had cost him Tessa. The world would be a better place, and the minds who contributed to the universal consciousness would be more joyful, more whole, than they would have been had he failed.

He tried to sense Bagdonis, but the afterlife was too vast. There was no physical reality, save what each mind dreamed up for itself. Bagdonis could be in a world of his own creation already, winning the war he had so recently lost, but Rick somehow doubted he would bother. His would be the only true mind there; everything else would be a reflection of his own thoughts.

Then again, maybe he would. That might be his idea of Heaven.

It wasn't Rick's. An artificial world peopled with figments of his imagination held no appeal whatsoever.

But Tessa could eventually join him here. He hung on to that knowledge, clung to it after he let go the grass and sat up. In forty or fifty years she would become pure information as well, and they could take up where they had left off.

But by then she would have another husband, a family, a full life of her own, in which he would be just a distant memory. He would be equally distant from her, in whatever way he chose to amuse himself.

He thought about reincarnation. Could he go back? But he didn't want to be reborn into another body. That would just separate them even further. He wanted his own body.

If he tried it, he would be a ghost. He knew that with the certainty of billions of people who had tried it before him. They had all given it up when they saw how little attention the living paid to beings of pure thought. A few of them with unfinished business had mustered enough support for their cause to manage a wispy presence, but that was the best they could do. Earth wasn't like this place. Earth had six billion people to lock down its consensual reality, and the dead weren't part of it anymore. He would have better luck haunting the Moon.

If he could find it. With all the minds around him, so many

of them alien, the notion of *place* seemed a little obscure. There didn't seem to be a direction he could strike out in. Direction was a meaningless term here, except for those he made up himself.

He looked up at the sky. The clouds were moving from one side to the other. He decided they were going east. He thought maybe he would go east for a while himself. Just walk. Explore the inside of his mind a little by exploring its external creation.

Or maybe not. It was pleasant enough right here. Maybe he would just watch the clouds a while longer, let his external creations come to him.

He lay back against the grass, but it didn't support his weight. A hole had opened up in his world. He yelled in surprise as he pitched over backward into the darkness.

CHAPTER 52

No flames!" he shouted, or tried to shout, but his muscles were so tight with fear that his voice was barely a croak. He felt a moment of disorientation, then came to rest on his feet, nearly falling over again. He wobbled, waving his arms to regain his balance, and smacked a computer monitor, sending it to the floor to explode in a shower of sparks and glass.

He looked up. Sonderby sat before the keyboard, a look of total astonishment on his face. Beside him stood King Arthur, Excalibur half out of its sheath as he waited to see if this new apparition was friend or foe. And on Sonderby's other side, rising up from her chair, Tessa—her face red and wet with tears—held her mouth open to speak but could form no words.

It was even brighter here than in Heaven. Rick squinted against the glare and took a step toward Tessa. "Are you okay?" he asked. "Is that really you?"

"Rick?" She stepped toward him, took his outstretched hands in hers, and looked at him in wonder. "Rick!"

She felt real. He gathered her in his arms and held her close to him, burying his face in the soft hollow of her neck. She smelled real. He backed away just enough to kiss her. Her lips were hot from crying. Oh yes, she was real. And somehow, so was he.

He wiped tears from her cheeks with his fingers, then realized his own cheeks were just as wet. "What happened?" he asked. "I was . . . well, I was dead."

She swallowed, sniffed, wiped her nose with her sleeve. "We saw you crash."

Sonderby cleared his throat. "Uh, Rick? Look over your shoulder."

He did, not letting Tessa go, and saw why it was so bright. Floodlights lined the wall, and three BBC television cameras were aimed straight at him. Of course; this was as close as they could get at the moment to where the war had been won, and this was where the survivors could be interviewed.

And apparently at least one of the casualties as well. Except his flight suit had not reappeared with him here, either.

He was way beyond embarrassment. "It's all right," he said to Sonderby. "The British don't mind nudity on TV. Right?"

"Er . . . right," said the man with the microphone, whom Rick recognized from the half hour they had spent with Arthur when he first showed up. Then he added, "But this is going worldwide."

Rick laughed. He couldn't help it. He was alive again! He had another chance. And he had just mooned the entire world.

He re-created his flight suit for the easily offended, then turned again to Tessa. "You brought me back," he said in wonder. "I really was dead. I saw the bright light, felt the presence of—well, I guess you could call it God, but it wasn't just one mind. I was still trying to figure it all out, and then I fell through the ground and wound up here. You brought me back, didn't you?"

She sniffed again. "I don't know what I did. I—he asked if you were really dead, and I said 'No.' I knew you were, but I couldn't bear to say it. So I said, 'No,' and then I looked over at Arthur and the next thing I knew you were here."

Rick followed her gesture. Arthur had slid his sword back into its sheath. He stood there watching Rick, his presence as commanding at five and a half feet as most men's would be at seven. He was obviously a king.

He was just as obviously from another time. Yet billions of people had been watching him stand there as real as anyone while Tessa denied Rick's death. Small wonder Rick had been pulled back into the here and now as well.

Just to make sure nobody got any funny ideas, he stared straight into one of the cameras and said, "In case there's any question, Bagdonis *is* dead, and he's going to stay that way. The only way he'll be back is if the whole world wants him back, and I don't think that'll happen anytime soon. While I was flying over the occupied territory, I could sense regret coming from his own people at what they were doing. He was losing his support even before I killed him."

He pulled Tessa close again. The warmth of her body against his was the most wonderful distraction in the world, but he tried to keep his mind on what had just happened. "You knew where he was before I found him. How did you do that?"

She nodded toward Arthur. "I guess you'd call it dowsing. Once he realized we didn't know where the enemy was, he asked for a map, and when they laid one out for him he held his sword over it and swirled it around until it dropped out of his hand and stabbed the same spot we were looking at."

Sonderby said, "Of course on that scale the spot he hit was still a mile or two across, so the RAF brought him over here and I called up a satellite image, and he did it again on the computer. Chipped the screen, but he pointed right at the house. That was about the time you made your first pass through the hot zone without finding anything, so we decided to send you over it and see what happened. You know the rest."

"But the world doesn't," the reporter said. "Rick, tell us what happened."

He looked into the camera, then took the microphone from the reporter's outstretched hand. "Well," he said, "it was quite an experience, that's for sure. And that's just the part *before* I died."

CHAPTER 53

The Pope was more interested in what happened afterward. Rick spoke with him the next day in Rick's and Tessa's room at Buckingham Palace. Rick supposed that meant he was *holding* the audience rather than *having* one, which somehow disappointed him. He had never wanted to be more important than the Pope. He didn't think he was. But the world did, and now apparently so did Thomas.

"If you saw the interview," Rick told him, "then you already know everything I do."

"Ah, but there's always another interpretation for the same set of facts," Thomas said. "For instance, are you sure you weren't in Purgatory?"

Tessa, sitting beside him in an ornate, high-backed couch filled with pillows, giggled. She'd been doing that a lot lately. She and Rick had both cried a lot last night, then made love furiously and scandalously right there in the palace, and that overwhelmingly physical reassurance that they were both indeed alive had stopped the tears. Now they were behaving like newlyweds again, and Rick had promised to do so for the rest of his renewed life, however long that would be.

"I got no sense of levels," he said. "The concept of 'place' didn't really seem important. If there was a higher plane of some sort, I wasn't aware of it."

"But it might have been there."

"You're stretching, Thomas."

"Damned right I'm stretching. I want to know how much doctrine to toss out, but I don't want to throw the baby out with the bathwater."

Rick leaned into a shaft of sunlight coming in through the

tall windows. Sunlight felt good. He liked the warmth of it against his skin. It could be thought of, he supposed, as the tender caress of a star. "You got one thing right," he said. "The more the merrier. Every mind that has ever been is still out there, and the universe grows more self-aware with each addition. But there's no rush. Keep birth control. And nix to the suffering and guilt stuff. Overpopulating the planet and making everybody unhappy is counterproductive, because all that negative stuff goes into the group mind. In the long run the quality of life is far more important than the quantity."

"I guess that's good news," Thomas said. "But how can I tell for sure? I don't know how any of this will be used by the people who come after us. It's kind of scary to realize that they can affect me even after I die."

"Everything is connected," Rick said. "You knew that before this, too."

"So tell me something I didn't know."

Rick closed his eyes and tried to remember the experience. It hadn't lasted that long, and he hadn't really opened himself up to the overmind. It was still out there, still connected, a hidden source of knowledge that had helped him create everything from apples to rocket ships, but with reality competing for his attention it was hard to even detect on a conscious level, much less understand. "Meditation might work," he said.

"What?"

"I think the Buddhists might be onto something. You should give it a try."

"If you will remember," Thomas said, "I suggested the same to you several weeks ago."

"So you did, but it's probably even more important than you thought. And karma is real, too, in the sense that what you do here will affect the reality you wind up spending eternity in. It's just not as one-to-one as most people think it is." He laughed. "So many people had it *almost* right."

"Like faith," Tessa said. Rick and Thomas looked over at her. "Faith can move a mountain," she explained. "Almost true, but not the way most people think. No amount of faith can help one person alone, but other people's faith in *you* can help you move a mountain."

"So how come so many religions want people to put their faith in God?" Rick asked. "Especially knowing what God is?"

Thomas laughed. "*Do* you know what God is? And even if you are right, how many regular people do you want with the ability to move mountains? Giving the power back to the cosmos is much safer."

Rick shivered and drew Tessa closer to him on the couch. Even the sunlight and her presence couldn't banish the memory of his night flight over Bagdonis's handiwork. "It's a good thing people like Bagdonis don't share their power," he said. "If there'd been two of them, we'd still be in trouble."

"Dictators don't think that way," Thomas said. "It's one of many pitfalls in their worldview."

"I wonder how long it'll be before another one shows up?"

He sighed. "I'm sure someone's at work building up a following even as we speak. But now that the world has seen what his kind of ambition leads to, I think it will be some time before another warmonger gains the power Bagdonis had. And if we use this breathing space to work toward making the world a better place, perhaps it will never happen."

Rick didn't share his optimism, but he didn't say so. Negative thoughts bring negative results, after all. He was willing to hope that Thomas was right, but he would be keeping his eye on the Middle East, and on China, at least until the world learned to live peacefully within the new paradigm that had been forced on it.

"Will you continue your space program after you go home?" Thomas asked.

"I don't know," Rick said. "Personally, I'd love to, and that's what the President wants, but there are so many things that need doing. I'm not sure what the best use for our ability really is."

"Your president is wiser than you give her credit for," Thomas said. "Giving people something to look forward to is the most important thing you can do. This power you've discovered is at once wonderful and terrifying. It changes practically everything. Without something big to focus on, uncertainty and fear will create another monster." He snorted. "Perhaps literally. For all I know, Godzilla could appear in Tokyo tomorrow if enough people believe it could."

Rick winced at the image his words conjured up. "Don't say that out loud to anyone else," he said. "In fact, you shouldn't have said it to us. We don't know what we're capable of either."

"Well, then, that's another good reason to go into space again. Using your abilities for something big will force you to learn more about it than if you simply make—"

He was interrupted by a knock at the door. It opened before anyone could rise to get it, and a woman stuck her head in. "Beg your pardon, but you're needed immediately in the library. Something's happened to Arthur."

"Arthur?" Rick asked. "*King* Arthur?"

"Yes. Come quickly!"

They jumped to their feet and rushed after her, down hallways and stairways through the six-hundred-room palace, until they found King William and the medieval scholar, Derek, standing helplessly beside the ghostly figure of Arthur, who had faded to the consistency of a gauze curtain.

"Quick!" Derek said. "Bring him back!"

Rick concentrated on doing just that, and Tessa stood beside him doing the same, but the ancient monarch continued to fade. Rick pressed his fingers to his forehead as if he could squeeze more power out of his brain the way a person squeezes water from a sponge, but it had no effect.

Arthur seemed ungerturbed. Sad, perhaps, that his visit to the future had been cut short, but he stood there stoically until he was nearly gone, then in a final gesture of good-bye he drew Excalibur and held it aloft in front of him. The sword glistened as bright as ever for a few seconds, then it faded as well and they both were gone.

"What happened?" Tessa asked. "What caused it?"

Derek looked like a child whose older brother had just smashed his favorite toy. He bit his lower lip, then took a deep breath and said, "King William and I were reading to him from T. H. White's *The Once and Future King*. I had just read him the section where Merlin turns him into an ant, and he was laughing at the bit where he learns that 'everything not forbidden is compulsory' when we noticed him starting to fade. He said, 'It looks like I am compelled to return to Avalon.' That's when we sent for you."

There could be only one explanation. "The threat to England was over," Rick said. When the remaining king looked over at him, he explained: "The legend says Arthur will return to aid Britain in its time of need. Bagdonis is dead, you were enjoying a quiet morning in the library, and we were talking about rebuilding. It was time."

"It hardly seems fair," Thomas said. "He was here less than a day."

It did seem unfair, both to Arthur and to the rest of the world who could have learned so much from him, but there was no contradicting the legend. They tried, but no matter how hard they concentrated on bringing him back, nothing happened. Too many people knew that the crisis was over, and Arthur's presence was no longer required.

After they finally gave up, Rick realized Tessa had grown unusually quiet. He looked over at her and was startled to see her staring intently at him, her pupils as wide as they could go and her eyelashes quivering. She was biting her lower lip.

"What's the matter?" he asked.

"Nothing," she said, but it was clear she was lying.

Then he realized why. He'd been avoiding the issue himself, but now that it was out in the open he supposed they had to talk about it. "You're wondering how much time *I've* got, aren't you?"

"You will live forever," she said, saying each word slowly and clearly, as if pronouncing a spell.

Rick certainly hoped so, but he doubted if their wish would be enough to assure it. Jesus Himself had only lasted a few months after his resurrection. The worldwide attention focused on Rick's death had given Tessa the power to bring him back, but how long would that attention persist? Had their emotional involvement been enough to push him over the threshold into permanence, or would he have to play the publicity game like an aging TV actor and stage wilder and wilder stunts to keep his ratings up?

He didn't know, and he wasn't sure he wanted to know. "Thank you for saying so," he said. "I hope you're right. I want to live forever, too. All the same, from here on out I plan to live each day as though it was my last."

They finally went back to their room, worn out from trying to recall the ancient king. The Pope excused himself to go prepare for his return to Italy, leaving them alone again with their thoughts.

"Are you going to be all right?" Rick asked as they sat back down on the couch in the sunlight.

"I don't know," she said. "I don't feel like I know much of anything right now."

"Me either." He laughed softly, and reached out to touch her hair as he said, "I know where we go when we die, and I know where the power comes from to work miracles, and I even know how to work miracles with that power, but I still feel like there's a million times more that I don't understand. Even if I do live forever, I'll never learn it all."

He looked at Tessa's left hand, where her ring still shone in the morning sunlight. It hadn't disappeared when he died. And presumably the Martian battle armor was still there in the Taos lab, and in the barn in New Jersey, mocking him with its very existence. Did he have what it took to stick around, too? Maybe that was something he could test. As soon as he got back to Taos, he would try to figure out a way. He might not know everything, but he could start learning.

CHAPTER 54

The Taos lab had become a holy shrine while they were gone. People came from all over the country to see the man who had returned from the dead and the woman who had brought him back to life. Rick and Tessa were both embarrassed by the attention, but Delia had them address the crowd as soon as they arrived.

"They won't give you a moment's peace if you don't," she said, "and besides, this way you've got a good excuse to call it off when you get tired. You *are* tired after flying all the way from London. So just go out there and make 'em happy for a few minutes and promise 'em more tomorrow."

They had to helicopter in; there would have been no way to get a car through the crowd once the people knew who was in it. As it was they had to address everyone from the roof of the building, because every square foot of space around the lab was packed with people. There were camera crews from at least fifty TV stations, probably twice as many radio, newspaper, and magazine reporters, and dozens of would-be biographers all asking for interviews, but the vast majority were just people wanting to bask in their glory, get their autograph or their blessing, or receive a miracle cure for some affliction or other.

Tessa started by suggesting that people who wanted to try alternative medicine seek out people who knew something about it, rather than trusting their lives to a couple of astronauts who still didn't know what they were doing when it came to psychic powers. She remembered the name of the woman who had shared the hot spring with them only a few days earlier, and suggested that people in need of healing go visit her.

Rick explained over and over again that he was no more divine than anybody, that he had just gotten caught up in events beyond his control, but people were having none of that. They wanted to see miracles. They wanted to learn the secrets of the universe.

"That's what we're all trying to find out," he told them. "Have some patience and maybe before long we'll get you some real answers."

As for miracles, he and Tessa resisted playing magician. They knew they could manifest a shower of rose petals or a lunar lander or even a Saturn V, but they didn't want to start down that road. Instead they patiently explained how they intended to build a genuine space program with the power they had been given, how they would use it to explore the solar system and give humanity a permanent foothold in space. They promised glorious things—a manned landing on Mars, a permanent Moonbase, maybe even a mission to the asteroids—but the more they talked about their plans, the more restless the audience grew.

Rick could see Delia standing in the stairwell leading down into the lab, frowning and drawing her finger across her throat, but he didn't know how to cut it short without pissing off the people who provided the power he intended to use.

He looked out at them, a sea of upturned faces, thousands of them stretching out so far into the sagebrush that they couldn't hear him unless they were listening to one of the radio or TV feeds. He looked at them, feeling frustrated and misunderstood, but as they looked back at him, waiting for him to say something more, he realized they wore the same expression as him. He knew why, too. He and Tessa were just as guilty as Bagdonis, at least in one regard: They were taking a gift that belonged to everyone and turning it to their own use.

No wonder the crowd was restless. Nothing had really changed for them. Once again, people in authority were taking what was theirs, telling them what was good for them, and ignoring what they really wanted.

"I think maybe we're barking up the wrong tree," he said softly to Tessa. "What do you think?"

"I think that's pretty obvious. So what do we do?"

"Give them what they want?"

"What? Bread and circuses?"

"Do we know that's what they want?"

"Isn't that what they always want?"

He looked back out at the crowd, growing still as they strained to catch what he and Tessa were saying. "I don't know. Why don't we ask them?"

She frowned. "Is that a good idea?"

"If it's not, then we just fought a war for nothing."

It took her a second, but she finally nodded. "Good point."

He took a deep breath, knowing Delia would probably kill him, knowing that the President would be next in line, and Allen right behind her. It could completely wipe out their chance to go to Mars, it probably *would* mean abandoning the whole idea of a Moonbase. The ice he and Tessa had found there might sit untouched for another million years before humanity decided to make use of it, but if that was their choice, was it really his place to tell them they were wrong? Was it anybody's?

"What do you want?" he asked the crowd.

There was a moment of silence, then somebody shouted, "Make another dragon!" Someone else yelled, "Make me a ring like Tessa's!"

Rick said, "I'm not talking about silly little magic tricks. I'm talking about the future. We've got this wild new ability, but it comes from you. It's *your* power, not ours. So what do you want us to do with it?"

"World peace!" someone shouted.

"That's your job. Try again. We've suggested going to space, but that's what *we* want. Tell us what *you* want."

If the crowd had been restless before, they became absolutely unruly now. People called out things right and left, but after the first few, nothing more was intelligible over the general din.

"Well, that did it," Rick said. He looked over at Delia, who was banging her head against the stairwell doorframe. Allen, standing behind her, rolled his eyes and made a pistol-to-the-side-of-his-head gesture with his right hand. Tessa slid her arm around Rick and eyed the helicopter parked behind them.

Then a flicker of motion out in the prairie drew Rick's attention. Something was happening out there beyond the edge of the crowd. Something big. Its shimmering outline looked like a glass skyscraper, tall and slender and gleaming in the sunlight, but as it solidified it became apparent that the gleam was from metal. Rounded silvery metal reaching upward in graceful curves and arches, its lines drawing the eye ever upward thousands of feet into the sky, where a single spire extended well beyond all the others, tapering to a needle-sharp point.

Tiny facets winked like jewels all along the skyscraper's flank. It took Rick a moment to realize they were portholes, and that the tiny sticks leaning against the base of it were ramps. There was no sign of engines, but mysterious bulges beneath the ramps fairly screamed of immense power waiting to be unleashed.

"Holy mother of God," Rick whispered. "Is that what I think it is?"

"I think so." Tessa giggled. "We were evidently thinking too small for them."

"Just a little bit."

Awareness spread in waves through the crowd. People turned, gasped in surprise, then totally freaked out. Rick saw several faint dead away. Others screamed and tried to run, but the crush of people was too thick to run through.

But a cheer rose up from a surprisingly large proportion of

the crowd, and people on the edge closest to the starship—for that's the only thing it could possibly be—started running *toward* it.

"Wait a minute!" Rick said into the microphone. "Hey, hold up a minute! That thing could be dangerous!"

Nobody heard him, or if they did, nobody heeded him.

"Damn, I think they're actually going to climb inside," Rick said.

"Looks like it," said Tessa. There was a wistful note in her voice that scared him.

"If it actually works, they could be in serious trouble."

"Mmm-hmm."

"I mean it! None of them have had any training. I'd be surprised if any of them have even flown a plane before. Not that it would do them any good anyway. That's centuries beyond anything we've ever dreamed of!"

"Apparently not." Her arm quivered until she pulled it tighter around him. "Somebody dreamed it up just now."

"But—but—they can't just take off in it! It hasn't been tested. It could disappear at any moment, if it even gets off the ground in the first place."

She nodded. "It could. Maybe we'd better go along and make sure they don't get into trouble."

"What?" Rick looked at her in complete shock. "You actually want to trust your life to something that just appeared out of nowhere?"

"I already did," she said. "So did you. Have you forgotten already?"

"That was different."

"Uh-huh. This time the people who want it are coming along with us. They can help us keep it together."

"But what about food! Clothing!"

Tessa snapped her fingers and a pair of blue jeans appeared, its pockets stuffed with apples. "What happened to your plan to live each day as though it was your last?"

"I didn't mean I'd try to *make* it my last."

Allen ran over to the helicopter, said something to the pilot, then rushed over to them, shouting, "Hurry up! If somebody pushes the launch button before we get on board, we could get left behind!"

"You too?" Rick said. "What's wrong with you guys? You could be killed!"

"Yeah, or we could make it to Alpha Centauri and back before our radio signal from there gets a hundredth of the way home. You think we're going to get another chance at this?"

"Do we *want* ... I mean ..." He looked back at the immense spacecraft. It looked like it was breaking the light-speed barrier just sitting there. It could run rings around the *Millennium Falcon*. "Sure we will," he said. "We got this one, didn't we?"

Allen laughed. "You won it with a loaded deck, buddy. You think the American public will let you do this again? The same people who abandoned Apollo at the height of its glory? Get real!"

Maybe they would. If regular people actually got to go, maybe they wouldn't give up on space exploration like they had before. But they certainly would if the first starship killed thousands of people. In that sense, Tessa was right. A couple of experienced astronauts might just help them get back safely.

The people in front were at least a quarter of the way to the base of the ship. It looked even huger than before now that he had some sense of scale. The Sears Tower could be hiding behind it and nobody would know.

The helicopter's blades were starting to move. "Come on," Allen said, running back over to climb inside.

"Come on," Tessa echoed, tugging on his arm.

"Are you sure?" He looked at her, saw the excitement in her face, then he looked back at the starship. He couldn't do this. It was crazy. They would all be killed. Nobody knew where the design came from, or how it worked. Allen was a certified genius, but could he understand *that*?

"Bus is leaving!" Allen shouted from the helicopter. Rick saw that Delia was already on board as well.

He realized his knees were shaking.

Then Tessa giggled again and said, "Eddie would go."

"What?"

"Eddie would go."

His heart hammered against his ribs. Damned if she wasn't right. Eddie would go.

Rotor wash whipped his hair back, swirled Tessa's around her neck. He grasped her hand and together they ran for the helicopter. Ran toward the future.

A few readers may have recognized Allen Meisner from a short story of mine entitled "The Getaway Special," published in *Analog* magazine back in April of 1985. In that story, Allen invented a faster-than-light engine which he tested on board the space shuttle by hiding it in a getaway special canister in the cargo bay.

What's he doing in this story? And where's his hyperdrive engine? That would have changed things considerably if I'd let him use it here.

Well, I've always had a fondness for him, and for his organization, the International Network of Scientists Against Nuclear Extermination. When I needed a hands-on administrator for Rick and Tessa's new space program, he applied for the job, and I hated to turn him away merely because his universe didn't fit the one I was writing in.

If this book has a message, it's that reality is what we make it. I decided that my reality was flexibile enough to contain a story in which Allen invents the hyperdrive, and another one in which he helps develop space travel in a different fashion. As Whitman said:

Do I contradict myself?
Very well then I contradict myself,
(I am large, I contain multitudes.)

I bring all this up only because I don't want anyone to think I was trying to palm off impossibilities on them just because this is a work of fiction. That one was artistic license. All the other unbelievable stuff in here is stone-cold fact.

Honest.

—Jerry Oltion, August 2000, Eugene, Oregon